CW01523210

WEREWOLF

ON THE RANGE

A Novel by

JEFF HOWARD

DEDICATION

To my exceptional wife,

Cheri Howard

Thank you for your continuous patience and
thoughtful criticism throughout this project.

I love you very much.

CONTENTS

Soon To Be a Major Motion Picture!

ACKNOWLEDGMENTS

Artwork by Will Sweeney

Editing by Cheri Howard

Manufactured in the United States of America

Library of Congress Cataloging-in-Publication Data has been applied for.

ISBN 13: 979-8-3452-6664-9

<u>WARNING!</u>

This is a work of supernatural fiction.

It is based on actual historical events... except for the werewolf.

WEREWOLF ON THE RANGE may not be for you if

you are triggered or offended by the following topics:

WAR CRIMES, GENOCIDE, MURDER, VIOLENCE,

GORE, SLAVERY, RAPE, ANIMAL CRUELTY, THEFT,

PRISONER ABUSE, PREJUDICE, RACIAL SLURS,

PROFANITY, WHITE PRIVILEGE, FIREARMS, CORRUPTION,

PROSTITUTION, SLAUGHTER, CRASS HUMOR, or MONSTERS.

YOU KNOW... AMERICA

This is not your father's Western Tale.

There are no silver bullets or moon cycles to save you.

This is Horror.

Saddle up if you dare.

Next stop: RETRIBUTION

DAKOTA TERRITORY – 1869

1

There is something inherently haunting about a prairie schooner frozen on the plains in the middle of nowhere, absent its usual motion and life. The covered wagon appeared unnatural, similar in many respects to its seafaring sisters, which froze in place during winters on the bay back home. With no trees or hills to distract our attention, our eyes remained fixed on the eerie wooden hulk stopped on the trail to nowhere. Torn canvas waved like a flag of surrender in the light breeze.

Mal and I approached on our horses, crunching through the light crust of ice-covered snow that glazed the windy grassland. As we drew closer, I reconsidered. It wasn't a flag of surrender but one of defeat.

I watched the plumes of steam issue from the nostrils of my Appaloosa, Styx, and Mal's Morgan, Luthor. The absolute isolation and lifelessness struck me. There was no campfire to warm the drivers and no sign of the horses or mules that should have been scratching at the ground nearby for something to nibble. Just a frigid breeze snapping the wagon's tattered fabric and piercing our full-length fur coats of bear and buffalo. Our beards offered our chapped faces little protection against the numbing chill.

I guessed at what might have occurred. Gold prospectors were secretive, traveling alone or in small groups to maximize profit and minimize claim jumping. They all hoped to strike it big in the rumored veins waiting in the forbidden Badlands of the Dakota Territory, and none wanted to share. The problem was their small numbers made them ripe for Indians desperate to hold onto their dwindling lands before the invading settlers came and took it all away.

The fact there were no animals present affirmed my initial conclusion Indians were responsible for whatever we were about to find. Raiding parties attacked easy targets and stripped them of their goods and belongings. That included healthy animals.

"Something's not right about this, Boss," Mal observed.

Mal had been with me since my escape from the prisoner of war camp in Georgia during the war. Though a sergeant, the highest rank a Negro could attain in the U.S. Army, I considered him my unofficial second-in-command and perpetual right-hand man. As with most things, he shared my gut feeling about the scene, and it nagged at me as I tried to pinpoint precisely what *it* was. I squinted against the sun, haloing over his head to give him my attention.

"How so?" The numbing wind against my face made my words feel ill-formed.

Mal looked me in the eyes, but as usual, I was drawn to the ugly scar that crawled from his hairline. It traced its jagged path from under his hat, down his forehead, mercifully sparing his left eye and landing on his left cheek. It was a constant reminder of his last few minutes as a slave.

"Indians would have taken the canvas, not shredded it like this," he suggested, hitting the nail on the head.

I nodded in agreement. The damage to the canvas was intentional. The bleached whiteness testified to its newness. It hadn't been exposed to the elements long enough to degrade and rip in the relentless wind. Indians were adept at relieving their victims of valuable supplies and materials. This was just wasteful.

The closer we got, the more agitated Styx and Luthor became. They didn't exactly shy away from the scene as they had been ridden into riskier battlefield situations. Still, as we closed in, they whinnied and raised their heads in alarm. Something spooked them, perhaps a scent they were catching that we could not.

Once we reached the derelict, we dismounted and found discrepancies that confirmed our initial assumptions. This was no Indian attack. We found three dismembered bodies dispersed about the wagon amid blood-soiled bedrolls, suggesting the attack came at night while they were at their most vulnerable. These men had not just been murdered. They had been devoured. Chunks of meat had been ripped from their torsos. Limbs had been torn free along with swaths of their clothing. There were no telltale arrow shafts to signify savagery, nor had the decomposition left enough exposed flesh to indicate a stabbing or throat cutting. Something else had been here.

"This look like anything you've ever seen, Mal?" My eyes darted between the shriveled wounds that could only have come from sharp teeth and claws. "Wolves? Bears?"

I surveyed the open grasslands around us. We could see for miles in all directions. In our geographical circle, no trees or rock formations were within view. Yet, I knew some animals lay low and unseen in grassy areas, waiting.

Mal pointed at the decimated corpse lying at his feet. "These men were near about hollowed out for their soft, sweet meat." The man's face had been chewed off, and his skull cracked like a walnut. His ribs were exposed, and the cavity all but picked clean. We had seen our fair share of war injuries. Men riddled with bullets and blown to pieces before our eyes, but this was a different kind of deliberate gruesome.

I unlatched the wagon's back gate to lower it and peered inside. Among the untouched items were barrels of pork, flour, lard, a gallon jug of molasses, and a few burlap sacks of potatoes. The prospecting tools included shovels, pickaxes, a sledgehammer, chisels, and gold pans for sifting out nuggets and flakes. I recognized the stamp on the goods from the general store in Lucian, the small town adjacent to Fort Charon. These men were well-provisioned and likely started out within forty-eight hours of their demise. This time of year would not have been my preference to journey north, but it was not unheard of either, especially by those who prized secrecy. Most out of place was a collapsed field camera secured to a sideboard. I'd seen the like employed by brave photographers documenting the war. Not something prospectors considered essential equipment.

"Have you seen any sign of an animal carcass, Mal?" I asked, knowing the answer but double-checking.

"No, Boss. Looks like the horses were the only things took." Mal gestured toward the corpses. "Other than these souls."

Mal walked to survey the other side of the wagon as I poked around inside. A small chest with a Wheeler-brand padlock was positioned in the middle and pressed against the interior buckboard. I was confident if I hit it hard enough with the pickaxe or sledgehammer, I could break it open and discover the identity of at least one of the unidentified men.

With a couple of well-aimed whacks, the lock broke off. Inside was a small amount of neatly folded paper money, almost $50 in coins, a map, and a sealed envelope with cursive writing on the front label: *In the Event of My Death: William Wilcox, Jr.* There were several other documents inside but nothing that immediately identified the other two men. I assumed the chest was meant to safeguard any gold dust or small nuggets excavated at Wilcox's claim.

"Hey, Boss," Mal called from the other side of the torn canvas. "You might want to look at this."

I hopped out of the wagon and walked around to Mal, who pointed at something on the exterior sideboards between the iron-rimmed wheels. Joining him, I saw a crisscross pattern of deep marks dug into the weathered wood by something very sharp and ungiving. The tears in the planks resembled a series of crude X's and W's. We studied them for several seconds before I raised my right and left hand and made swiping motions with each in turn to mimic the patterns I observed. "Look about right?"

Mal nodded agreement. Whatever did this had been in a frenzy and was responsible for the tattered canvas.

"So, what have we got?" I asked Mal. "Indians that attack and kill without leaving a calling card but take the horses and leave valuable foodstuffs and supplies behind?"

"Don't sound like no Indians I ever heard of."

"Maybe they got robbed by someone after their claim," I suggested, tilting my head to one side. I tilted it back and countered, "Then why not take the strongbox containing maps, money, and documents along with the horses?"

"Horse thieves who don't take everything that's not nailed down?" Mal shook his head. "Don't sound right either."

I didn't see anything conclusively pointing to Indians doing any of this, but Indians would eat the blame because that's how things were. As I tried to reason out an explanation in their favor, I shook my head because deep down, I knew no one would ever accept that. I waved the envelope I found and asked Mal, "The name William Wilcox mean anything to you?"

"Isn't there a William Wilcox from New York City owns a railroad?" Mal furrowed his brow. "I remember the name from looking for a porter job before you roped me into this big adventure." Mal laughed and jerked his chin toward the wide-open space around us.

"That's why it sounds familiar," I said, more to myself than Mal. "If one of these dead men is the son of William Wilcox, we're going to have some blowback out here." I shook my head. That's all we needed, the scrutiny of some rich asshole whose son got himself killed in pursuit of gold on Indian land.

We used the prospectors' tools to bury their bodies in the frozen ground, then offered a few words. The shovels were useless until the pickaxes penetrated the icy six inches to soft soil. It was like breaking up granite boulders with the first dozen swings. The iron picks vibrated sharp pain through the wooden handles to our gloved hands. The chore took us closer to sundown than anticipated. At the beginning of the job, I considered returning to the fort and sending out a group of younger men to handle the task and salvage what they could, but we were already here. In the time it would take for us to return and send others, we could have them all buried.

As a result of our diligence, we were only an hour into the four-hour journey back when darkness fell, and the setting sun gave way to a waxing moon. This provided plenty of light to find our way safely along the reflective snow-covered terrain. Of course, with the dark exchange of celestial bodies came a cold that bit even deeper.

We concentrated on the horses' rhythmic breathing and cadenced hooves crushing through ice-glazed snow. Each puncture brought us another foot closer to a hot meal and our warm beds. The barren landscape lacked living sounds except for the wind whisking grains of ice and snow over the frozen desert.

Here and there, I caught the shrill cries of coyotes in the distance, communicating in their high-pitched yips and barks that many compared to a baby's wail. As if babies wouldn't have better sense than to prowl the Dakotas tundra at night. Styx and Luthor quickened their pace without being nudged.

A short time later, the occasional yelps were drowned out by a deep, haunting howl of something much larger and unknown. It issued a prolonged bay in the distance that carried across the territory from no discernable direction. The horses reacted with perked ears, widened eyes, and elevated heads. It called out again, but its location became no more apparent. Mal and I shared a glance and a shiver that had nothing to do with the cold as I asked the question that was in both our minds, "What the fuck was that?"

Mal's eyes darted from one corner to the other as he shook his head, checking his three and nine o'clock positions. We heard nothing more from it for the rest of our trip and were grateful, but we knew we were being watched.

.

2

Days later, our horses thundered through fresh snow powder, snorting clouds of steam from their nostrils and bridled mouths into the frigid air. The biting cold made my dark beard feel brittle and scratchy against my skin. I was thankful for Styx between my knees, which kept me somewhat warm by contact. I unbuttoned my bearskin coat for easier access to my holstered pistol, letting the accumulated heat escape. Though conscious of the cold, my thoughts of comfort faded as I focused on the brutal task ahead.

My fifty men looked smart in dark blue cavalry blouses and gray slouch hats. They spread out in lateral alignment and maintained silence as we descended into the valley and Indian encampment of tipis below. It wasn't the first time the Buffalo Soldiers were enlisted to do the dirty work of attacking defenseless women and children. To my dismay, some of the men enjoyed the murderous assaults, but I lost the stomach for killing long ago. Killing Rebs and their supporting populace during the war was one thing. The South launched an unprovoked attack upon the country and our way of life to split the Union and start a separate nation on the backs of slaves. Killing rebels was the right thing to do in a time of war, but this dark morning was something else - a moral abomination justified by black ink.

As the Indians awakened to the approaching danger, buffalo skin tipis flipped open, expelling people from their warm interior fires. Women fled in desperation, clutching small children to their breasts, across the frozen field to the cover of woods with no protection or weapons against capture or certain death. Their few worldly possessions were abandoned. I was suddenly overwhelmed by the wrongness of what we were doing. We were robbing the nomadic tribes of the resources and land they inhabited for hundreds, if not thousands, of years.

6

The few warriors in attendance grouped with primitive spears, knives, and wicked hatchets. They clutched a few rifles among them, but the Indians were notoriously limited on ammunition. The firearms were procured from dead soldiers, settlers, and miners, with the only rounds being those chambered or pilfered from bodies at the time of acquisition. More often than not, the unloaded rifles were converted into ornate clubs. If they were lucky, the bayonets remained affixed, making them crude lances to impale.

A handful of warriors lay prone in the snow, taking aim with single-action rifles. Flashes and crackles of gunfire erupted from the tipi camp. Bullets whizzed invisibly through the air. To my right, a horse bellowed in pain, and one of my Buffalo soldiers cursed, "God dammit!" in response.

Without breaking stride in our attack, the men shouldered and fired their Sharps carbine rifles. Our battle-hardened horses were oblivious to the loud reports. The lack of reaction directly opposed their natural inclinations and had been challenging to train out of them. The surest way has been to associate gunfire with a call to feeding. Nor did the horses slow their gallop as their riders slackened the reins to steady their carbines with both hands for accuracy.

A volley of bullets was fired almost simultaneously by my men, cutting down the few warriors who took a stand. The Indian survivors either fell back or fled outright, some losing their buffalo robes in flight. Our superior armed forces quickly rounded up those who continued fighting. The men shouted, "Stop or die!" and emphasized the commands with gunfire. Some of the Indians obeyed, recognizing the implicit threat.

As we reached the edge of the camp, a fraction of the men dismounted and checked each tipi for stragglers. Those foolish enough to resist or put up a fight were quickly shot or stabbed to death in cries of pain and shock. Contrary to my orders and moral code, some of the men resorted to personal attacks on the women.

Rape, torture, and abuse of the Indians were tactics quietly ordered by some of our more brutal post-war commanders. Instilling fear in the enemy was an unwritten holdover from the war of Southern aggression. *By any means necessary*, a whispered justification for outright cruelty. These were among the lessons instilled in the Negro Buffalo Soldiers commissioned after the war in 1866 at Fort Leavenworth, Kansas. The U.S. government armed black men, many former slaves, such as my sergeant, Malcolm Butler, and sent them out to tame the West.

On the hierarchy of humanity, it was whites above Negroes, and Negroes above Indians. The Chinese held a position slightly higher than the

Indians, but only because they worked laying track for the railroad. Everyone except whites was generally considered expendable. Well, perhaps not Southern whites. This is how the Buffalo Soldiers came into existence, dispatched to clear the West of what was sometimes called the *Indian infestation* in the Indian Territory west of the Mississippi River.

It was the first time Negro soldiers were given authority over other men. Apart from battle, attacking whites was forbidden and could result in lynching or worse. Attacking and killing Indians, and in some cases, Chinese, was something they were given tacit approval to execute. Some of the Negro soldiers relished the domination over others. A privilege they were not previously afforded.

I galloped toward the tree line with my weapon raised, wary of a possible trap. Ahead of me rode Corporal Axil Smith, one of my more aggressive soldiers, a former slave from North Carolina. He chased after a buckskin-clad young woman with silky, jet-black hair. She frantically pulled the hand of a similarly dressed mother, whose inky raven braids were decorated with colorful beads that bounced on her shoulders as she ran for her life. The older woman had trouble keeping up because she was clutching a squalling infant to her breasts with her other arm. Slowed by snow drifts, they were no match for Axil, whose horse swiftly gained on them, his weapon leveled. At point-blank range, from atop his mount, he fired his pistol into the mother's head. As the top of her skull exploded, all forward motion in her body ceased. She slumped into the snow, painting it red with her blood and brains. I could hear the muffled cries of the baby in the snow under her lifeless body.

Released from the grip of the dead woman's hand, the running girl gave the fallen pair one angry, pitying glance over her shoulder. Perhaps she considered a quick rescue of the babe before changing direction into the thickening trees to outmaneuver Axil. He didn't slow down as he pursued her and lined up a shot to erase her from existence. When I saw what he planned, I yelled a commanding, "Axil, no!" and drove my heels into Styx's ribs in a vain effort to gain on him before he compounded his atrocity.

Instantly distracted, Axil looked back at me, then refocused and fired twice after the girl. She avoided both rounds with stealthy changes in course that seemed to anticipate each discharge. Bark exploded from a tree trunk nearest her shoulder. Internally, I cheered her escape, but beneath the surface, I felt searing shame.

Axil pointed his sidearm safely into the air and cocked the hammer on the single-action pistol as his horse trotted and snorted to a stop. He scanned the trees and seemed to consider dismounting and charging into the thick woods in pursuit. "Can't believe I missed. She's a fast one." His horse snorted to regain its wind as Axil peered into the darkness. "I should go after her. Maybe get me some of that," he chuckled and grinned.

My back stiffened involuntarily at what he suggested. "Let her go," I ordered. "She'll turn up." I gestured toward the carnage behind us. "We need to make sure the camp is neutralized. Treat any of our injured. Round up and secure the prisoners. What you did was wholly unnecessary, corporal."

Axil holstered his weapon, giving the woods a glance of disappointment. "Yes, sir, Captain Kincaid, sir."

"Retrieve the babe." I pointed to the Indian mother he had just murdered. "We'll place it in the care of one of the prisoners."

Axil scowled just enough to let me know he didn't care for that order. As a rule, fighting men did not consider caring for a babe to be soldier work. I figured since he killed the mother, the child had become his obligation. He dismounted to follow my instruction as I surveyed the area to ensure we were clear of any threat.

"She's still warm in all the right places, Captain."

I turned to see what he was referencing. Axil had rolled the body over and exposed two ample but blood-spattered breasts below the lolling ruination of her head. He cupped one of the breasts and smiled up at me, squeezing it.

I was disgusted. "Corporal, this is not why we're here." I stopped myself as my war years flooded my thoughts. I stared absently at the bloody snow and into my past. The cycle of destruction and senseless killing was repeating itself. The realization of my participation overwhelmed me. I returned my gaze to Axil with a heavy sigh. "Just grab the babe, and let's go."

Wearing a devilish smile, Axil unsheathed his bowie knife. Like a snake about to strike, he swiftly poised the gleaming blade above the swaddled child. It issued a simple, defenseless grunt as steam issued from its mouth.

"Don't you do it," I snarled with a stony glare, raising the Colt still in my hand and inching Styx a few menacing steps toward him.

His grin faded, and the blade was lowered. He returned the knife to its leather sheath and collected the infant. "It's just an Indian, Captain. Another mouth to feed."

All I could do was stare at the defenseless child cradled in Axil's arm, and the dead mother cooling in the snow and wonder how it had come to this. My intentions were noble when I joined the army following the rise of the Confederacy. Defeat the enemy. Reunite the Union and retire to peace while getting paid in the process. Secretary of Defense Stanton and the recruiters promised a quick war to whip the Rebs back in line. The South was a bunch of farmers, ill-equipped for a sustained conflict with a better armed, better fed, more industrialized North. I envisioned myself in a clean uniform with shiny buttons and a few war medals once the dust cleared. Maybe find a new wife and raise a family out west in the wide-open space. True freedom built from scratch with my own two hands. It never occurred to me that dream would require the elimination of an entire race already occupying our promised land.

I hadn't counted on a drawn-out bloody war. My clean uniform did not stay clean for very long. Nor did my soul, for that matter. I did things and ordered deeds I was not proud of. How many people were killed under my command? My soldiers, their soldiers, unarmed and armed civilians. Then, my capture by the Rebs and internment as a prisoner of war. I shivered at the memories. I knew starvation. I knew torture. I knew cruelty. All came firsthand. Killing in war came easy and routine. A man becomes jaded to the process of killing.

After the war, a lot of soldiers were looking for work. Clearing the West of the Indian threat felt like a natural continuation of what we had done during the war years. Indians attacked settlers, interfered with commerce, and tore up railroad tracks. They were the new enemy, and I would explore a part of the country I had never seen before.

It wasn't until I reported for duty that I discovered what I'd gotten myself into. Though the Indians were brave, strong, cunning, and knew how to live off the land, they were vastly outnumbered, out-supplied, out-armed, and unorganized compared to the United States Army. They didn't stand a chance. This was not righteous. We were the invaders. We were in the wrong. Ultimately, I was responsible for atrocities. Freezing there in the snow on Styx, I swore I would make changes. Anything was preferable to this.

I shook off the memories and stared into the dark woods, not consciously looking for her, but just in time to see the Indian girl step subtly behind a tree some distance up the hill. She had been studying me as I gazed into my past. Had she seen what Axil was about to do? Had she seen me almost let him?

Then she was gone. I waited a few minutes and searched for her among the shadows as I holstered my weapon. I did not spot her, but I was sure she was still out there, wary of us and watching.

<u>3</u>

I returned to the scene of the Indian encampment to find my men at work collecting any valuables among the Indian's abandoned possessions. We were always interested in the weapons the Indians accumulated. They were indicators of where the Indians had been. One of the first things most gun owners did was carve their names, initials, hometowns, regiments, significant dates, sweetheart names, and the like into the wooden stocks and handles. On occasion, we identified victims and missing persons in that way.

Sometimes, we found journals the Indians snatched during their raids. Often, the pages were torn out to kindle campfires. Occasionally, we found sketches and writing authored by the Indians themselves. It did not occur to me the Indians had a written language until Mal recovered the first journal. The drawings were usually done utilizing charred wood, the Indian's most readily available instrument for writing and sketching. Colors originated from berry juice, soil, grass, or even blood. The men gathered what they found, and we would later look through the materials at the fort or camp when time and light allowed.

Most popular with the men were the buffalo blankets and other hides the Indians used daily. They were of great value. The Negro Buffalo Soldiers were paid a handsome wage of $13 per month by the government with a signed five-year enlistment contract. Far more than they could ever hope to earn in any civilian job, as Negroes were routinely paid less than whites.

Buffalo blankets and hides were worth up to $3.50 each. In cash! A soldier could easily trade such a blanket for food, clothing, liquor, and other goods or trinkets not supplied by the military. The buffalo blankets were readily exchanged for sex at the various brothels that catered to non-whites in the mining camps and railroad towns. Also worthy of trade were pieces of intricate beadwork, as some of the Indian art was exquisitely detailed.

Therefore, the soldiers were very thorough in their inventory of the Indian camps. Anything not found to be of value was burned. That included the bodies of the thirteen or so Indians we killed that day. By the time the sun rose above the valley, we had a substantial pyre blazing. My rule was to leave nothing that could be used against us later.

Mal rode up to me in his open buffalo coat, revealing his dark blue cavalry blouse. He was a very dark-skinned man in his mid-thirties who appeared older due to hard years in Georgia fields. I usually called him *Mal* when the men were not within earshot. We had been together for a long time. He was a solid and muscled man of nearly six feet and shy of two hundred pounds. A product of hard labor. Mal's most recognizable characteristics were the scars on his face and back that contoured a roadmap of pain and misery detailing a life born into slavery.

Mal found me after my escape near his master's cotton farm, between the prison and a small Georgia town. Mal characterized it as his rescue, but Lincoln emancipated the slaves in January 1863. The farmer, while beating Mal, had no legal right to hold him against his will or assault him. After liberating each other, we made our way north.

Mal tipped his slouch hat above his brow and leaned forward in his saddle. "None of the men were injured. Booker's horse was grazed in the shoulder. He patched it up sufficient, Boss."

I nodded. That must have been the horse I heard cry out when the shooting started.

"We have forty-two prisoners. As far as I can tell, all appear to be Wolf Clan Sioux. Mostly women and children. Three bucks survived. One was badly injured and may not make it. The third is an old man."

"I expected more. Where do you think the others are off to?" I looked at the empty, snow-covered landscape around us.

"They could be anywhere." He followed my gaze and shrugged. "Hunting, maybe? There wasn't much food in their camp. The way the companies are going after the buffalo around here, I'm sure the Indians have to travel farther than usual to find game while steering clear of the buffalo hunters." He paused before emphasizing, "And us."

By the companies, Mal meant the government's policy of facilitating the wholesale slaughter of buffalo to separate the Indians from their primary source of food. It was another outrage we were committing that I disagreed with. Generals Grant and Sherman felt the destruction of the buffalo was the key to eradicating the Indians once and for all. There was a time when the herds blanketed the plains of the Indian Territory, defined as the area from Texas to Michigan and from the Mississippi River to the Rocky Mountains. As with the buffalo, the tribes were being eliminated, broken treaty by broken treaty, and the Indians themselves moved to relocation camps the government referred to as *reservations.*

"I guess we'll need to watch our asses until we make it back to the fort."

Mal nodded. "I've assigned a couple of men to keep an eye out. What do you want to do about their horses and ponies?"

"Let's take anything that can travel with us and figure out what we've got when we return. We can break their horses for saddle riding and slaughter the others to feed the prisoners." I looked from Mal to the forty-two Indians taken into custody. The adults were bound and strung together with rope to discourage escape. "Use your judgment on how you mount them for the ride. I don't want anyone walking in this snow. They'll slow us down."

"Excellent, Captain." Mal gave me a quick nod of approval. He knew I frowned upon prisoner abuse. We had both been there. Me as a prisoner of war, and Mal as a slave.

"And Mal," I added earnestly. "I want you to talk to Axil and the rest of the men about shooting unarmed non-combatants. A woman was running with her children. He blew her head off and aimed to stab the babe in her arms before I stopped him." I tightened my lips and shook my head in disgust. "There was no reason for it. Neither was a threat."

Mal nodded with a frown. "Yes, sir. Understood. I'll see to it."

4

Mal placed up to three Indian prisoners on each horse or pony, with one adult and a small child or two. Those old enough or determined enough to attempt an escape were bound securely and positioned facing backward on their bareback mounts. The Indians did not use saddles. Mal further ordered the men to loop a rope around the necks of the Indian horses and secure the other end to their saddle horns. Half of those men led a horse on either side. Indians considered to be problematic were secured similarly by one soldier each.

We acquired twenty-three good horses, mostly Appaloosas. Some of the men considered Appaloosas to be *Indian* horses or *garbage* horses. I found them reliable, effective steeds. My horse was an Appaloosa I named Styx. I figured I'd crossed into hell enough times the name was apt. The men who didn't understand the reference to Greek mythology or the spelling called him *Stick*. From his head to his hindquarters, he was midnight black, where the milky white field on his rump was dotted with black spots. His forehead was emblazoned with a white starburst.

The cooperative Indian horses were tied together on a line and used to cart the bundled, pilfered items from the encampment in typical packhorse fashion. The uncooperative or lame horses were shot. I learned a long time ago not to leave horses behind for the use of stragglers. The day-long ride to our base camp would be long enough in the snow without an attack riding up from behind. The addition of prisoners and looted bounty made us a slow-moving target.

As was customary, I led the procession out of the valley towards our base camp with Mal by my side. It was a clear day, and the sun shone brightly. I pulled the brim of my hat down to shade my eyes from the intense glare

14

thrown by the snow. I estimated we would make camp before nightfall and meet up with the rest of my squad, consisting of a few trusted men left with my lieutenant, Joshua Witwer. I knew the men quietly referred to Lieutenant Witwer as *Witless* because of his poor instincts, lack of experience, and privileged upbringing.

Witwer was a young man in his early twenties, fresh out of the Military Academy at West Point. The son of a prominent New England family, his father had pulled strings to get him in. Witwer had been too young to serve in the war, but like most kids graduating these days, he seemed to think he knew more than the enlisted veterans he commanded. Thus far, he had not been involved in any confrontations, Indian or otherwise. He served better functioning with a handful of men guarding the supply wagons, extra horses, and equipment.

Additionally, Witwer was the only other white officer in our squad, as it was customary not to leave Negro soldiers unsupervised. Therefore, I could not have sent him to engage the Indian encampment this morning. I could only imagine what a disaster that might have been, probably resulting in the wholesale slaughter of all the Indians and several casualties of our own. I knew Witwer was anxious to *do some killing*, as he put it, presumably to brag to any available young ladies and family back home that he was an Indian fighter and killer, not unlike the heroes portrayed in the popular dime novels.

"I'm going to review the men and prisoners, Mal. You take the lead," I said after a half mile of slow travel. The snow was six inches deep in spots, developing an icy crust in the sun. It caused the horses to raise their shod hooves higher than usual with each step to punch through. The drifts were up to three feet high in places and took even greater effort.

"Yes, sir, Captain Kincaid!" Mal responded loud enough for the men to hear. As a Negro, Mal took enormous pride in being placed in charge of our company. Mal wasn't just my most trusted Negro. He was a trusted friend as well. We had been through a great deal together. Mal may have considered me his rescuer in Georgia, but I owed him my life. I could not have made it north without him. We were fugitives together on our trek. Equals then and now, separated only by the fortunes of race and the fiction of rank.

As I hung back on Styx, a young, fresh-faced private named Marcus Jefferson, our flagbearer, trotted even with Mal. Our flag was red over white with a white 9, for 9th Cavalry, in the red field, and a red D in the white field, for D Company. The men liked to call us Dread Company.

The Buffalo Soldiers were dubbed such by the Indians shortly after they first appeared on the plains because of their dark skin and curly hair, which resembled the manes of the buffalo. It was said the Indians feared the Buffalo Soldiers more than they feared white soldiers because of their foreign appearance and ruthless demeanor.

"Did the Captain just put you in charge, Sergeant Butler?" Jefferson teased in delight. "A Negro?"

"Just out front for a while is all, Private," Mal responded quietly. "Nothing irregular."

"A Negro leading the U.S. Army. I never thought I'd see the day," Jefferson added in a half-mocking tone.

I smiled to myself as I moved out of earshot. Styx stood in the snow to the side as the soldiers and prisoners passed me by. The men made eye contact as they moved along, each acknowledging my presence with a quick nod in my direction and a respectful Captain or Sir thrown in for good measure.

As the prisoners paraded by, I noted how lean, tired, and beaten the Indians appeared. Though each was wrapped in a warm buffalo robe, their faces were gaunt and eyes hollowed. Cheekbones protruded more in the older women than the others. Only one of them dared look at me. He was a defiant young man who could not have been more than nineteen years old. He refused to blink as he stared at me from a passing Appaloosa, hands securely bound in his lap. He was muscular and wiry with an abundance of shoulder-length, raven hair. He tried to stare me down with his black eyes. There was a great deal of hatred etched into that face and a slight downward curl at the corners of his mouth. Under the circumstances, I would have hated me, too. I squinted against the glare from the snow, determined not to be the first to blink or look away. The sun was behind him, giving the young man a slight advantage.

The soldier escorting the lone Sioux man, a round-faced Private Jackson from New York, saw what was happening and gave the Indian a hard slap across the face with the slack in the rope connecting his saddle horn to the neck of the prisoner's horse. "Eyes down when you see an officer, red!"

The young man gritted his teeth in anger. He said something in his native language that was probably the English equivalent of "Fuck you, asshole!"

"Eyes down when you look at us too, motherfucker!" Jackson gave him another slap, and though he continued to grit his teeth, the younger man thought twice about escalating his challenge.

Seconds later, Corporal Axil Smith passed me. On either side of his horse, he escorted a downcast, adolescent Indian girl. It was no coincidence

Smith was escorting them. Clutching each young woman around their waists from behind was a much younger child, a boy and a girl, each between the ages of six and eight. They were sobbing softly against the elder's back.

"Got me a couple comfort girls, Captain," Smith's smile broadened. "No need to freeze in our tents tonight. Take your pick. These two are ripe." His lascivious intent was clear.

"There'll be none of that, corporal." I scowled, looking from one frightened girl to the other and back at Smith, "Understand?"

Smith's smile disappeared. "Whatever you say, Captain, sir. Whatever you say."

Better watch that one, I thought to myself.

As the caravan continued, I scanned the ridge and tree line for movement and silhouettes. As expected, I saw nothing but wasn't fooled into a false sense of security. The Indians were expert outdoorsmen, hunters, and trackers. If they weren't out there now, they would likely follow. Our tracks in the snow were distinct, even to the untrained eye.

5

As anticipated, we arrived at our base camp by 4:00 PM. Lieutenant Witwer rode out with one of the men to greet us. He was well-fed but not fat, of average height, with a sharp nose and blond curls poking from beneath his military hat. Witwer tended to ignore the men as though they were invisible and made a beeline for me. His uniform was impeccable, and his riding boots spotless. That wouldn't last long in this snow.

Witwer threw up a salute with a gauntleted hand. Even his leather gloves were pristine and in a state of golden newness. My own were well-worn and soiled on the grasping surfaces. I saluted him back, or he would have held his hand to the brim of his hat all day.

"How did it go, sir?" He inquired with excitement.

"As well as expected," I tried to dampen his enthusiasm. "Did Buff make it out?"

Witwer seemed confused by the question. I don't think he knew who I was referring to. He was not good at remembering the names of anyone with a lower station or rank than his own.

"I need him to translate for me. I want to question some of these prisoners."

His eyes widened in recognition. "Ah, the Indian Scout. Yes, he arrived this morning." Witwer lowered his voice. "I think he's been drinking. Do you want me to put him on report?"

Or maybe he's just tired. The scouts were stretched thin. They were also targeted during Indian attacks. It was a source of constant stress. "No, he doesn't need to go on report. He's a hard worker."

"Yes, sir, Captain." He took a breath and changed the subject. "Did they put up a fight?"

I sighed and gave in to what he wanted to hear. "They fired upon us. Booker's horse took a hit. None of the men were injured. We killed about a quarter of the camp before they gave up."

"Wish I could have been there to help out, sir." His blue eyes lit up at the prospect. "I just want to get some experience." He probably meant what he said, but I was suspicious of his motives.

"Don't be too eager for that kind of experience, Lieutenant. We're not here to kill these people. The mission is to relocate them to the best of our ability." Officially, we weren't supposed to be killing them. Still, many in the hierarchy seemed to know it occurred and preferred that outcome.

Witwer tipped his head back in acknowledgment but did not nod or express agreement.

"Have you ever killed anyone, Lieutenant?" I studied him carefully, my eyes narrowing.

I think he thought about lying to me but answered truthfully in a quiet tone. "No, sir."

"Don't be in too much of a rush. It's not a pleasant feeling that follows. Guilt will nag you for the rest of your life." I held his eyes for a beat. "Regardless of the circumstances."

I'm sure he didn't believe me, so I gave him an order before he could respond. "See to securing the prisoners. Get them fed and make sure they're provided warmth. We'll head back to the fort in the morning. Hopefully, we won't get any more snow."

Puzzlement passed across Witwer's face as he considered his tasks, signaling to me the formulation of a question.

"Sergeant Butler will help you with all of that," I added before he could ask.

6

"He says I'm a traitor to my people," Buff translated for the young man who tried to stare me down earlier. So far, we learned his name was Angry Eagle – no surprise there – and Buff was a traitor.

We sat by a fire near the heavily guarded prisoners. Buff and I were seated on a fallen tree, with Mal brandishing a rifle behind me. Angry Eagle sat cross-legged on the ground facing us, his demeanor seething defiance. He wore dark buckskin clothing under a buffalo robe.

The Indians were allowed to relieve themselves. Witwer and Mal provided them army rations and melted snow for drinking water. Some Indians poked suspiciously at the food, which consisted of heated beans and hardtack biscuits until they saw their guards eating scoops from the same ladling pot. Satisfied they weren't being poisoned and the foreign food was indeed edible, they licked and bit awkwardly at the tin plates balanced in their bound hands. Eating while tied was challenging but a necessary precaution. Only the tiny children were untied, as they tended to stay near trusted adults.

I wasn't sure what tribe Buff was from, but I knew his actual name was Tankama or something similar. He told me it meant Buffalo Man but to call him Buff. He was in his forties, heavier set than the average Indian, dark-eyed, and short of stature. He wore dark buckskin pants and a matching overshirt with tassels strung through beads. Buff was among the best Indian Scouts employed by the Army - a good tracker but a better translator. His translations were verbatim, back and forth. Others I'd employed tended to engage in long, drawn-out conversations, and all I got was, "He said he doesn't know." Which told me I wasn't hearing everything I needed to determine relevance. Buff wasn't like that. Sometimes, he injected humor and opinion into his translations. That worked for me, too.

"Correction, I'm an old *ass* traitor," Buff added with a note of sarcasm. "He's about nineteen years old." Buff looked me in the eye. "He's not telling me this, but I gather his father is probably a leader in their band. Mr. Angry here is fairly intelligent... and dangerous. He sees himself as a future leader. He would kill us if he had half a chance. His band is Wolf Clan, and he's pretty proud of that."

"What does that mean?"

"All Indians are part of a clan, no matter their tribe," Buff explained. "I'm Buffalo Clan. There is the Snake Clan, Eagle Clan, Bear Clan, Wind Clan... It's a long list. He's Wolf Clan. The various clans from each tribe don't necessarily have the same roles. In some tribes, Bear Clan are the protectors. Mr. Angry's Wolf Clan is a protector clan for his tribe."

"Ask him where all the men from his camp are. Tell him I want to bring them in safely. They should surrender," I directed.

Buff laughed, knowing the query would go nowhere, but he spoke to Angry Eagle in their shared language. I studied French, Spanish, and a smattering of Latin in my school and military training days, but nothing they said to one another sounded anything remotely related to the romance languages. Buff's tone was soft and measured. Angry Eagle's was cryptic and, well, angry.

"Ha!" Angry Eagle forced a laugh, spit into the crackling fire, and launched into a manifesto Buff tried to keep up with. "He says the blue coats are cowards without guns and no match for Wolf Clan. Never mind where Wolf Clan warriors are because they are the least of your worries. It is blue coats who should surrender to Wolf Clan and leave our lands. He says something is coming that we have never seen before, and blue-coat guns will be useless against it. We will know it when it comes." Buff shook his head in confusion. "That's an odd way to phrase a threat. I don't know what that's supposed to mean. I think he doesn't know where the warriors are, and if he did, he wouldn't tell us. We should probably be on the lookout for an attack or ambush between here and the fort."

"That goes without saying," Mal scoffed.

"He has a question for you." Buff's eyes found mine. "He wants to know if you killed the bear for that coat you're wearing or if you're a coward."

Angry Eagle gazed upon my coat with something akin to envy.

I laughed, amused at the young man's aggressive tone. "Tell him I did, and the bear nearly killed me."

Buff started his translation.

"Tell him I didn't just take the hide. We ate that bear. It was like venison, only sweeter, and kept us fed for a week." I said this because I knew the Indians did not respect the slaughter of animals simply for their skins. It also happened to be true.

Buff nodded and continued the translation. As Angry Eagle listened, he formed a slight smile of grudging approval. Based on my description of its taste, he recognized that I had actually eaten the bear meat.

I considered his warning and stroked my beard. "We will know it when it comes.".

7

The sky was free of clouds and fully illuminated by a crescent moon. My long-dead wife Rebecca loved to stare at the moon, comment on its beauty, and wonder if anyone was up there looking back. The light from above bounced off the snow-covered earth to cast everything else in dark relief. Consequently, it was easy to keep track of everything in the vicinity. It also created the disadvantage of making us stand out from afar. We glowed like a small town beside our fires and lanterns. Guards were stationed on the perimeter, with shifts changing every two hours.

There was little banter amongst the men as we sat warming ourselves, drinking coffee, eating beans, and trying desperately to fight off the frigid temperature. When fighting against equals, I have noticed soldiers excited and proud of how they both escaped and doled out death. Boasting always followed occasions of combat. It is the nature of the beast, but there was little pride in what occurred during the morning hours. The men were mostly silent, except for Witwer, who quizzed them about the battle.

"They opened up on us, Lieutenant," Booker provided. "Hit my damn horse in the shoulder. But there wasn't much to it. Some of us returned fire as we rode in, but the Indians don't have much in the way of ammunition, so it was kind of one-sided." The snapping and crackling of burning wood occasionally resounded like gunshots in the frozen air to give Booker's narrative sound effects.

"Did you kill anyone, Private?" Witwer asked hopefully.

"I might have. I was pretty mad when Rex was shot. I love that horse. The first horse I ever called my own. I fired three or four times at where the shots came from."

"Negro, you didn't hit shit! I shot one of them fuckers that was laying

23

in the snow," Private Taylor laughed. "I know I got him 'cause he wasn't getting up when I rode past him. I was ready to plug him again when these two bucks came out of their tent."

"Shows what you know," Booker retorted. "Indian tents are called *tipis*. They're made out of buffalo skin with the fur scraped off and an opening at the top to let the smoke out. I'm pretty sure I got one of them, though. Revenge for Rex."

"I'm beginning to think you might be queer for that horse," Axil chimed in.

"Ain't your horse anyways, Book," Taylor added. "It's the Army's horse. They just let you ride him."

"Is so, my horse," Booker insisted. "I take care of him. I trim his hooves and make sure his shoes are tight. I comb his mane and give him plenty to eat."

"Do you fuck him too, Book?" Axil laughed. "Bet you back him up to a fence and fuck him up the ass when nobody looking."

"Oh, fuck you, Axil!" Booker responded in disgust. "Where you get that shit from? Is that how it is in North Carolina or Mississippi or wherever the fuck your black ass is from? Fucking horses and shit?"

"Sex with a horse is a violation of the military code of conduct." Witwer tried to keep a straight face. "It's called bestiality. It means sex with an animal. Buggery."

Axil just laughed. The other men joined in at their Corporal's expense.

Witwer questioned Taylor. "Two came out of a tipi after you? What did you do?"

"Shit, Lieutenant..."

"Yep," Axil interrupted, "Private Taylor shit himself. We share a tent. The smell..." He waved his hand in front of his flared nostrils.

The men howled with laughter.

"Fuck you, Axil!" Taylor said. "Sorry, Lieutenant, shouldn't swear in front of an officer. I shot one in the face." Taylor raised his arms like he was aiming his rifle. "Pop! Down he went."

"I got that other one with my pistol when he raised his tomahawk, or whatever they call it, to chop your little pinhead off," Jefferson said, inviting himself into the conversation.

"I blew a squaw's head off," Axil bragged. "Exploded like a ripe pumpkin—only red."

The comment put a chill on the good-natured back and forth.

"She was going to poke me with a knife she was hiding," Axil added in self-defense. He demonstrated by holding his hand against his chest where she had been holding the baby.

"Those Colt .45s do some damage, that's for sure," Witwer observed.

"Sure do, Lieutenant," Axil agreed. "Sure do. Would have liked to poke her with something else, if you know what I mean. She had some big old titties."

"Man, you got nothing but sex on the brain, Axil," Booker shook his head.

"Speaking of sex with animals, you know a couple of those Indian girls look mighty tight," Axil tipped his head in the direction of the prisoners.

"What makes you think they tight?" Grant asked, intrigued.

"Because Indian boys got little bitty dicks, stupid. How could they be anything but tight if they ain't never had a good stretching by a big Buffalo Soldier dick?" Axil schooled them.

This resulted in laughter from all involved, including some of the men listening in and not participating in the conversation. Boys being boys. Most of them were eighteen to twenty-two years old. Still, Smith's predilections for violence toward women disgusted me.

"Whatchoo laughing about, Book?" Smith continued, "I bet you haven't even had a woman yet. Unless her name was Rex!"

The laughter exploded again but trailed off when the horses became agitated. They were loosely tethered near a frozen stream cutting through the woods and away from the campfires. At first, they stirred as horses do when fed rations of hay and oats from the supply wagons in strange surroundings, but the mild whinnies and grunts became more alarmed. Like a mother able to pick up her child's cry from a noisy crowd, I was immediately aware Styx was frightened and moving toward wild-eyed panic. Something was out there, and the horses were terrified.

Across from me, Mal paused in mid-scoop of his last spoonful of beans, listening intently. His eyes darted toward the disturbance, the whites glowing from the campfire in contrast to his deep black skin. "Something's at the horses, Axil."

"Maybe a bear or coyote smells the food cooking?" Smith suggested, tensing.

"Take some men and check it out," Mal ordered. "We can't afford to lose no horses."

"Right away, Sergeant," Axil acknowledged, becoming all military business, scrambling to his feet, and checking his belt for his pistol. "You boys, come with me." He directed Booker, Taylor, and Jefferson with a gesture.

Mal wiped his mouth on his sleeve and picked up the Sharps carbine sitting next to him. With his other hand, he waved to include everyone in his general vicinity. "Grab your rifles. More eyes we got, the better chance spotting whatever it is. Might be those missing Indian warriors you've been itching to fight are sneaking up, Lieutenant."

"Warriors?" Witwer whispered, the color leaving his face.

"Indians are too smart to scare horses," Buff reasoned. "It's an animal. It'll take maybe five minutes to run off."

I wasn't so sure. I'd never heard Styx in a panic, and there was no doubt I heard him among the fifty or so we had corralled with the Indian horses. I reached for a nearby lantern and turned it down to barely an ember, not wanting to make us sitting ducks if it was indeed an Indian attack.

We moved down the leafy, snow-covered hill, spreading out with our rifles and pistols pointed safely toward the sky. I cocked the hammer of my gun back in readiness to fire. The men kept their fingers outside their trigger guards per their training to avoid an accidental discharge.

Corporal Smith also grabbed a nearby lantern, turned down its flame, and grumbled something unintelligible as he hastily led the way into the darkness beyond the reach of the campfire flames. A horse in the distance screamed in fear at what I estimated by sound distance to be the far end of their tether.

I squinted into the dark toward the commotion and lowered my lantern to waist level. This made it more difficult to see, causing a light glare upon the snow and darkening the shadows behind the tree line. Too focused on what I might find ahead of me, I tripped on a branch concealed just under the surface of the snow and almost fell on my burning lamp. "God damnit!" I swore under my breath.

"What in the fuck!?" Axil yelled from a distance ahead.
The soft glow of Axil's lantern illuminated a group of anxious horses stomping and rearing to pull free of the rope line. A couple rose on their back legs and kicked at the air before them, obscuring whatever Axil saw. Axil's lantern was either dropped or set down in the snow. "Get back!" he yelled.

"Oh, lord!" The men flanking Axil said in tandem. They punctuated their exclamations with a series of rifle reports, which were followed by a roar that chilled me to my core. It was deep and angry and came from something enormous that I still couldn't see. The bear that became my coat sounded like a whimpering puppy in comparison. There was a vibration to the sustained roar that boasted size, strength, and a lung capacity unmatched by any animal I had ever heard. My mind recalled the unseen creature bellowing in the night a month ago.

"Sound familiar?" Mal suggested, reading my thoughts. We looked at each other in open-mouthed wonder as though that would improve our hearing and give us a better sense of what we were dealing with. The scar on Mal's face stood out in twisted relief against his suddenly sweaty skin. Whatever it was snarled savagely as a man screamed from the pitch darkness. More rifle shots and muzzle flashes were followed by additional, agonized human cries and wailing horse shrieks that set Mal and myself into action. We took several running steps toward the sounds before everything went silent. A lantern ahead barely cast a glow from the snow where it had been discarded.

My eyes adjusted to the low light. Trees stood as dark, unmoving silhouettes against the moonlit sky. Patches of snow glowed below the canopy of denuded limbs. The horses raised their heads and snorted in fright as an identifiable, shadowy mass. The men close by swiveled their heads from side to side, trying to locate fresh sounds and shadows to gather a fix on whatever it was in the dark. We were greeted by nothing but the snapping of our abandoned campfires and the whispers of men crunching through snow-covered leaves.

"Mal!" I yelled, breaking the silence and startling myself with my voice as I continued in the direction we last heard the commotion.

"Corporal, report!" Mal ordered Axil in the silence.

"What the hell?" Witwer complained from a few feet away and to no one in particular.

Mal broke through the crust of the snow, striding quickly toward the men he sent into harm's way. As we advanced, the horses at the other end of the rope line snorted, whinnied, and panicked to a guttural growl. Whatever it was sounded vicious. I turned my head to look over my shoulder. The sounds were now coming one hundred and eighty degrees from the gunfire and roars we had been pursuing.

"Are there two of them?" someone suggested.

"It's circling us," Mal surmised with certainty.

"Baxter! Book! You boys go with Lieutenant Witwer and check the other end of the tether," I directed. "One of you men, run back to the camp and grab more lanterns so we can see what's happening."

"I'll do it, sir!" Taylor volunteered, running toward the campfires.

The privates around me suddenly looked their ages. The law and the Army considered them men, but they were each less than five years from the end of their childhoods. They wore expressions of fear and hesitation and looked to Mal and me for direction and calm, though I felt neither.

Taylor returned in record time with a cluster of lanterns. They burned brightly and threw out three hundred and sixty degrees of illumination that painted everything in the foreground a luminescent white and cast all else into pitch silhouette. Mal grabbed a lantern from him, and I directed Taylor to take the remaining lanterns to Lieutenant Witwer and his group of men.

"Corporal!" Mal called out. He paused for an answer he didn't get. "Axil, answer me!"

Corporal Axil Smith was not responding. Something was wrong.

By lantern, we made our way into the woods toward the tether. The horse's eyes reflected the light of the lanterns in glowing black orbs as they shied away. Yet, in their way, they seemed reassured it was us.

Behind the last horse lay two uniformed bodies in the snow. One was moving and gurgling with his hands holding his own throat. It was Jefferson. Blood spilled from his mouth and through his fingers as he futilely tried to stem the crimson flow. "Help me," he gurgled with his last breath. But there was no helping him. I knew from the war that there was no way to stop that kind of bleeding. By Jefferson's eyes, it was clear he found himself in that cruel limbo between life and death. He was conscious enough to know he was mortally wounded while equally aware he was not going to make it.

I turned up my lantern light and waved it over two more bodies. One was decapitated, and the other was twisted around with his torso torn open and his entrails dragged onto the snow in bloody ropes. Deep tracks trailed away, coated with steaming blood. Is this the hell that befell those prospectors?

I was suddenly pushed forward from behind. Turning sharply, I leveled my pistol at the perceived threat. I was relieved to find it was only Styx nuzzling me in appreciation. I un-cocked and holstered my weapon and stroked his soft muzzle. He pressed his nose against my hand for affection and reassurance. "It's okay, boy, I'm here."

From the far end of the tether line came more cursing, yelling, rifle shots, an animal's threatening bay, and men screaming unintelligibly. "Mal!" I yelled and ran as quickly as possible through the snow in the new direction, holding my lantern out to see.

Horses neighed and stomped, trying to get away. "Shoot it! Shoot it! Kill that motherfucker!" Witwer's high-pitched voice ordered in panicked terror, using language not generally in his character.

I elbowed through the crowd of soldiers to the forefront. I raised the lantern overhead to reveal the source of the powerful, bone-chilling snarls. A demon arrived from hell itself. It looked as if God had created the devil and given him a mouth full of razor-sharp teeth and a pair of fearsome black claws.

It stood upright like a man but was a creature of incomparable proportions. Its shorthaired coat consisted of thick, black, wiry fur. Its high, pointed ears, at first glance, resembled devilish horns. From its neck flowed longer black hair tangled about its shoulders and chest. Its head was more prominent, broader, and triangular than a horse's. Its powerful jaws parted to reveal a flash of ivory fangs, salivating with menace. Below its moist, black, lupine nose were two threatening canines. Its furious eyes glowered red as it bellowed with rage.

Mal flung his lantern at it. The soot-crusted globe shattered, and the kerosene within splashed over the creature's chest and burst into flame. The monster's brow angled in rage. It looked like a demon from the bowels of the underworld. It launched itself toward Mal, raising a massive claw to inflict punishment. I drew my Navy Colt and fired into the burning demon as it swiped downward with its sharp talons and raked Mal's face and upper torso. The whip scar from Georgia was obliterated and replaced with life-threatening trenches that opened up pink and quickly filled with inky blood. Mal went down, grunting in pained deflation, pulled to the ground by his flayed wounds. He dropped his weapon and clutched his face to stem the blood flow. I fired two more shots into the monster's burning chest. There was no reaction from the beast towering over us.

It batted at the flames with its paws, then dove into the snow, chest first, to extinguish the blaze in a calculated roll back and forth to smother it. Just as quickly, it regained its feet and rose in a cloud of singed and smoking fur. Overall, it had the features of a massive timber wolf with the size and brute strength of a standard horse or buffalo. It stood in a half-man, half-animal crouch and advanced with a bellow, sweeping a bushy black tail behind it. In that split instant, I knew no matter what I thought we might do, we stood no chance against it. That realization filled me with a hollowed-out horror of helplessness reminiscent of wartime battlefields and overwhelming odds. At least on those occasions, I had faced mere men.

Shielded by a nearby tree, Axil was revealed to have taken up a position of cover, aiming his rifle directly at the creature's head. He hadn't responded to our calls because he had been tracking the animal for a shot and did not wish to alert it to his presence. The monster took a menacing step toward me and raised a claw when Smith fired into the side of its skull. Fur fluffed, but again, there was no visible effect other than distraction and rage. Now, Smith was the focus of its ire.

"Oh, shit!" Axil exclaimed as he quickly worked the action of his rifle for another shot. The two men flanking me dropped to their knees and fired their rifles simultaneously.

As the creature tore grooves into the piney bark beside the branch upon which Axil had positioned his weapon, the sharpshooters struck the monster in its back and shoulder. Again, no injury was noted. Axil was hit in the head by the butt of his weapon in a teeter-tottering motion from a follow-up swipe. His rifle was knocked from his hands and into a drift. Tufts of fur plumed outward from the creature with every bullet strike, but there was no blood or meat ejected from a normal gunshot wound. Were the rounds absorbed into its hulking mass or losing their velocity against an immovable object and dropping harmlessly into the snow?

I raised my pistol and leveled it as the men beside me cocked their rifles, ready to fire again. I shot into its face as I stared into its hellish red eyes. It bellowed more in surprise than pain and advanced, literally slicing the man beside me in half from his forehead to his abdomen. The soldier had no time to scream. It backhanded a second man in the shoulder with a bone-snapping crack that sent him reeling into a tree, where he slumped into the snow unconscious.

Witwer managed to fire a shot or two with his pistol as it plowed through us and directly into the heart of the camp. It dodged horses and trees and slashed its claws through any man within reach. It leaped over campfires and tore through tents, looking for men to attack. The soldiers around me desperately fired their weapons after it, few bothering to take careful aim.

"Watch what you're shooting at!" I ordered the remaining men as they tracked the target and pulled their triggers in reckless volleys. Each searched for something to blast and fired for the sake of shooting. During the war, I witnessed too many anxious men firing their weapons because they drew reassurance from the gunfire. Adding to the confusion were terrorized cries for help from the men in camp. Screams melded into the sounds of the creature's attacking snarls, roars, and half-barks of anger. And then... silence.

The men continued to swivel their heads in anticipation of assault, but the night eased into a solicitous, unnerving calm. It remained quiet for several minutes before one of the men hesitantly asked, "Is it gone?"

"What the fuck was that, Captain?" Axil rose from the snow, holding the side of his head where his rifle struck him. He retrieved his weapon. It now had a noticeable bend in the barrel, testifying to its uselessness.

I shook my head in response. "Check for wounded," I ordered, kneeling beside Mal. His face was torn open from the top of his head, through his left eye and cheek, and into his left shoulder, as though sliced with three straight razors positioned side by side. A fresh, devastating injury erased the old bullwhip scar. Though bleeding badly, he was still breathing. My hands hovered over him, not knowing where to apply pressure. Life was draining from my friend as I wasted precious time hesitating. "Get me a medical kit!" I finally yelled in frustration and anger.

Mal was in shock, his remaining eye staring upward and unblinking into the nothingness above as though waiting for his soul to exit his body. It was not fear that defined his demeanor. It was his craving for the approaching eternal peace. I'd seen this look before. An indescribable level of agony so great a man can no longer feel his pain yet causes the observer to feel it for him. Merciless suffering you know will be there when you wake up but manifests only as a numb ringing in the ears while in the moment.

Private Wilson, our field medic, dropped to his knees beside me, urgently grabbing out materials and applying cotton gauze and cloth bandages to Mal's wounds. We took turns adding absorption levels to pack and stem the blood flow. With each layer, the off-whiteness of our compresses soaked with blood. My hands stained as we worked, but the bleeding continued. We applied layer upon layer until the fabric stopped staining.

Even as we worked on Mal, I knew the threat was still out there and could attack again. But I didn't care. My best friend was dying at my feet, and I refused to abandon him. It took a night of work, but before dawn, the bleeding was under control, and it was apparent Mal would survive. We piled on the buffalo blankets, and finally, his remaining eye closed in rest.

The others who were attacked were not so lucky. I lost nearly a third of my squad in the time it took the average man to shave his face. Mere minutes with a living nightmare. A wolf-like creature that had no business existing. It had not fled because of anything we did. Our defenses were useless. It was unstoppable. It left because it had done what it came to do.

Then, Angry Eagle's warning… threat…, taunt echoed in my thoughts: *Something is coming that you have never seen before, and blue-coat guns will be useless against it.* What were we going to do if it came back?

8

The remaining men spent the night awake, rifles at the ready and on edge. Once the morning sun chased the shadows away, there was a general feeling of exhausted relief. Yet there was no guarantee the creature would not return in daylight. I ordered the dead wrapped in canvas and stacked in the wagons for transport to the fort. Mal was gently loaded into a wagon with other wounded.

While the men were striking camp, I inspected the scene of the attacks. There were few clear tracks, but the best of what I found were measured and diagrammed in my field diary. Beneath the drawings of the dead men's injuries, I wrote their names and date of death. All had the same slashing tears of razor-sharp talons to varying degrees. What remained of their uniforms were soaked with blood. Some had bites that tore large chunks of their flesh and clothing away. Only Baxter, the man decapitated, appeared to have been fed upon in earnest. The creature bit into his shoulder and neck, severing his spine and detaching his head. Then it ripped through his ribs and into his torso to get to his soft interior guts. This left no doubt that the same creature was responsible for the deaths of the prospectors.

It struck me odd that none of the horses suffered so much as a scratch. One of them would have been a much easier kill and satisfying meal. The creature could have drug one off, and we probably wouldn't have noticed, especially one of the Indian mounts we weren't familiar with. It didn't have to reveal itself to us. It had deliberately attacked us to create fear. That troubled me all the more. Was I attributing logic to an animal? Animals can't reason.

The prints were five-toed with a significant heel measuring eight inches long and seven inches wide. I checked my measurements with the prints where Mal, Grant, and Baxter were attacked against those where the other men went down. All were more or less the same size, though some not as evident in the snow as others. This confirmed in my mind there had only been one creature. I wished I had a photographer to record the pawprints as evidence they existed. I then recalled the camera in the prospector's wagon, now in storage at the fort.

That was another concern. No proof. Other than the word of myself and Witwer, the only white soldiers in attendance, there were no witnesses anyone was going to believe. That was just the reality of it. Negroes, even those in army uniform, were considered lesser men - superstitious liars under the best of conditions. Who was I kidding? No one was going to believe this story. Monsters in the Indian Territory? A blurry photograph of a footprint in the snow would be meaningless even if I had the bulky equipment necessary to complete the complicated task. There would be no proof if not for the wounded and mutilated bodies.

It disturbed me that I could find no blood I could attribute to the creature. I saw it shot, I don't know how many times, reacting with pain and anger. Its fur ruffled upon impact and exploded outward where the bullets struck. I assumed men of science could look at blood under a microscope and deduce whether it came from a man or an animal. I was less confident as to whether species could be differentiated. Still, it wouldn't matter because there was no blood to examine.

I checked the snow and found small strands of thick black fur near the spot Mal was attacked. Removing my right gauntlet and a clean white handkerchief from an inside pocket, I collected all the fur I could find and folded it up for protection. I made a mental note to segregate the handkerchief until I found a more suitable evidentiary envelope at the fort. I tucked it carefully into my breast pocket for safekeeping.

We followed the tracks as best we could, but they only led us to the scene of the previous massacre. The snow was badly trampled and abutted a field of scrub that led nowhere. Buff was our best tracker, but I didn't want to send him into the unknown unprotected. There were other everyday dangers besides the preternatural variety, including a missing group of vengeful warriors whose camp we captured and destroyed. I ultimately decided a tracking party was out of the question. At least until we got our wounded, dead, and prisoners to the fort. Most importantly, Mal needed a surgeon. We had to move out immediately.

"Did you see these tracks over here?" Buff pointed beyond the horse tether.

"No." I made my way around horse droppings to join him. The tracks were intermittent and less pristine than those I examined and diagrammed. I followed slowly behind him as he studied the ground with a practiced eye. Here and there, I saw partial prints, but most of it was nothing to me.

Several minutes later, we found ourselves in the small area we set aside for the captured Indians. Only now, they were all untied and warming themselves by blazing fires. There remained just a single guard posted. Our prisoners had become the least of my worries in all the confusion. None had tried to escape. Even Angry Eagle stuck around. He approached us, trying not to gloat as Buff continued to survey the ground. He spoke to me through Buff. "You see, I was not lying."

I glared at him and spoke in a stern voice. "Where did it go?"

"You don't find it. It finds you. As you learned last night." He grinned smugly.

"It has to be destroyed. It's dangerous."

"It's no danger to him or his people," Buff translated.

Axil marched up to us. "We're about ready to move out, just as soon as we get these people…" Axil noticed the Indians were no longer restrained and were moving around freely. They grew interested in the conversation between Angry Eagle, me, and Buff.

Axil looked to the lone sentry on duty and directed his ire upon the young man, Private Arnold Wilson. "Why aren't these prisoners bound and tethered, Private?"

"This is how I found them this morning, Axil, I mean, Corporal," Wilson explained, swallowing uncomfortably. "There wasn't anyone here when I reported for my shift."

I knew seeing to the prisoners was something Mal usually took care of personally, but in all the excitement overnight, the task had been neglected. Angry Eagle said something that caused Buff to scowl. He seemed reluctant to translate. He opened his mouth to speak, licked his lips, and closed his mouth.

"What is it?" I asked.

"Yeah, what is it?" Axil repeated in a more menacing tone, moving in to tower over Angry Eagle.

"He says he untied everyone and gathered wood for the fires because we left, and the women and children were growing cold."

Understandable, I shrugged.

"He says his people didn't run because they have nothing to fear. The soldiers guarding them ran like little girls. White bluecoats are cowards. Maybe Buffalo Soldiers are more cowardly than we thought."

Smith looked from Angry Eagle to Buff.

"His words, not mine." Buff pointed to Angry Eagle and took a cautious step back.

Axil stepped close and backhanded the boy to the ground. "You don't call anyone in the 9th Cav a coward around me, red!" Axil moved in to kick Angry Eagle in the stomach.

I grabbed Smith's muscular arm. "Axil, let it go!"

"You don't have any yellow soldiers, Captain. He's not going to run his mouth. We fought that thing! It ran from us!" Axil drew his boot back enough to make the boy flinch.

"That's enough, Corporal. He's just a mouthy kid stung by capture."

"Ha! Angry Eagle retorted through Buff. "It didn't run from you. It will be back… to kill all of you because that's what you're doing to us." The other Indians were crowding in but maintaining a safe distance. They subtly nodded and grunted their agreement with Angry Eagle.

"You seem to know a lot about this thing," I said directly to Angry Eagle.

"I know enough, "Buff translated. "I know it won't stop until it has killed every last one of you! That is what one of your generals promised. 'We will kill every last one of you!'"

I knew he was correct in spirit. General "Little Phil" Sheridan said something like, "The only good Indian is a dead Indian." In the early 1850s, California Governor Peter Burnett said, "A war of extermination will continue to be waged between the two races until the Indian race becomes extinct." There had been others, but those two came immediately to mind.

"It will keep attacking you to your fort. Then it will attack your fort until all of those cowards are dead. And then it will climb on your trains and kill every last white…"

"Shut the fuck up, red!" Angry Eagle didn't stop threatening until Axil punched him in the face. This time, Angry Eagle stayed down and didn't look so smug. He wiped his mouth and looked at the blood on the back of his hand.

"Until you are all dead or leave our lands," Buff finished.

"Yeah, well, that's not happening." Axil yelled at Wilson, "Private, get some more men and tie these motherfuckers up tight. Especially this piece of shit." He punctuated his order, jabbing at Angry Eagle.

"Axil," I said, raising my voice, "Go supervise the men and cool off. We have injured men who require medical attention. I want us back before nightfall."

Axil stalked off. When he was out of earshot, I addressed Buff again, "How much farther do these tracks go? I can barely make them out in this snow."

Buff eyed me earnestly. "We've walked the entire path." He cocked his head toward the prisoners, now being tied and tethered. "This is as far as the tracks go."

"Does that mean we lost it? Are there more tracks somewhere else?"

"No. This is where the tracks end." He gave a noncommittal shrug.

That didn't make sense, but we didn't have time to investigate further. Mal needed help, and I was going to ensure he got it.

9

We were all on edge from the minute we broke camp. The men constantly looked over their shoulders and surveyed the horizon for signs of danger. As we entered the open plains, the tree cover thinned out. Obstacles became few and far between, allowing us to see for miles in all directions. There was a palpable easing of tension.

Light cloud cover protected us from the brutal glare of the sun reflecting off the snow. The dormant tall grasses and shrubs poked through the blanket of white, like sparse hairs on a balding man. Absent the snow, this area was an ocean of swaying, tall grass, weeds, and other prairie vegetation. More importantly, we could see anything coming for us.

Hours and miles later, we came upon a scene that was becoming more common - a field of approximately one hundred dead bison lying half-exposed in the snow. By the looks of them, they had been killed shortly before the last snowfall and obscenely stripped of their valuable skins. The largest beasts were missing their heads. Taken for trophies, they would likely wind up in saloons, brothels, or other public places. Other than their tongues, considered a delicacy by some, none of the majestic animals had been harvested for meat. If any flesh was missing, it was from scrounging coyotes, wolves, bears, or carrion-eating birds, like vultures and eagles.

Lieutenant Witwer interrupted my thoughts, sidling up to me, following his hourly ride about the perimeter to check the men, prisoners, and equipment. "Looks like one of those hunting companies has been through, eh, Captain?"

I nodded without taking my eyes off the killing field. I imagined them alive, simply grazing the prairie without a care. "I would hardly characterize it as *hunting* when they just stand there oblivious, gunned down one after another," I responded in disgust. "Something about them doesn't register with me as dangerous." I knew that wasn't entirely true. Bison were known to run as fast as thirty miles per hour and could outmaneuver a horse. Their horns were capable of killing both man and beast. Nonetheless, it seemed senseless to slaughter them into extinction.

"The railroads encourage passengers to shoot the animals from their railcars. The engineers slow the locomotives so children can take their shots. Thrilling!" Witwer said this with admiration. "Stupid animals don't even know enough to run for their lives."

"They say there was a time they blanketed this land, and a man could travel miles without touching the ground simply by walking on their backs." The wonder of that fascinated me. I tried to imagine how plentiful the bison had been that one could step from beast to beast to the horizon. "But those days are long gone."

"We have to make way for the railroad and settlements," Witwer explained, telegraphing his side of the issue. I think he was wondering if I was a loyal American or an Indian sympathizer. Someday, I might explain it to him. Andersonville changed me in profound ways. Like many gone to war, I was not the same coming out as I was going in. Killing changes a man. Being held captive and tortured changes him even more. I don't think anyone who's experienced those things can ever go back to who they were.

"They're doing it to exterminate the Indians," I countered. "Rob them of their primary resource. The Indians use the buffalo to feed, clothe, arm, and shelter themselves." It was no secret many in Washington agreed the destruction of the buffalo was the solution to their Indian problem. So long as the buffalo roamed, the Indians would follow. For every buffalo killed, there would be one less Indian. Or so they said.

I steered Styx to a cluster of dead beasts and came to a stop. The animals had all been expertly drilled through their necks or chests with a .50 caliber Sharps Buffalo gun—an efficient killing mechanism for big game. I scanned the hills for the highest and closest point, then rode up a quarter mile. Witwer followed, glancing back at our wagon train of troops, prisoners, and horses.

"Let's have a look from the *hunter's* point of view," I said, emphasizing the word to express the fallacy. Where was the sport and skill in mowing down a group of sitting ducks?

Once we arrived at the top of the hill, I climbed off Styx and kicked at the snow until a discarded tin can poked through. It had probably contained beans. The small area was matted down, as evidenced by the smooth, unblemished snow covering it. This is where the shooter laid and picked off the grazing buffalo, one after another. I got down on my knees, keeping my eyes on the killing field below, then laid where I guessed the hunter had lain and lined up a shot with an imaginary .50 caliber rifle. The model I was familiar with was about four feet long and weighed under ten pounds. An experienced shooter could get off up to ten shots in a minute. More if he was willing to burn his bore and ruin the rifle, as many of the greedy idiots did. Though manageable and designed as a shoulder weapon, this kind of shooting was likely accomplished in a sniper's position from a bipod or some other prop. Shouldering such a weapon for a sustained period was tiring, and there was no rush. The best bison killer usually shot a fat cow through the chest where it stood and bled out. The other buffalo would smell the blood and move closer to see what was wrong. Then, the killer would shoot them dead through their necks one by one as the other bison watched their companions drop in between bites of grass. An inexperienced man could have killed all of these animals in about fifteen minutes.

"This was likely a team operation," I schooled Witwer. "The real time consumption comes in skinning the animals." A single man was unlikely to roll a full-sized bison over to pull all the hide independently. "Two, at least. Three if they're efficient. That kind of work wears men out."

"They must have had a wagon," Witwer suggested.

"Likely at the bottom of this hill and out of sight." I rose and dusted the snow off my bear coat. "Shoot, skin, scrape, and load the capes. An hour for each buffalo?" I looked up at Witwer, knowing he had no idea. He probably hadn't participated in much buffalo skinning in New England.

Witwer shrugged noncommittally, considering something.

"Out with it."

He swallowed hard, choosing his words carefully. "Do you think a buffalo gun could have brought that thing down last night, Captain?"

There was an uncomfortable pause before I answered, "I'd like to think so." I'd been working that through myself. "But I have some serious doubts." I searched his face. "How many rounds did the men pump into it?"

Witwer shook his head and shrugged, "Twenty? Thirty? More?"

"It hardly took notice. I didn't find any of its blood in the snow this morning. I don't think we even managed to penetrate its hide. Let alone wound it."

"I've never seen anything like it. I mean, we shot rabbits and deer on our farm in Vermont. And I've had a deer or two run off after a bad shot, and we would follow it until we found it to finish it off. Sometimes, we didn't find them. But I've never heard of an animal taking fire and not being killed or mortally wounded. I know they have elephant guns for elephants in Africa, but… this was nightmarish. Our bullets had no effect." Witwer looked at me in near desperation. "What in the hell was that thing?"

I shook my head. "I've seen bears stand upright for minutes but not run on two legs. I think we all know this was no bear. The animal last night looked more like a wolf, but I never saw it on all fours. What's your estimate? Seven feet? Three hundred to 400 pounds?"

"It seemed bigger than that." He took a shaky breath, eyes darting about the prairie snow. "I just want to be ready for it if it returns."

When it returns, if Angry Eagle was to be believed. The boy promised further attacks.

"At first, I thought it was after one of the horses," Witwer reasoned. "But it didn't harm any of them. Something it could have done easily if it was just foraging. If it wanted a human being, the Indians were easier targets."

I nodded my agreement. He was echoing my thoughts from earlier.

Witwer continued, "On one level, I feel it set out to attack us. The soldiers. Ultimately, it only attacked the Negroes."

"That was just the luck of the draw. It could easily have taken a swipe at any one of us. I was within reach of Mal when it tore him open." I smiled and looked Witwer in the eye. "Being the only two whites out here doesn't make us any safer if that's what you're getting at."

He almost looked disappointed. "No, I don't suppose it does."

"Are you attaching intelligence to it, Lieutenant?" I asked, entertaining the nagging notion it knew what it was doing.

"I hope not," he whispered.

10

I ordered Witwer to take the lead of our wagon train from Axil and made the rounds myself, checking in with the men. They were doing well, having fallen back into the travel routine. I was confident if everything continued as planned, we would arrive at the fort before sundown.

I checked on Mal. He was as comfortable as we could make him in the wagon of wounded men but was by far the most severely injured. His bandages were now lightly stained with dried blood rather than wet and fresh, which I took as a good sign. Either that, or he was low on blood. I'd gladly give him my own if I thought there was a way. The men were pulling for him. He was looked up to as a father figure by many of the younger men. Having survived and escaped slavery put him on a pedestal at near folk hero status in their eyes.

"He's doing about as well as we can expect under these conditions," the medic, Wilson, reported. "I'm hoping he holds on until we get him to the fort infirmary and the doctor. There's not much more I can do. I gave him morphine for pain, but there wasn't much to begin with."

The Buffalo troops were notoriously shortchanged in supplies, provisions, and medicines. If there was something better, it went to white troops. We usually ended up with discards, defectives, and straight-up broken gear. Medicines were either half-used or so old they lost their effectiveness. We were lucky to get any at all. Food was usually spoiled or of substandard quality. The list went on. The thought of that bison meat left to rot made me physically ill. Properly butchered and preserved, it could have fed my men for months. The nutritional value of buffalo meat was well-known. It was leaner than beef and chicken. A little went a long way.

"I know you're doing your best, Wilson. He's got you to thank for getting him this far." It was no exaggeration. If Wilson hadn't started treating Mal immediately, he would have died in the snow where he fell.

Most troubling to me was the loss of Mal's left eye when the creature raked its claw down his face. Luckily, it was not his sighting eye for shooting. He would likely end up with a glass replacement or a patch like many war veterans wore. At least he wasn't in danger of losing a limb. So long as we made it safely to the fort, I felt the biggest threat to his life would be infection. Medicine had progressed to a far better state since the war. Some would say it had progressed because of the war.

"We're going to get you to the fort as soon as we can, Mal," I said softly to reassure without disturbing him. I hadn't expected a reply, but I got one.

"Thank you, Boss. Appreciated," he rasped.

"You're still with us!"

"Always, sir."

"You just rest, Mal. Won't be much longer."

Boss is what Mal called me in times of privacy and confidence. At first, it had been a title of verbal respect applied to any white man who crossed his path, instantly elevating that man above Mal's slave station. Later, it was spoken in a way specific to our friendship.

Back on Styx, I continued my review. Axil led the same two Indian girls with the same small children via tether. As before, he eyed each girl intermittently with unconcealed lust. I shook my head and reminded myself I couldn't police a man's thoughts.

"Captain," he acknowledged politely upon my approach.

"Corporal." I just moved on.

Axil was not the only soldier doubled up on prisoners. With our losses overnight, the men were saddled with two or more prisoners on horseback. Anyone with more than two also had a couple of children. I ticked off a head count as I passed each one.

Even Buff assisted with prisoner transport, though it was not one of his regular duties. He had drawn Angry Eagle, which was admittedly at my suggestion.

"He's been asking when you'd be back to talk," Buff offered. "More like gloat."

"Well, here I am." I maneuvered Styx to look Angry Eagle in the eye and hear Buff's translation. "Might as well cut to the chase. Ask him what that was last night."

"He likes Styx, by the way. He asked if you know Appaloosas are Indian horses."

"So I've been told," I said under my breath. Repeatedly.

Buff translated my question and the reply.

"The Wolf-god is our Protector." His untranslated tone sounded like boasting. "Where was your God last night?" He smiled at me like he had a secret I would never guess.

"Where did it come from? Where did it go?" I didn't expect much.

"It comes when it is needed. It is seldom seen. It is not my place to understand its ways. My sister knows better where it is from and where it goes."

"Who's your sister?"

Buff explained. "He means sister in the Indian way. Most of these people are related, but to add to the confusion, he might refer to all the girls from his age group as sisters. The girls he's grown up with. The older adult women, his mother's peers, are referred to as aunties. In the white man way, you would say cousins."

"Ask him to point her out."

Angry Eagle shrugged. "He hasn't seen her. She ran off with a baby when you first came yesterday morning in your cowardly way."

He was trying to bait me, but I was more concerned that Axil had shot and killed the one person who might best answer my questions. "Who else here might know?"

"Maybe the elder. Little Bear. But he is not right in the head. Who knows what he'll say." Buff stated for Angry Eagle.

"What does he mean by that?"

Buff thought. "I don't know the word white people use for it. It's when elders don't remember their lives. Crazy?"

"Dementia or senility," I supplied. "If it protects them, why wasn't it there when we attacked?" I asked rhetorically. I hadn't intended for Buff to translate the question.

"It has its reasons," but Angry Eagle seemed uncertain.

"I don't think Mr. Angry knows as much about it as he wants you to believe," Buff opined. "Just between you and me, Captain."

Angry Eagle said something unexpectedly that caused Buff to laugh before he translated. "He wants you to know all that meat you left back there is going to waste. He says the women could have found the unspoiled parts, and we wouldn't have to eat disgusting beans."

If only we had that kind of time. I ended my questioning and continued my rounds. Angry Eagle was number thirty-seven. There would be more time to talk to the prisoners and take thorough account of them upon our arrival at the fort.

At the end of my review, I counted my last prisoner under my breath. Forty-three. I rode up to Witwer. "Forty-three?" I asked myself and scowled in thought.

"Pardon, sir?"

"Did you happen to count the prisoners on your rounds today?"

Witwer cleared his throat and replied sheepishly. "No sir, I'm sorry. I did not."

I glanced at him with disdain. How could he not count the prisoners? There wasn't much else to do, and he made four rounds since we broke camp. I kept my tone even. "Okay, how many prisoners did we count after we took the Indian encampment and rendezvoused with you? Do you recall?"

"No, sir. I apologize," he stammered. "Sergeant Butler usually takes care of that. Forty-some sounds right," he nodded, not committing to a figure. But it didn't sound right. Forty-some was not the same as forty-three. With everything going on, I couldn't remember the count.

I side-eyed him. "He usually writes it down."

"Hold on, Captain." He sounded hopeful and overly formal, buying time. "You are correct. Sergeant Butler did indeed write it down for me to report to you. I forgot, and then there was the incident. I think I have it here." Witwer dug into his uniform pants pocket and pulled out a torn paper. It appeared to have several notes on it. After flipping it around a few turns, Witwer found what he was looking for.

"Forty-two, sir. Forty-two Indian prisoners and twenty-three captured Indian horses." Witwer considered me. "Why, what's wrong? Did we lose one?"

I sighed. "No, we've gained one."

As we moved onward to the fort with our Indians and injured, I thought back to my period of captivity. To the insult and abuse heaped upon myself and my men by the Rebs as prisoners of war. Did the Indians look at us the same way despite the allowances I made to spare them some of the indignity and horror? Long rides took me back.

ANDERSONVILLE – 1864 – Part 1

11

The war ended for me in early May 1864 in a shithole called Spotsylvania, Virginia, in what was later labeled the Battle of the Wilderness. The newly appointed General-in-Chief, Ulysses S. Grant, was pushing General Robert E. Lee back to Richmond, the Confederate capital. I was a lowly second lieutenant in the Union Army. My enlisted men were just kids. One was only sixteen, having been sold a bill of goods to fight the stupid fight and send money home to his family in Michigan. The war involved a lot of back and forth for inches of ground that ultimately cost thousands of young lives.

The woods in Spotsylvania were thick with heavy oaks and pines, which were difficult to see between but provided exceptional cover from rebel gunfire. For a region of country hunters, I didn't find the Rebs to be particularly good shots. We dug trenches and spent many days in wait. When the fighting finally started, it was more brutal than expected. The air thundered with the crackle of musket shots and exploded with cannon fire. A thick, consistent cloud of gun smoke hung like an artificial fog of poisonous gas. For three long days, we coughed and wheezed for fresh air. With each explosion, we dove to our bellies to avoid having our heads taken off by flying chains and other wicked shrapnel. Day after day, the Rebs blasted away, pummeling trees and shredding horses and men.

We charged the enemy with affixed bayonets when we ran low or out on ammunition. I got pretty accurate impaling Southern boys through the chest and throat. The trick was knowing a single spearing wouldn't put a man down immediately. Without repeated follow-up jabs, the Rebs could fight back and do real damage to us before bleeding out. No matter how good you got them with that first stab, they still had a minute or two of fight before the color drained from their dirty faces. It was then they realized they had mere seconds to say a prayer, whisper the name of their betrothed, or, more often than not, call for Mama. A soiling of the britches usually accompanied this. I advised anyone who would listen to go for the head after that first jab. An impaled brain killed a man instantly.

The joke of the Wilderness Campaign was how the Rebs shot their own General James Longstreet during the fight. The year before, at nearby Chancellorsville, the Rebs shot and killed another of their famous generals, Stonewall Jackson. We hoped they would gun down old Lee next so we could all go home, but Grant kept pushing us and the Rebs south. Wilderness was a nasty area of thick vegetation consisting of seventy square miles of intertwined trees and brush. It was a lot of miserable territory to fight through day and night.

It turned out some of us pressed too far south because the Rebs got the drop on us and took us prisoner. Us being me and my squad of what started as a couple of dozen men between the ages of sixteen and twenty. Just kids and me, the old man of twenty-seven. I remembered hearing an estimate of about three thousand soldiers being taken prisoner by a flood of Rebs. Sometimes, you have no choice but to surrender in the face of a superior force. That's just how it was. Me wearing the bars that put me in charge earned me a rifle butt to the face to knock me out cold. It was a warning to my men that compliance was king. I woke in a wagon headed south, young faces watching me return to life. I swore I would ditch my officer status the first chance I got, knowing the Rebs would separate me from my inexperienced charges.

"Welcome back, Lieutenant. You, okay?" My eyes focused slowly on Rice, the sixteen-year-old farm boy. He was scrawny, with gawky features, bad acne, and a protruding Adam's apple. He appeared hopeful at my regaining consciousness. The others looked uncertain and fearful, with slack jaws and baggy eyes.

I stared up at the blue sky and the trees overhead. The sun's position told me we were headed south. "Splitting headache." I touched the tender, swollen side of my face where I'd taken the rifle blow. The wagon jostling on the trenched road wasn't doing me much good either. Each bump and pothole drove daggers into my brain. "Where are we?"

"Headed to Richmond." Rice looked to the boys around him. "We've been taken prisoner."

"I don't expect we'll be there long." I shaded my eyes with an elbow across my face, hoping for the best.

Also in the wagon was a badly wounded sergeant not of my squad. With the assistance of my soldiers, I swapped coats and the accompanying rank insignia. This would ensure I remained with them and upgraded the unresponsive sergeant to an officer's level of medical treatment. I figured he would stand a better chance of surviving that way. Hopefully, I would not regret the act. "Congratulations on your battlefield promotion, Sergeant."

Being a prisoner of war was a short adventure of a few months in the early years. The agreement was both sides would treat prisoners with humanity and respect and provide medical care, shelter, and decent food. Prisoner exchanges were a matter of course. Soldiers on both sides had to promise not to return to fighting before release, but most returned to their old units and picked up where they left off. As the war drew out, exchanges grew infrequent. Eventually, Grant decided to stop them entirely because it benefited the Rebs more than the Union.

We were first held on Belle Isle, a shitty fifty-acre island in the middle of Richmond's James River, where the enlisted men were kept. Most of us didn't get a tent, a blanket, or rations, but working as a team, we made out and found a way to endure the ordeal. The worst part was being at the mercy of the elements without protection from the wind, sun, and rain. At night, we warmed ourselves with whatever we could find to burn. Much of it came from the river and had to be thoroughly dried. Drying things like wood and clothing left them open to theft by the other wretches who occupied the same miserable plot. It was like being marooned on a small island in the middle of the ocean with the same feelings of loneliness, starvation, and abandonment, yet dry land was visible and within a leisurely swim. For many, it was a death sentence.

I could see Libby Prison on the Richmond shore from Belle Isle, where the officers were held. It was an old warehouse with bars in the windows, no glass, and no better heat. We understood it was tight quarters, crammed with too many officers. From the island, it seemed a damn sight better than our city of makeshift shelters. I wondered how the newly promoted sergeant with whom I'd swapped ranks was faring.

A few months later, we were transferred to a new prison in southern Georgia called Camp Sumter, a hastily constructed facility cut out of the woods in the middle of nowhere with virtually no local population. Andersonville Station was a small whistle-stop on the Central Georgia Railroad, located a quarter mile from the large stockade but well away from any fighting, which meant no hope of liberation by Union forces. The trip from Richmond to Andersonville was about 650 miles by train, involving nine separate railroad lines and a week of travel. They moved four hundred of us with each trip. It's when I first contemplated escape. We were required to camp at night as we waited for our next ride. If we were going to flee, the cover of night would be the perfect time. Unfortunately, we were all chained and well-guarded. I didn't see myself getting far with leg shackles. In addition, our Reb guards seemed anxious to shoot any man who rose without permission.

Sumter, better known as Andersonville Prisoner of War camp, was built by slaves on twenty-six acres and consisted of fifteen-foot or taller pine logs buried close together, penning us in. It was so new I could detect its fragrant, piney scent as we marched toward the gates. We were the fresh fish. The new prisoners.

Set about one hundred feet apart along the top of the impressive logs were sentry boxes, where the guards watched and dared us to move within the twenty-foot deadline. The deadline consisted of posts and a single rail fence that ringed the interior perimeter to keep the prisoners clear of the walls. We were warned by the dispassionate guards that if we stepped or even reached into that no-man's-land between the rail and the wall, there was a bored sentry in those boxes above, happy to gun us down and break up their otherwise monotonous day. Once inside, the shackles came off, and the rules were explained. Obey or get shot. Try to escape, get shot. Attack a guard, get shot. Simple.

The prison was constructed for ten thousand men. While I was there, the count quickly doubled. Eventually, it was triple. The area had been a thick forest, but the trees were cut down to build the enclosure. As a result, there was no shade, and the walls blocked any breeze that might have wafted in on a hot afternoon.

Overall, the prison had an unfinished and disorganized look about it. The Rebs were originally going to build barracks, but they either ran out of money, wood, or both and never got around to constructing actual shelters. If a man was lucky enough to find a blanket, he could build a makeshift tent with scrap wood. Most of us were constantly exposed to the elements with no relief. At that point, Belle Isle didn't look like such a bad option, and the rumor was the island had been losing up to twenty-five men a day to starvation and exposure.

Our water supply was a simple stream that flowed through the prison. It was fouled long before my arrival and steadily became more unsanitary as the population grew. The Rebs used the water for bathing, laundry, and disposal of other waste before it reached us. I noted the water passed under wooden breaks in the wall and wondered if there was a grill, barbed wire, or some other barrier to stop a man from swimming through to the outside.

Rations of hardtack, peanuts, bacon, and cornmeal were few and far between and often resulted in fistfights among the prisoners. Fights some of the guards encouraged for their entertainment. There were fights for food, blankets, clean water, and fights for the sake of fighting. Due to the weakened condition of the malnourished, the fights often resulted in death. I knew from my stay in Richmond the Rebs were having a hard enough time feeding their soldiers and livestock, let alone Yankee prisoners. We quickly found our place at the bottom of the pecking order.

The guards were an interesting lot, providing insight into what was happening within the Confederacy. They were not soldiers, not disciplined or competently trained. They consisted of the very young and the very old, the youngest hovering around fifteen and the elders being grandfathers of fifty and above. There was little in between. That told me the Rebs had the rest of their men engaged at the front.

One of the exceptions to the rule was a guard named Miller. He was a bully by any other name. He took great joy in telling me if I wanted to eat decent food, I was going to have to pick a fight and beat another man to death or suck his cock. God may judge me, but there comes a point wherein hunger trumps your moral code not to kill another defenseless wretch. Living another day feeds the hope you might eventually break free of an impossible situation.

It was bad enough we lived like pigs in our filth, but as many as thirty to fifty men died daily in those abominable conditions. On one sweltering and memorable morning, we were told one hundred men died the day before. Death was the one inevitable constant.

We shared our rectangular pen with mosquitos, flies, and fleas. If they had been big enough, we would have found a way to eat them in our desperation. The humidity and stench of shit and death made the hell of it all the more intolerable. About half the men developed dysentery in short order. It was impossible to get clean. There was no soap, even if you were lucky enough to get to the water. The men shit where they stood or where they slept. Diarrhea was a curse visited upon every other man.

The conditions turned good men cruel. If you wanted to survive, you had to resort to harsh measures. Gangs existed among the prisoners, generally made up of men from the same units, companies, regiments, states, or whatever. But as factions sprouted, recruitment became a necessity. In the survival of the fittest, the gangs wanted the biggest and strongest men who came in so they could steal food, blankets, and meager shelters from the weak.

Fresh fish were only good for healthy gang recruits and war news. Upon arrival, the new prisoners were quizzed about where they had been captured and how the war was going. Generally, it was a lot of back and forth with no significant gains or losses other than lives. The town of Fredericksburg, Virginia, had changed hands North to South and back again so many times we lost count of who held it currently. Fredericksburg, the boyhood home of George Washington, was of particular interest because the Rappahannock River that ran through it was perceived as the line dividing North from South. It was approximately fifty miles south of Washington, DC, and fifty miles north of Richmond, Virginia.

Throughout our ordeal, my boys gravitated to me for guidance and protection. They knew I had been good to them up north, and they naturally expected me to continue my job during our incarceration. I wasn't going to abandon them in a swamp of human depravity. If things weren't bad enough, the basest urges of men refused to take a holiday. Boys were popular among men who were used to having women available. Some in our midst served under General "Fighting Joe" Hooker, the famed commander who ran a loose operation that allowed women of soiled virtue to set up residence in his military camps, figuring regular carnal knowledge kept the men happy. The prostitutes became known by General Joe's last name. Appetites die hard, even in the confines of a prisoner of war camp. Thus, I became the defender of the young and the weak.

Pontificating the rights and wrongs of certain behaviors generally didn't last beyond sundown. Once it was dark, it was easy for a gang to pick at a weaker group, a lone man or boy. That's generally when the gang rapes occurred. I developed a system where my group staked out a spot to defend against raiders until dawn. During the day, we scrounged for food and set up a new rendezvous for the evening. Staying in motion and moving our camp kept us safer.

I got on Miller's shit list early on. I'm unsure what I did to draw his attention, but he zeroed in on me the day I entered the prison. He was smaller than most of the other guards, with a much lighter complexion and nearly albino in appearance, except he didn't have the beady pink eyes. Just by being a guard, Miller drew healthier food rations than we, the prisoners, on the days we got fed. If he only maintained his strength, he would eventually be capable of overpowering me, as I was losing five pounds per week upon entry. Less food was only going to make me weaker faster.

"Look alive, federal," he would say to us for a good laugh.

"Look alive" became a crushing taunt when you watched yourself and the men around you slowly wasting away into walking skeletons.

On a campus of twenty-six acres, it was easy to go unnoticed for a time, but the guards had those perches in the sentry boxes at the top of the stockade and nothing but time. Time to watch for marks. Eventually, Miller was going to spot me. But as time passed and the notion of Miller's taunt echoed in my head, it struck me in a new way. "Look alive," I said under my breath, chuckling as an idea came to me.

The first soldiers to informally report to me were Rice, Collins, Yates, Phillips, and Mackey. All young privates from our company captured at Wilderness. They were a loose band, scrounging the camp for food and clothing to steal, but needed leadership and organization. I hadn't seen them since we were separated in Richmond, as we were placed in separate groups for transport to Georgia.

"You boys gather around." Within a week of my arrival, I got a general feeling of how the place operated. "Just because you're in here doesn't mean you're not soldiers anymore. We're still fighting. We fight together for each other and our survival. We fight smart."

I advised them to watch for the sickest of prisoners and get them moved in closer to our campsite once we set up something of permanence. Though the natural inclination among the living is to steer clear of the dying, cultivating relationships with the dying was precisely what we would do. Rather than immediately reporting a man dead to a guard, I wanted them to report that dead man only to me. We would make the dead look alive for as long as possible.

Rice cocked his head and squinted his eyes at me. "Why's that, sir?"

"Because the living gets fed and the dead don't eat. So long as the guards ration food to the sick without verifying they're still alive, that's just more food for us."

The boys smiled as the simple math of it dawned on them.

Yates, an eighteen-year-old, nodded his agreement. "We can make the sick a barrier to keep the predators and thieves out. Make them out as worse off than they are."

"Exactly." I pointed at him so everyone would notice what he was saying. "Advise anyone around that these men have dysentery, yellow fever, typhoid, measles, or smallpox. No one will chance it. They'll steer clear."

"Won't they ask why we're such good Samaritans?" Phillips, a freckled seventeen-year-old with a painful-looking sunburn, seemed skeptical.

"Tell them he was in our unit, and we owe him. Or say you knew him from back home."

Phillips nodded as it sank in.

"You lie," I clarified. "You want to live, you lie. Just make it a good lie."

After a few weeks of following my orders, the boys saw how my plan worked. I wouldn't say we grew healthier, but we weren't deteriorating as fast as the others. At one point, we were hoarding thirty dead that we tried to make look alive. It was a temporary fix to a long-term problem.

Eventually, we had to rotate our dead. That was phase two. The guards had designated areas to pile the corpses. After relieving the bodies of any money, clothing, boots, or other valuables we could use or trade to the guards for food or privileges, we inquired about assisting with the burials. Burials occurred in long trenches outside the stockade a quarter of a mile away.

I instructed the boys to count the guards at any given time and take note of their approximate ages. We expected there to be at least one in every sentry box. The only time guards came into the enclosure itself was to feed the prisoners and take care of a work project, like removing the dead. I knew that if the guards were older, they would be more likely to order assistance from the prisoners.

"Lieutenant," Yates informed me one day, "Some guards look older than my pap. I asked one about burial, and he said they have darkies who do that work."

I thought about that for a minute. "If you see that guard again, ask him if he doesn't think a white man should see to burying a white man with the respect he's earned as a veteran."

"How's that going to help?" Yates asked quizzically.

"Whether he agrees with you or not, ask him if he or his son deserves to be buried by a white man rather than a Negro," I explained. "These Rebs look down on Negroes. We can use that to our advantage. Tell him you'd be glad to bury our own and say a prayer over their graves."

Yates smiled and nodded his head ever so slightly in agreement.
"In fact," I continued, "Tell him you've got a handful of like-minded comrades who would be honored to assist first thing the next morning."

Sweetwater Creek Branch flowed off the Sweetwater Creek into the stockade, supplying our filthy water. We referred to it as Shitwater Creek because it was. One evening at sunset, while on the platform over the creek that abutted the deadline railing, I made the mistake of reaching through for water with an old bean can, forgetting it was the demarcation line—the deadline. A shot rang out, and the wooden plank I knelt on exploded in a mass of splinters. I jumped back, dropped my water can in the creek, and sprinted into the crowd before the sentry could reload.

"Where you going, federal? You trying to escape? It was Miller. He had a good chuckle but didn't take another shot. I was lucky. I'd seen him shoot men through the head from that distance for similar offenses.

The following morning, I learned a prisoner named Hough had taken advantage of the distraction to roll into the creek and swim out of the enclosure via the creek outflow. It answered my question about whether the creek could be used as an avenue of escape. I cursed myself for not being the first to try, but my boys were unlikely to follow without us being discovered.

There was a commotion over Hough's escape. Someone had informed the guards. There was no other way they could have known. Under these conditions, starving men would do almost anything for an extra ration of food or a blanket at night.

Hounds belonging to a posse of slavecatchers were set after Hough, and the guards made sure we knew it. They were going to make an example of him. Slavecatchers made their living tracking down runaway slaves. Though Lincoln had officially set the slaves residing in the Confederate States free with the Emancipation Proclamation in January 1863, the South did not recognize the northern law and continued to enforce property rights. Slaves who ran were caught many times by slavecatchers, who returned them to their owners for a bounty. Owners meted out punishment that took many forms. Slaves had monetary value, so the health of the slaves was weighed against the need for punishment to discourage future escape attempts. A maimed or executed slave was a financial loss.

Unfortunately, Northern prisoners had no monetary value to the Confederacy. They were only valuable in their exchange for Southern prisoners held in the North. By this time in the war, we achieved a negative value because we were a draw on Southern resources. We waited to see how Hough was treated if caught. We all prayed he would make it to freedom.

Two days later, a nude Hough was returned. He was rougher looking than upon his escape. To say he was thin was a meaningless descriptor. We were all emaciated. He was of average height and had long, stringy, lice-infested hair. The grueling race for his life left him exhausted and pale. By the looks of him, he fled through brambles and branches as his naked body was scathed to resemble a detailed road map. Miller and one of the older guards roughly clapped Hough into a set of wooden stocks, locking his head between his hands in an uncomfortable standing position and on display as a warning for all to see.

An hour later, Miller showed up with a bullwhip, which he cracked menacingly at us, and gave Hough ten lashes that striped his back in bloody crisscrosses. Four armed guards ensured no one would come to Hough's aid. Hough stopped howling in pain after the third lash, having passed out at that point. His body convulsed with each bite of the whip. When Miller finished, he addressed the silent crowd. "That ought to learn you federals not to attempt to escape from Camp Sumter!" He coiled the whip, adding, "Ingrates!"

Once the guards left, we got Hough out of the stocks before he strangled himself with his meager weight fully on his neck. We moved him to our inner circle of dead, weak, sick, and terminally ill and made him as comfortable as we could, careful to lay him belly down so as not to infect his lacerations in the filth. The fleas we shooed away from the dirt quickly relocated to his bloody wounds. Hough regained consciousness hours later and received paltry medical attention from an older guard who said he once worked as a farm hand and treated injured animals. Hough's wounds were going to need to scab over and remain clean.

I quizzed him about his escape. "How far did you get?"

"Maybe ten miles. I followed the creek east until I got to the Flint River. That's about five miles. After that, just bad luck and more bad luck." He filled me in with the particulars.

"You did good."

"You gonna try?" He challenged, proud of his accomplishment.

"They started stringing barbed wire through the water where you got through. I don't think that's an option anymore."

"You know what I mean," he said slyly. "There's other ways."

I just smiled. I managed to keep my plans between me and the five boys who clung to me like baby ducks. I didn't want word getting out. I wanted the guards to think making an example of Hough was a deterrent.

"Wait until I heal up. I'll be ready to go again."

I didn't think Hough would fit into my plans. If he regained his health, the guards would have an eye on him at all times. Escape artists, like leopards, keep their spots. As it turned out, I needn't have worried. A week later, Hough died of infection.

12

I shook off the memories as we got within sight of our destination. The heavy log doors of Fort Charon stood wide open. Charon was not the newest or most impressive fort, but it was adequate for our needs. Located within a mile of the town of Lucian, all appeared business as usual. An armed guard in the nearby tower saluted me as we drew close. Though ten years old, Charon retained a newness that reminded me tenuously of Andersonville, absent the latter's unsanitary conditions. We rode through the wide wooden gates and entered the parade grounds to interested glances of visiting merchants and stationed soldiers alike. Witwer and I tied our horses to the rail outside the officer's quarters. Next, I directed Witwer to have Axil and the others take the prisoners to the expanded stockade area for offloading.

Once cataloged, the Indians would be relocated to their assigned reservations. It was a cold, impersonal task akin to tagging cattle. The Bureau of Indian Affairs, commonly known as the BIA, recorded the names, ages, and relationships. The children would be marked for boarding schools to learn English and service work. The expediency of this depended on the work ethic of the assigned BIA agent.

At present, we do not have a BIA agent assigned to Charon. The last one, McClain, had been promoted back to Washington, DC, two months ago and shortly afterward arrested. The rumored charges were for subverting food and supplies earmarked for the Indian reservations to outside entities in exchange for bribes and kickbacks. In addition to physically abusing the Indians, BIA employees often found ways to further victimize them by depriving them of necessities in exchange for personal profit.

My men and the Indians called the BIA "Bossing Indians Around."

More often than not, an accurate assessment. Without an assigned agent, the Indians we brought in would not be moved anytime soon. Under the best of conditions, it took months to move things along. In the meantime, they would be ours to feed and supervise—a drain on our meager resources, not theirs, creating a sore spot between the federal agencies.

Sorting and organizing the Indians for the relocation before BIA involvement was usually left in Mal's capable hands. It was a task he approached with compassion. He went out of his way to keep family units together. Many in the military frowned on the practice, thinking it resulted in alliances and scheming that promoted resistance among the Indians toward federal authorities. I disagreed. In my experience, a well-fed, well-treated, and informed prisoner was compliant. Treating captives like human beings had been my philosophy before my internment during the war, and I knew Mal was like-minded.

The separation of children from their parents was always a flashpoint for aggressive conflict. The Indians were particularly sensitive in this regard. Mal was mindful of the practice because of his slave days and the selling of slave children from their families. More often than not, women and girls found themselves singled out and isolated in circumstances that left them with little to leverage other than their bodies, at the expense of their dignity and self-worth. It was an abominable side issue of relocation the government ignored.

Given the unique circumstances surrounding the Wolf Clan, I resolved to handle the matter personally. Buff would be integral to the process, handling fifty percent of the communication. One more thing added to my plethora of duties.

I shook off my ever-increasing mental notes as the acting officer of the day, a young lieutenant and new arrival whom I had never seen before, approached. He was an Irishman with close-cropped red hair and a smattering of freckles, trying to grow a mustache, perhaps to make himself look older. It wasn't going very well. The facial hair consisted of orange peach fuzz over his upper lip. The army seemed to send nothing but green cadets fresh out of the Military Academy to tame the frontier. He gave me a sharp salute, which I returned.

"Good afternoon, Sir. Lieutenant Carpenter, Officer of the Day. How may I be of assistance?" He tried to smile, but it fell away when Wilson, the medic, fell in beside me and saluted Carpenter. It was an all-too-common reaction to the Negro troops.

"I have several wounded soldiers to quarter in the infirmary and be tended to immediately. My sergeant is in urgent need of care and necessary surgery." I looked to Wilson for confirmation.

"Yes, sir. Sergeant Butler will require surgery to properly address the loss of his eye. The others have serious bites and claw marks that need cleansing, dressing, and suturing," Wilson ticked off. "I did what I could but didn't have much to work with."

"Ah… I don't think that's going to be possible, sir," Carpenter stammered. He was uncomfortable talking to a Captain of my age and experience. I saw him glance at my service stripes, which told him I was a war veteran.

"Why wouldn't it be, Lieutenant?" I said this more aggressively than was necessary, but I felt we were wasting time, and any delay in Mal's care made me angry.

"The infirmary quarters are currently occupied," Carpenter explained cautiously.

I paused in anticipation of an explanation I would not receive without prodding. Had I missed some catastrophe in the few days we were away? Had the creature already attacked the fort or town? "Show me," I ordered.

I walked shoulder to shoulder with Carpenter to the infirmary barracks. Wilson followed a few steps behind. I couldn't fathom why the infirmary would be full and unable to accommodate battlefield patients. Upon our arrival, Carpenter pushed open the door to reveal an empty room except for a lone man on a cot at the back, near a door I knew led outdoors to the four-hole privy behind the building. I looked around at the nineteen empty cots that evenly lined the log walls on either side of the room. Each bunk had a stack of bedding and a single uncased pillow, ready to be made up for the new patients.

"It's empty." I gestured to the obvious and looked to Carpenter expectantly.

Carpenter nervously pointed to the man on the far cot with his back to us and swaddled in an army-issue blanket. "White man," he proclaimed without further explanation.

"So?" I raised my hands in surrender.

"Sir, I assume you are Captain Kincaid of the 9th Cavalry Buffalo Soldiers?"

"Yes," I agreed testily, missing his point.

He eyed Wilson as he spoke. "Sir, I assume your injured are nig…"

My knitted brow and pressed lips must have telegraphed a line he ought not cross.

He swallowed before continuing. "Negroes, sir?"

"Negro soldiers," I emphasized.

"Be that as it may, sir, army regulations prohibit mixing the races even in an infirmary setting."

"Are you fucking kidding me?" I exploded. "What's wrong with him?" I demanded, pointing towards the apparent invalid. I marched to the end of the aisle to confront the man lying in bed. He rolled over to look at me in his first sign of life. He was gaunt and extremely pale, with a dark shadow cast by his unshaven face. "Dysentery, sir." He winced and placed a hand on his lower stomach. He smelled like a warm outhouse.

I looked him over as if he were a live bomb. Dysentery was always a problem. Half the prisoners at Andersonville had it, and the Rebs refused to treat us. Thousands died. But this man, whom I did not recognize, appeared to be a civilian and a secondary concern to my wounded.

I turned to Wilson, "Start getting our men into these beds, Private. Grab whoever you need to help you. Have someone round up that lazy fuck of a doctor." My anger was rising, and I consciously tried to tamp it down before I said or did something unfortunate.

"Yes, sir," Wilson smiled, shuffling and saluting as he exited. "Right away, sir."

Carpenter grew concerned, "I'm sorry, Sir, but you can't do that with a white man here."

"The fuck I can't! The white man is leaving," I growled. "I'm declaring him safe for travel to other quarters. Preferably one near a shitter." I looked upon the man. "What's your name?"

"Flynn, Calvin Flynn, Bureau of Indian Affairs." With each word, he reacted as though bayonetted in the gut. Our replacement agent had arrived like a thief in the night. He stuck his hand out to shake mine.

I took a step back, fearing he might actually touch me. "I'll pass on the handshake for now. I'm Captain Kincaid."

Flynn nodded, tried to smile, and winced again. "Relief can't come soon enough, Captain. I'll buy you a drink. We can discuss the Indian situation."

"Just brought a fresh load in for relocation."

"I'll get myself to my office and out of your hair." He sat on the edge of his bunk with the blanket draped over his shoulder. "I've got a bed and quick access to a privy." Flynn rose unsteadily to his feet and leaned forward, holding his ample gut.

I wasn't sure why he thought I needed to know all that. If that were the case, why did he need a bed in the military infirmary in the first place? "Sorry for the inconvenience," I apologized without sincerity.

Flynn shuffled gingerly toward the back door. When the blanket on his shoulder unwrapped from his body, I saw the back of his drawers were stained brown. An awful odor permeated the area around him. "I'll make my way to my back door down the alley."

As the door closed behind Flynn, Wilson held the front door open for four soldiers carrying Mal on a makeshift canvas stretcher.

"Put him on the cot closest to the potbelly stove," I directed.

I looked at the tainted cot Flynn vacated. I didn't want to touch it with my bare hands, so I hooked a wooden leg with my boot, dragged it to the back door, and kicked it out into the alley where it could be properly disposed of later. I didn't want any of the men plagued with dysentery in addition to their life-threatening wounds.

Wilson checked Mal as the soldiers departed to assist with the others. I moved to the other side of Mal's cot. "You still with us?"

Mal found me with his soupy remaining eye and gritted his teeth with a slight nod.

"How we coming on the Doc?" I asked Wilson.

Wilson moved the curtain from the window to peer at the parade grounds. "Here comes Gatewood now."

Private Gatewood huffed as he stepped inside. He had been running. Looking from Wilson to me and back, he took a deep breath in frustration. "Dr. Nagel is at the Mess Hall. He says he's eating his dinner…"

I swore under my breath, thinking if the following words weren't, "…and he's on his way," I would lose my temper.

"And he said we could just wait." Gatewood finished with a sigh.

It wasn't what I wanted to hear. Still, I didn't quiz Gatewood as to whether or not he relayed the urgency of the matter because I knew my men had to tread lightly with white officers. The Union may have won the war, and Lincoln may have freed the slaves, but white officers were never going to share their totem pole with Negroes.

"Officer's mess, you said?" I moved toward the infirmary door.

"Yes, Sir," Gatewood confirmed.

"I'll be right back with him," I said over my shoulder and marched across the parade grounds.

13

I burst through the heavy front door of the officer's mess, surprised to find Dr. Albert Nagel, the lone diner. A steward, Private Leonard, stepped out of the kitchen adjacent to the bar. His dark skin stood in sharp contrast to his white tunic. "Good evening, sir. Something to drink? Something to eat?"

"Maybe later," I said gruffly, striding across the thick plank floor to Nagel's table. I stood impatiently awaiting his acknowledgment of my presence.

Nagel cut a piece of meat with his steak knife, speared it with his fork, placed it in his mouth, and began chewing before looking up at me with irritation. "Captain."

"Doctor."

"How may I help you?"

"I believe Private Gatewood has already explained that to you." I remained standing but leaned forward to place the palms of my hands flat on the table across from him.

His eyes rose to find mine. "He did, and I explained to him I would be along once I've finished my meal." Nagel dug at something in his teeth with his tongue and cut off another bite from his buffalo steak. He placed it into his mouth and began chewing anew.

"Then apparently, he did not adequately relay the urgency of the matter." I placed a finger on his dinner plate and gently slid it two feet toward me and out of his reach.

Nagel set his utensils down, drooped his shoulders, and cocked his head, considering a response. Nagel was in his mid-forties, wore glasses shined to crystal clarity, and kept his dark beard closely trimmed. His demeanor was scholarly. His build was non-athletic, but he kept himself trim. I knew he was from the Richmond area of Virginia but fought for the Union during the war. I was not clear on the motivations behind that decision.

"My men were attacked just under twenty-four hours ago and are in desperate need of expert medical attention," I explained, keeping my tone even. "They've lost a lot of blood. One of those men is a friend who once saved my life. I intend to repay that debt."

Nagel looked at me with something akin to apathy. In a condescending tone, he said, "Aren't your men just a bunch of darkies, Captain?"

I took a step back and tried to focus. Was he disparaging my men to my face? I think he took my momentary silence as either agreement or a lack of resolve because he followed the comment up with, "They're a dime a dozen. One out, one in. They're interchangeable." He stood to reach for his plate and issued a haughty half-laugh.

That pushed me over the edge. I darted around the table, grabbed his throat with my right hand, and forced him back into his sturdy wooden chair. He choked as I squeezed his windpipe. He grabbed my hand ineffectually with both of his. I pressed him steadily backward until the back of his neck was firmly set against the chair's headrest. "I'm not going to kill you, Doctor, because you have essential work to do in the infirmary, but you are not to demean my men ever again. They are the toughest soldiers I have commanded. They do the shit jobs no one else seems able to stomach. Show some fucking respect!"

I released him with a shove. He caressed his throat tenderly, coughing and gasping. He slid his chair back in escape. "Are you out of your mind?" He rasped. "I'll report you for this."

"You anxious to take my job? Feel free. In the meantime, grab your coat. You've got a long night ahead of you."

I had to give Nagel credit. Once he arrived at the infirmary and dispensed with his pouty attitude, he was efficient and all business. He quickly assessed each man's injuries and started treatment with Mal. I would have insisted if he hadn't started there.

Wilson brought Nagel a stool and hooked a lantern to a metal arm attached to the wall. Nagel looked over Mal's bandages and unbuttoned his shirt to reveal dried blood on the gauze underneath, where the creature's claws caught his shoulder. "Whoever packed these wounds and bandaged this man did a fine job," Nagel observed.

"Thank you, sir." Wilson puffed with pride, and a tight smile flashed across his lips.

Nagel appeared taken aback that the work he was complimenting had been completed by a Negro. Nagel glanced from me to Wilson. "Are you the company medic?"

"Yes, sir." Wilson gave him a quick nod.

"Good, you're going to assist me. Go to the storage room and bring me two bowls and a kettle. Fill the kettle with water and set it on the stove to boil. We'll use one bowl for the water and the other for discarded gauze and bandages. Bring a stack of towels. This will be messy. We'll remove your hard work, clean the wounds, and sew him up. We'll also need the morphine and anesthetic."

As Nagel worked to remove the bandages, he revealed the jagged tears from Mal's head to his chest. "This was an animal?" He looked up questioningly. "I thought you were fighting Indians." He looked from me to Wilson and back to Mal.

"Indians first. After dark, an animal attacked."

"Must have been a grizzly?" He guessed.

"Looked more like a wolf."

He laughed. "Wolves claws are not generally long or sharp enough to cause this kind of tearing. Bears, though…"

"Bears have five toes. Wolves only have four." I pointed to the grouping of four side-by-side cuts in Mal's flesh to illustrate. "Nevertheless, it was wolf-like."

"Big wolf."

"Monstrous," I confirmed. "Is rabies an issue?"

Nagel shook his head dismissively. "Rabies is rare in wolves and bears. That's the least of this buck's worries. Infection is the greater risk."

"If any of these men need a blood transfusion, I'm volunteering."

"I don't think that'll be necessary. Yes, they've lost blood, but these wounds look worse than they are." Nagel cocked his head and changed his tone. "The bites may be a different story. The one man there at the end…"

"Private Dixon?" Wilson supplied.

"He's not going to make it. His pallor, his injury… The damage is beyond my expertise. I'll try, but…" He shook his head in the negative.

"While I'm thinking of it, I have a favor to ask."

"Name it," I said without hesitation.

"I'd like to examine the bodies. Not tonight. Sometime tomorrow will be fine."

"No problem. May I ask why?"

"I want to assess the damage to the dead men. I'm assuming they're in worse condition than these survivors?" He nodded to the men on the cots.

I almost laughed out loud. "Without a doubt, the dead are in worse condition." It came out sarcastically, but I hadn't meant it that way. "One man had his head bitten off and a good portion of his torso devoured."

He snapped his head up to look at me with widened eyes and a gaping jaw. "Devoured?" His tone rose an octave, incredulous. "Are you serious?"

I nodded.

"I'm curious to see the inflicted wounds."

"Do you have a microscope here, Doc?"

He raised an eyebrow in puzzlement but did not look up from the blood and puss he was cleaning from Mal's wounds. "I do."

"I collected some hairs from the snow near the attacks. When you have time, could you look at them and determine what kind of animal they came from?"

"I'm no expert, but I'll take a look," he said grudgingly. "Still, it would have to have been a hell of a big wolf."

Nagel spent hours working exclusively on Mal. He started with a battlefield dose of ether, tipping the open bottle against a rag and pressing it under Mal's nose until Mal went limp. I'd seen the technique used many times in the medical tents. During the conflict, hospitals were merely open canvas tents raised to protect the injured from the elements. Wooden benches and doors on sawhorses served as surgery tables. Leather straps or horse reins held the thrashing patients in place but were never tight enough.

During the war, more often than not, a bullet wound resulted in amputation. There were several occasions I had been one of the four to six men necessary to hold a man down while the doctor sawed off a limb as the patient screamed in agony. Anesthetics were in short supply. Our infirmary was much better equipped than the battlefield tents. Almost luxurious by comparison.

In the meantime, Nagel directed Wilson on what to do with the other men. Those with slash wounds like Mal's were a simple matter of cleaning, anesthetizing, and sewing up. Wilson was becoming a frontline doctor before my eyes. He had a knack for it. When it came to a deep injury that damaged bone or invaded a body cavity, he politely sought Nagel's direction. The bite wounds were another matter. Punctures required thorough cleaning and sewing. All of Nagel's expertise was required in areas where chunks of flesh were ripped away.

"These bites give a good idea of the size of this thing." He pointed to two identical puncture wounds that were seven to eight inches apart in the man adjacent to Mal. "These were its upper canines." He paused to do the math in his head. "My god, the jaws on this thing. Enormous."

"To say the least." I thought back to it raging over us.

"It would make quite the trophy for a big game hunter." Nagel worked on removing Mal's mangled eye with his scalpel. "Could you grab one of the lanterns, Captain? Hold it about here," He held his hand two feet from Mal's face, "So I can see into the socket. There will be some delicate stitching to do. Then, I'll pack it with cotton and gauze. Once it heals, he'll have to invest in a glass eye to maintain a normal appearance."

As if claw marks on Mal's face could ever be characterized as *normal*.

"Were you and your men able to get a shot off at it?"

"Several."

"Any chance it wandered off wounded and died?" He looked up at me earnestly.

"Doubtful. Our small arms seemed to have no effect on it whatsoever."

Nagel stopped working and looked at me with an expression of disbelief. "Is it possible you just missed?"

"We shot it from point-blank range multiple times. We didn't miss. There was no blood. I looked in the snow at first light. Nothing. It barely reacted. More annoyed than injured."

"Faulty ammunition, then? Sometimes, the manufacturers skimp on powder to increase their profit margin," he suggested.

"I'd be surprised if we all experienced sub-standard ammunition simultaneously. I can attest that the recoil I felt when I fired my weapon was normal."

"Perhaps you require more powerful weapons? You know there's a buffalo hunting company operating in town. Run by a man named Grogan. He may have come across something like what you're describing. He might have suggestions."

"I would hope our government could provide us with adequate weaponry," I said, but I also knew the Negro soldiers were not furnished with state-of-the-art equipment. Everything we were provided was essentially a hand-me-down.

As Nagel finished up with the men, I lay down on one of the open cots, realizing I had not slept since the morning before we took the Indian camp of the Wolf Clan. I tried to calculate exactly how long I had been awake and quickly drifted off mid-thought

14

I awoke not because I had rested well but because I needed to find an outhouse. The infirmary was dark except for the soft glow of a lantern hung near the potbelly stove. Wilson, too, had fallen asleep on a spare cot. There was no sign of Dr. Nagel. The bloody gauze, bandages, bowls, and surgical equipment had been cleaned up and put away.

Out the window, I saw the light rising from somewhere beyond the fort's walls. It was morning. In my head, I ticked off my tasks for the day. Seeing to burial and services for the dead would be my first priority. My Buffalo Soldiers were not of a station in the social order that their bodies would be sent home. Nor would the town church allow us to bury our soldiers within the fences of their distinguished cemetery. They said it was because of the limited space, but in reality, it was because the dead men were Negroes. Buffalo Soldiers were lucky if they got markers. As a rule, they were buried in a small Negro cemetery established outside the walls of the fort. I took it upon myself to write to any surviving family members.

I also needed to make time to report to Colonel Kirkwood on the circumstances of the deaths. An after-action report would typically be filed in the official military record. I struggled with explaining what occurred without sounding like a lunatic. My anger often put my career on shaky ground. This might result in them taking an even harder look at me.

Later, I would arrange for replacement soldiers. Glancing at the injured occupying the bunks around me, I wondered how many would be physically able to return to military service. Better than half if we were lucky. I did not figure Mal would be among them and wondered where he would go with only one good eye. He would likely move to Washington, DC, and reunite with his wife, Mia, who worked as a domestic for a congressman.

I braved the cold in favor of an empty bladder, using the privy behind the building and thinking about heading to the officers' mess for breakfast. My stomach growled at having not been fed since the attack, but I decided it could wait. Once I returned to the warmth of the infirmary, I lay back down and fell quickly back to sleep.

When I awoke the second time, it was to the injured men being fed by Wilson and Leonard, the steward from the officers' mess, where I confronted Dr. Nagel. Was that just last evening? It seemed like days ago. My mind and thoughts were foggy. Leonard served me a bowl of watery oatmeal on the stool where Nagel sat while attending to the wounded. Once I poured myself a tin cup of black coffee, I started to wake up and think with greater focus.

A short time later, Axil arrived. "I've seen to the gravedigging, Captain. The town chapel won't allow us to hold services. We'll have to do it outdoors. Revival style."

"The bodies are in one of the livery barns closest to our cemetery, aren't they?"

"Yes, sir."

"We'll have our service there if you think it's large enough to accommodate everyone."

Axil nodded his agreement. "And if it's not, we'll open the barn doors.

"Good thinking."

"In the meantime, I would like you to separate the two or three corpses from the others – the ones you feel suffered the greatest trauma." Before he could ask why, I added, "Dr. Nagel wants to see the wounds on the dead for comparison purposes."

"That would be Baxter, Tuney, and Cleveland. "Christ," Axil swore, "Baxter's head…"

"He needs to see them for himself to understand our story."

"Whatever you say, Captain."

"We'll have our service a little after noon. I'll say a few words. We have a chaplain among the men, but his name escapes me. Please notify him." I pivoted to head back, then pointed at Axil with an afterthought. "And please see to it that each man receives a proper marker with his name and rank on it."

"Yes, sir, Captain." Axil saluted and left to take care of the burial arrangements.

I checked on Mal, who was still sleeping and, by all appearances, resting comfortably. He seemed to be breathing with relative ease. I expected he would pull through and function in some capacity after he had time to heal.

Shortly thereafter, I walked to the Doctor's quarters. He was shaved and dressed but still looking weary from his long night. "Good morning, Captain."

"Good morning, Doctor. Are you ready to look at those bodies?"

"Yes, I am." Nagel bundled up in a store-bought bearskin coat of lesser quality than mine and picked up a black leather medical bag by the door. We walked briskly across the parade grounds and out the open fortress gates to the livery barn. It was about a quarter-mile walk.

Upon arrival, we found the barn doors open and Corporal Smith and Private Jackson sorting through the body canvasses. Fortunately, someone had written the last names of each deceased on the fabric in the upper chest area. It looked like whoever did it dipped a finger in an inkwell and applied the letters that way.

The canvas death shroud for Baxter stood out because it was headless and, therefore, had an oddly stunted shape. It was also saturated with blood. Two other canvasses marked CLEVELAND and TUNEY were also generously soaked with blood.

"Let's start with this one," Nagel pointed at Baxter.

"You mind doing the honors, Axil?" I directed.

Axil nodded and removed the Bowie knife from the sheath on his belt. It was the same one he used to threaten the Indian baby. He cut through the twine, wrapping the canvas. After removing the binding, he and Jackson rolled the body until it was exposed, still in its tattered uniform. Baxter's head had been unceremoniously positioned in the body cavity for easier transport. Covered with syrupy blood, the eyes were gray where they should have been white, and the lids were slightly open. A slip of his bloody teeth showed between his parted lips.

Nagel set his bag on the ground, opened it, and removed a dark butcher's apron and two bloodstained leather gloves that reached halfway up each forearm. Situating the protective gear, he knelt beside Baxter and pulled away the torn uniform to expose the man's ashy, torn flesh. Nagel huffed and coughed, turning his head to the side. "Smells," he said in a nasal voice. "Never get used to it."

Nagel brushed at the coagulated crust of blood to reveal ragged meat where Baxter's collarbone met his neck. He inspected the stump of the spine where the vertebrae had been splintered into bits. He lifted Baxter's head out of the cavity, which caused a grotesque sucking sound. The face was mauled, and his nose bitten off. There were deep wounds on the side of his head from gnashing teeth. I could still hear the growls and snarls from the attack.

"Fangs did this." He traced the gaping wounds with his gloved index finger. "This tearing here, outside of the skull, that's from an upper canine." He turned the head to one side. "Bit off this ear, too." He fingered around the spine, then turned the head over to consider the point of separation, revealing bright white bone. "This is over one thousand pounds of pressure that did this. I'm surprised…"

Nagel pushed on either side of Baxter's head, revealing an unnatural sponginess. "The skull is cracked. It bit down on this man's head and crushed his skull like a nut. Extremely powerful. A human being is not built to withstand this kind of attack."

No shit, I didn't say out loud.

Nagel tugged at the arms tucked into Baxter's bowels. He pulled hard enough to reveal a stump beginning at the left wrist. "This is from raising his hand instinctively to protect himself. All he managed to do was get it a bit off. The pain and blood loss from this alone would have rendered him unconscious." He set Baxter's head next to a hip on the canvas. "Brutal."

Nagel separated Baxter's rigid arms and pulled away the torn fabric covering Baxter's midsection. The lower portion of the ribcage was stripped of meat, and his insides were missing. "It bit through here, shattering these lower ribs, and hollowed him out in what I estimate were two or three deep bites." He looked up at me from his kneeling position. "Heart, lungs, kidney, stomach, intestines, all gone. As you said, *'devoured.'* This is unbelievable. I've never seen anything like this."

"Let's have a look at this one," Nagel pointed to the canvas marked CLEVELAND and Axil set to unwrapping the corpse. Once rolled out, Nagel got back on his knees to inspect the wounds. The difference in the attack pattern was immediately apparent. Cleveland suffered savage claw wounds. Grooves crisscrossed each other multiple times, starting at the chest and tearing down to Cleveland's groin.

"Now this man was clawed repeatedly," Nagel observed. "See these marks on his head and face?" I leaned in. Axil and Jackson peered over my shoulder and swore softly.

Nagel demonstrated as he explained his theory of what occurred. "It held his head down with one paw and then raked him with the claws of the other paw repeatedly in a downward motion, starting mid-chest and carving through his ribcage. Not like a dog digging at the ground with its forepaws one after another, but stroke after stroke with one claw."

Nagel counted the various incisions. "I see sixteen razor-like cuts here, which divide into four separate swipes if we go with a wolf instead of dividing by five with a bear, as you pointed out last night, Captain."

He looked up at me and removed the blood-smeared gloves. "Therefore, a wolf-like creature with bear-like claws. Interesting."

Axil pointed at the third body with a questioning look on his face.

"No, thank you, Corporal. I've seen enough carnage at this point."

I reached into my coat pocket and carefully removed the handkerchief containing the fur I found in the snow. "This is the fur I collected. If you get a few minutes with your microscope."

Nagel carefully took the handkerchief from me and stuffed it into a tight compartment in his black bag. "I'll unwrap it later. No sense losing it to a gust of wind."

Nagel removed the butcher's apron and gloves. "About how long was this attack?"

I thought for a moment, eyeing Axil. "Five to ten minutes?"

Axil nodded agreement.

"Fights always seem longer when they're happening, probably seven, start to finish."

"Nine wounded in the infirmary, and how many dead?" Nagel looked up at me.

"Sixteen dead," I said, gesturing to the pile of canvased bodies.

"Roughly, three and a half men killed or wounded in each of those seven minutes. Those injured men got off easy, I'd say. It wasn't trying very hard when it attacked them."

Hopefully, we would never meet it when it was killing to its potential. The creature's attack paled compared to the killing machine of the war, where the bodies piled up day after day. It just depended on how you preferred your death—fast and furious at the claws of a preternatural monster or slow and torturous at the hands of an apathetic enemy.

ANDERSONVILLE – 1864 – Part 2

15

In late August or early September, wrapped in my filthy hole-riddled blanket, Rice shook me awake. "Lieutenant, wake up. That old guard, Levering, is looking for a team to bury the dead. Over a hundred men died yesterday. They need extra workers."

I was immediately awake. This was the chance we'd been waiting for. "Wake the others before Levering gets another crew," I instructed.

"Way ahead of you." Rice gestured to the other boys, Phillips, Mackey, Collins, and Yates, who were kneeling in a circle around me.

"I'm ready." I climbed to my feet. One of the luxuries of owning nothing except the clothes on your back was you were always fully dressed and ready to leave everything behind.

Rice clutched a small bundle I knew to be our stash of money, buttons, and other small trinkets purloined from the dead over the many weeks. Items we could not leave safely behind while on a work detail. We would use the money and valuables to buy or trade for food and assistance on our road to freedom. If everything went as planned, we would not be back.

We assembled at the deadline where Levering sat parked in a horse-drawn wagon. Most of the bodies were tagged with the corpse's name, rank, and date of death. The overall stench was overpowering, and we had trouble taking a breath without gagging. Swarms of buzzing, blue-black flies stirred as we picked up body after body and tossed them into the wagon bed. The dead wretches were only slightly worse off than some of the walking dead that lay around our camp. Some of them had been in our camp. The worst of the bodies broke apart and spilled gore all over as we picked them up, which released an odor fouler than I thought possible. Mackey threw up, and the rest of us intermittently gagged, fighting the urge to join him in emptying our stomachs. Fortunately, the bodies were lightweight. Those dead the longest were lightest.

We loaded thirty when Levering cut us off. "That's enough for this trip. We'll come back for the rest. These horses aren't in much better shape than the six of you."

Levering wasn't kidding. The horses' ribs were showing, and they didn't appear to be the healthiest specimens to begin with, but the distance to the cemetery was short, which was both good and bad. It was not the most taxing of trips for the horses, but the work was exhausting for us due to our malnourishment. If we had to make more than one trip to bury the dead, there was going to be little energy left to attempt an escape.

"You can ride with the dead or walk," Levering informed us. "I'm good with either."

We gave each other hard looks. We wanted to ride, but the smell was horrendous. Mackey shook his head in defeat, but they all took their cues from me. We needed to conserve energy for the work ahead. "Ride," I answered.

Passing through the gates was just a formality for the guards, who seemed listless and uninterested in their jobs. None of them bothered to make sure all the corpses were dead men. Could we have snuck an escape-minded prisoner in the bunch and gotten by with it? Probably.

I scanned the area outside the stockade walls for the first time in over a month, taking deep breaths of the fresh air. Fewer soldiers were moving about than I remembered upon entry. It could have been the oppressive heat and humidity keeping them indoors. Still, there were other signs of a slowing pace and population decline - fewer horses, fewer wagons, and an overall atmosphere of desertion. It looked like the Rebs were running low on everything. With over 25,000 prisoners in residence, we had the numbers to overrun our guards if we were of a mind to storm the gates and take heavy casualties.

As Levering steered onto the north road to the prisoner cemetery, my feeling of good fortune ended abruptly with the sound of a horse clopping up behind us. It was too much to hope that the six of us would be left in the custody of a single distracted guard long past his prime and in possession of a single pistol and ammunition belt. Approaching at a gallop was Miller, with a Sharps carbine, two side arms, and a wide grin on his too-white face. He maneuvered his chestnut mare even with Levering but kept a wide enough berth that none of us couldn't jump him, which appeared of genuine concern to Miller.

"Why are these federals riding in the wagon, Lev?" Miller asked.

"Not like it's a treat, Jake. You get a whiff of these dearly departed? I thought they stunk before they expired. Lordy." Levering coughed up some phlegm and spat between the horses and the wagon. "They need to save their energy for the work ahead. I don't want to be at this all day in this heat if we can speed things up."

Miller leered at us. "Ain't nothing but a lot of Yankee foot-draggers. Until I showed up, they was probably plotting how they was gonna kill you and escape. Especially this one." Miller reined his horse to drop back even with me.

"After the way you whipped that boy the other day, I doubt anyone would try." Levering's tone sounded more like wishful thinking than conviction.

"These blue devils are scheming. Don't turn your back on them. Not for a minute." Miller grinned a mouth of rotting teeth and patted his rifle. "But if you do, I'll be watching."

When we arrived at the cemetery, we found two long trenches about six feet wide and four feet deep, with a six-foot space between them. A detail of Negroes had done the digging the day before in preparation for us. The job suddenly became much easier than anticipated. The bodies were piling up so fast there wasn't room at the dead house, the usual first destination for the deceased. Our task was to remove the bodies from the wagon, lay them side by side in the trenches, and record their grave marker numbers and toe tags. We passed the information on to Levering so the exact location of each body would be recorded. A prisoner from Minnesota devised the system. It was better than the mass graves I expected from the Rebs.

Once we unloaded all the bodies and placed them shoulder to shoulder, we set to fill in the occupied spaces with the loose dirt piled on either side of the trenches, careful not to bury the markers. The day's heat increased by the hour, and we sloughed the sweat from our eyes almost as often as we tossed a load of dirt. Shovel work is hard on the hands but easier than if we had done the initial digging, too. The six of us got our first thirty buried by noon, and our hands were raw and blistered. We left the shovels graveside and climbed into the wagon for our ride back for another load. We ached from the exertion. Before becoming prisoners, we could have done the work without a second thought, but in our weakened state, it was grueling.

Miller managed not to run his mouth much as we worked. Even with his hat to shade his pale skin, he seemed to have as much trouble with the sun and humidity as we did. His first complaint of the afternoon waited until Levering drove us to the dead house where there was some shade and a horse trough of water. "What the hell are you doing now, Lev?"

Levering ignored Miller and positioned the horse for a drink. "You men can wash up in this trough and get a drink. I'm gonna find you something to eat." Levering jumped off the wagon, tied the horses off at the trough, and headed toward the bakehouse, a small log cabin-like building just outside the north gate of the stockade. I could smell fresh bread baking from across the road, which made my stomach rumble. The aroma alone made me faint.

Incredulous, Miller yelled, "You just gonna leave them here unattended?"

"No, I got you watching my back, remember?"

After Levering entered the bakehouse, Miller turned to us but settled his eyes on me. "That man's too soft on y'all," Miller growled. "You're up to something. I know it."

Maybe he wasn't as dumb as he looked, but Miller was definitely off in the head. Likely, whatever it was, someone thought him unfit for regular military service, so here he was at the prison. That, or he had a high-placed daddy keeping him safe from actual combat. Whichever it was, I held my tongue until Levering returned with two fresh loaves of bread.

Levering bit into one of the loaves and handed the other to me. My fingers practically tingled with the warmth of the crust. How long had it been since I'd last had something freshly baked? Miller grabbed for the loaf and knocked it in the dirt as he shouted at Levering, "What in the holy fuck do you think you're doing, Lev? These are federals. They're the enemy."

"Sweet Mother Mary," Phillips exclaimed at the sight of the bread now powdered with dirt. He dropped to his knees and snatched it up to dust it off.

"They're starving men that did a hard day's work and got more ahead," Levering dressed Miller down. "We have it in our power to feed them, so I'm giving them bread." Levering pointed at Phillips but spoke to me. "Divide that up with your men, Kincaid, that's yours."

The boys moved in like a ravenous pack of dogs as Phillips tore the loaf into six equal portions and doled them out. We each bit into our chunk and started chewing, afraid Miller would take it away if we didn't eat quickly. We instinctively tore a chunk off and stuffed it into our trouser pockets for later.

"You can't do that!" Miller protested, his albino cheeks turning a bright pink.

"Just did," Levering laughed at him. "It's the Christian thing to do. Do unto others, Jake. Like they teach in church." Levering took another bite and tore off half for Miller. "It's how I'd want them to treat my boy who's prisoner up north."

Miller snarled. "These men aren't like your boy, Lev. These are federals. They're trying to take away our rights. Free our slaves to rape our women and think they're as good as white men."

If Levering had an opinion on any of that, he kept it to himself.

"And this one is a liar and a schemer. I've heard these boys call him Lieutenant at least three times. Once today at the cemetery and two other times that I remember for sure. What's a federal officer doing with enlisted if he's not scheming an escape?"

Levering kept his mouth shut and looked me over, deciding how to respond. An uncomfortable moment later, he asked, "That true? You an officer, Kincaid?"

"Battlefield promotion," I lied, thinking fast. "I only make a sergeant's pay. Happens all the time with heavy losses. I'm sure they do the same in your rebel ranks, Sergeant Levering."

Levering nodded acknowledgment if not acceptance. "Sounds reasonable to me." Levering turned to Miller. "Battlefield promotion. Happens all the time. Old Lee himself was getting promoted every other month, it seemed like. Now he's top of the heap."

"Same with General Grant," Rice offered, smacking his lips through a mouthful of bread.

"Don't eat it all at once," Levering advised. "Your stomachs won't keep it down. You've been going without for too long. I need you all to bury another load, which'll be it for the day."

Levering seemed willing to let Miller's revelation go, but Miller didn't. After we loaded another thirty bodies from the growing pile in, we were greeted at the gate by not one but two additional guards. They seemed friendly toward Miller, and I didn't see six unarmed prisoners overpowering four armed guards. We had missed our opportunity. We could have killed Miller and Levering in the cemetery and taken our chances in the daylight. But now, knowing what I'd learned about Levering through the kindness he'd shown us, I was glad it hadn't gone that way.

16

Nagel packed up and left when Lieutenant Witwer arrived, looking dapper in a clean uniform. He watched as Axil, Jackson, and another man rewrapped Baxter and Cleveland for loading into the wagon with the others. When it was time, the bodies would be transported a few hundred feet to be interred. I was heartened that Witwer made it to the service. It showed the men he respected them. "Good afternoon, Captain," he saluted.

"Good afternoon, Lieutenant. Good of you to be here. You just missed the show." I gestured toward the bodies as Axil and Jackson tossed Baxter's bloody shroud into the back of the wagon. "Dr. Nagel just performed an impromptu autopsy."

"I would like to have seen that," Witwer said in a way that indicated he thought that was something he was expected to say.

"You didn't miss much. He agreed a large predator attacked us, but I think he's under the impression it was just a grizzly, and we were mistaken."

Witwer walked with me to inspect the graves. There were four rows of four pits with piles of soil heaped on canvas for easy refill. A few shovels and pickaxes were intermittently inserted in the piles. Standing on the cold, snow-covered graveside, I appreciated—from recent personal experience with the prospectors—the trouble the gravediggers faced in breaking through the icy ground to get to the softer soil below.

"In many ways, this is the hardest of obligations." Witwer got a far-off look in his eye. The manner of their deaths remained unreal to both of us. "I wish I could have done more to fight the thing."

"We stood about as much chance against it as we would have stood on a railroad track trying to stop a speeding locomotive," I pointed out.

We returned to the livery barn, now acting as a short-term morgue, funeral parlor, and impromptu chapel. All the men not otherwise assigned showed up wearing their best and cleanest uniforms to bid their comrades farewell. I dusted at my own half-heartedly. There wasn't time to go back to my barracks and change.

Corporal Little, who doubled as the troop's unofficial chaplain, arrived carrying a well-worn bible with ribbons marking select verses to be read over our fallen. A purple pastor's stole draped over his shoulders fluttered in the light breeze. He pulled a sturdy equipment crate to the front of the wagon of dead soldiers for a stage.

Wasting no time, Little climbed onto the crate and cleared his throat loudly for attention. "Let's get started, please." His voice was a pleasant baritone that suited the somber occasion.

"Fall in!" Witwer commanded.

The men moved into the barn and assembled in uneven rows as best they could. Those who could not fit inside stood looking in at the open barn doors. Witwer and I moved in close to the side of the assembly.

"Good afternoon," Little began. He preached words of encouragement and praise, some of which were Bible quotes, and others clearly written before the occasion.

"God has called home His weary servants…" He gestured to the heap of dead men behind him. A wrinkled American flag was draped over the bodies. Little named the fallen from memory, giving their ranks, months and years of service, and cities and states of origin. These courtesies had not been extended to our dead at Andersonville. "Yea, though I walk through the valley of the shadow of death, I will fear no evil: for thou art with me…"

But God had not been with us that night. Never had I felt so helpless and abandoned by the Almighty. There were many occasions during the war when I felt nothing but the absence of God despite all the church-going jingoism to the contrary. From my own experiences, I agree war is hell. Still, the creature's attack felt as though we had wandered into hell itself and been confronted by a godless beast: The manifestation of Satan's hellhound. In Greek mythology, Hades' guard dog, Cerberus, was described as a three-headed, dog-like monster stationed to prevent the dead from leaving the underworld. Was it such a stretch that our creature, plenty dangerous with one head, was ushering men in?

I shivered as I relived the attack. Perhaps it was the devil himself. I was beyond trying to convince myself the events hadn't happened as I stood among the lives it had so efficiently reaped. I found no comfort in Little's words regarding God's promises.

The service concluded with a man playing taps on his bugle. A horse similar in appearance to Private Booker's beloved Rex was attached to the wagon of dead men and guided by Axil to our cemetery.

17

After the service, I reported to Colonel Kirkwood's office. He returned my salute without looking up or rising from behind his large oak desk, littered with papers, maps, parcels, telegraph reports, and envelopes. Kirkwood was usually easy to get along with but understandably abrupt on this occasion. "Sixteen killed. Nine seriously wounded. What the hell happened out there, Kincaid? I sent you on a relatively simple assignment. Round up a small band of renegade Indians and take as many prisoners as possible for questioning and relocation."

I didn't see any point in sugarcoating it. "We were attacked by something in the woods. Something I can't explain."

Kirkwood's blue eyes rose from the paper providing him with the figures he confronted me with. "Some… *thing*? Indians? Bears? A Pack of wolves? Cannibals? What?"

I drew a breath to speak, then paused as I chose my words carefully. This information would not go over well. I took some comfort from my conversations with Dr. Nagel and his calm acceptance of what I told him. "I don't know what it was. It wasn't any animal I'd ever seen before. It stood upright on its hind legs like a man but much more muscular. It had the features of a wolf but was taller than a horse and weighed several hundred pounds."

Kirkwood blinked and considered my words. "Did you kill this wolf-man and bring him back with you? I'm hoping the answer is yes." His tone changed, but it didn't register until later.

"No. It got away…" I sighed. My shoulders slumped, and I shook my head. "No, that's incorrect, sir. It didn't get away. That would imply that, at some point, we were in control of the situation. We were never in control of the situation. It attacked, killed, and wounded several men and left when it was done. It showed no fear of us or our weapons."

Kirkwood squinted his skepticism. "Do you hear the words coming out of your mouth?"

"I could lie and tell you it was Indians or a pack of wolves, but the men know otherwise and deserve better. I don't know that this thing won't turn up again, and I figure we warn those who need warning and prepare ourselves for a future confrontation." I exhaled, having reduced my level of tension. I said what I had to say and would take my lumps, lose my command, and be relieved of duty. Whatever they wanted to do to me.

Kirkwood nodded non-committal. "I have a lot of respect for you, Kincaid. You generally follow the rules, but you always follow your conscience. You take on tough assignments and are highly regarded by the soldiers, past and present. They trust you... I trust you. So, I'm going to level with you. This creature you're describing... there have been unsubstantiated reports going back years. From prospectors, travelers, settlers, railroad men, and drunks. No credible firsthand reports, mind you. Campfire stories and rumors, really. That sort of thing."

That came out of nowhere. There was an uncomfortable quiet between us as the information sank in. Kirkwood continued, "With all the unexplored territory out here, who knows what kinds of animals remain undiscovered. Maybe what you saw was a freak of nature."

"To say the least," I said just above a whisper.

"There have been several unexplained disappearances. It's rugged country, and to be expected. Most are attributable to Indian hostility. Animal attacks are inevitable. Many traveling to California are wholly unprepared. Perhaps some have fallen victim to this wolf creature that attacked. But until we prove its existence, it would be prudent to be vague in the official report."

Kirkwood tapped the ledger on his desk with his index finger. "We'll just say men were killed and injured during an operation involving hostile Indians and indigenous wildlife. Not exactly a lie, but it'll give us some breathing room. We can amend the report when it's killed. It would be better to have a carcass under these circumstances."

"I see." I pressed my lips together to say no more. He was going to need me to sign off on this. A carcass and photographs would make it believable and spare the men ridicule. I could already imagine the taunts, calling my men lazy, superstitious, and cowardly Negroes, concocting ghost stories as an excuse for failure. "I suppose there's no rush to file a final report."

"Agreed." Kirkwood bit at his lower lip. There was more. "Full disclosure, Kinkaid. Unofficially, a wealthy man in New York has posted a substantial reward for this thing. Alive."

I laughed involuntarily at the insanity. "And do what with it?" My anger leaked into my tone as I recalled the horrifying encounter. How would anyone stand a chance taking it alive?

Kirkwood pursed his lips and shook his head just enough to indicate he had no idea.

"Did Washington know before sending us here?" I tamped my temper. "Unprepared?"

Kirkwood's held my gaze. "How would you prepare, having fought it?"

The question had consumed my thoughts since the attack, but I had no answer. We glanced at each other for several seconds, saying nothing.

Finally, it was Kirkwood who broke the lengthy silence. "In the meantime, some good news." Kirkwood dug into the pile on his desk and found an unwrapped parcel previously opened and crumpled closed. "This came for you while you were away." He handed me the package. "Congratulations, you are officially reinstated to the rank of Major."

I opened the parcel to find two embroidered field duty shoulder straps of gold oakleaf signifying the rank of Major and two similarly adorned epaulets. They were the pairs I'd given up when I was demoted. Kirkwood set them aside for this eventuality. "Thank you, Colonel."

"Don't get too excited. Your assignment won't change. You'll remain in your current capacity, but there will be a pay bump. In the meantime, try not to assault any more ranking officers for insulting your men," he laughed.

"Maybe I should just return these now, then," I huffed, handing them back. "I assaulted Dr. Nagel yesterday evening. He threatened to report me."

"What happened now?" He sighed in exasperation, waving away the insignias.

"He was dragging his feet when I ordered him to attend to my injured soldiers and used an offensive slur while disparaging them."

Kirkwood considered that before responding. "Sounds like he had it coming. You didn't break any of his fingers, did you? He needs his hands for surgery."

"No, I'm not stupid. I just choked him until he got off his ass."

Kirkwood laughed, genuinely amused, covering his mouth with a fist, knowing he shouldn't. "Well, Nagel is more of an honorary Major denoting his position as the company doctor. Not exactly a leader of men. Technically, you were reinstated a month ago when the War Department signed the orders. Therefore, you were of equal rank when you assaulted him. I'll smooth it over if he makes waves. Maybe it'll improve his disposition."

I nodded. "Thank you, sir. He treated the wounded and examined the deceased. I believe he's willing to corroborate the unique and unusual nature of the injuries sustained."

"That will no doubt prove valuable. Keep up the good work."

As the door closed behind me, all I could think was, they fucking knew there was something out here and didn't warn us. They knew!

18

My next stop was the stockade to take inventory of the Indian prisoners. There, I would learn their names, get to know them, and build trust. And possibly glean insight into the whereabouts of the creature and the missing braves. I aimed to safely round up the Indians and determine if the animal had a hidden lair.

The stockade was built inside the twenty-foot wooden walls of the fort and reinforced with thick pine poles sunk deep enough into the ground that horses and determined men could not work them loose. They were set close enough together that a man could not see between them. It was initially intended as a corral and stable for our horses in case the fort fell under siege. To date, that had never happened. Our presence served as a deterrent to the Indians and a magnet for settlers, merchants, and prospectors.

The adjacent town of Lucian, named by one of the first men to arrive who thought himself prominent enough to do so, was growing by the day. The train stopped once each week, bringing more people and goods.

Livery stables for the horses and barns for wagons and equipment were popping up close to the fort to accommodate our growing herd of riding horses. Area homesteaders were beginning to provide us with a steady supply of hay, oats, and foodstuffs. Provisions that couldn't be procured locally were brought in weekly by train. Fort Charon was no longer an isolated outpost in the wilderness. It wouldn't be long before we became a city with all the problems a population brought to nearby forts. Cities meant government, politics, and organized discrimination against the Negro soldiers protecting them.

An observation tower resembling a small log cabin overlooked the stockade area at the outermost corner. Initially, the structure was designed to monitor what might be approaching from the northwest prairie. Now, those sentries kept watch over the Indian prisoners immediately below them. It reminded me of Andersonville. Only here, the men did not taunt the prisoners to cross a deadline to shoot them. An alarm bell was affixed near the tower doorway to be rung in case of an emergency, riot, or escape attempt.

Because of BIA inefficiency and personnel issues, over one hundred Indian prisoners were making their temporary homes in stables designed for horses. The floors were dirt, and piles of dried manure had long ago been pushed against the walls. The Indians used it to burn in their fires for warmth, the way they used buffalo chips when following the dwindling herds. The whole place stunk of horse, but not as bad as it would when the temperatures rose in the spring. We had yet to make other accommodations for them. The BIA was not generous in supporting Indian prisoners.

I entered the liveryman's office, which had been converted into an intake and interview room. A blackened potbelly stove full of glowing coals sat in the corner, radiating ample heat. The nearby coal box was stocked to overflowing. Much of it was collected from the tracks, spilling out of coal cars. Axil rose from behind the desk and saluted me. "Captain, sir!"

I smiled and lowered my shoulder, tapping my new epaulet with some degree of pride.

Axil smiled back, displaying gleaming teeth, and saluted me anew. "Correction, Major, sir. Congratulations. I'll make sure the men are informed." It was clear Axil was bucking for Mal's job. I knew he stood next in line in seniority, but I wasn't sure he was the best man to replace Mal. Axil's temperament towards the Indians disturbed me, particularly his treatment of women.

Next to enter the small office was Private Jackson. He aligned himself with Axil as a close ally. I found his demeanor and treatment of the prisoners equally troubling. I shrugged off my concerns. Maybe I was being too hard on them by comparing them to Mal, the gold standard of subordinates.

Jackson saluted, and I caught Axil signaling him with a nod toward me, tapping his shoulder. "Good afternoon, Major. Congratulations."

I saluted him in return. "Thank you both. I want to speak to the new prisoners and gather information." I removed a bound ledger from under my arm as Axil slid from behind the makeshift desk of leftover planks to give me the only chair available in the room. This was usually a task performed by Mal, and it took me a few seconds to mentally check off the things I would need. "Call Buff and tell him to bring them one at a time." I didn't have to add Buff would be translating. That was a given.

"He's out in the yard gathering them now, sir," Axil said, anticipating my plans.

I raised an eyebrow in surprise at Axil's initiative. "Very well, let's get started." I sat behind the desk and opened the ledger to the ribbon marking the last set of entries made in Mal's neat, printed handwriting. I pulled a fountain pen out of my inside pocket, which kept it warm. Leaving such things to the cold tended to freeze the ink, causing them to bleed and malfunction. I shook it to get the ink flowing, then wrote the interview date and date of capture at the top of the next blank page. I marked the second line down a numeral one for the first new prisoner.

Buff entered with the elder Indian he previously described as senile. They positioned themselves in front of the desk. Buff was looking around for a place to sit. I took the hint. "Private, do us all a favor and grab some chairs or stools. Enough for each of you, Buff, and the prisoner. We will likely be at this for some time."

"Right away, sir." Jackson stepped out of the office without missing a beat.

"Thank you, Cap… Major." Buff's sharp eye caught my change in rank.

"What's his name?" I poised my pen.

"It translates to Little Bear." Buff supplied, having already inquired.

I wrote the name in careful cursive.

"Age?"

There was some back and forth between Little Bear and Buff. "He's confused, but you can safely say he's in his sixties."

I wrote, *60?* next to his name and considered he appeared at least a decade older than that. Life on the plains took its toll on the Indians. "Does he speak any English?"

There was additional back-and-forth, which caused both men frustration. Buff frowned and shook his head. "I think you should move on from this one, Major."

"Agreed." I looked up to Jackson. "Next." I wrote, *Senile. No English* next to the age column. Jackson ushered the aged man out the door.

Angry Eagle was pulled in roughly by Jackson and shoved to the stool. He sneered at us. I recorded his name and a *19*, which Buff provided earlier. I added, *Made threatening predictions...*, and stopped writing. Should I use words like *creature* or *wolf* in an official document? Kirkwood had facetiously said *wolf-man*, and I wasn't about to write that anywhere. I settled on *predictions of attack*, feeling that was sufficiently vague.

"English?" I moved on.

Angry Eagle laughed, "Fuck you! Coward! Blue belly! Thief! Raper of women!"

Buff threw up his hands in aggravation. "I guess we asked for that."

Jackson backhanded Angry Eagle from behind. Angry Eagle turned with a scowl, gave him a dirty look, and laughed. Jackson drew his hand back for another slap.

I raised my hand to stop him. "That's enough."

I stared Angry Eagle in the eye. "I intend to be civil and expect the same from you."

"Buff, tell him I'd like to know where the creature is."

There was the obligatory back and forth. I could tell by his tone Angry Eagle was posturing and making threats.

"He says it is everywhere and will return when you least expect it. This is not the only place it has business. It doesn't live in a cave where you will catch it sleeping."

"So just more of the same. How about the missing warriors from his camp?"

"Those men went hunting. They knew of white hunters slaughtering the buffalo, so they took a hunting party and a war party. About twenty men led by his father, White Mankiller or Whiteman Killer. I'm not sure which. He has killed many whites, but not as many whites as you have killed Indians. Angry Eagle was left in charge of the camp while they were away. We took them by surprise."

"Where might they be now?"

"They are near. They know where we are."

"How would they know that?" Jackson asked.

"Tracks in the snow," Buff answered, stating the obvious. "You guys aren't exactly subtle when you travel."

True enough.

"He says if you want to know about the wolf god, you should ask his sister."

"I thought she ran off?" I looked from Buff to Angry Eagle and back again.

"Her name is Ajiah. She's outside in line," Buff said in a matter-of-fact tone.

"Get her in here, please," and ordered Axil.

"Ajiah? What does that mean?" I asked. Buff usually supplied the

English equivalent of the Indian names without being asked.

"I don't know." Buff shook his head. "There is no equivalent."

"Tell him to point her out," Axil instructed Buff as he yanked Angry Eagle to his feet.

"One more thing," I added. The men looked at me. "What does he know about a wagon of prospectors attacked northeast of their camp?" There was back-and-forth between Angry Eagle and Buff, followed by a knitting of Angry Eagle's brow.

"He claims he doesn't know what you're talking about." Buff seemed skeptical.

"Thank you." I nodded and waved them off, then scratched the information into the ledger, underlining *Whiteman Killer* and *20 Braves*. They would be a handful.

I shook the pen and looked up when the girl walked in. All eyes were instantly upon her. She was by far the most beautiful Indian girl we had ever seen. Axil was noticeably aroused by her, taking in every inch of her with his lusting eyes. He unconsciously rose from his seat as if a lady of means had entered the small office. Her assessing eyes were a smoldering brown. She had a pleasing build, with firm, high breasts that stretched her buckskin tunic temptingly. Her hips were well-defined in her matching tasseled pants. There were beads on the tassels but none in the silky black hair between her shoulder blades. A leather strap held it in a loose ponytail.

I gestured she should sit on the stool just vacated by Angry Eagle. She licked her pouty tan lips, glanced at the seat, and took it. Her confidence and intelligence were immediately apparent. She did not have the usual doe-eyed look of confusion and fear displayed by most captives. She was somewhat darker complexioned than the others in her clan, and her overall features were more refined.

Her skin was free of blemishes, dryness, and scarring. Her lips were not chapped. She radiated health and well-being. Unlike the others, she did not appear to be suffering from starvation or exhaustion. I mentally chalked that up to her being well-cared for and receiving special treatment. It seemed desirable females received privilege and deference in all societies. I estimated her height to be five feet six inches and her weight to be approximately 120 pounds. She was well-proportioned but not as heavy as most men preferred.

"How do we spell Ajiah, Buff?"

"I'm not sure, Major. Never been a good speller."

"A-J-I-A-H." Her tone was pleasing, confident, and direct.

I was stunned. "You speak English?"

"Yes, I speak English. I am Ajiah."

"How is it you speak English?" Several possibilities occurred to me.

She looked me directly in the eye and spoke without hesitation. "I was kidnapped by whites who murdered my family. They were in a wagon train heading west. They taught me English to better serve them."

I looked her up and down again with a nagging sense of familiarity.

She glanced at my ledger and could read it, even upside down. "Eighteen years." She pointed to my hovering pen. "Is what you should write there. And I speak fluent English." She looked up from the page and met my gaze, ready for my next question.

I wrote out her answers without a second thought. I was mesmerized by her appearance and demeanor. I cleared my throat to break her spell over me. "What can you tell me about the creature that attacked us the other night?"

"I've never seen it. The others have spoken of it, and the entire Wolf Clan is enamored and worships it, but I have never seen it."

"Enamored?" Axil asked. The word broke his lustful stare from his object of desire.

"It means they love it. It protects them," she gave him a condescending glance.

"I know what the word means," Axil said defensively. "I'm just surprised you do."

She locked her gaze with him. "Not all Native women are ignorant vessels to satisfy your lust, Corporal." Her tone was cold and shut him down.

Axil was taken aback and scowled. He wasn't used to a woman speaking to him that way.

"What is it?" I wanted to stay focused on the task at hand.

"The Wolf?" She searched her thoughts. "Protector. The One Who is Many." The shrug she threw in at the end indicated she didn't attach importance to what the creature was.

"The One Who is Many?" I keyed on. "What's that supposed to mean?

"It means different things to different people." She moistened her lips with her tongue as she explained. "To some, it is a protector; to others, it is vengeance, power, or savior. Currently, its ire is focused on you whites and your many abuses."

"So far, it has only killed and injured my Negro soldiers," I pointed out. I reminded myself I was losing sight of the original intent of my question: What were we dealing with? I needed to circle back to that.

"Your Buffalo Soldiers do the dirty work of the whites." She tilted her head slightly in thought as she ticked off her grievances. "Take the lands belonging to their rightful owners by killing Natives and the buffalo they depend on. Natives don't believe in land ownership as whites do. Natives see the land as a gift intended for the use of all. Whites see land as free for the taking and send the dark-skinned people to wipe out the red-skinned people. White people have concluded non-whites are expendable."

Ajiah looked over her shoulder to Axil and Jackson directly. "You Buffalo Soldiers are here because Whites do not want armed Negroes who helped fight their war in the east. You are here to die and will receive nothing in return."

I agreed with her assessment. Based on their expressions, Axil and Jackson were turning her words over in their heads, perhaps coming to a hard realization for the first time.

"Forty acres and mule," Jackson croaked weakly, followed by a hard swallow.

"If you knew your history, you would know that will never happen. Your President Johnson rescinded the promises made by President Lincoln. If you think you will find your reward in the West…" She shook her head, "You are working for a lie."

She turned her attention back to me. "You see Natives as uncivilized and uneducated, but they existed, flourished, and survived here for thousands of years before Whites invaded. They grew crops, maintained game preserves, and established tribal boundaries. You call us Indians, yet we are not from India. This is based on ignorant geography. Who is the truly uneducated?

"The Wolf is your comeuppance. It is Death. Don't waste your time looking for it. It will find you." Beautiful and educated, with a healthy dose of anger and resentment. Her accusations stung like an acidic mist. The silence grew long and uncomfortable.

"Will you all take turns raping me now?" She dared us. It seemed an expectation. A verbal slap across the face laid bare carnal thoughts of her. "That will not happen," I declared. "I assure you."

She scoffed. "I see how you look at me. Especially him." She pointed at Axil. "To you, Native women are to be raped and murdered. Not necessarily in that order."

I thought back to Axil gunning down the fleeing woman and fondling her dead body. *She's still warm in all the right places.* She heard him. This was the girl who ran from me and Axil into the snowy woods when we raided the camp. She watched me from the shadows. It was her. Axil didn't recognize her, but there was no reason to point it out.

I then realized she was not among the captured. She came later. She ran off and returned. She was number forty-three. She must have rejoined the group when the captives were unsupervised during the attack. Her appearance was so mesmerizing I would have noticed her. As I thought back upon my rounds of the prisoners while we traveled, I couldn't place her with any of the men. I remembered consciously thinking the two women Axil had tethered were the most attractive among the captives and no accident. How did he miss Ajiah?

"Maybe we should take a break," I suggested.

The three men nodded their agreement. They hadn't recovered from their thoughts being exposed. She had them questioning not only their actions but the trajectory of their lives.

She slid a buckskin pouch on a thin hide belt on her waist to her lap. She opened the flap, removed two dark morsels of meat, and placed them in her mouth. After chewing, she added, "If you're not going to rape me, is it your intention to starve us? We haven't been fed since before we got here. I have too little from before to share."

"What?" I looked to Axil.

"That's the BIA man's responsibility once they're delivered," Axil explained in excuse.

I was angry. "Well, find his outhouse and get him off his ass. Flynn's his name. If you can't find him, figure something out. Slaughter one of their horses if you have to. That's one of the reasons we brought them along." If we're going to confine and relocate them, we have a responsibility to treat them humanely. I remembered the long days of starvation during my captivity, and I wasn't going to visit the same abuse upon others.

"Buffalo meat would be best," Ajiah insisted.

I admired her cheek. "I'll see what we can do."

She rose, and I asked my last question. "What do you know of a lone wagon of prospectors attacked north of your camp?"

She studied me. There was no knitting of her brow as with Angry Eagle. She gave a slight shrug. "Maybe they were where they should not have been."

<u>19</u>

I dismissed Axil and Jackson to feed the captives a hot meal and provide clean, warm water. They would likely have to make do with our disgusting beans and whatever meat could be butchered and cooked in short order.

Considering Ajiah's request, I thought back to the dozens of dead buffalo left to rot by the buffalo hunters. I shook my head in disapproval. It was wasteful and wrong. Angry Eagle said the women could have salvaged edible portions and fed them all for weeks. A wagonload of carcasses would have provided a feast for my soldiers and the captives.

With Axil and Jackson gone, it was just Buff, Ajiah, and me in the office. As I considered her, it occurred to me she didn't smell like the other Indians either. Indians tend to bathe infrequently, especially in the winter months. My men and I grew ripe over time, bathing only with bowls of warm water and soap when available. It was more our clothing that retained odors, but I was conscious of the different aromas people carried. With two uniforms issued to each of us, the closest thing to clean clothes were those being worn. Dirty clothes were usually sitting in a pile somewhere awaiting laundering. Overall, Negroes smelled their way, the Chinese theirs, and the Indians too. I supposed whites did as well, as I thought about it. I attributed this to the differences in sweating out the foods we ate and personal hygiene. I shrugged. Or maybe that had nothing to do with it.

Ajiah's cleanliness made her all the more appealing. Her smell was not soapy, freshly washed, or perfumed by herbs and flowers, but a freshness I couldn't put my finger on. Something akin to the way a baby smells clean and fresh.

"Perhaps your inventory would go faster if I assisted?" Ajiah suggested. "If you give me your ledger and fountain pen, I could do it for you."

I felt suspicious and guarded as several questions came to mind. "You can write?"

"Of course, I can write."

"How long have you been with these people?"

"About five years."

"And how long were you with the whites who adopted you?"

"Kidnapped," she countered with a sneer.

"Fine. Kidnapped. How long?"

She considered the question carefully before answering, "Five or six years."

That made her a mere child of eight or so at the time she was taken from her murdered Indian family. I had many follow-up questions, but I needed to focus on the necessary, so they would have to go unanswered. "I know you can probably provide names and ages for each person, but I have other questions to ask them."

"None of them can speak much, if any, English. They will tell you things Angry Eagle and I have already told you. What more is there to know?"

"Where is it?" The question lingered, and I didn't care about their denials. It had to be somewhere, and I couldn't help but think at least one of them had an idea where that might be. That would give me a place to start searching.

"Then your man, here," she indicated Buff, sitting in silence, "Should feel free to talk to them at his leisure, but he won't learn anything new."

Buff nodded. I knew he would question the others no matter what.

"Why do you want to help me with this?" I had to ask.

"The sooner you have cataloged us, the sooner we will be fed."

That made sense. "Very well. Let's get to it. But I'll do the writing. I want to place faces with names."

"Buff, please queue them up, and we'll move this along. Feel free to question whoever seems promising."

"Yes, Major." Buff stood, put on his buffalo robe, and stepped out into the cold.

When we were alone, I turned to her. "You were the girl that ran into the woods and watched me from the trees."

She studied me carefully, looking from my left to right eye and back again. I was struck by how bold this young woman was to look me in the eye without fear, shyness, or deference. As an equal. Or adversary. There was no judgment in her words. "And you were the captain who allowed his underling to murder a mother with a child in her arms without consequence."

A wave of shame burned in my cheeks. At the same time, it was clear she knew I was a captain then, though Buff had just addressed me as Major. I let the question go.

"Where did you get to? Why rejoin us?"

In a somber tone, she taunted, "Maybe I went to summon the Wolf and set it upon you." The words ignited a cold dread I tried to deny, but wasn't that precisely what I desired to learn? Where? How?

She broke the tension with the well-timed laugh of a flirty young woman and smiled at my silly fear. Her teeth were clean and pearly. "I hid! What do you think? I didn't want to get shot and killed. Where would I go alone with all I know taken or burned?"

I exhaled the building anxiety.

The door opened, and Buff ushered in the two attractive young Indian women Axil had tethered to his horse on our journey. When they saw Ajiah, their downcast demeanors perked into a brief conversation with her. Ajiah was notably more appealing and intellectually astute with all three girls together. She gestured to my ledger.

"This is Tanka. She is twenty years old," Ajiah introduced the taller girl. She wore her hair in braids adorned with beads. Both girls wore buckskin tunics over buckskin pants of a similar, flattering cut, but Tanka's clothing was darker.

"This girl's name would translate to Plenty Holes. She is twenty-one years old. Although you should know, Natives do not track age as whites do. I'm estimating."

"Plenty Holes?" I verified. "What's that supposed to mean?"

"As in many wounds. Though female, she is considered a fierce fighter."

"Maybe we should call her Plenty Wounds instead," I suggested. I didn't explain my rationale, nor did I want to engage in a conversation about the sexual implications of a woman named Plenty Holes with her.

"Oh, I see," Ajiah absorbed, nodding. "Plenty Wounds would be more appropriate."

"Agreed."

Buff grunted a half laugh of approval.

Plenty Wounds wore the lighter clothes and her hair in free-flowing tangles. Her build was athletic, and she had a tomboyish air about her. Again,

I couldn't help but compare the two women to Ajiah. Their faces were ruddier and weathered, yet only a few years older. I didn't know how to read into that. I dutifully recorded their information into my ledger and asked, "You don't track age?"

"No."

"Why not?"

"There is no value to it."

I let that sink in. "Do they have any children?"

She didn't have to consult with either of them to answer. "They each have two children." Ajiah provided the names and approximate ages of each of the four children. My math told me they each bore a child around fifteen. Somewhat younger than the average white mother.

"Tanka's mother now cares for the orphaned baby." Her eyes narrowed with the unspoken accusation. The information was an unexpected blow. As I recorded the child's name with the others, Ajiah dismissed Tanka and Plenty Wounds. Buff followed them out.

"Do you have any children, Ajiah?"

"No." She shook her head and pinched her face in thought as though troubled. "I would like to have many children, but I am not capable of childbirth. I have tried many times to become pregnant but without success."

"Is your mate among the captives?"

"I do not have a mate or husband," she explained. "Because I was raped while with the Whites and incapable of bearing children, I have no value to quality men. Because I have no family with the Wolf Clan, I have nothing to offer in status or station."

"But you're so beautiful," I spoke without thinking.

She watched me closely for a moment before answering. "Beauty has no value among Natives. The ability to work quickly and competently and cook skillfully are desirable traits. It's said that a man who marries for beauty only marries her looks, but my inability to have children doesn't stop men from wanting to be with me. Until recently, I slept with our Chief, Whiteman Killer, and his wife, Jumping Elk, the woman your Corporal shot."

I caught my breath. "I'm so sorry." The burn of shame returned to my cheeks.

She shrugged. "Jumping Elk was jealous of me. We were not close. My tears are for the young one robbed of her mother. That was senseless and cruel."

"It was." I nodded my agreement.

She considered me, closely searching my eyes. "Do you have children,

Major?"

I was not used to being questioned about my personal life, especially by an Indian, but I answered anyway, choosing my words carefully. "No, due to a war injury, I, too, am incapable of fathering children. My wife and child died shortly before I went to war." I decided that was enough information, and she seemed to sense I was ill at ease with the topic. Rebecca had been struck down with yellow fever not long after announcing herself with child. She was dead a week later. All I had known and planned was gone with their passing. I entered the war hoping I would be killed and my pain erased.

"I understand loneliness," she whispered.

War injury, I scoffed to myself once she left, and I was alone with my thoughts. Ajiah looked after her people as though they were her children. My children were my young soldiers who depended on me for guidance and protection from the unknown. Only Mal reciprocated and looked out for me.

Buff opened the door as I snapped my ledger closed and rose to leave. "Anything else?"

I shook my head. "No, any thoughts?"

Buff laughed with a grunt. "I think you're smitten. Watch out."

ANDERSONVILLE – 1864 – Part 3

20

When we returned to camp, I was exhausted from the work and made sleepier from a full belly. Being gone all day resulted in our meager belongings being picked over and spirited away. My shoddy blanket was gone. I bit off a piece of my bread and curled up in the dirt to sleep, feeling somewhat content for the first time in a long while. The promise of another day of work and maybe more bread carried me into a deep, hard-earned slumber.

It was dark with a full moon overhead when I was jolted awake by a commotion around me and a gloved hand over my mouth. A cold substance smelling of shit mixed with mud was shoved into my mouth.

"Lieutenant, look out!" Rice called me in a panic from the shadows, but it was too late. I heard the sound of a muffled cry for help and a series of blows administered to nearby bodies.

At least two grown men were holding me down. A hooded head of dark canvas whispered a threat in my face. "This is what happens to federals who lie about not being officers so they can escape to kill more Southerners."

It was Miller. I could smell his rotting teeth, even through the offal he smashed into my mouth. My pants were pulled down, and the threat forgotten as a searing pain burned my genital region. A cold knife was plunged into me. Miller was cutting me in a deliberate way. "This is what we do with uppity hogs on the farm, Kincaid. If you hold on tight, maybe you won't bleed out." He cackled like a lunatic.

I was released just as quickly as I'd been attacked. A mixture of excruciating pain, the egregious violation of my body, and the embrace of shock pulled me into unconsciousness. I heard Rice and Phillips make futile pleas for help in between curses as it all faded into a consuming black void.

When I regained consciousness, it was daylight, and I was aware of two things. I was in a room that smelled of medicine, where alcohol and antiseptics competed for dominance, and I had to urinate. The dull throb from my wound reminded me that my last conscious thought had not been a dream. I had been viciously stabbed. I tasted something strange on the back of my tongue and surmised I was given a painkiller. It was either laudanum, the cure-all of alcohol mixed with opium powder, or a straight-up shot of morphine. Whatever it was, it was wonderful.

As I tried to rise, I heard a pair of boots approaching on the wooden planks of the hospital floor. An older man with thin, graying hair, wearing a white shirt and dark vest, put his hand on my shoulder. "Go easy there, son. You don't want to tear out my stitches."

"Gotta pee," I rasped. My mouth felt like dry cotton.

"Let me get you something." The man, whom I assumed was a doctor, reached under my cot and pulled out an old cooking pot. "Use this and take it easy with your equipment. Someone did a number on you."

I took his advice and was happy to find my plumbing was still working properly, though painfully.

"I hope you've had all the children you planned on, soldier." His tone was lightly sarcastic but grim. As I finished up, I gave him a serious look of concern.

"You've been castrated."

The news was going to take time to absorb. I was a widower with no prospects back home. Another wife and child were something I assumed would come after the war. Now, that possibility was stolen from me. What woman would want a man that could not give her children?

"Your job now is to heal up and not get an infection. Take it easy. Don't expect you're in a rush to return to that hellhole they're running across the way." He motioned toward the stockade outside the window. "I'll keep you here as long as possible, but it won't be forever.

"No," I said, "I'm in no rush to go back." The hospital was a welcome taste of normalcy I hadn't experienced since well before my capture.

The doctor was good enough to bring me a cup of water before dosing me with more morphine. I watched him inject the liquid into my arm with a fancy glass and silver needle and was immediately overtaken by well-being and drowsiness. I lay back down and fell into a dreamless sleep. I slept into the next daylight and awoke to Rice and Phillips standing over me.

"Can you walk, Lieutenant?" Rice whispered. "We need to get you out of here."

"I think I can." My mind was cloudy from the morphine, and my genitals were comfortably numb. I was anxious and confused.

Phillips leaned in close to my ear and whispered. "Levering is helping us."

I sobered up a degree but would need several hours to clear my thinking. They stooped on either side of me and adjusted my elbows around their necks to gently raise me to my feet.

"You men be careful with him," the doctor instructed. "He's going to be tender for a while. I'm not understanding the rush to move him." He provided medical instructions as if I was headed to a comfortable chair. "No running and no heavy lifting." He held a small envelope close to my face, then pushed it into my front pants pocket. They were still coated with dried blood from the night of the attack. "For the pain. Use sparingly."

The boys walked me slowly out the door to the waiting wagon. It was stacked with another load of stinking corpses. Mackey and Collins helped Rice and Phillips lift me onto a space in the pile of dead men, stirring up a cloud of flies.

"Are you going to bury me alive?"

Levering snapped the reins, and the same malnourished horses from before jerked the wagon forward before the five boys were safely situated on the edges of the wagon walls around me. I craned my neck and found we were without an escort this trip. Levering did not press the horses to move faster than was comfortable, perhaps not wishing to attract undue attention.

We arrived at the cemetery in short order. The boys moved the bodies one after another, processing them from the wagon to the trench, shoulder to shoulder, recording the marker numbers to the dead soldier's identification tags, handing the tags to Levering, then offloading the next body. Once all the bodies were unloaded, the five boys covered them with dirt as quickly as possible. I watched through a haze of flies from the wagon with my back against Levering's seat. They were the picture of efficiency.

Hours later, when the bodies were adequately buried, Levering gave the men an earnest look and set the reins down. He climbed off the wagon seat and dropped to the ground. From a haversack on the toe board, Levering exposed four loaves of bread to me. He tore off a chunk and took a bite. "I've given this a lot of thought since I heard what happened to *Sergeant* Kincaid here." He emphasized my fictitious rank. "I got a son not much older than you five up in the Maryland prison. The conditions here are criminal, and I'm sorry to say no one sees an exchange coming anytime soon. I'd like to think there's a guard up there looking out for my boy." He shook his head until the thought went away, his eyes watering.

"Y'all seem like decent men. I can't say that about most of the prisoners here, and I can't say that about men like Miller, either. We may be on the same side, but that don't make us the same. I'm a Christian man, and I live a Christian life."

"So, what's your plan?" I looked up at him expectantly.

"I'd like to part ways with you here, but that doesn't give you the best chance, so I'm going to drive you along Sweetwater to the Flint River. There're some boats tied up there, less than five miles away. Anyone sees prisoners driving this wagon, you'll get stopped for sure. At least with me along, we can tell nosy neighbors I got you on a road repair."

Levering climbed back into the wagon's driver's seat and picked up the reins. "All aboard, who's coming." The men jumped into the filthy wagon bed with me. Levering snapped the reins, and the old horses started the journey.

"How are you going to explain our escape?" I craned my neck to look at him.

Levering shrugged his shoulders. "Mugged. It happens."

"Won't they question Miller or some other escort guard not coming with you?"

"That can be hit or miss. After you got stabbed, I think the general feeling was prisoners would be damn fools to try anything," Levering explained.

I wondered if it didn't make more sense that prisoners would become considerably more desperate in their behavior, but I wasn't going to talk him out of helping us.

"Y'all take this bread." He lowered his elbow to the sack. "You'll want to let the current take your boat as far south as possible to ditch the dogs coming after you."

"Downriver?" Yates asked.

"Current flows north to south, and if you tried to pole or row your way north, they'd find you quick," Levering explained.

"Hopefully, the guards will assume we're making our way north," I said. "Maybe buy us some time. Meanwhile, we'll find a safe spot to go ashore down south and figure a way north."

"You think that'll work?" Collins asked.

"Better hope so, or we'll likely get what Hough got."

"Or worse," Yates agreed.

We shared knowing nods.

There were afterthoughts between us, but we were determined to make the most of the opportunity by the time we arrived at the dock. A neglected dirt road led to a clearing in the heavily wooded area. As we approached, I whispered some last-minute instructions to Rice and Phillips. The men helped me gently to the ground. I was stiff from sitting, and the pain from my crotch was clawing to make itself known.

Levering remained in his driver's seat as Phillips came up behind him in the wagon and put him in a powerful headlock. Rice grabbed the man's sidearm from its holster before Levering could reach for it. "Sorry, Sergeant Levering."

"What the hell y'all doing?" Levering became suddenly angry and afraid, his eyes wide.

Yates saw what was happening and grabbed the reins to keep Levering from doing something stupid with the horses. Rice jumped down and handed me the pistol. I pointed it at Levering and told Phillips he could release him. "If you're going to say it was a mugging, we had best make it look that way by actually doing it."

I directed Rice to check under Levering's seat for a rifle. I knew teamsters kept larger weapons close at hand and out of sight. Levering didn't seem the type to break with tradition. Rice pulled a weapon loose from a rifle sheath underneath and smiled at his find.

"Are you gonna to kill me now?" Levering asked, rubbing his neck where Phillips choked him. He sounded worried.

"No, I'm trying to save your life and make your story look more credible." I waved the gun for him to get down from the wagon. "Take off your uniform coat and cap."

Levering reluctantly did as he was told but complained, "I had to pay for my uniform out of my own pocket."

"If they think you conspired with us, they might hang you." I took the oversized gray wool jacket from him, put it on, and placed the cap on my head. The ensemble smelled of sweat and grime.

Levering nodded. "Maybe you should hit me so I can say I was overpowered."

I nodded at Phillips to go ahead and do it before Levering saw it coming and changed his mind. Phillips walloped Levering in the face with a dirty fist, causing a bloody nose and what would become a swollen lip. Levering fell to the ground from the sudden assault and put his hand to the injury, touching his fingers to the blood and looking at it. "God damn it," he said in a dazed tone.

Yates unhitched the horses from the wagon, removed their tack, and slapped them on their flanks to send them galloping off. Levering watched the horses flee. Yates considered tossing the tack into the river but threw it in the back of the wagon instead.

"Use those leather reins to tie him up," I instructed. "Not so tight you cut off his circulation, though."

Yates and Phillips nodded and did as requested.

"I'd appreciate it if you'd wait until we're out of sight downriver before you start in on freeing yourself, Sergeant Levering," I suggested. "Maybe take a nap. Pretend Phillips choked you into unconsciousness with that headlock. Give your neck some time to bruise up."

Levering rubbed his face, pinched his nose to stop the bleeding, and nodded his agreement. Yates tied the man's hands behind his back with the leather. We each bid Levering farewell and expressed our thanks and blessings.

"Good luck," Levering's nose filled up. He appeared unable to get his rear end comfortable on the wagon's soiled planks.

The rowboat was small with wood slats that looked near rotting. Something obviously used for fishing. There were two oars, but one was broken in half and was all paddle with no handle. Once we were all in the boat, Collins cast off the rope that tied us to the rickety dock post and hopped in. Collins and Yates pushed us away, and we rowed into the eddies of the shoreside current. We all took turns glancing back at Levering until we turned a bend, entirely in the grip of the growing current.

21

Days later, I was summoned to Kirkwood's office by way of Lieutenant Witwer regarding an urgent matter involving the buffalo hunting company owned by a flamboyant businessman known as "Little John" Grogan. Little John was anything but. He stood six foot, four inches, nearly three hundred pounds, and known for his healthy appetite. He had a head of wiry brown hair and a thick, unruly beard he only trimmed when he visited the barber for haircuts, which was infrequent. He generally wore a dark buffalo skin coat of the highest quality, a walking advertisement for the garments his company harvested and produced for sale, primarily in the East.

Quick-witted, jocular, and a frequenter of saloons, brothels, and restaurants, Grogan was known to buy drinks for anyone inclined to listen to his far-fetched stories of the West. He was a talking version of the popular dime novels. Absent all that, he was a profiteer, pure and simple. When the government showed an interest in obliterating the bison from Indian Territory, if not from the face of the earth, Grogan saw dollar signs. Why just kill the beasts when their hides could be stripped from their carcasses and manufactured into expensive coats? He had a side enterprise that ground their bones into fertilizer.

Grogan was known as a big game hunter in Africa, wantonly killing exotic species for trophies and skins. Unlike most hunters who sailed across the ocean and trekked the jungles to shoot the first unlucky creature to raise its head or show its spots, Grogan employed a network of scouts and guides. He didn't rely on luck when hunting. He wanted a sure thing. When he made his trips, he knew beforehand what he would bag and ship home. Once he scored his trophy, he moved to the next unlucky species on his kill list.

In this way, Grogan methodically acquired lion, tiger, rhino, elephant, leopard, water buffalo, hippo, and giraffe trophies for advertisements in America and Europe. Grogan discovered early in life he could profit handsomely by attracting wealthy men into the sport of gunning down large animals to mount the heads on their walls and cover their furniture with skins. He minimized risk in his safaris by ensuring in advance the hunters would never be in any actual danger. The operation was more a catered vacation with fine foods and wines, expert guides, and a conscientious security team than a hunt.

It was rumored Grogan's guides baited the animals, drugged them, and employed hidden sharpshooters to ensure the obligatory kill shot. This was necessary as most bankers, railroad men, speculators, manufacturing magnates, and other robber barons had never killed anything under duress or in the wild. If all else failed, Grogan's men trapped the desired animal for an impatient hunter to shoot while it was safely confined. Wealthy men could then tout themselves as brave explorers defending against wild animals while being in no real danger. Imagine the thrill of bragging to your affluent peers—and potential future customers of Grogan—over cigars and liquor how you killed a ravenous predator on the dark continent. Oh, the backslapping, congratulations, and impressionable young ladies at your homecoming party.

Grogan had several partners in New York, Philadelphia, and Boston who ran his hunting operations. Concurrently, he established himself in the Wild West as a buffalo hunter and Indian fighter. Once west, Grogan calculated the profit margin in slaughtering bison for their hides and paying skinning crews just north of starvation wages, yet more than the average East Coast factory laborer.

I walked with Witwer from the infirmary, where I was checking on the men, to Kirkwood's office, comparing what I knew about Grogan with what Witwer told me.

"They say this man Grogan has shot more big game than any man alive. He's well respected in Europe and New England. He sent my father on a hunt to kill a charging black rhinoceros. Its head is mounted over the fireplace at our Connecticut home. They say the beast's horn can be ground into a powerful aphrodisiac to keep a man erect for hours. It's practically a dinosaur." Witwer tittered like a schoolgirl. "The stories he told about that hunt were thrilling."

"How did it taste?" I never understood the appeal of shooting an animal for the sake of shooting it. It was cruel.

"Taste?" Witwer didn't seem to understand my question.

"My grandfather told me a man should never kill something he wasn't going to eat."

"Well, he didn't eat it, Major. It was a trophy, after all. My father and his business partners have gone on safari every other year since well before the war. It's a sportsman's contest to see who can outdo the other with the biggest and meanest beast."

He thought I was impressed. No wonder the men referred to him as *Witless*.

"Where were all of these skilled killers during the war?"

Witwer realized by my rhetorical tone that I was critical and not admiring. "Well, seeing to their various business interests and supporting the war effort that way, sir."

"Made a tidy profit, too, I'll wager, while brave men died by the hundreds," I scoffed. "How about right now? What are the brave hunters up to this very minute?"

"I have no idea." He blanched and became mildly defensive.

"Maybe you could send a Telegraph message and invite them out here to help us with this creature that waded through us like we weren't even there. Imagine what that head would look like over the fireplace in Connecticut. Provided it doesn't tear their heads off in the process."

Witwer reached for Colonel Kirkwood's door handle and opened it for me. He stammered, "If I've said something to offend you, Major, I'm truly sorry."

"I'm weary of killing for killing's sake, Lieutenant," I waved him off as we stepped into the dark office. I directed my attention to Kirkwood in his chair and the man lording over his desk. It took a few seconds for my eyes to adjust from the bright sunlight to the pseudo-gloomy interior of the colonel's office.

"Ah, here he is now," Kirkwood proclaimed, half rising from his chair and gesturing an open hand to me. "How are the injured men coming along?"

We exchanged salutes all around, and I reported on the men. "Sergeant Butler is doing as well as can be expected. He can walk without assistance. The others have a few weeks of bed rest and light duty ahead of them. Private Dixon has died, as Dr. Nagel predicted."

"So, seventeen dead now. I trust we won't lose anymore." Kirkwood's tone expressed his concern at the heavy loss of life. There was a hint of a scowl on his brow that softened as he made the introductions. "Major Kincaid, this is John Grogan."

Grogan reached out, grabbed my hand, and began pumping it vigorously, "Please, call me Little John; everyone does. I look forward to working with you to locate my missing men."

I eyed Kirkwood for an explanation. As a rule, the army didn't escort civilians unless it was an organized wagon train through Indian-threatened territory. I wasn't interested in playing safari guide to Grogan. "What's going on?"

Grogan was not one to allow others to do his talking. He dove into his story. "I sent a crew of ten men to do some buffalo hunting and skinning out west about twenty miles from here. That's no more than two days of riding with wagons. With my men, it's usually less.

"A small herd was reported out there, and I sent them after it. I run a quality operation. Thirty buffs for thirty skins each day, no more, no less. We don't rush it like some of these fly-by-night operations that are just out to kill as many as they can for some sick personal best. Cutting out tongues for a quick buck and doing a shit job of skinning by either stretching the capes out of shape with a horse or tearing the hides is not our way. That's bullshit, and I find it repugnant. My men do quality work.

"That's what I tell my men, anyway. Thirty per day, don't rush it, come back early if it gets shitty weather-wise, Indian-wise, or otherwise." He laughed at his own joke. "*Otherwise*, is all the shit you don't expect. Bottom line is be back by the fourteenth day. Don't get greedy. The longer you're out there, the more time you have to paint a target on your back for thieves, Indians, or both. Sometimes, the Indians are the thieves." He laughed again.

"Which makes them overdue by how many days?" I got to the point, hoping to wrap up.

"Which makes them overdue by four days," he continued. To make matters worse, I got a telegraph message from North Platte Station that smoke was sighted in the area of the herd my men were operating. That's not good. It's not good even if it isn't my men, as you know."

It wasn't good for another reason. The area Grogan described was within a half-day's ride of our Wolf Clan attack. Those twenty braves led by Whiteman Killer were still out there. I also suspected it might be where the creature lurked, though I didn't visualize it starting a fire.

"So, I need you to escort me and my Cowboys to see what's what," Grogan concluded with a good-natured smile. Grogan was one of those men who likely got his way more often than not by being the loudest person in the room.

I scowled and glanced at Kirkwood for an explanation. "What do I need you for?" My suspicious eyes returned to Grogan.

"To assist me with the collection of my property and fight off any redskins liable to molest us." He said the words slowly and distinctly as if he were trying to explain something to a simpleton. A less enthusiastic smile punctuated the statement.

"I can look for survivors without you," I pointed out. "Probably do it faster, too." I kept my eyes trained on his. There was something he wasn't sharing.

"But will you collect my property and return it to me? That's the thing, Major. I have valuable guns and scopes out there. I want my employees back alive, sure, but those guns and scopes are high-dollar. The scopes were made in Germany. Hard to replace. And, of course, any harvested hides." He took a deep breath. There was no smile this time.

I was getting the distinct impression Little John was only interested in his property. The men were expendable. "If your employees came under Indian attack, your guns are gone, and they are likely dead. I don't need you along to determine that."

"I don't trust your soldiers," Grogan blurted, leaning over to place his hands on the edge of Kirkwood's desk and use as a barrier between us. His disapproval was cracking through his salesman's facade. "Coons have a reputation for thievery. Same as Indians. There, I've spelled it out for you."
"Maybe you should go alone. You're supposed to be some super cock hunter. It doesn't get more real than Indians fighting for their lives," I challenged, checking my temper.

Grogan blanched and swallowed hard. In a way, I was pushing him toward certain death and daring him to admit he lacked the stones to confront the threat.

"I defer to your expertise of the terrain and tactics, Major," Grogan said diplomatically, backing down.

Kirkwood saw the steam about to explode from my ears and nullified my predictable response. "Your orders are to escort Mr. Grogan and his team in a thorough search for his men, Major. Any questions?"

I managed to bite my tongue. "None, sir. We leave at first light."

What was it with Kirkwood putting himself at the beck and call of rich assholes?

22

I assigned Lieutenant Witwer to organize the expedition to save Grogan's men, provided they were still alive. I disagreed it was a military matter to provide an armed escort for a profiteering company like Grogan's. In my opinion, associating the army with hunting companies bolstered the legitimacy of slaughter. Grogan was welcome to go it alone as far as I was concerned. But an order was an order, and it would allow us to look for Whiteman Killer and the Wolf.

As I returned to my office to prepare and write a condolence letter to Private Dixon's family, I was distracted by a canvas bundle inside my door. It was a dark blue carpet bag. Inside were the compiled papers, journals, books, and correspondence found in the Wolf Clan tipis seized in our raid. It must have been dropped off by one of the men. The items still required sorting for names and intelligence that might provide insight into the Wolf Clan's travels. I had just the group of sedentary soldiers in mind to do the work.

I carried the carpetbag to the infirmary and unceremoniously dropped it beside Mal's bed. "Good afternoon, Sergeant. Have I got a job for you." I said it with a note of sarcasm because I didn't expect he would find it terribly interesting.

"Two visits in one day, Major?" Mal laughed but winced at the stretching of skin beneath his bandaged eye. "Must be important. What have you brought me?" He eyed the carpetbag.

"It's the correspondence and related items from the Wolf Clan camp. It still needs a review." In a joking tone, I said, "I figured while you're lying around with nothing to do, you and the rest of the men could process it."

"Not a bad idea. Divided up eight ways, we should be done in no time." Mal sounded thankful for something meaningful to pass the time. It wasn't exciting, but it was necessary.

"In the meantime, Dread Company is ordered to go on a rescue mission for a group of missing buffalo skinners who work for Little John Grogan. Remember that field of dead buffalo we passed the other day?"

Mal nodded. "I do."

"My guess is that was their handiwork. Grogan has an overdue crew. The railroad reported smoke in the area they were likely *hunting*." I said the word with contempt.

"Probably find them all dead and their wagons and hides burnt to the ground," Mal surmised. "Bet it was those missing Indians. Sounds like they'd be in range of each other."

"That's what I was thinking."

I stepped in close to Mal so no one else would hear. I checked the room for anyone nearby and lowered my voice above a whisper. "Kirkwood said Washington has known about the creature for years."

Mal was incredulous. After a lengthy stare, he spoke. "What?" he asked under his breath.

"And," I emphasized, "There's some rich fuck in New York that wants it captured alive. Which is a big secret for some reason." I nodded at the absurdity.

Mal shook his head slowly in disbelief. "Good luck to anyone dumb enough to jump in that meatgrinder." His surviving eye found mine. "Why?"

"That was my question. Didn't get an answer. Makes me wonder what this little excursion with Grogan is really about."

"You be careful out there, Boss," Mal cautioned.

"Always."

As I left the infirmary, I saw something I immediately didn't like. The BIA man, Flynn, strolled across the fort's parade grounds with Madam Beth Crossly toward the stockade. *Madam* was her professional title and went with the territory of her brothel business. Flynn looked much better than the last time I saw him. Hopefully, that meant he discovered soap and water and a general improvement in hygiene. I still considered him a dysentery threat.

Beth Crossly was not the most attractive of women, but she managed to accentuate what she had. Heavy makeup to cover blemishes and rough skin from years of hard living, and dark clothing that fit tightly enough to remind men she had ample breasts and curvy hips. She was well known to the area as a supplier of welcome female companionship. Crossly started as a dreg looking to wash, sew, and cook but abandoned honest labor for the lucrative pay of laying with men. She found out quickly she could name her price and get it. She started working the tents of mining camps to feed and clothe herself, soon realizing her most desirable commodity was in high demand among the lonely men traveling west for work and to seek their fortunes. If there was one thing missing in abundance in the boomtowns, it was women. Single girls looking for husbands were in short supply. Thus, women of less than average appearance and willing to make accommodations were treated like queens and paid generously for services rendered.

In just fifteen minutes on her back, Crossly made what used to take her an entire day of toiling to achieve chapped hands, sore fingers, and disparaging remarks about her cooking skills. She made a steady income rivaling the most industrious men in no time. Along the way, she learned how to coax and coach other down-on-their-luck girls into the life, with a cut of the payments going to Crossly for management fees. Soon thereafter, Crossly employed a security man or two to make sure the customers paid, and the women got out from under them alive.

It was well known among opportunists there was nowhere to find steadier work than near a military camp. There was a limitless supply of horny young men who were single, lonely, regularly paid, and all too willing to spend it on young ladies. Crossly constructed a small empire and moved into a low-rent hotel with plenty of available beds. It was a progressive step up from the tents and cots she started in and on. The women she employed didn't have to be particularly attractive, just available, and willing.

As the Indian relocation program intensified, Crossly found it no longer necessary to recruit desperate women via newspaper advertisements in the East to travel west by train. Desperate women were being brought straight to her doorstep by the U.S. Army, free of charge. All Crossly had to do was make an unscrupulous deal with the BIA agent for warm bodies. The girls didn't have to agree because they had no choice. White women were reluctant to sell themselves to Negroes. Crossly found Indian girls broadened her market, popular with both the whites and the Negroes, and she didn't have to pay them unless she felt generous. Most of the girls seemed happier with the warm beds and regular meals than the uncertainty of life on an unfamiliar reservation miles from the land they knew. It was easy to ignore any complaints because Crossly didn't understand, nor did she bother to learn, their native tongues. It was well known emancipation didn't apply to the Indians, and the laws for white people were different for those of color. In other words, the law was only relevant if the offended was white.

With the constant flow of captured Indian women passing through

Crossly's brothels, there was plenty of variety and turnover, which increased business. The girls who wanted to stay in the upgraded accommodations learned to work harder and became favorites among the regular guests rather than be sent to a harder life of poverty on a reservation. Crossly also learned to select children twelve years of age and above to perform domestic work and graduate to the sex trade when they had sufficiently matured. Or not. Why send them to government-run boarding schools when they could be home-schooled at the Crossly brothels?

I approached the pair as the required military escort into the fort was nowhere to be seen. I pulled my gloves on in anticipation of Flynn's greeting. "Good afternoon. May I help you?"

They stopped walking, and Flynn stuck out his bare hand for his customary handshake. "Major, good afternoon. How are your men convalescing?" I still detected the faintest stench of diarrhea about him.

With gloved protection firmly in place, I accepted his grasp. "Coming along, slowly but surely. Thank you for asking."

"Miss Crossly," I tipped my hat. In addition to her heavy makeup, she was drowning in cheap perfume. It did a passable job of masking her unwashed body odor.

"Major, please call me Beth," she greeted in her lilting tone. "When might I expect you to visit one of my establishments? My offer of first visit on the house still stands," she added warmly. "I'll give you the pick of any girl that suits your fancy."

I took her gloved hand gently and bowed my head but did not kiss it. "Very generous, Beth, but a visit is unlikely."

"I'm starting to wonder about you, Major. You don't know what you're missing." She teased, "I might be willing to come out of retirement for you if you tried to persuade me."

I had a pretty good idea of what I was missing. Venereal diseases put military men at serious risk. The men were merely educated on the health dangers and advised to exercise caution. Women found to be infected were routinely locked up in hospitals for lengthy stays.

I'd heard of male shields or rubber condoms, but the military made them challenging to obtain, and there was the nuisance of finding a physician to fit them so they wouldn't slide off mid-stroke. Protection aside, women with plain old fleas and crabs remained a problem.

"Nevertheless," I responded, sticking to business. "Do you require assistance?"

Flynn piped up. "I was just about to show Madam Crossly the newest prisoners."

"Whatever for?" I challenged feigning ignorance of their intent.

"I would just like to see the Indians." Crossly smiled, trying to evade my question. "I have an interest in bettering their situation."

"Specifically, the girls?"

"Why, yes, Major. The girls in particular. Nothing quite as exotic as Indian maidens."

"I can't allow that, I'm afraid. Regulations state that Indians are not to be abused or exploited in any way nor separated from military custody once captured.

"Perhaps the Indian girls would like to make those decisions themselves?" Crossly countered. Or maybe something temporary. A try-out period, so to speak?"

"I'm not sure they're in a position to know what's best for them," I pointed out. "Especially after so recent an internment."

"Please, Major, they are better off with me than on some filthy reservation with inadequate food, heat, clothing, and predatory individuals skulking about, and you know it." Her tone was haughty. She absently placed her hand above her left breast and clutched at the pearl necklace around her neck.

In a way, I suppose she had a point, but predators weren't confined to the reservations. I had two standing directly in front of me.

"I'm sorry to say, Major," Flynn said defensively. "But the decision is that of the Bureau of Indian Affairs, not military discretion. In a word, me." He looked me over judgmentally, tipping his head back. "I wasn't aware the army employed Indian sympathizers."

"The army employs all kinds, but I consider myself more of a Christian who actually believes in doing unto others." I was also intimately familiar with being at the mercy of captors. "The Indians are not to be frivolously removed at the whims of civilians."

Because I couldn't exactly stop them from taking a look, I accompanied them to the stockade. I climbed the steps to the lookout tower, assisting Crossly up the steep ladder to the upper deck. I was determined not to leave them to interact with the prisoners or to their own devices. I knew what they had in mind and was certain Crossly promised Flynn a bribe or favor to assist in procuring new girls. Probably both.

"Mr. Grogan tells me you have at least three young women I might be interested in employing," Crossly informed me.

There it was. Someone under my command was discussing the

captives with Grogan. This was the first confirmation that Grogan and Crossly had some association, though I wasn't surprised. Lucian was a small town.

"The girls mentioned were Tanka, Plenty Wounds, and Ajiah," Crossly provided. Of course, their names must be changed to something more conventional. Well, maybe not Ajiah. Such a unique name. Unique equates to mysterious, which translates to interest and word of mouth. We'll have to see about that one. My understanding is they are all rather lovely."

From the top of the tower, Flynn and Crossly could see the Indians milling about in the dusty yard below. Some stood or sat in groups, talking among themselves in the sun, occasionally glancing up at the watchful guards looking down from their stations. Others walked the perimeter of the confining walls. Many remained in the horse stable, sleeping their predicament away. With confinement came a great deal of anxiety.

"Might you be so kind as to point them out to me?" Crossly glanced at each female, sizing up their desirability.

I saw no reason to delay the inevitable and pointed out Tanka and Plenty Wounds. "There." They were supervising a group of small children occupying themselves by tossing a beaded pouch to one another. "Ajiah must be in the stables where they've set up semi-private living quarters."

"They appear a bit on the lean side. Is there any way I might meet them and get a closer look?" Crossly was pushing my good-natured hospitality to its limits.

"I'm thinking this is enough entertainment for one day. I have duties to attend to, and I can't leave you unescorted, the Indians being savages and all," I added with a note of snark.

Crossly pouted her disappointment but did not argue. Flynn took an audible breath and opened his mouth as though he might protest but didn't. If they were talking with Grogan, I was sure they also knew I was leaving soon, and it would be easier to push their agenda at that time. I would have to talk to the Colonel about barring them from visiting the Indians. I escorted Crossly and Flynn to the gates and went to see Kirkwood.

23

I later spoke with Ajiah in the liveryman's office, where we first met. Crossly was right. She was lovely, smelling fresh and clean. She watched me with uncertainty, assessing my intent.

"Some people from town have expressed an interest in you, Tanka, and Plenty Wounds. Their intentions are not pure."

"Are your intentions pure, Major?" She was direct as she stared into my eyes.

The singe of embarrassment stung my cheeks. Buff accused me of being smitten, but I told myself I wasn't. She was nearly twenty years my junior, but her piercing gaze and bold demeanor made her easy to talk to on an informed level. "Of course they are. You're young enough to be my daughter."

"That would not stop most men."

"Nevertheless," I continued, "Do you know what a brothel is?"

"It is where women are raped for money." Her voice was filled with judgment. "Are you selling me into sex slavery?"

The accusatory statement took me aback. Still, a woman in her position might see it that way. "You don't hold back, do you? No, I have no intention of allowing that, but a woman in town has designs on you and the others. She intends to recruit the younger girls to work as domestics in her establishments and graduate them into her system. I'm just warning you."

"Are you telling me this because you want me for yourself?" Her smoldering brown eyes remained unblinking as she continued to assess my motivations.

"No," I said flatly, "You're a child. I'm concerned for your well-being."

"If you were truly worried for my well-being, you would have left me where you found me." She tilted her head to make another point. "You to release us." She paused briefly. "But you won't do that either, will you?"

"No, I can't. I would be relieved of my command and court-martialed. Then, someone with no sympathy would be appointed to take my place and hunt you down. The best I can do is protect you. Will you let me do that?" I was not doing a very good job of reassuring her.

"My experience with men who say they want to protect me is they often become the person I need protection from. I can take care of myself." She sounded determined, but her demeanor relaxed as her shoulders lowered.

I nodded, feeling we were making progress. "We're riding out to the field of dead buffalo we passed last week. Men are missing. Buffalo hunters and skinners. Whiteman Killer and the others are likely in the vicinity. If I bring you along, I feel I can convince them to surrender peacefully and without bloodshed."

By the rise of her eyebrows, I deduced that was not the proposition she was expecting. Her eyes got wide with intrigue. "You desire my presence for purposes of communication. Is that your only desire?"

"Yes," I said firmly. Well, that and getting her as far from Crossly as possible. "I thought if he saw you were safe, he might entertain surrender. You indicated he values your company."

She considered that. "You would do better to take Angry Eagle for that purpose. Either way, you are wasting your time. The men you seek are likely dead at Whiteman Killer's hand. If so, would you still want Whiteman Killer alive?"

"Dead or alive, it has to happen." I was honest with her and nodded. "Better sooner than later. Other Indian leaders in other parts of the country have surrendered under similar circumstances." I paused before asking, "Why bring Angry Eagle when I have you?"

She smiled. "You overestimate the value of a concubine above his blood son. If his son can assure safety and convince Whiteman Killer it's no trick, you might achieve your goal. Alone, I will only arouse suspicion."

"You will both be bound," I added. "I can't risk an escape. Especially Angry Eagle."

"I expect you are not a fool."

"And once we've accomplished that task, I would like to be pointed in the direction of that thing. It's a confrontation that will eventually occur."

"You'll have your hands full with Whiteman Killer. If the Wolf

114

appears, none of you will survive. As a military man of war, I expect you would choose your battles more carefully."

It had been my experience my greatest battles tended to choose me.

"I will try to convince Angry Eagle surrender is the best way. He will likely see this as an opportunity to escape and join his father." She raised her hand before I could protest. "That alone will get him to agree to cooperate. I'm merely warning you what motivates him."

I nodded. "Understand that an escape attempt will result in his being shot. We will restrain him in a way that will make escape impossible."

She considered my proposal before answering. "I will assist you as long as you guarantee your goal is peaceful surrender. If your intentions change or you go back on your word, our agreement dissolves, and I can promise you will suffer fatal consequences."

Her certainty left me startled. Though I knew I had the upper hand in manpower, weaponry, and strategy, her words filled me with doubt and dread. I couldn't get over the nagging fear I was ignoring something painfully significant that would make me eternally sorry.

24

We rendezvoused at first light. Lieutenant Witwer assembled forty soldiers, three wagons loaded with supplies, extra ammunition, and the two prisoners. He commandeered half a dozen buffalo rifles and ample ammunition from town. I complimented him on his planning and organizational skills. Our provisions were streamlined to last us five days on the trail, which was more than enough. Little John arrived with four Cowboys and a wagon of their own. We didn't know how many bodies we might transport in addition to Grogan's precious equipment. For all of our planning, we could not prepare for every contingency. Witwer suggested bringing Dr. Nagel in case there were wounded to treat. I nixed the idea because it exposed the doctor unnecessarily to harm, and our medic, Private Wilson, was plenty capable.

Witwer wanted Buff to accompany us, but that presented an unnecessary risk to Buff as the mission was to rescue survivors. Regarding Buff's tracking abilities, I was confident Grogan would know best where his men might be found. If negotiation became necessary, I would ask Ajiah to do it. The argument against that was whether Ajiah could be trusted to translate accurately and not place us in danger. We would learn quickly if Ajiah was not being truthful and take corrective measures.

Scraping together forty men, including myself and Witwer, resulted in a skeleton crew of tired soldiers remaining behind for day-to-day operations. The loss of seventeen men and eight convalescing was a severe blow to Dread Company's forces. It took all of my powers of persuasion and a stern, "That's an order" to dissuade Mal from joining the expedition. He needed a good week or two of healing before he would be out of the woods. At the very least, I wanted to avoid his stitches bursting open.

Grogan's Cowboys were trail-weathered veterans from Texas and probably former Confederates. All appeared to be around thirty, making them prime soldiering age during the war. Each wore a soiled, deep yellow duster I recognized as military issue. I spotted belts, shirts, weapons, and boots on all four that looked like Confederate surplus. On one, I spied a CSA belt buckle. I tried not to read too much into the condescending looks they gave Axil, Jackson, and the rest of Dread Company.

Grogan rode a well-fed roan quarter horse that shouldered the man's girth and heft with relative ease. He wore a clean buffalo coat that would probably not remain so for long. He introduced the Cowboys by their last names: Jordan, Spooner, Tarling, and Bennet. I wasn't clear who was who and didn't much care. Upon first introduction, they seemed interchangeable, but for their hair length and facial hair. Grogan spoke mainly with the one in a soiled ten-gallon hat whom he called Mr. Spooner. The one with the CSA buckle.

Dread Company was chatting and laughing as they often did upon gathering. Spooner said in a voice too loud for the occasion, "No one said we was riding with the emancipated." He spat a stream of brown tobacco juice into the melting snow to punctuate his contempt. Jordan, Tarling, and Bennet grumbled their unintelligible agreement. Dread, to a man, went stone silent. The four Cowboys immediately realized their mistake.

I ambled Styx within feet of the men and said, "You Southern heroes are welcome to go it alone if you're picky who you share the trail with. We'll mind your bodies for burial on our next patrol." I paused for effect and made deliberate eye contact with Grogan and his hired guns.

"If we ever find them," Axil added, trotting his mount behind me.

It angered me that the people who expected protection when they ventured from the fort's safety turned around and maligned the men protecting them.

Grogan sidled up to me on his mare. She snorted her greeting as she drew near Styx. "We appreciate your assistance, Major. You and your men." Grogan eyed Spooner, "Apologize, Mr. Spooner."

Spooner looked stung but kept his eyes on me and mumbled, "Sorry."

I looked to Axil, who moved a few feet closer. He understood what I wanted.

"Apology accepted." Axil made stony-eyed contact with the Cowboy, refusing to look down in deference to a white man from the former Confederate States.

"Don't forget," I said to Grogan and the Cowboys. "You're

outnumbered out there." I gave them a tightlipped smile for emphasis. "On both sides."

By the looks on their faces, my point was made.

"I do appreciate this, Major," Grogan said in a conciliatory tone. "As a business owner, employees take on a familial relationship. They're grown men, but I feel responsible for them."

"You can't just abandon them. I understand completely."

I called out to Axil. "I'll address the men, Corporal."

"Gather round!" Axil yelled. "Gather round for the Major." Dread company crowded in. Some on horseback, some not.

"I want to accomplish this mission as quickly as possible, though we are provisioned for five days. We are to rescue or determine the whereabouts of ten buffalo hunters." I looked at each man's face. "As you know, we face unusual obstacles. An Indian war party of at least twenty braves is still unaccounted for." I paused to let that sink in. "Additionally, the creature that attacked us and took a third of our number represents an unknown quantity. We don't know anything about it or where it might be. Keep your eyes open. I consider the creature the greater and more probable threat."

"What's he talking about?" Spooner asked Grogan.

"If you see Indians," I continued, "Do not open fire unless fired upon. My goal is to achieve communication and take them into custody peacefully." I predicted that would not be well received.

"That's not likely," Cowboy Tarling griped. "Only good Indian is a dead one." His three compatriots laughed. As well as some of Dread Company.

"So, let's move out and get this done." I looked to Witwer to give the order.

"Let's move it out," Witwer yelled officially. He and I rode side by side in the lead positions. Axil took up the rear to ensure the wagons and men fell in line.

Grogan and his men traveled loosely to my right, where I could hear bits and pieces of their conversations. Spooner was the most vocal. "What's he talking about, Little John? What's out there?"

"Nothing we can't handle," Grogan assured. "We have superior firepower."

Bennet piped up for the first time, sounding worried. "He said it killed twenty-five men."

"A big bear or freak wolf or something," Grogan said, keeping the threat of the creature vague. He was deliberately minimizing the danger like he knew something. The New York connections occurred to me for the first time. "We got something for its ass. Probably just Indians, anyway."

The Cowboys continued to complain among themselves. I didn't see any reason to explain further the horror lurking in the vast countryside. They wouldn't believe me anyway. Secretly, I hoped ours was a one-time encounter, but deep down, I knew I was kidding myself. There would be an inevitable confrontation, probably at the worst possible time. What Grogan chose to share with his men was his business.

Several hours later, we were within two miles of the field of dead buffalo. I took the opportunity to drop back and check on Ajiah and Angry Eagle. They were in our chuckwagon, steered by Private Gatewood, our cookie. Private Wilson was at the other end of the spring-mounted wooden bench with Ajiah sitting between them, jostled by every bump in the rutted trail. Their feet were firmly planted on the toe board for support. Ajiah's wrists were not bound, but her ankles were shackled under her buffalo robe. The snow was melting, yet the air still held a chilling bite.

Angry Eagle peeked from the canvas flaps of the covered wagon behind them. He had a pair of sturdy pirate iron handcuffs on his wrists, which were visible as he held onto the wagon box with both hands to steady himself. He wore shackles around his ankles that matched Ajiah's to prevent them from running off. I hadn't seen the point in handcuffing Ajiah because I didn't believe she would lash out or attack the soldiers.

Ajiah eyed me curiously. I wondered what she was thinking. Did she believe I would keep my word to take the Indians alive? Did she think I would betray her trust? Was she counting the minutes to sundown to attempt an escape? Or was she hoping the creature would return and kill us all? Time would tell, but I was sure she wasn't going anywhere in those shackles. At least not without the key dangling from the strap around Gatewood's neck.

As we approached the dead buffalo, Styx galloped to the front of the line, where we came to a stop. Everyone dismounted to stretch their legs and relieve themselves as necessary. The buffalo appeared the same as we found on our last pass. The only difference was scavenging animals had been at the exposed meat. I saw in the distance a pack of coyotes gnawing at a carcass. With the warmer weather came the fragrance of rotting flesh.

Grogan looked over a handful of the exposed bison as though inspecting the stitching on a refined garment. "My men did these. I can tell by the care in the skinning," he proclaimed with pride, pointing to a nearby carcass. "See how no chunks of meat or fat are torn away here? This was done by a practiced hand. Pulling too fast or using a horse can spoil an entire robe.

My men do a quality job." Grogan pointed at the neck wounds of the three beasts nearest him. "See here, a single shot to the neck? Every one a clean kill. That's Bob Foster's work with a .45-120-550 Sharps rifle married up with one of my 10-power, German-made telescopic sights. He sets up a special bipod shooting stand and picks them off individually. Usually from about 200 yards or so." Grogan pointed to a nearby hill. "A spot like that up there would be prime."

Spooner rode up the same hill while shading his eyes against the horizon. He pulled a small military telescope from a pouch on his saddle, elongated it, and peered through.

"Just out of curiosity," I asked, "Why don't you harvest the meat while you're at it? Couldn't you sell it too?"

"Each one of these monsters produces about 425 pounds of meat. Do you have any idea how long it would take to butcher, smoke, cure, or brine all of this?" Grogan tossed his arm in a sweeping arc to encompass all the dead animals.

I'd done my share of hunting and knew it was a process.

"Too long, that's how long. We're an in and out operation." He laughed. "Kind of like Beth Crossly's brothels, only a different meat product."

"There's a reason ranches and cattle are popular," Grogan pontificated. "Cattle cooperate. We can drive them to slaughter and kill them all in one place. The only thing you can count on from bison is unpredictability. They run one minute and turn on you the next. A rule of thumb is if you see a bison's tail stand up straight, you better run."

Grogan shook his head at the dead animals. "Truth is, I'd love to bring all this meat to market and ship it east. But it would take wagons, men, and a steady supply of railroad cars. Skins are much easier to take and transport and more profitable, too."

"Such a waste," I said under my breath. I thought of the Indians. I thought of the rampant starvation while at Andersonville prison.

Spooner collapsed his telescope and descended the hill to report to Grogan.

"What've you got?" Grogan asked.

"Based on the railroad reports of smoke, this killing field, and known heard migration patterns, I'm thinking we need to travel northwest to pick up their trail."

Grogan nodded his agreement and turned to me. "Let's get to it, Major."

25

Spooner distinguished himself as a skilled tracker and map reader. Within three miles, we picked up the distinct tracks of wagons and horses on the matted, snow-covered grass. Upon cresting a series of hills, we happened upon a treelined creek and an abandoned, burned-out wagon sitting askew on a broken spoked wheel. The upper deck had been set ablaze and charred into an unrecognizable mass. As we drew closer, I detected the distinct odor of burnt animal fur and buffalo hide, overpowered by kerosene, the likely accelerant to set it all aflame. The stink of it grew in intensity as we drew closer. Upon inspection, it became clear the wagon was filled with bailed buffalo skins, destroyed like a book thrown into a fire to char the outer edges. The flames snuffed out before touching the innermost section of the hides. The wagon's iron-reinforced skeleton poked out where the wooden planks had been reduced to ash.

"That's one of mine," Grogan announced, surveying the wagon.

"There's a body here," Spooner called, pointing at a corpse lying in the tall grass where the team of horses would have been attached to the wagon tongue. "Took an arrow in the back."

Tarling dismounted his horse to inspect the body. The corpse's arms were tucked under the dead man's chest. Tarling tugged on a rigid elbow to break the body free of the ice and snow adhering it to the ground and revealed a purple face of pooled blood clenching its teeth in agony. The man was so severely bloated I could not estimate his age. Both hands clutched the broken shaft of a second arrow protruding from his chest.

"It's Potts, the cook," Tarling said. "Looks like the last thing he did was release the horses before he got hit, probably hoping to ride one out of here. Fucking redskins!"

"The others wouldn't have abandoned him unless under attack," Grogan speculated.

"Cookie's always the slow poke of the group," Tarling said matter-of-factly.

"Watch this treeline," I ordered, pointing west. "We can't assume it's safe." I turned Styx to affix my gaze on our D-Company chuck wagon, specifically the prisoners therein. It was closing in with two soldiers on horseback trailing behind. Grogan's chuckwagon labored loosely nearby, with Bennet driving the team.

Grogan and his mounted Cowboys moved toward the trees briskly and without caution, Spooner in the lead. He pointed to nothing I could see and yelled, "I see another wagon."

Grogan and the other two mounted Cowboys cantered after Spooner without a word to me. I understood their urgent desire to find their friends, but whatever happened occurred some time ago. The area was unsecured, and they were recklessly ignoring the possible threat.

I turned to Witwer, who was hanging back, looking for direction and not taking any initiative. He had no idea what he should be doing. "Stay here. Have the men remain vigilant. Spread them out. We can't assume this area is safe. Eyes on the perimeter."

"Yes, sir, Major," he responded, glad I'd given him something to do.

"Axil!" I yelled, knowing he was nearby.

"Here, sir!" He steered his horse clear of a group of soldiers.

"Grab three men and follow me!" I broke away in pursuit of Grogan.

"Yes, sir!" He gestured to the men closest to him. "You three are with me."

I caught up to Grogan and his Cowboys, clustered around a badly burned wagon near a frozen creek that separated us from the trees. The closer we got to the woods, the more ominous the shadows became. I could only see the front tree line as the sun had fallen behind the hill they blanketed. This was a bad spot. We were sitting ducks for any enemy hidden in the woods or behind the hills.

The structure of the second wagon was burned to the ground. The surrounding snow melted to the turf. Nothing discernable remained but the iron supports framing the wagon and rimming the spoked wheels. Charred wood provided some definition to the husk, but overall, it had burned to black and gray ashes. Lumped in and coated with ash between the wheel remnants were three sets of human remains. Each was positioned behind a rifle reduced to metal bores and parts. Two men had taken a position of concealment between the spoked wheels to shoot into the woods. The third man lay to fire at whatever was attacked from behind. If there had been any arrows, they all disintegrated in the fire. I again detected the heavy odor of kerosene accelerant.

Tarling pointed at what was left of the men. They were so severely burned they appeared childlike in size. "Can't even tell who they were anymore."

That was four confirmed dead and six unaccounted for.

"Where would the heavy guns and your scopes have been stored for the ride?" I asked Grogan. "They wouldn't have been strapped to the horses, would they?"

"No, those guns weighed sixteen pounds each," Grogan advised. "They'd be safely nestled in one of the wagons."

We stared at the piles of ash that had been the wagon. With complete disregard for the appearance of my polished riding boots, I waded into the debris, bits of fur and hide, and kicked into a series of rigid objects. I yanked my gauntlets from their pockets, pulled them on, and reached for the pipe-like objects buried in ash. I came up with the barrel of a large bore rifle and a once shiny brass tube with heat-cracked glass. "This one of your scopes and buffalo guns?

"Shit!" Grogan swore as I tossed the scope at his feet and felt around for more.

I found another large-bore barrel and tossed it after the first. Grogan's look confirmed I'd found everything. The big guns had been stored while the men carried their lighter arms.

Without a briefing, Spooner and Jordan drove their horses through the iced stream in a rush to wade into the woods for more clues. Shod hooves punched through the thinning ice. The temperature was hovering just above freezing, but I anticipated it dropping as the sun sank into night. We would have to make a camp before darkness fell.

"Your men might want to hold on until we get organized and do this correctly," I suggested to Grogan. "Running into the woods willy-nilly is a fool's errand. You requested us for force and numbers. We're here. Let's put my men to good use."

I was surprised Grogan allowed himself to be ruled by emotion. He was getting caught up in the chase. This was not hot pursuit. I knew he wanted to know what happened to his men, but he had to understand the necessity of acting methodically. A group of forty soldiers and five Cowboys had likely not gone unnoticed by anyone within a few miles radius.

Grogan flashed a scowl of annoyance that quickly softened to a nod of agreement. "That's probably sound thinking, Major."

Before I saw what he was doing, and thus, before I could stop him, Grogan drew his revolver, cocked it, and fired a shot into the air. "Spooner!"

Spooner and Jordan reined in their horses and stopped their forward progress. They looked back, drawing their weapons in anticipation of attack.

Grogan had their attention. "Wait! We'll coordinate with the army." Grogan turned his attention to me and noticed I was staring at him in a scolding manner. "What?" He asked.

"No more unnecessary gunfire. If there's anyone in the vicinity that didn't know we were here before, they sure as shit know now." Or any *thing*, I thought to myself.

"Agreed." He sheepishly holstered his weapon.

I turned to Axil, "Go back and tell Witwer we're going to fan out on this side of the creek. I don't want the men bunched up on top of each other. Every man should be where he can see the man next to him. Eyes peeled three-sixty, understood?"

"Yes, sir, Major." Axil road to Witwer to deliver the message.

"I see another body a few yards into the trees, Mr. Grogan," Spooner called. His horse spun around as he pointed.

I turned to a young private who was new to the unit and with whom I was unfamiliar. He was as black as midnight. "What's your name, son?"

"Webb, sir, Private Gary Webb." His voice quavered nervously. He bladed his shoulder toward me, apparently thinking he needed to prove his rank by displaying his lone chevron.

"How about we ride over there and see this dead body, Private?"

"Yes, sir, but honestly, I've seen enough dead bodies this month to last me a lifetime."

"I'm with you there, Private. I'm with you there."

We rode across the creek to Spooner's position. Spooner climbed off his mare and loosely draped the reins over a nearby tree branch. Webb and I followed suit. Spooner pushed a pine tree bough aside and pointed to a blanket of dead leaves and pine needles lightly sugarcoated with granular snow. I looked to the canopy overhead, where water dripped from the snow-laden boughs protecting the area. A few yards away was a prone, lifeless man in cowboy boots, jeans, and a dark flannel shirt. I knelt and squinted as my eyes adjusted to the lower light level. Except for the occasional patter of melting snow striking dried leaves, there was no sound but our breathing. Was silence here typical? It's funny what occurs to you when you're uncertain of your surroundings.

Beyond the man were two more bodies, a corpse dressed like a white man on his back and another in buckskin atop him, obviously an Indian. They appeared to have been locked in mortal combat when they died. As I drew closer, I noted the first man lying prone was not wearing a dark flannel shirt but a shirt so sodden in blackened blood that its true colors were unidentifiable. Spooner pulled at the man's collar to reveal his throat had been cut to his spine. "It's Bates."

Spooner worked to separate the corpses, rolling the dead Indian off the man on his back. The Indian had a bowie knife sticking from his chest and had bled all over the man beneath. The buffalo skinner had deep cuts to his hands, wrists, face, and throat. The blood was black and tarry. "Evans," Spooner identified him. "That's more than half our guys we've found so far."

"Not looking too good for survivors." I grimaced.

Spooner gave the dead Indian a swift kick in the face and was rewarded with a clump of pulpy gore on his boot. "Motherfucker!" he swore, wiping the mess on the dead man's clothing.

"How do you think it went down?" Jordan asked Spooner.

Spooner looked through the trees the way we entered. "They came up from behind and hit Potts, then snuck up on those three under the wagon. These two got chased into the trees here, where more were waiting. Redskins probably took the horses." Spooner stepped outside the tree line, stared at the horizon, and spat a stream of tobacco juice on the dead Indian.

"Grogan said a man named Foster was your best sharpshooter," I told Spooner. "Where do you think he was set up when all this happened? A man like that would find a position."

"That's what I was thinking," Spooner agreed.

"Could he have been one of the men under the burned wagon, where I found the telescopic sight and the large-bore rifle?"

"I hope not," he said, carefully scanning the overlooking hills. "I'd like to think he killed at least a few of the sons-of-bitches." He pointed to a hill that looked promising for a sniper. "A spot there would have given him the advantage."

I noted it was well behind the line of fanned-out soldiers. And that's when the first Indian appeared. He stood as a two-dimensional silhouette with no features. A short distance behind him was another wraith, creeping up on horseback. Upon spotting us, the second Indian dismounted. The first Indian raised a fist to signal others unseen to stop moving forward.

"We've got company," I said.

"Shit," Spooner responded, but keeping his cool.

I glanced at our chuckwagon. It could not have been farther away, as luck would have it. I mounted Styx and rode for it at a speed not to telegraph alarm. "Hold fire!" I ordered. I pointed at the silhouettes. My men dropped to their knees, fumbling with their rifles.

"Hold fire!" I repeated louder. The order was passed down the line. I waved for Gatewood to move the chuckwagon closer so I could intercept Ajiah and communicate with the Indians. Thanks to the impatience of Grogan's men, we were positioned in a precarious spot.

Ajiah stood on the wagon's toeboard and strained to look at the watching Indians. She yelled something at them I could not understand. I hoped it was a friendly greeting. When she called to them again, a response echoed off the trees. "It is Whiteman Killer," she confirmed.

"Tell him I want to talk peacefully."

"He knows why you're here," she said firmly.

Angry Eagle stuck his head from the wagon canvas and said something heated to Ajiah. She pushed him back into the wagon, but he resisted, shouting into her face. Ajiah's words meant nothing to me, but her tone indicated she insisted he calm down.

Ajiah turned to the men in the distance and shouted. One of them yelled back.

Ajiah sighed dejectedly and addressed me, "The men you seek are all dead."

No surprise there.

"They demand you release us and leave."

"That's not happening," I said.

"They will fall back and attack you in the night. You will lose many men," she cautioned.

At this point, I knew there hadn't been enough back and forth to communicate all that. She was basing this on her intuition of the Wolf Clan leader.

Out of the corner of my eye, I registered Grogan signaling his wagon, directing it to roll down to the creek, possibly to gain a position of easy defense or just to put something between himself and the threatening Indians.

There was a shout from the Indians that intoned a question. Ajiah was about to explain, "He says…" But the balance of her sentence was cut by gunfire. Bennet, Tarling, and Jordan all raised their rifles and fired up at the two Indians. The Indian standing in the foreground doing the talking fell to the ground, and the man behind him ducked out of sight.

"Goddamn it! No!" I yelled. "Cease fire!"

But the response to my futile order was gunfire and muzzle flashes from just inside the woods, which mowed the three Cowboys down from behind and devolved the situation into pandemonium. Spooner dropped to safety behind a stout tree trunk and watched for a shot at his attackers. My soldiers fell to their knees and fired into the trees toward the gunfire. Whooping came in response, followed by more Indian gunfire and arrows flying from the shadows. At least five of my men fell to the ground in a way that told me they were gravely wounded.

"No!" I yelled, digging my heels into Styx's ribs, sending him down to the creek where I could better support my men.

Grogan remained on his horse and kept the wagon between himself and the action. Spooner gave up his position of cover, darted to Grogan's mysterious wagon, and climbed in. Within seconds of disappearing behind the cream canvas cover, Spooner pulled the fabric away to reveal one of the vilest machines ever invented. It was a Gatling machine gun sporting several rotating barrels that spun around a stabilizing cylinder. The weapon was secured to a tripod and presumably bolted to the wagon floor. Spooner swiveled the wicked weapon with ease toward the trees. His hand operated a cranking lever on the right side that set the barrels into motion, spitting fire and bullets into the shadowy woods. He yelled profanities at whoever might be on the receiving end. "Eat shit, motherfuckers!"

Chunks of bark and wood chips exploded from the trees, taking the brunt of the onslaught. If Spooner was hitting anyone, there was no way of knowing over the deafening .45 caliber explosions raining destruction. Each round blasting from the lethal weapon reverberated like a man hammering an iron skillet. I knew from the war a man operating a Gatling could fire a hundred rounds in the time it took a single skilled soldier to load his musket and fire once.

A chorus of whooping and a hail of arrows fell from behind the hill, piercing a shoulder here and a back there among the exposed Buffalo Soldiers. We were being assaulted from two fronts, and the only way I could see to stop it was to go after Spooner, who started it all.

"Take cover!" I yelled to anyone within earshot. "Take cover!" It was the most natural thing to shout, but even as the words left my mouth, I knew no one would hear or heed them.

Grogan trotted his roan mare a conservative distance from the Gatling and out of range of the arrows raining from the hill. His eyes bugged, and he grinned maniacally at the mayhem initiated by his Cowboys and their weapon of war. A weapon that represented a grotesque embodiment of overkill.

As Spooner exhausted his first magazine of approximately forty rounds and fumbled to reload with a fresh one, the ringing in my ears was met with a new cacophony of horror. A deep, throaty howl echoed through the trees and bounced between the hills. Every man on the battlefield paused in silence, trying to identify the origin of the menacing cry.

"Oh mercy, Jesus, please, not again." A soldier from my ranks exclaimed.

"It's back!" Another warned, crystalizing all of our thoughts.

"Fuck!"

It let out an echoing roar all around, further confusing us about its location. Horses whinnied and reared in fear, wanting to escape but held in place by their experienced riders. Their men uttered comforting words in nervous tones. "Easy, girl, easy."

To complicate matters, the sun abandoned us, replaced by a half-moon.

26

The creature moved quickly from man to man with slashing claws and gnashing teeth. Each gunshot erupted in flashes, illuminating its inky coat, ivory fangs, and gleaming eyes. It grunted and roared with each bullet making its mark, but nothing slowed its progress as it reaped every man in its path. Razor talons ripped through clothing like tissue paper and sliced deeply into torsos. Although I couldn't see the injuries the beast was inflicting in the dark, I easily imagined the traumatic wounds Dr. Nagel examined during his horse barn autopsies. The monster inflicted fatal injuries with a ferocious intensity and fury. The men responded in varying pitches of pain and terror.

It moved like a horse at full battle cantor, expertly eviscerating each target with deep, cutting swipes of its powerful claws. It intermittently batted rifles away, snatched men between its massive forepaws, and sank its snapping jaws into unprotected throats, producing screams drowned by vomited blood. No man struck remained standing. Occasionally, it paused to ravenously devour portions of its victims.

Spooner slid another magazine stick vertically into the Gatling's receiver, swung the lethal weapon around, and searched for a target. He fired toward the growling shadow, leaping into shrieking men, and lit up the area with rapid gunfire as he cranked the handle. Chunks of turf kicked into the air as each precious projectile missed its mark. Spooner used the strafe to zero in on the creature and produced the first unmistakable vocalization of a large animal in pain as bullets repeatedly struck the monster's legs and torso.

Until this development, Grogan had been staring over his shoulder in slack-jawed disbelief at the creature from his saddle. With cause for celebrating, he yelled with glee. "Eat that, you godless abomination! We've got you now! Get him, Spooner, get him!" Though excited, Grogan continued his retreat to safer and higher ground, away from the attacking creature and raging gunfire.

The creature stumbled but did not lose its balance. It used its missteps to dart swiftly out of the path of bullets, veering toward Spooner and alternating its approach. Spooner hesitated the cranking of the handle to spare ammunition until he reacquired his target and fired into the monster's torso. Each time he went for the large head and muzzle, the creature shook its face from side to side and batted at the rounds like a man wading into a swarm of hornets. It was a waste of ammunition but resulted in a satisfying howl of pain. Incredibly, it continued to hurl itself toward Spooner, confined to the weapon bolted to the bed of the exposed wagon. With Bennet dead in the driver's seat from Indian gunfire, the wagon wasn't going anywhere.

"I'll blast you back to the hell!" Spooner's words were perfectly audible as the crank clicked on a rotation of empty receivers. He might have stood a chance if accompanied by a partner feeding the weapon fresh ammunition magazines, but Spooner was alone. The creature crashed into the wagon's side, upending it and raising two spoked wheels into the air. The dual-horse team screamed as the wooden tongue tying them to the wagon snapped loose, allowing them to flee. Spooner lost his grip on the weapon and tumbled backward to the ground as the Gatling lolled like a strangled cat.

"Fucking hell!" Spooner yelled, rolling through the grass and snow and into the creek.

The creature leaped over the spilled wagon after him. Spooner managed to draw his pistol and fire ineffectually into the creature's chest and jaw as it grabbed him by the throat with its elongated fingers and stunted thumb. The hulking beast lifted Spooner entirely off his flailing feet and looked the man in the eye. Its vice-like grip choked off whatever epithet Spooner tried to spew. He shivered as paralysis took hold of his crimped, cracking spine. Unable to raise his arm, Spooner fired once into the ground before the weapon slipped from his grip. The animal responded by chomping down on the former Reb's face, crushing his head like a ripe melon. Spooner's body convulsed with a disturbing quiver and went limp like a marionette on slack strings.

I stupidly fired my pistol into the creature's back, which had no more effect than any of the other shots fired into it. The round served only to alert it to my presence. It finished Spooner off by tearing his head free and tossing the flaccid body to the ground. It locked its gaze on me with wicked intensity and lupine annoyance. Styx shuffled backward to get away, but the creature lunged forward and gave my shrieking horse a sudden shove to the chest, knocking him backward to the ground with me underneath. I braced myself but felt my ribs crack under the total weight of the Appaloosa as he rolled on his side and over my body. My left hip and leg jolted with sudden pain and an audible snap of breaking bone. Styx scrambled to his feet with me unsaddled in the snow and stomped on the knee of my injured leg in his haste to get us away. I tried to get to my feet, but the pain was excruciating and debilitating. My leg failed to bear weight, and I was unable to rise. I knew then my right hip was broken. I slumped onto my back, looking up at it, trying to dig my heels and elbows into the ground for purchase in a futile effort to push myself precious inches away.

The creature loomed over me with a menacing glare. Its fangs gleamed in the moonlight as it snarled and sniffed at the air, working its moist black nostrils to read my scent. I'd managed to hang onto my pistol but saw no point in shooting it again and pissing it off further. I holstered the weapon in a laughable attempt to show it I meant no harm. I tried to scoot away from the monster in an elbow crab crawl but couldn't even make my muscles do that with any effectiveness. I wondered how badly injured I was that I couldn't force myself away from the embodiment of death. At that moment, the absence of fear surprised me the most. I was completely at its mercy, and we both knew it.

The creature's bushy tail swished as it regarded me with interest. I imagined I saw a spark of intelligence behind its darting red eyes. It was heavily muscled and well proportioned, built for the destruction men are ill-prepared to withstand. On some deep level, I couldn't help but admire it. "What in the holy fuck are you, you magnificent beast?"

It gurgled a guttural growl and twitched its devilish ears.

"Major! Are you all right!? Are you out there, sir?" I heard Axil call from the dark.

I didn't see any point in trying to answer. I just shook my head in wonder as I looked up at it in fearful respect.

"Is it gone?" Someone yelled with a hint of hope.

"Oh, shit, it's got the Major! Shoot it!"

The night exploded in rifle fire from a dozen different points. The creature looked up and roared in anger. Then it glared back at me, almost as though considering what to do next. It looked upon me with something like recognition mixed with irritation. It snarled, cocked its over-long arm, and backhanded me with a heavy paw. My head detonated in a flash of both light and pain, with a growing ring rising in my ears. Deafness drowned out the crackle of gunfire around me. I thought I was going to vomit from the shock of the blow as the fading darkness of unconsciousness swallowed me completely.

I awoke an undetermined time later to quiet all around me with a mane of dark bristles on my face. The creature was stooped over me, holding me to the ground with its great weight, crushing breath from me, pinning my arms with its heavy paws and a shin across my thighs to secure my legs. A searing pain pierced my neck and left shoulder as it became clear its fangs were sinking deep into my flesh. The pain of the bite pulled me briefly back into consciousness. I felt a numbing fear and a sense of utter helplessness. I experienced a burning sensation, as though liquid fire was being injected into my veins and throughout my unresponsive body, transporting me to another vivid trauma. A dream-like fugue with clarity beyond simple memories enveloped me. The creature pulled my thoughts from me, reading my lifeline, knowing my history, humiliations, emotions, agonies, fears, and failures. Then, there was pitch darkness.

Andersonville – 1864 -Part 4
<u>27</u>

The woods on either side of the river were lush and green up to the water's edge. It had been some time since we'd laid eyes on so much greenery. Occasionally, we were permitted a view of the surrounding countryside farms through the trees. Still, for the most part, the area was wilderness. We kept ourselves concealed from nearby roads so even a random passerby would not get a clear look at us.

We washed our hands in the clean river water and grabbed a few palmfuls in cupped hands to relieve our thirst and scrub our faces. Clean drinking water was hard to find at Camp Sumter, and now it was all around us. As we guided the small boat downriver, we dipped our clothes and swabbed our filthy bodies. I couldn't recall when I last bathed or when the general area around me didn't smell like shit, sweaty men, pine, or death. I felt like a human being again. Vast open space instead of cramped close quarters was a welcome adjustment.

We talked fancifully about resting on some shore or sandbar and basking in the sun with the river washing over us, but we couldn't risk it. We needed to get as far away from Andersonville as possible. We were free of the prison, but we weren't free of the South. We were in greater danger in many ways, hundreds of miles behind enemy lines.

The shadows grew long as the day wore on and reached across the river. The temperature dropped slightly, but the humidity remained oppressive, and the air became just as thick with evening mosquitos. We discussed traveling as far as we could at night, but there was concern about what might lay ahead. Fallen trees, branches, and the rocks of a shallow river bottom could easily punch holes in the weathered boat if we were not vigilant. We were unprepared to make repairs if we took on water. The simple boat would eventually sink and strand us. Still, the temptation to continue in the dark and put as much distance between us and the prison was appealing. If I remembered my waterways correctly, it was theoretically possible to float the two-hundred-fifty miles to the Gulf of Mexico and find some remote locale to wait out the war. We contemplated the possibilities over half a loaf of bread.

Once it became too dark to navigate, we ran the boat ashore and tied up, figuring it best to remain within until first light. We had no idea how far we were from civilization or what kinds of animals dwelt in the woods. We wanted to avoid walking where we could not see where we stepped. Georgia was known for rattlesnakes and water moccasins. Before Virginia, troops were warned of copperheads, though none of my soldiers ever suffered a bite. Of course, getting shot by the enemy was the more significant concern, and greater worry.

We made ourselves as comfortable as possible low in the small boat and tried to get some much-needed sleep. Still, we remained on edge, knowing the Rebs were hunting us. I pulled Levering's smelly uniform coat around me and tilted his cap close to my eyes to protect my exposed skin from the ever-present mosquitos. The unfamiliar sounds echoing in the woods from unseen birds and animals made our slumber fitful at best. I tried to focus on the throaty, rhythmic bullfrogs croaking to each other on the river's banks. In my mind's eye, they lay unconcerned in their muddy hiding places, inhaling and exhaling soothing music. When they paused, possibly sensing danger, I found myself alert and listening for whatever silenced them. When they began anew, I was lulled unconscious and past the pain in my throbbing groin.

Some hours later, I awoke to a series of cracking branches in the brush of the opposite bank. The frogs went silent, leaving only the crickets to pulsate around us. One of the men was snoring lightly in a deep sleep. Water gurgled and meandered by with a soft whoosh. Was something walking around in the scrub and dead leaves? A deer, a bear, a raccoon, or a skunk? I detected a growl or snarl in the distance, but it was impossible to estimate how far away it might be. Nothing was visible in the pitch darkness. I closed my eyes and tried to fall asleep when nothing materialized.

Later, I detected a splashing sound. It was either a fish turning over and flopping its tail at the river's surface or something falling into the water. Innocuous sounds during the day promised menace at night. It's just the wildlife, I thought to myself. Nothing to be alarmed about. Something like a branch or drifting log bumped against the side of the boat. I was embarrassed by my jumpiness and let it pass.

At first light, the men stirred and stepped onto the shore to relieve themselves and splash the cool river water into their faces.

"On mornings like this, my father and I would build a fire, make some coffee, go fishing, and eat our catch," Phillips reminisced.

We all grinned or nodded, sharing similar memories.

"Untie us, and we'll shove off," I instructed Collins, the last to make his way from behind a bush on shore.

Collins pulled the rope at the bow loose from a nearby tree to set the small boat free. It moved an inch or so but wouldn't budge more than that. "Are we stuck in the mud?" He gave the boat another push, putting more effort into it.

Yates looked at the water side of the boat. "There's a log pressed up against us," he said. "Man, that's some wicked-looking bark."

I looked over the side and saw an uneven six to eight-foot log of green and black breaking the river's surface. The bulk of it was submerged in cloudy water. At first glance, I thought it was a pine tree with branches and sprouts neatly stripped away. Its craggy surface consisted of several uniform rows running lengthwise. There was a sneaking familiarity about the pattern as Yates swung his legs over the side to plant his boots on the log. "I'm just going to kick it away so we can…"

The water and the log thrashed to life as I realized too late why the surface of the thing appeared so orderly. It wasn't bark. It was the hide of a large reptile. An enormous, elongated head with beady raised eyes emerged from the water behind a pinkish-white mouth of jagged yellow teeth and whipped around. Yates lost his balance, yelped, and fell overboard. The thing growled, clamped its jaws onto Yates' legs, and pulled him under. The monster twisted its pointed tail to maneuver itself and Yates toward deeper water. Yates broke the surface, screaming in panic. With the obstruction clear, the boat was freed from the shore. I jerked involuntarily to get to my feet and experienced a stabbing pain in my groin.

"What in the fuck-all is that!?" Collins yelled at anyone listening.

"Jesus Christ Almighty!" Phillips called out.

Rice reached for the rifle and pointed it at the river as the thing dragged Yates below the surface. The screams of pain and fear turned into drowning gurgles as man and monster submerged in a subtle wake. Rice waved the rifle like a divining rod, trying to locate something to shoot. "Where is he? Where'd it go?"

A hand broke the surface about twenty feet out, grabbing at whatever might be available. Behind the hand was a renewed thrashing as the river creature pulled Yates into deeper water to drown him into submission. I struggled to think what it was called. I'd seen drawings in books and came up with *alligator* or *crocodile*. It was between twelve and fifteen feet in length.

"Yates!" Rice cried. "Yates!" Rice shook Levering's rifle, desperate to shoot something or catch a glimpse of his friend. "We have to find him!"

The boat moved along the shore as we watched the flowing water for signs of life. What could we do? Go in after him? Where there was one, there would be more. It was foolish to think there was anything we could do unless Yates miraculously broke away and started swimming for us. After several minutes of waiting, it was clear that wouldn't happen, and none of us were confident enough to dive in and take a look.

"Alligator," I muttered.

Andersonville – 1864 -Part 5
<u>28</u>

We sat in stunned silence as the current pulled us downriver. Phillips and Collins steered us with the oar and a half to avoid any obstacles in the water. The rest of us watched the shoreline. Now that we were looking, we saw them sunning themselves here and there. Reptilian eyes watched, and gnarled backs were highly recognizable now that we'd seen one up close. We came to a hard realization. The water was alive with danger. We were much more cautious about reaching in with cupped hands, imagining something else rising to snatch us from the boat.

Hunger abandoned us after Yates's violent demise, but we ate small pieces of bread anyway. My point of view changed. The trees I dismissed as background vegetation took on an alien manifestation of long, angling limbs loaded with dripping bundles of moss. Some of it hung low enough we could grab it. Still, even that seemed risky now as dark snakes were just as prevalent upon closer inspection among the various birds nesting in the overgrowth. "This place is fucking creepy," Collins said, putting into words what we thought collectively.

As we meandered downriver, I shook off the trauma of Yates' death by alligator and noted the pull becoming more powerful. Eddies swirled around us, and the shoreline grew rockier. Collins and Phillips made more frequent adjustments to keep the bow pointed in our direction of travel. The trip grew tense as we were not in a position to see changes in geography or threats in advance.

Before we knew it, we approached rocky shoals, white water, and a bridge in the distance. The first sign of trouble came when the bottom of the boat hit a large rock. Phillips and Collins tried to adjust course, but the current had us in a firm grip. Rice and Mackey got on their knees and braced themselves on either side of the bow, watching for danger. I stiffened against the rudderless stern and grabbed both walls as the water grew rough. The boat struck another unseen rock with a loud thud.

"Huge rock poking out just ahead," Mackey warned.

Phillips and Collins scrambled to avoid it, but it came up too fast. The starboard side slammed into something heavy and ungiving.

"Another's coming up here to port," Rice called out as we crashed into it.

The impact jarred us from our seats and briefly stopped our forward motion. I felt another stab of pain in my groin. The stern of the boat swung around, and we continued sideways against the starboard side with cold water splashing into our faces. Phillips and Collins each grabbed their sides of the boat and raised their oars out of the water.

"Pull the oars in before we lose them," I instructed.

They followed the order and held the side tight with both hands. The stern rose as the bow dipped, and I spotted a field of rocky white rapids ahead. One I didn't think the aging vessel was designed to withstand. I made sure Levering's pistol was secure in my waistband and cinched my belt as tight as I could. "Rice, keep hold of that rifle if we go into the water."

"Yes, sir," he called out over the triple set of thuds that hammered at the bottom of the bow, stern, and port.

I took my eyes off the rough water ahead and glanced at my boots, alerted by a sudden change in temperature at my feet. Half an inch of standing water now occupied space it hadn't a moment ago. "We're taking on water. We'll likely be in the river when we clear these rocks. One of you want to grab the bag of bread?"

"Got it," Phillips volunteered, securing the rucksack to his chest.

The boat righted itself with the bow pointing forward. The bow slammed into another rock head-on. I heard wood crack somewhere up front, and water flooded the floor. The boat spun clockwise three hundred and sixty degrees, taking several hits. As we rotated, I saw a wooden bridge ahead. There, men on horseback watched us careen through the rapids. They had rifles and dogs that bayed over the rough water, cracking wood, and my cursing men.

"We got company on this bridge up ahead," Phillips warned everyone.

"Fuck!" Mackey swore.

"Just keep your heads," I cautioned. "If we make it past the bridge, we might stand a chance." To my chagrin, I found the water in the boat rising.

It would not stay afloat. "Once in the water, find the safest way to shore and run. Do what you think is best. Don't bunch up. You'll stand a better chance if we separate."

The men looked at me with dread. We were in dire straits. This could be the end of the line for all of us. Our luck ended as we hit the last field of rocks before the bridge. The boat broke apart like a bundle of sticks freed of their binding. We slipped into the water and floated apart. I took a quick breath before rolling under. My clothing drew close, wet and cold, as I surfaced and turned to look up at the bridge. There were three men in Confederate guard uniforms armed with rifles searching the rapids for us. At least five bloodhounds bayed but were careful not to let their enthusiasm carry them over the edge to a thirty-foot drop.

"There they are!" One of the guards called as he raised his rifle to his shoulder. He led his shot to match our whisking in the current and pulled the trigger. Mackey cried out as his head exploded, turning the white foam around him pink.

I went limp and washed over a smooth, algae-slickened boulder, allowing Levering's coat to billow in the water. I wiggled out of it as quickly as possible to make it an appealing target and guided myself between two bridge footings. The Rebs fired more shots. A couple of them glanced off rocks or whistled through the water. Two bullets splashed near me just as I flowed into cover. Once under the bridge, I grabbed an entanglement of mossy branches caught on a cluster of rocks and released the gray coat into the current.

As Levering's coat flowed away from me, it took the shape of a man floating face down, arms extended. It cleared the other side of the bridge and moved into the sunlight, where it drew fire and plumed small waterspouts.

"Got him!" Someone celebrated from above. I hoped with the commotion, no one would notice there wasn't a man in the coat. More gunshots were fired. One of my boys cried out.

I pulled myself toward the steep array of rocks reinforcing the banks and supporting the bridge against erosion. I climbed the vines and weeds that spiderwebbed the stones up to the woods, ignoring the men and dogs on the bridge. I kept quiet, low to the ground, and out of sight. Fortunately, the pistol was still secure in my sodden pants.

I concealed myself behind a tree and risked a look to see how my men faired. At least two bodies bobbed motionless in the water, taking additional fire. Shots rang out from the other side of the river, presumably another man being pursued through the brush. I didn't expect there was any chance Rice maintained his hold on the rifle. It had taken both hands for me to maneuver over the rocks and avoid splitting my head open.

I sighed in exhaustion and tried to take quiet breaths. The pain from my stab wound was deepening with my despair. To make it through battle on so many fronts, become captured and incarcerated with the same group of boys, to survive a brutal prisoner of war camp, and then escape with them, only for it to end so cruelly was demoralizing. I pressed on, figuring it would not be long before the hounds on the bridge caught my scent and ran me down.

My injury found relief in the cold river water but screamed now that I was limping along on dry land. I found a dirt road near the bridge, decorated with fresh, fly-swarmed horse droppings, indicating a recent rider. I crossed to thicker woods on the other side of the road and found a deer path to follow. I cared to remain silent and not rustle dry leaves or break dead branches. That I was forced to take shorter steps because of my injury worked to my advantage. Up ahead, a horse whinnied and snorted. I lay prone among scrubby bushes beneath a tree and peeked around the moss-covered trunk.

Saddled atop a familiar chestnut mare was the albino guard Miller with his Sharps rifle across his lap, watching the road I had deliberately avoided. I ducked behind my tree, hoping he hadn't seen me. His horse snorted again and clopped in place. I heard the distinct click of a rifle hammer cocking. Miller called out, "Come on out, federal. I see you hiding there. I knew you stupid fuckers would come this way. All we had to do was wait you out. And here you are."

I shook my head. A missing boat and no scent for the dogs to follow, it must have been obvious we were on the water. All they had to do was wait for us at the rocks. They knew we'd get hung up there. I grabbed the handle of the pistol and slid it from my waistband. My pants were stained with fresh bleeding. In all the excitement, I'd pulled my stitches. Well, I wasn't going down without a fight. There was no way I'd let Miller take me.

"Show me your hands!" Miller demanded.

I peeked around my tree, keen to keep the pistol out of sight as long as possible. Instead of a gun pointed at me, I found Miller looking in the opposite direction. His rifle was leveled at something down the hill. I hunkered back and turned my head to find Rice propped behind a thick trunk, bleeding from his upper torso and cradling Levering's rifle with a bloody arm.

Miller nudged his horse a few steps toward Rice and sighted his rifle on him. "I said come out and show me your hands, you federal piece of shit!"

Rice was unsteady but made himself as small as possible behind his tree. "I got a rifle, too," Rice said, sounding exhausted.

That startled Miller a bit, but he recovered in an instant. "A rifle that's been in the river? There's a reason they say to keep your powder dry, stupid." Miller laughed and fired a shot into the middle of Rice's tree, blasting away bark chips. Miller cycled another round, ready to fire again. In the distance, I heard the hounds barking their approach.

Rice looked at his rifle with open-mouthed doubt. I eyed the pistol in my hand, calculating how much time it spent submerged in the river. "Shit," I whispered.

Nevertheless, Rice raised the rifle with newfound determination. Miller ducked behind the head of his horse and was rewarded with a resounding click of the rifle hammer falling on a water-soaked cartridge. Rice cocked the hammer and pulled the trigger again and received an identical response. "Fuck!"

Miller laughed a nervous cackle and nudged his mare forward to corner Rice. "Get down on your knees, federal!"

Miller remained oblivious to my presence. I snuck from behind my tree and moved up behind him as quietly as I could. I was confident I could cover the hundred feet that separated us before he could notice and react. If the pistol didn't fire, I would grab his rifle and tear him off his horse. Hopefully, Rice would be able to assist at that point.

I made a lame run for Miller, grimacing in pain and aiming myself at a blind spot to the mare's rear to keep him at a disadvantage. My attack had the unintended effect of coaxing Rice from his cover when he saw me advancing. Oblivious to me, Miller shot Rice. The rifle explosion resulted in a cry of pain and a spray of blood from Rice's shoulder. Rice dropped his gun and fell backward. Inky redness spread over his shirt.

I growled involuntarily in anger and frustration as I closed in on Miller and his mount. He spun the horse around and tried to level the rifle at me, but I was close enough to keep clear of the barrel. I raised the pistol with my right hand and reached out with my left. He adjusted himself in his saddle to force the rifle toward me just as I pulled the trigger. A satisfying explosion launched the projectile into Miller's throat as his eyes registered recognition and realization. I got my left hand on the rifle barrel and felt a waning strength behind it. Miller dropped his reins and clapped his supporting hand to the geyser of blood pouring from the gaping wound in his neck while trying to form words that stopped at "Fed..."

I held onto the rifle as much for support as to avoid the panicking horse spinning toward me. I cocked the Colt revolver's single action for another shot and was met with an impotent click. And then another. I dropped my gun and grabbed Miller's rifle with both hands and put all my weight into jerking him off his horse. With the second tug, he pulled the trigger, and too late, I noticed the barrel aimed at the left side of my chest.

The rifle spat fire, and my ears rang. Pain exploded in the muscle outside my left breast as part of me opened up. My hands registered stovetop-level heat on the barrel. The horse bucked up its forelegs to kick at me. I fell backward in possession of the rifle. Miller rose above me wide-eyed and clapped his other hand to his throat to stem the flow of blood oozing between his fingers. As white as the albino was, he grew paler than freshly fallen snow with blood loss. The frightened animal threw Miller off and jumped away.

I leveled the rifle, cycled the next round into the chamber, and pointed it toward Miller's fallen body. From the other direction, Rice was closing in with Levering's rifle, smiling at me with blood-covered teeth. He said something I could barely hear through ringing ears, but it looked like, "Lieutenant!"

We both arrived at Miller's prone body at the same time. The blood was still trickling from his wound, but his hands were not clasping as tightly. His lips moved, and he whispered, "Mother. Fuckers," as two separate and distinct words. His eyes drooped, unfocused.

Rice's face snarled in anger, tears streaming down his cheeks as he clubbed Miller with the useless rifle that failed him moments ago. I raised a hand to block the splattering blood and gore and stepped away. Miller's face caved in after a series of swings from Rice as he emptied his rage on our tormentor. I gestured to him when he seemed too exhausted to raise the rifle for another. "We have to go, Rice." My voice sounded distorted to my numb eardrums.

My eyes gravitated to the pistol holstered in Miller's gun belt. I unbuckled it, slid it from under his lifeless body, and strapped it around my waist. I was gratified to find fresh cartridges in each ammunition loop.

I stepped to Miller's mare and grabbed her reins. She calmed quickly in the aftermath of the commotion. She was well-trained enough that she hadn't fled her rider. I sheathed Miller's rifle on the saddle and checked my fresh gunshot wound. My shirt was sopping with blood under my left armpit. Although there was pain and numbness from the trauma, it felt as though the bullet had passed through the meat and not shattered any bone.

I hoisted myself into the saddle and maneuvered the mare to Rice with significant effort. I reached out with my right hand to grasp his. Between the two of us, we got him situated behind me. He was losing a lot of blood, but we needed to put some distance between us and our pursuers before taking time to address our wounds. As the ringing in my ears abated, I heard the dog barks getting closer and men shouting behind them.

We made our way along the deer path that paralleled the road but eventually moved to the road, heading south. We started at a canter until I felt Rice's grip growing weak on either side of the gun belt. I reined the horse to slow her gait. I didn't want to lose Rice or wear the horse out. She did not seem well cared for, as her ribs were showing, and her hooves needed a good trimming. With Miller as her owner, I was not surprised.

As we made our way, I did an inventory of Miller's saddle. I found extra ammunition for both the rifle and pistol. There was some jerky and hard tac in one of the pouches. As Miller was not a soldier, I was disappointed but not surprised there was nothing in the way of emergency medical gear. No bandages or medicines of any kind. Then I remembered the envelope given to me by the doctor at the prison hospital and pulled it out. The exterior was stained red with my blood. I fingered the wet paper open. The river reduced whatever the doctor gave me to a pale white paste, tinted pink. I shrugged and scraped a bit of the gunk onto my lower teeth. My tongue worked over it, and I found it bitter. I hoped it would dull the pain.

"Take some morphine, Rice." I held the paper over my shoulder, but he did not accept it.

Rice mumbled an unintelligible reply and renewed his grip on my gun belt. I returned the envelope to my pocket. We had to find a place for Rice to lie down. We both needed tending, and I had no idea where to go.

Andersonville – 1864 -Part 6
<u>29</u>

We had the road to ourselves for hours, and in that time, we did not encounter another human being. I assumed it would eventually happen and planned to veer off into the woods somewhere and wait for them to pass or make up some plausible lie. My ultimate fallback was the fact that I was armed. We were wounded Union soldiers; there was no escaping that. Anyone running across us would be alarmed and alert the authorities.

Rice tried to stay atop the horse but could not maintain consciousness. In the time it took us to travel another half mile, Rice slipped to the ground. I felt him going but was in the worst possible position to catch him. I eased myself to the ground through growing stiffness. Moving my left arm aggravated the rifle wound. Whether it was through and through or not, it needed cleaning, treatment, and stitches. The clotting was scabbing over, but the simple movements of my arm caused scabs to break open and ooze anew.

One look at Rice told me the boy would not make it. His wound was draining fresh blood. I tried to bandage and pack it as best I could with torn strips of cloth from our shirts, but it would become infected without proper care. Even if a field hospital were nearby, it would make no difference. I knew I should probably abandon him, but I couldn't bring myself to do it. Nor was I in any condition to load him back on Miller's horse by myself.

Minutes later, a large wagon rounded a bend in the road at a comfortable rate of speed. It was pulled by two mules, one white, one black, and driven by a lone Negro slave in ragged, hand-me-down clothing. He wore an old black hat with a wide brim that shaded his eyes. His wagon was laden with recently picked cotton on its way to a gin for weighing and sale. It was an assembly of unfinished and discarded wood planks, with extra sideboards to hold the cloud of white cargo in place. The slave sat about ten feet off the ground and had a perfect vantage point to see me, Miller's horse, and Rice on the ground. There was no time to stage any of it.

The whites of his eyes contrasted against his dark skin as he stared at me in unblinking surprise. He knew what we were. All I could do was wait and see how he reacted. As he made his way toward me, he pulled back on the reins to bring the mules to a halt.

"Afternoon, Boss," he said matter-of-factly. He gave me a slight nod, keeping his eyes downcast now that we were close. Negroes in the South were conditioned not to look whites in the eye or suffer the consequences. "Afternoon," I rasped.

The man seemed uncomfortable with my not steering the conversation. "Are you in need of assistance, Boss?"

"Depends on your brand of assistance," I said cautiously.

"You and the young man look like you been shot, Boss. Medical assistance."

"I'd be obliged."

He took a deep breath before probing further. He eyed the guns on my hips. "You're wearing a Southern cap and riding a horse with a Southern saddle, but you sound like you're from the North," he said, quickly adding, "No disrespect, Boss."

For the first time since my escape and after all we'd been through, I realized I was somehow still wearing Levering's cap.

"Are you the men the soldiers from the prison are looking for?"

I placed my hand on the butt of Miller's pistol and made sure he saw it and understood the implication. "We are. Does this information change your offer of assistance?"

"No, Boss." He smiled softly. "I know a safe place for y'all. You can call me Mal."

"I'm Kincaid." I reached up to him, extending my hand.

He acted like he had never shaken hands before, but when he took my hand and gave it a firm shake, I realized he had never shaken a white man's hand.

"Probably be best if I stick to calling you Boss around these parts."

His name was Malcolm Butler. He was one of five slaves working a small, struggling farm. The cotton in the wagon represented a day of work. He estimated it at one thousand pounds. It represented roughly 200 pounds picked by each slave. I tried to imagine what kind of backbreaking work that must be. I had never spoken to an actual Southern slave before.

Mal showed me a secret compartment. A false bottom was concealed beneath the cotton-laden wagon bed. It was essentially a shelf with an oversized board to hide the opening at the rear. The lower level of the wagon was big enough for up to four men to lie side by side. It was lined with straw, and I saw a dirty blanket wadded up in the back. Mal helped me load Rice inside, with Mal doing most of the work. Rice didn't stir as we moved him, but he still breathed in short, panting breaths. I used the blanket to cover him. Once closed up, Rice was not visible from the wagon's exterior.

"Is he your son?" Mal asked.

Did I look old enough to have a sixteen-year-old son? Mathematically, it was possible. "No, he's one of my soldiers. His name is Rice. Private… Rice," I said lamely, realizing I didn't know Rice's first name or had forgotten it.

Mal invited me to hide in the compartment, too, but I was reluctant to do so until I was confident I could trust him. Once inside, I wasn't sure I'd be able to get out. We removed the saddle and tack from Miller's horse and set it in the compartment with Rice. We shooed the horse into the woods, free to graze and find her way. I concealed myself in the raw cotton and settled in the corner of the wagon nearest Mal as he drove the mules.

"You'll have to join Private Rice before we get to the gin," Mal said, slapping the reins on the backs of the mules to set them in motion. "First thing they do is unload the cotton. We'll have to watch out for patrols on the way back."

"Patrols?" I asked from my cotton layer.

"Slave patrols. Make sure my pass in order. Make sure I'm not up to no good," he laughed.

"You help a lot of escaped and wounded enemy soldiers?"

"Nah, you're my first ones, and you ain't my enemy," he pointed out. "According to President Lincoln, I'm free."

"We just need to convince President Davis of that."

"It'll happen," he said confidently. "You're breaking them."

His perspective interested me. But before I could ask any questions, I passed out.

30

I did not wake from my nightmare so much as I endured a fitful, restless slumber filled with jarring jerks and twitches. Unpleasant memories inflicted themselves upon me in uncomfortable dream sequences. The thing did not bite me in half with the fangs piercing my throat and shoulder. Instead, it slowly withdrew from me, producing a slightly erotic sensation of pain bordering on titillation as my wounds sealed like fleshy sheaths. The creature sniffed at my face and nudged my chin with its wet snout as if assessing my level of unconsciousness.

Once it freed its fangs from me, the searing burn of a paralyzing venom diminished in my body, and all my injury-related pains returned. The cracking of my ribs, fractures to my hip, the shattering of my kneecap under Styx, the penetrating punctures, even Miller's years old bullet wound and gutting of my genitals flared. My system struggled past a numbing head-ringing to tamp down the agony and plunged me back into the abyss of blackout. Fear overtook my sensations of pain when I realized the hairy brute was lifting me from the ground with the ease of enormous strength. I felt as though I were taking flight as I drifted back into unconsciousness.

The fitful vision that followed was of the Indian girl, Ajiah, fully nude, drenched in blood and gore. I worried she, too, was injured. Yet, she reached for me with helpful hands to make me comfortable by positioning my limbs and straightening my uniform. She gave me a coy smile and laughed as I slipped into darkness. For an instant, I thought my soul was leaving my body.

Later, she fed me a savory stew of barely warm, rare meat chunks in a light broth seasoned with some unfamiliar herb. "This will give you strength and help you heal," she soothed. I took what she gave me and drifted off again.

When I awoke, it was to the soft light of daybreak and the gentle jostling of a wagon moving on the open prairie. I was bundled in buffalo blankets salvaged from the carnage of Grogan's skinning operation based upon the mild fragrance of singed fur and kerosene. I touched my neck and found the oozing, scabbing wounds of the monster's bite, a mess of tacky blood on my fingertips. It had not been a simple nightmare. I had suffered a grievous injury, and my body throbbed throughout. My head pounded, and my ears rang from the blows I received during the creature's attack.

Styx was tethered to the back of the wagon, occasionally looking in on me through the open canvas flap with his big, curious horse eyes. I noted a section of the wagon floor was smeared with dried blood. Was it mine? I tried to rise, which set off shooting aches and pains down the entirety of my left side. In the corner was a twisted piece of metal the size and shape of a horseshoe, but I dismissed it as unimportant, given the overall strangeness of my situation.

I tipped my head to get a look at the driver of the wagon and was utterly shocked to find Ajiah holding the reins. She was not naked, not bloodied, but adorned in her usual buckskin tunic and hair tied in a neat ponytail. There was no sign of Wilson or Gatewood or any other soldiers. The only sounds were of Styx, the two lead horses, and the creaking wagon in which I lay incapacitated. The murmurs of men talking to kill time during travel were missing. Also absent was the accompanying ruckus of other horses stomping, snorting, and whinnying by.

"What's happening?" My voice was an inaudible whisper. I cleared my throat and croaked louder. "Where are we?"

She glanced back at me but returned her gaze to the road ahead. "I'm taking you back to the fort so your doctor can heal you. Everyone else is dead or fled."

I pondered the information as it sank in. "What?" I managed, with some anxiety.

"Whiteman Killer came. The Wolf came. Many men were killed. Angry Eagle went with Whiteman Killer. I'm taking you to your medicine man."

"None of my men survived the attack?" I was alarmed.

"Some survived and fled," she repeated. "I would accuse them of cowardice, but to face certain death would serve no purpose. Those who left acted sensibly."

"Forty men dead or missing?" I was incredulous and horrified it could accomplish that kind of slaughter, yet I had witnessed much of it with my own eyes.

"You've seen what it does. It is death. It will destroy your world as you have destroyed ours." She said the words without anger, but the condemnation was there.

"You could have gone with Whiteman Killer and regained your freedom. Finished me off." That's probably what she should have done. If the creature and the Indians killed as many men as she claimed, the result would be the arrival of more soldiers, more deaths, and more Indians killed. "Why are you helping me?"

She gave my question brief consideration before answering. "It's true. I could have abandoned you, but you were badly injured. I couldn't leave you to die. You hold the others captive. I need to be with them. The day will come when you aid me. In some ways, you already have." She said it with an air of certainty.

"What makes you so sure? You've said yourself, we're responsible for devastating your way of life." I paused before adding, "Irrevocably."

"That is true. It is not a change the Wolf Clan considers good, but there is a decency about you, Kincaid. You don't want to see us eradicated any more than you wish to see the mighty buffalo wiped out. All things have a purpose. We need honorable men like you to guide us through the change so we may survive and rise again. More people will die. More people must die. You and I are kindred in that realization. There is a plan for you as there is for me."

"Is that why it didn't kill me?" It occurred to me I had not suffered the same fate as my men on two separate occasions. I had not been clawed. I had not been torn apart or otherwise maimed. Nor was I clear on why it had bitten me the way it did and why the wound was not fatal. I didn't kid myself into thinking the color of my skin or the rank on my shoulders meant anything to the monster.

"If it wanted you dead, you would be dead." That occurred to me as well. In a roundabout way, Ajiah confirmed my suspicions. The creature possessed an unnatural intelligence.

"You say it has a plan?"

"Anything that acts with cunning plans, Kincaid."

That made it all the more terrifying. It had superior physical strength and appeared invulnerable to modern weapons. Though it registered pain, it withstood Grogan's Gatling gun unscathed. No one was going to believe that. I wouldn't believe it if I hadn't been there.

Well before sundown, Ajiah fed me more of her cold stew. I preferred meat cooked medium, but it was tender and delicious. "It's good. Thank you." She must have scavenged something from the cook's wagon and added spices.

Later, we arrived at the fort. Soldiers moved me to the infirmary. Ajiah was taken into custody and returned to the enclosure to rejoin the other Indians. They led Styx to the livery for hay, oats, and water. With so few remaining soldiers assigned to the fort, I didn't know how I was going to explain another massacre to Colonel Kirkwood. Whether the creature was acknowledged in Washington or not, I would be relieved of duty and court-martialed for another colossal failure. The army could not ignore the enormous loss of life under my command nor allow the incident to go unexplained. Command would scapegoat me, and my Buffalo Soldiers, already derided by the upper echelons of the Department of War, would be seen as incompetent cowards. The Indians would be blamed for the casualties and made to pay. No one in the East would be satisfied with stories about a monster wolf.

Before Dr. Nagel examined me, I was sure of my prognosis. My cracked ribs would heal in time, but my shattered kneecap and broken hip would leave me a lifelong cripple. If I were lucky, I would one day climb back on Styx, but my military career was over.

Nagel arrived and did a cursory examination.

"It happened again," I started to explain.

"Your wolf friend?" He joked, finding humor in the situation. Or was it my failure?

"It knocked Styx on top of me. Then it bashed me in the side of the head with its paw and bit my neck." I tugged at the sticky shirt collar of dried blood adhering to my throat.

Nagel looked at the bite wound and stepped away to grab a bowl of water and antiseptic. He dabbed at the injury, cleaning it up. "Looks about the same size as the bites on the victims from the first attack, minus the tearing. It could easily have ripped your throat out." He scowled in thought. "I'm wondering why it didn't."

"Don't sound so disappointed."

He laughed. "It's not that. It just strikes me as odd."

"I wondered about that myself," I admitted.

"I'll clean it up as best I can, but these punctures are deep. My main concern is infection." He wiped at the wounds, dipped his rag into the water, and wiped some more.

I didn't know how to articulate that the creature had not only sunk its teeth into me but suckled me. I wasn't sure how to describe the burning sensation in my blood.

Nagel continued cleaning, cocking his head to see through the bottom of his glasses. "Do you think you have a concussion?"

"You're the doctor," I pointed out.

"Headache, ringing of the ears, loss of consciousness, nausea, vomiting?"

"All of those, except I don't remember vomiting. Felt like it, though. I thought my head was going to explode when it backhanded me."

He finished swabbing at my neck, wiped his hands on a dry towel, and touched my bruised and swollen face where the beast struck me.

"Backhanded?" Nagel raised an eyebrow.

"Back-pawed?" I suggested.

"Not clawed, like your men," he pointed out.

"No."

Nagel was drawing the same uncomfortable conclusions.

He put his hand on my ribs and told me to take deep breaths. The total inflation of my lungs felt like icepicks jabbing. I winced with each inhalation. Shallow breaths were easier to tolerate, and how I regulated my pain. He thumbed my kneecap firmly with both hands, igniting renewed jolts of agony. Even I could feel it was no longer in one piece when it separated and floated over the swelling.

Nagel sighed. "You've no doubt guessed, broken ribs are the least of your worries. Bed rest and take it easy for that. I'll splint up your patella, or kneecap, and order you off of this leg. It will take up to two months to heal."

"Goddamnit," I swore in frustration.

"Are you ready to address this hip?" He stared until he had my attention.

"Doesn't sound like I'm going anywhere."

"When this happened, you couldn't get to your feet, correct?"

"Yes."

"Are you experiencing pain in your hip and, or groin?"

"Definitely. Just laying here hurts."

Nagel nodded acknowledgement. "Can you remove your pants?"

"I can try." I unbuckled my belt and unbuttoned my uniform trousers. The act of sliding them down was excruciating. When I exposed a large purple bruise on my left hip, I stopped, unable to move them down further.

"That's enough." Nagel placed his hands on my hips and dug in with his thumbs.

I grimaced and clenched my teeth. "Right there."

He pressed several spots on my hips and pelvis, then made his way down my leg to the ankle. "Any other pain in your leg?"

"No." The stabbing sensation remained in just one spot deep in the upper portion of my left hip, above the joint of my left leg.

"The good news is you appear to have only one fracture to the left femoral neck."

"And the bad news?"

"Six months to a year until you fully recover."

"Goddamnit," I repeated.

"It could have been a lot worse. You got off cheap. The greatest threat to your overall health is infection. The good news on that front is none of the men bitten previously have developed infections. This animal, wolf, monster, whatever it is, has a clean mouth."

"That or your impeccable medical skills."

Nagel curled his lip in a half smile as he washed his hands. "I'm sorry you lost Wilson, your medic. He seemed competent." It was the most complimentary thing I had ever heard him say of a Negro.

I nodded. "I lost a lot of good men."

Nagel helped me get my pants off, then put a splint on either side of my knee and secured it into place with bandages he wrapped around and around, nearly cutting off my circulation. "Your dancing days are over," he joked. "I'll mix you up some laudanum for the pain and to help you sleep. Your brain needs rest to heal from the blow your head took."

Minutes later, I was downing a healthy swig of the doctor's bitter laudanum concoction and soon fell into a deep and desperately needed sleep.

When I awoke hours later, I found Mal seated at a small table by the potbelly stove, watching over me. He looked to be in much better shape than when I left. Only a day ago? It seemed longer. He carried his chair to my bedside. How quickly our roles had reversed. He had a soft, black leather patch over his empty eye socket. It was held in place by a leather strap tied around the back of his close-cropped head. He saw I was staring at the eyepatch.

"Like it?"

I nodded. "I do. It makes you look distinguished. And mean. Any man with an injury like that is a tough motherfucker."

We laughed. Of all the adjectives to apply to Mal, *mean* was not one of them. When the stitches came out, he was going to have a wicked scar from his forehead to his cheek. Worse than the erased bullwhip scar. "I imagine the young ladies will be lining up to hear your story."

"I think Mia would have a thing or two to say about that," Mal chuckled.

I shouldn't have said anything. Mal and Mia had been through a lot and were faithfully devoted. When the moment passed, I changed the subject. "It happened again, Mal. That thing."

Mal nodded and pursed his lips. "Can't say I'm surprised. You went back to almost the very spot we first encountered it."

"Grogan brought a Gatling gun." I shook my head. "Even that didn't bring it down."

Mal leaned forward with his elbows on his knees and exhaled, slowly wrapping his mind around the statement. His lone eye searched mine. "After all we've been through, the battles and the skirmishes, I could not have imagined anything like this."

"I was reminiscing about everything that led to our first meeting." I reconsidered that. It was more like a vivid dream. Every detail was crystal clear. You called me Boss for the first time." I lowered my voice to mimic him. "Afternoon, Boss. Are you in need of assistance?"

Mal laughed. "You were a dead man walking. Got blood all over my damn cotton that day." His smile faded. "I'm surprised that young private made it as far as he did."

"He was only sixteen." My voice softened, and I lowered my head to the memory of Rice falling off Miller's horse. "If it weren't for you, I never would have made it out of there." I got a little choked up and teary-eyed. It was probably the laudanum.

"Water under the bridge, Boss," he dismissed humbly.

I cleared my throat to regain my composure and noticed a book tucked under his arm. It was too thin to be his worn Bible. "What are you reading there, Mal?"

Mal pulled the tattered volume from his armpit and turned it over in his hand. It was a bound journal of blank pages that appeared several years old. It was dirty from water and mud damage. "All that material you asked us to look through, this is the only piece interesting."

"How so?"

"It starts as a diary of a young girl named Emma Franks. Her first entry is dated May 1846, in Independence, Missouri. Emma was on a wagon train headed to California."

"May's pretty late in the season to set off on a drive to California."

"I thought so too, but this girl, Emma, was part of the Donner-Reed Party. They were the folks caught in the mountains who supposedly ate their dead to survive. I've heard so many versions of the story, it's hard to know what's true."

I was a schoolboy in 1846, but everyone knew the Donner Party story. It was repeated at night around campfires all through my youth. It came up during lulls in the war. Some said they didn't just eat their dead, they killed the living for food. People crave lurid and sensational stories. Cannibalism satisfies that desire.

"Anyway," Mal continued, "This girl started on that wagon train. There were nine wagons and thirty-two people in her group. Five hundred wagons were ahead of them. They left earlier in the spring. There was talk of a shortcut that some of the guides decided to take, thinking it would get them to California faster. There were the usual Indian sightings and some related violence. Indians that came too close got shot." Mal paused before continuing. "A large howling animal stalked them at night and attacked their livestock."

My mouth went dry, and I felt a shiver not from the laudanum.

"Men on the wagon train rode out to investigate and didn't come back. People were terrified every time the sun went down, afraid they would be the next to disappear."

This part of the story I had never heard.

"At one point, they got into it with a group of Indians paralleling them on the trail. Men on the train decided enough was enough and rode out to confront them. Shot the Indians up and took on an Indian girl orphaned in the fighting."

"Who brings a kid out to fight with trigger-happy settlers?"

"The Indian girl, whom Emma dubbed Jade because she couldn't pronounce or spell her Indian name, seemed friendly and claimed to have been captured by the Indians. Jade said she was abducted from another Indian tribe before that."

When Mal didn't continue, I raised my eyebrows in anticipation. "And then what?"

"That's where the journal ends." Mal flipped it open and showed me written pages that took up the book's first third. "And then it switches over to drawings. There's no more text. It looks like the book went to a new owner who used the blank pages for sketches. Many of the pictures look like different people made them at different times. It's those pictures you'll find the most interesting."

Mal handed me the journal. The written portion was in a young girl's precise penmanship. She used a pencil as her writing utensil, which was lucky because if she had used ink, it might have blurred from water damage. The dried-out pages were wrinkled in places but legible. I flipped through several blank pages to the last quarter of the journal, where the drawings appeared. Turning the book around and upside down where the clean pages would have started, I found a new beginning.

The drawings were startling in both their detail and subject matter. They were disturbing images similar to the monster that attacked us. Nothing approaching photographic realism, but skillful sketches of the creature, primarily in charcoal. Sharp fangs, pointed ears, menacing talons, dark fur, bushy tail, and penetrating eyes. Only the stance of the thing seemed off as if the artists did not have a clear picture of the animal below the hips.

More disturbing were the depictions of what appeared to be a person with some of the creature's attributes. No, that was incorrect. The drawings were of what seemed to be a person becoming the creature. *Transforming* was a better word. Quite an imagination, but it bothered me how closely it resembled what we'd seen.

I held the depictions at arm's length to get a better sense of it, not believing my eyes. "Mal, is the artist of these sketches wanting us to believe a person turns into this wolf creature?"

Mal nodded reluctantly, sharing the opinion. "Look at the smaller pictures in the corners. Every page is just a little different from the last."

I paged through the book. A good portion had nearly identical pictures.

"You're supposed to flip it, Boss."

I looked up at him in confusion. "Flip it?"

"I'll show you." Mal pulled his chair up beside my cot and held the book. He lifted the corner pages with his thumb and let them flip into place like a deck of cards. The flipping and nuanced changes in each detailed drawing produced motion, depicting a person growing a long snout and fangs, pointed ears pushing out of the head, and wiry hair bursting out of the skin. A tail blossoms, its chest expands, talons pop from the ends of elongating fingers, muscles rippled, limbs lengthened until it rose as the creature that clawed Mal's face, bit me, and killed so many of our soldiers. A human being transforming into the living nightmare of the wolf creature.

I thumbed through the well-worn pages, realizing we had not been the first to complete this exercise over the life of the drawings. Then I flipped it in the other direction. The wolf transformed back into a person. "Quite ingenious."

We stared at each other for several seconds, daring the other to ask the question aloud. Finally, I broke the silence. "These sketches are pretty accurate, Mal, and this book was with the Wolf Clan before we first locked horns with the creature. Why would they suggest something like this..?" I waved the book in my hand between us.

"Craziness." He shrugged. "People were hanged in Salem for witchcraft. In my slave days, there were whispers of voodoo raising the dead. Even in the Bible, Jesus brought Lazarus back to life," Mal reasoned. "Indian superstition. Maybe they were trying to understand it."

I flipped the pages again. "If someone could..." I shook my head. "This is ridiculous."

"They would have to take their clothes off." Mal offered.

"If they did that, they would have to know it was going to happen," I said. "If they didn't, they would grow out of them..." Something from my wagon trip nagged at me—a twisted piece of metal.

"You got a look, Boss."

"Were you there when they brought me in from the wagon?"

"Yes."

"Did you happen to look inside the wagon?"

"I took a peek. A lot of blood. I was mainly worried about you."

"Would you be willing to check something?"

"Be glad to get me some air." Mal rose. "Stuffy in here. What's you need?"

"There was a twisted piece of metal in the wagon. I want to take a closer look at it."

Mal wrinkled his brow, which looked odd on a man wearing an eyepatch.

"You'll know. It was about this big." I held my hands six inches apart.

"I'll go look now."

31

Mal wasn't gone five minutes before Lieutenant Witwer walked in, harried and out of breath. "Major, sir," he saluted me. "You're alive!" He sounded surprised, relieved, and embarrassed all at once.

Admittedly, I felt the same way and joked, "Lieutenant. So are you!"

"I'm so sorry, sir. I saw that thing standing over your body. It hit you in the head. You weren't moving. Our weapons were no use. The buffalo guns were in the wagon. There was no time to get them. I ordered the men to retreat, but it came after us." Witwer spoke rapidly, justifying his actions as though he had done wrong.

I raised my hand. "It's okay. You did exactly the right thing. How many did you rescue?"

"Rescue?" Witwer seemed distressed by the word. "Sir, I deserted you. I had no idea you were alive. I never would have left if I had known."

"If you stayed, it would have killed all of you." I pointed out. "How many men escaped?"

"Eleven, sir," he started to calm down. "It came out of nowhere. I don't know if it was in the woods or following us. It must have come from the woods. The men always watch for Indians creeping up from behind."

"Eleven, including you, or would you be number twelve?"

"Twelve, including me, and now with you, thirteen survivors," he reported.

I shook my head in disbelief. We lost thirty. The figure knocked the breath from me.

"Mr. Grogan got out of there so fast we never caught up."

"Grogan's alive?" Given his cowardly behavior at the scene, I wasn't surprised.

"Yes, sir." After the Indians killed his men and the creature tore Mr. Spooner apart, he didn't look back."

"Did the Indians come after you?"

"Never came down from the hill that I saw. I think they were as terrified as…" Witwer caught himself, revealing his state of mind at the time of the assault, and corrected his wording, "Concerned about the creature as we were."

I needed to interview the survivors. I wanted to know who saw the creature arrive, its movements, and its point of origin. There may be clues to defeat it. Defeat it? Was there a way to defeat this monster? Before I could give Witwer the order to assemble the men, Mal returned with the piece of twisted metal. He held it up as he entered the infirmary.

"This what you wanted, Major?" Mal turned it around in his hand.

"Yes," I said as he handed it over. It was one cuff and two chain links of a leg shackle. An intact shackle consisted of two cuffs affixed to the prisoner's ankles with ten links in between to allow limited mobility. The cuff was bent, and the ratchet was stripped from the locking mechanism. Dried blood coated a good portion of the metal surface.

I held it up to Mal. "Looks like something grew out of it."

Mal nodded slowly in agreement."

Lieutenant, would you go to the stockade and bring the Indian girl, Ajiah? I have questions. Unfortunately, I'll be off my feet for a while." I patted my sore thigh for emphasis.

Witwer took a nervous step back and looked down. "I'm afraid I can't do that, sir."

"Why's that?" I half expected he would inform me Colonel Kirkwood had relieved me of my command and neglected to notify me.

"Because some of the Indian girls and children were removed from the stockade by Mr. Flynn of the BIA shortly after we left on our ill-fated expedition."

That didn't make sense. "Ajiah drove me here in the wagon. She wasn't in the stockade."

Witwer shook his head, "I assure you, sir, she is not among the captives."

I looked to Mal, who shrugged. He was not consulted or advised.

"Then where is she?" My tone was testy.

"That might be a question for Mr. Flynn," Witwer answered.

"Fetch him," I ordered, trying to keep my temper under control.

"Yes, sir. Right away." Witwer saluted and moved quickly to the door.

"And Lieutenant," I added, "I'd like to interview the survivors in the meantime."

"Right away, sir." He saluted again and was out the door before I could think of more.

I found myself growing agitated about Ajiah's whereabouts and well-being. It disturbed me Flynn made this move immediately upon our taking leave to search for Grogan's missing men. Grogan, who was evidently among the survivors. Not such a brave hunter after all.

"I'm drawing some uncomfortable conclusions about this beast, Mal." I shook my head as I struggled to express my theory aloud.

Mal nodded in reluctant agreement. "Yes, Boss.

Shortly thereafter, the door opened, but instead of Flynn, Dr. Nagel entered. "Forgot my watch." He went to the back room where he kept supplies, found what he was looking for, and returned, carefully winding a pocket watch. "My grandfather gave it to me."

"Hey, Doc? Did you look at those hairs I gave you the other day?"

He snapped the timepiece shut. "Yes, the best I can say is they're not human. If hair comparisons are being done, I'm not privy to the current science." He smiled dismissively.

"How about blood? Can you tell the difference between animal and human blood under a microscope?"

"Unfortunately, I cannot. I can tell the difference between red blood cells and plant cells, but that has more to do with coloring and cell shapes." Nagel shrugged. "I'm sure more powerful microscopes will one day be developed, but what you're looking for is unavailable *today*."

I looked at the blood on the broken shackle and felt stupid for thinking it could be evidence of an unknown or supernatural creature. I glanced at Mal's journal and thought about sharing it with Nagel. I held Mal's gaze for a moment. He shrugged.

"Got a minute to look at something?"

"Sure." His curiosity piqued, he stopped fiddling with his watch, slipped it into his pants pocket, and gave me his undivided attention.

I pointed at the journal. Mal handed it to him. Nagel paged through the volume and stopped at one of the more detailed charcoal drawings. Nagel contemplated the depiction closely before commenting. "This image is rather frightening. Is this what you saw out there?"

"Twice." I raised my chin to Mal. "Show him how to flip the pictures."

Mal drew close and demonstrated how to set the pictures into motion. Nagel took Mal's book and flipped through it several times, clearly finding it intriguing.

"Very clever. Where did you get this?" Nagel looked from me to Mal.

"It was collected from the Indian camp we raided. When this began."

"I've seen these novelty books before. They're usually cartoons, clowns, or animals. I've never seen one featuring a werewolf before."

Trying to sit up as best I could, I winced as pain jabbed my hip with the sudden movement. "What did you call it?"

He handed the book back to Mal. "It's a werewolf."

"What's a werewolf?" Mal and I asked in unison.

Nagel looked from Mal to me as though addressing two mental defectives. "A werewolf is a man who changes into wolf or man-wolf. There are various iterations in European legend. I'm no expert. I read it in a book of superstitious nonsense when I was at medical school. *Lycanthropy* was the word."

"Is that possible?" Mal beat me to the question.

Nagel's face soured with irritation. "Of course not. A caterpillar can spin a cocoon and become a butterfly. Mammals change as they grow. But nothing with the speed your flip book suggests. This is fantasy." He clapped the book shut.

I considered Mal and nodded acknowledgment but decided against sharing my theory.

"Obviously," he said, underscoring his point.

"So, this werewolf you read about... Was there some special way to deal with it?" He probably found my question ridiculous.

Nagel's brow knit against his glasses as though assessing my sincerity. "Shoot it? Spear it? Cut off its head?" He shrugged. "The usual, I suppose. It's folklore based on superstition. A curse transmitted via a bite from the afflicted and possibly triggered by the moon. It was attributed to people with mental disorders. The criminally insane. Not an actual living breathing monster." Nagel sighed in annoyance with the topic. "If you ask me, based on your sketches, excluding the flip, it's some freak of nature you're dealing with. It has to be. Legends, by definition, are unauthenticated drivel."

Mal and I nodded our understanding.

"In other words, it's not possible?" I wanted to be precise.

"A human being that turns into a monster? In a physical sense? Absolutely not!" He pronounced. "There is no such thing as werewolves." He chuckled to himself and moved for the door. "Now, if you'll excuse me."

"Thank you, Doctor."

Nagel stopped at the door and pointed at me. "I gave you that laudanum for pain, Major, but you should be careful with it. It's addictive and can interfere with your ability to reason clearly." There was a serious warning tone in his voice.

"I'll keep that in mind."

I spent the rest of my day interviewing my soldiers about the werewolf attack. I seized upon Nagel's word for it. Knowing what to call it reduced the mystery and comforted me. I wanted to get my hands on a book about it.

Each man of Dread Company, or what remained of it, apologized profusely for leaving me behind and at the monster's mercy. I was repeatedly assured it was not deliberate. I absolved each of any guilt. What else could they have done? I was down, and the creature was on top of me. It sank its fangs into me. By all appearances, I was a dead man. There was no other choice but to flee. Lieutenant Witwer issued the sensible order to retreat.

Their stories were in alignment. The first sign of trouble came from Whiteman Killer's braves, both in the woods and over the hill, instigated by Grogan's men, who attacked the Indians. If Spooner and the Cowboys hadn't started shooting, the operation might have succeeded as planned, with Whiteman Killer surrendering safely and without bloodshed. What needed clarification was where the werewolf came from. Not one man reported seeing the creature emerge from the woods. Not one man saw it come from the direction of the Indians attacking from the high ground. The first sign of it was reported by Axil, also a survivor, at or near the wagon in which Ajiah and Angry Eagle were shackled. This was consistent with my theory. It explained the blood on the wagon floor I noticed during my transport. However, that blood could have come from Gatewood and Wilson, who had been in the wagon just before pandemonium erupted. All the more reason to confront Ajiah. Only Ajiah could tell me what transpired immediately before and after the werewolf appeared. Questioning her was the priority.

None of the escaped soldiers were injured. All that survived the encounter were unscathed, leading me to wonder how many were left for dead because they were assumed dead. Ajiah said the men were either dead or fled. I found myself questioning if that was true.

Even Kirkwood visited me. Surprisingly, I was not demoted, nor was there talk of court-martial. Kirkwood's position was that we, as an outpost in the wilderness of Indian Territory, faced formidable odds with the Indian threat. Kirkwood wanted me to continue my duties as best I could as a paper pusher, producing official correspondence supporting our mission.

I would not lead any men in the field nor go anywhere near a horse for some time. Kirkwood pledged to up his request from fifty fresh Buffalo Soldiers following the first tragedy to one hundred with the latest massacre. There was no denying we no longer had sufficient forces to conduct our primary function. It troubled me the overwhelming threat was attributed to the Indians, and no mention would be made of the werewolf. I understood Kirkwood's reservations, but new troops prepared to take retribution on Indians did not address the actual danger. It withstood the onslaught of a Gatling gun. Throwing more ill-prepared men at it was not going to neutralize the problem. It would just increase the body count. After making his desires known, Kirkwood asked me to write up the necessary paperwork and get it dispatched to the War Department via telegraph and mail. Often, the telegraphed messages were unreliable or miscommunicated. Mail by train took longer but was spelled out in written documents.

Witwer would be promoted to Captain as no seasoned white officers were available to assume the position. Lieutenant Carpenter would replace Witwer. This I found troubling. Witwer lacked the experience to confront these unusual challenges. I would provide Witwer advice as best I could under my current limitations. In other words, there would be very little time devoted to recovery. My responsibilities would increase. I got permission to delegate work to Mal. He was willing to assist and had a level of experience second only to my own. I asked if Sergeant Butler could be promoted to Lieutenant, as promotions of enlisted to officer in dire cases were not unheard of. That request was denied. My most qualified and experienced man was barred from command solely because of the color of his skin, though it was blamed on his injury.

Overall, I spent the day speaking to everyone I intended to interview except for two people: Mr. Flynn, the BIA agent, and Ajiah, the Indian girl. I only wanted to talk to Flynn long enough to determine Ajiah's whereabouts. After additional time passed, I requested Mal remind Witwer of my order or track Flynn down.

Within thirty minutes of my request, Mal produced Witwer, now wearing Captain's insignia. Witwer saluted me, looking proud of himself.

"Congratulations are in order, Captain Witwer," I emphasized his fresh rank.

"Thank you, sir." He puffed up his chest, swelling with pride. "I won't let you down."

"I'll be at your disposal whenever you find yourself in need of advice."

"Colonel Kirkwood instructed me to seek your counsel liberally, Major."

"Very well." I exhaled, ready to change the subject. "Have you located Mr. Flynn?"

Witwer flushed. "No, sir, I have not. A Chinese laundry boy from town advised me the Indian girl was escorted to Madam Crossly's establishment, where several of the captured Indian girls were taken in the past. I think that particular brothel is called the Treasure Trove."

"What?" Mal asked. He was highly sympathetic to the plight of the Indian women and familiar with the dangers. His wife's difficult circumstances at the cotton farm came to mind.

"It's my understanding," Witwer continued carefully, "Mr. Flynn and the Crossly woman have an arrangement. Crossly pays Flynn to assume responsibility for specific female Indians. Children are routed to boarding schools to facilitate their assimilation into society. Crossly diverts others to her employ."

"In other words, he sells the girls into prostitution and the children into servitude," I surmised. I felt a deep foreboding and sense of loss I had not experienced since the premature death of my pregnant wife, Rebecca, before I left for war. Rebecca was only a few years older than Ajiah when she died. Was that why I was experiencing such a gut punch of loss? My affection for the young woman with the sad orphan's story was unexpected. Some might consider it an unprofessional attachment, but she rescued me from certain death.

Witwer lowered his eyes and folded his hands behind his back. "It would so appear."

Mal vigorously shook his head. "Boss, this is wrong. I can't abide enslaving these people and pressing them into prostitution. You know how I feel about this." He huffed a breath, venting frustration. There was more he kept to himself.

I was in complete agreement. "I'm with you, Mal. Both of you, help me up. Find me a crutch. We're going to stop this right goddamn now!"

32

Mal and Witwer could not dissuade me from traveling into town. I knew I was exercising poor judgment, but restless anxiety seized me, compelling me to find Ajiah no matter what. Rising to a sitting position, I experienced immediate pain in my hip and knee, accompanied by a slight wave of faintness. My broken ribs made it difficult to take a full breath. I took a hard hit from the laudanum bottle and hoped it would last me the entire evening. Mal found a crutch in the infirmary storage area. Witwer located a small carriage for us to ride into town. I wasn't going to delude myself into thinking I could hobble the mile to Crossly's brothel on a broken hip, crutch, or no crutch.

Riding with Mal reminded me of our first meeting and his engineering of our escape north with his family. It was a significant chapter in our shared history. Since rejoining the war and the Buffalo Soldiers afterward, we had ridden together only on horseback.

Due to my many duties and responsibilities, I rarely spent time in the town of Lucian. The military met my humble needs for shelter, food, and clothing. Any necessary services were provided by requisition or some other capacity. The soldiers, being Negroes, were not welcomed by the town populace unless they were spending money. And the quicker they spent it and left, the better, as far as the white townsfolk were concerned. Because laws banned the Negro soldiers from white-serving establishments, entrepreneurs erected separate accommodations.

Following the war, the South enacted the Black Code to segregate Negroes with state and local laws. These laws forbade when, where, and how Negroes could work, be served, gather, and with whom they might associate.

Separate entrances and facilities were the rule and not the exception. Lucian was not in the South, but the attitudes and ordinances were equally restrictive.

Negroes were barred from formal dining rooms unless they were waiters or otherwise assigned to servant tasks. Absolutely never as patrons unless it was a Negroes only dining room, of which there were none in Lucian. If my soldiers wanted meals in town, they were restricted to backdoor service and instructed to eat in the alleys.

Negroes could be barbered and bathed, but never in tubs used by white patrons. And under no circumstances could Negroes and whites share the same women. A Buffalo Soldier seen or even suspected of merely gazing upon a white woman, never mind speaking to one, risked impromptu lynching.

Crossly discovered a clever workaround to these institutional prejudices by introducing Indian girls as an option of desire at her establishments. Many in the white community did not consider Indians to be actual human beings. There was widespread confusion in the wording of the 14th Amendment adopted last summer. As it pertained to voting rights, many whites considered Negroes and Indians to count as only 3/5th of a person.

The offspring of whites and non-whites were viewed as a mongrelization of the white race. In the kindest of terms, any white persons creating children with a non-white were shunned, and the children disparaged mercilessly. These factors created a loophole for bordello owners such as Crossly. She learned to service non-whites with Indian women while simultaneously offering them to white clients desiring a taste of forbidden fruit. Negroes were generally charged more for the same services and regulated to *Negro Only* rooms, beds, and linens. It was a deliberate facade, so the brothel could not be accused of encouraging young ladies to entertain gentlemen of differing races interchangeably. Whites could not complain because the argument set forth was that Indian girls were employed to service non-whites. If whites wanted to sample exotic goods, that was their choice, and the brothel management was not held responsible.

Crossly further avoided trouble by setting up her businesses with shared walls and double doors or by locating establishments across alleys from each other. Her ideal design was to utilize shared halls that created the illusion of separate businesses, kitchens, and employees running separate sets of customers. In reality, there was but one set of employees serving Negroes and whites simultaneously, with neither clientele aware of the other. Whatever it took to support the spirit of capitalism on the prairie.

Beside a boisterous whites-only saloon called the Broken Spoke and sharing a back hallway, as previously alluded, was Crossly's crown jewel of Lucian brothels, the Treasure Trove. Men at the Spoke, drinking themselves into inebriation would wander to the Trove for a look, or more if tempted, and spend the remainder of whatever lined their pockets on female favors. It was outside the Trove that Mal brought the carriage to a halt. Mal and Witwer assisted me to the boardwalk, separating the hard-packed dirt roadway from the entrance.

At the door was a tall, brawny, bald man named Saul. His mustache was carefully curled with wax. His white sleeves were rolled above swollen biceps and crossed over his barrel chest. He gave us a quick wink and flashed a smile of gold fillings. He blocked Mal's entry with a twirl of his finger. "You'll have to use the service entrance, round back, Sergeant. Rules."

Mal made a face, held his tongue, and assisted me with finding a comfortable stance against the crutch. Once I was situated, he headed to the adjacent alley. I instructed Witwer to remain with the carriage while I reacquired the girls to my custody. Saul opened the heavy entrance door, which jangled a bell into a liberally perfumed foyer adorned with silky pink, red, and rose drapes softly lit by a single kerosene lantern. "Enjoy your evening, Major."

"I don't intend to be here long, Saul. Thank you very much." He knew I wasn't a patron, but he was required to be polite to every potential customer. Sweat broke out on my brow. My efforts were more painful than I could have imagined. Merely leaning on the crutch with my leg dangling was excruciating. I steeled myself to the task and took painful breaths that were fresh blows to my ribs.

Somehow, I knew Ajiah was in this place. It wasn't a sound or visualization, just a compelling feeling she was in the brothel and required help. I worried she was being defiled and degraded sexually every second I delayed. An irrational anger simmered deep inside me.

I pushed through a beaded entrance into a large sitting room decorated with an elegant oriental rug surrounded by velvety couches, settees, and overstuffed chairs. In the corner was a generously stocked bar of various spirits in crystal decanters. A light fog of opium smoke hung in the air, emanating from two pillowed hookah stations positioned in opposite corners. Over the magnificent redwood mantle was the largest bison head I had ever seen. It gazed over the great room with dead marble eyes. No doubt a gift from Grogan. A fire burned at a comfortable temperature in the brick hearth below.

This room, too, was lit by kerosene lanterns at a level meant to erase any physical flaws or signs of aging displayed by the women working therein. Ten women were costumed in variations of sheer bed clothes and frilly undergarments, leaving little unexploited. Four were Indians, two of whom I recognized from our most recent raid as Tanka, the Buffalo Girl, and Plenty Wounds. All four Indians were cleaned up and thoroughly painted with makeup to lighten their complexions and soften their features. These efforts did nothing to mask their discomfort and shame. Tanka looked at me, trying to assess my intentions, and assumed the worst.

The other six women ran the gamut of ages, hair coloring, build, and confidence. They were busy flirting with potential white customers and coming to terms. Half sat in the men's laps and rubbed their breasts in eager faces or squeezed the men softly between their legs. One by one, they drifted off with men of various ages and stations in life. My interactions with the town citizenry were infrequent. None of the patrons were familiar to me. Even with a space cleared on the couch between Tanka and Plenty Wounds, I refrained from making the painful attempt to sit with them. Knowing they did not speak English, I kept my question simple. "Ajiah?"

They looked to me excitedly, "Ajiah? Ajiah?" They thought I would bring Ajiah to them. I looked around the sitting room for an attendant. The girls were inexperienced, and it stood to reason someone should be watching over them. If for no other reason than to discourage escape and ensure payment. Perhaps the other two Indian women mentored them. Just as I reached out to grab their arms and coax them to leave, Beth Crossly sauntered from behind a curtain I had mistaken for a draped wall.

"I'm so glad you decided to visit, Major. Have you found something that interests you? I see you've selected Tammy and Pamela, as I've renamed them. I have a special rate if you desire both at the same time. A fantasy of many men, it seems." She gave me a salacious expression meant to demean my character. She eyed my crutch but ignored it as a topic of conversation.

"Where's Ajiah?" I demanded, more forcefully than I intended, my anger rising.

"She's not quite ready for gentleman callers, Major. Perhaps one of the other Indian maidens? I see you have an eye for the indigenous."

"I warned you to stay away from the Indians, Miss Crossly." I felt a flash of energizing rage. The adrenal rush burned off the lingering numbness of laudanum and bolstered my resolve. Dr. Nagel was right about the mixture dulling my mental faculties. The effects were wearing off.

"It's simply not your call once they're at the fort, Major. They are under Mr. Flynn's BIA authority. I've checked with a knowledgeable attorney in town regarding the legalities. Your role is security. You don't own them." She patronized me in a pleasant tone of voice.

I tried to tamp my ire and measure my pitch. "I have a strong sense Ajiah is here. Please take me to her. Whatever your arrangement with Mr. Flynn, you don't own them either."

Our interaction disrupted services as patrons discontinued their flirtations and glanced at our increasing animosity. Crossly also noticed and waved me to follow her behind the curtain she just emerged. Unbidden, Saul joined us. At this point, I wondered where the exit was. I leaned on the crutch to absorb some of the pressure building in my injured limb. A change of position did little good in alleviating the pain.

"May I inquire what it is between you and this Indian girl, Major? You seem to have an unnatural fixation. A rare beauty, to be sure. Is she simply the one you must have?" She nodded in an attempt to egg me on. "I'm planning an auction for her favors. She is in high demand among prominent professionals, including Mr. Grogan, Mr. Flynn, and the mayor. Even your Corporal Smith has expressed a lusty interest, not that he has the means to win the bidding. Now you?" She paused to look me over. "However, I don't expect any of you will outbid Mr. Grogan."

The words came out of my mouth before I could stop them. "You're auctioning off the privilege of being the first to rape her?"

"The first to enjoy her," Crossly rephrased in a practiced manner. "It's only rape if she decides to fight the winner. Frankly, some men prefer a spirited go when rogering a new girl," she said out one side of her mouth.

"I won't allow it," I decreed.

"Then I will be glad to entertain your bid when the time comes," Crossly cooed. "In the meantime, I'm happy to introduce you to one of the other girls."

"NO," I thundered in a guttural tone that was not my natural voice. "I'm not leaving without her." Crossly started and appeared alarmed by my insistence and sudden intensity.

"I think you'd better leave, Major," Saul said, speaking for the first time as the brothel bouncer. He reached for my left biceps, bearing all my weight on my injured side.

In trying to pull away, I jarred my hip, nearly collapsed, and cried out in pain, "Damnit!"

"Major Kincaid, are you here?" I heard Mal calling to me from behind a nearby wall.

"Don't hurt him, Saul, he's already injured," Crossly said. "I don't

168

want trouble with the military. Just escort him outside quietly, please."

Rising anger consumed me. There came an audible crack, which I initially attributed to the grinding of broken bones in my leg. Instead of pain, I felt a jolt of exhilaration and euphoria wash over me. Additional crackling came like muffled gunshots under my skin and caused Crossly and Saul to take cautious steps back. They appeared concerned whatever was wrong with me might be contagious. My molars convulsed at the back of my mouth, causing a pleasant roiling sensation in my jaw. My teeth lengthened and grew sharp around my expanding tongue.

"Are you all right?" Saul asked cautiously, renewing his grip on the shoulder that rode the crutch. His face registered alarm.

I released my grip on the crutch without considering the consequences and shoved Saul's hand away. As I did, I realized two things: my hip no longer hurt, and I was metamorphosizing into a larger, more powerful being. The muscles throughout my body thickened and enlarged. My left hand and wrist grew out of the cuff of my coat, sprouting thick, wiry brown hairs. My fingers wriggled, cracked, and elongated. Blood dripped from my cuticles as my nails thickened and spiked from the ends of my fingers. Paws formed from my expanding hands.

I tried to say, "What's happening to me?" But the question manifested as a deep guttural growl. Crossly and Saul stared at me with visible horror, unable to process my transformation. They should have run, but they couldn't tear their eyes from me.

My ears toughened, sprouted hair, and pressed upward into velvety horns that instantly enhanced my hearing. I now detected their quickening breaths and rapid heartbeats. My pores unsheathed thick, sharp hairs, sending electric tingles from the top of my head and along my spine to my emerging heels.

"Boss!?" Mal yelled, getting closer. I could hear his breathing now.

The front of my face and jaw tightened as my skin stretched, and my skull erupted to create a protruding muzzle below my eyes. I worked my mouth until my teeth fit with my bite and touched my face with heavy paws in fascination. My nose expanded black and moist. I became consciously aware the three people nearest me were sweating to various degrees and emitting pheromones, telegraphing their rising fear. I even detected Crossly coming to the end of her menstrual cycle beyond her heavily perfumed sex.

My clothing constricted and ripped away as my musculature swelled. I took a series of deep inhalations, which expanded my ribcage and burst the seams of my shirt and coat. The pain in my broken ribs was chased away. My trousers burst their buttons and tore free as my thighs thickened with muscle. The transformation erased the throbbing in my hip and knee. A bushy tail emerged from my tailbone and waved unhindered behind me. My feet expanded through my leather boots, ripping away to reveal thick, black nails digging into the bare wood floor.

The growth of my body didn't slow until I'd gained a good two feet in stature and an estimated three hundred pounds in weight. Where was the mass coming from? With the question came a predatory desire to feed. Crossly and Saul looked up at me in open-mouth astonishment when they should have been running for their lives.

Crossly uttered a fearful squeaking sound, unable to form a coherent word beyond "What...?"

Mal batted through the curtain and into the room. He looked upon me without recognition. "What in God's name?" He fumbled for his sidearm but left it in his holster, knowing it was useless and previously cost him an eye. Then he raised his hands to show me his palms and backed away.

Crossly eyed him with horror but found her voice. "For fuck's sake, shoot it!"

Raw power surged throughout my new body, and I wanted to know what it could do, but foremost in my mind was driving hunger. It gnawed within, all-consuming and symbiotic. I tried to warn Mal to run, but my voice was nothing but an angry roar of threatening violence. I knew who I was but also what I had become. Unfortunately, my predominant emotion was rage at not getting what I craved. My eyes narrowed on Saul as he reached for his sidearm. I snarled and raked him from his throat to his midsection with a potent swipe of newly formed claws. The bald man screamed and split open in bleeding rows. Tangled, bloody intestines spilled from him even as he dropped his weapon and attempted to stem the flow with his puny hands and shaky fingers. As his life drained out, he fell to his knees. I swatted him again, hard across the face, tearing much of it free. Half his jaw and several gold teeth flew against the wall and clattered on the wood floor like dice.

Part of me wanted to devour the soft parts of my fresh kill and sate my ravenous appetite. My sense of smell increased one hundredfold and overrode the hunger. I caught the fresh scent of Ajiah. She was in the building, and I was compelled to find her. Feeding on men would have to wait. I pushed Crossly roughly aside as she rediscovered her ability to scream. Something deep within warned me not to kill her until Ajiah was safe. Mal pressed himself against the papered wall, his mouth agape. I detected movement in the rooms above me. Men and women engaged in intercourse hastily dressed to flee or investigate the disturbance on the main floor.

As I crept through the hall, the scent of Ajiah grew keener. She was somewhere below me, comingled with smells of soil, iron, and other substances unknown to my new acute sense of smell. I raced to a set of darkened stairs at the end of the hall and bound down them to a landing. I found another set of stairs in the shadows, which I took three at a time to a dirt floor and wooden door. I crashed through the door without effort or hesitation, revealing a small room. Embedded in the dirt wall was an iron door with a dial, lever, and heavy loop handles. The safe was as large as an oversized wardrobe, and I knew without seeing Ajiah was inside. I slammed my powerful paws into the safe door, but the plating was too thick to penetrate even in my potent werewolf form. I roared angrily, frustrated at the obstruction, and sensed Ajiah knew I was there. Her heartbeat calmed.

"I knew you would come," I heard her whisper.

I swiped my claws at the formidable door, but it had no effect. The iron was one-half inch thick at minimum. The safe was solidly set in concrete on either side of the door. It was built burglar and fireproof. For an instant, I wondered if I could communicate with Mal and get him to force Crossly to dial the combination and open the safe. I considered running away in the hopes I would soon transform back and return to force Crossly to open Ajiah's cell. But there was no guarantee what I would find upon my return. Crossly knew the werewolf and I were one and the same. Retreat was not an option.

Instead, I clawed at the outside of the concrete and into the dirt walls surrounding the safe. The pressed dirt crumbled away under my ripping claws. I tore at the soil savagely until I exposed not another sheet of protective iron but more concrete. The cement required several piledriving blows from my fur-covered fists to crack. I clawed the chunks away in gritty pieces. Debris buried my monstrous feet. Beyond the concrete were layers of other substances, presumably there to protect the contents from fire. I tore through insulation and plaster and found an iron-reinforced skeleton.

"Let me out!" Ajiah yelled from inside.

I punched into the safe's side between the iron ribs. This gave way to a thin sheet of metal lining the interior wall of the safe. I pushed it inward and dug my nails into the sheeting, crumpling it to reveal Ajiah's worried face. She bent the sheet downward from the inside to expose her cramped space. I detected the residual odors of old papers, coins, and currency that previously occupied the safe. Also lingering were the smells of other girls similarly imprisoned on past occasions. I surmised Crossly used it to punish uncooperative women pressed into a life of prostitution.

More troubling was the eight-inch by eight-inch rebar squares comprising Ajiah's cage. For all my newfound strength, I knew I couldn't tear the metal loose or bend the bars enough to free her, nor could she squirm between them. As unstoppable as I felt, something like this cage would be adequate to imprison me. Someone would have to open the door in the usual way for Ajiah to escape.

There came a commotion at the door where I entered. Half-dressed men gathered at the bottom of the stairs, squinting into the darkness, cautiously advancing. I realized I was seeing in the dark without the benefit of lanternlight and held an advantage in the shadows.

"What's down there?" A familiar voice asked nervously.

The minimal lighting from the lantern in the hall at the top of the stairs backlit the group, which included Grogan and a couple of other men I did not know. I recognized the nervous voice, sour sweat, and stench of shit from the speaker's soiled underwear. He had recently engaged in intercourse, and I detected a mixture of seminal fluid and female lubrication about him. It was Flynn, the BIA man. He was somewhere near the closest landing and out of sight. My mouth salivated at my immediate desire to kill and devour him. Instinctively, I knew I would have to eat soon to maintain my strength and support my form.

I detected Mal's scent as well. He was hanging back at the top of the stairs.

"Anyone get a look at it?" Grogan asked. He was fully dressed and smelled of cigars.

"It sounded like a big dog," a middle-aged man tucking in his shirt added. He wore a suit of clothes attributed to a banker or man of means. He stunk of bourbon.

"Someone fetch a lantern so we can see what we're dealing with," Grogan ordered.

Mal rushed to the task and stepped down the stairs from behind the other men with a lantern turned up to full brightness. His eyepatch sucked the light away from his dark face like a black hole. In his other hand, he clutched my bloody coat, indicating to me Mal suspected what happened to me. I moved into the corner where I could watch the door, but anyone entering would have to step into the room to see me.

"Let me out!" Ajiah yelled again, waving her hand through the hole I created.

"There's a girl inside?" Grogan asked.

Mal entered the room, focused on the safe and the damage I'd done. He contemplated her waving hand, then swung the lantern to illuminate me. Mal stiffened and took a breath before swearing. "What in the unholy?" He was afraid and fascinated but suspected he had nothing to fear so long as he made no sudden moves.

"What is it, Sergeant? What do you see?" Grogan called out.

I uttered a low growl from the back of my throat.

"Y'all may wanna keep back," Mal advised. "Better yet, it might be best if you go upstairs and about your business. Maybe go on home." Mal was using their ignorance of the situation to his benefit. By the sounds coming from the stairwell, at least one person took the suggestion to heart. Boots resounded on bare wooden steps upward.

Ajiah whispered to Mal, "If you get that witch Crossly to let me out, it will leave."

Mal stared at me with his unblinking eye. "I don't understand what's happening." He shook his head in disagreement with his observation. "No, I don't *want* to understand."

Mal stepped away from the door and into the hall to address the other men. "I need the Crossly woman to release this child."

"What?" Grogan asked in confusion but moved no closer to the unknown danger.

The banker staggered through the other men to Mal. "What's all the mystery you're creating, buck? Make way."

Whether it was the inebriated remark or knowing resistance was futile, Mal let the intoxicated man pass to take a look. "What goes on?"

"That Crossly woman is crazy," Ajiah said, waving to make her presence known and, perhaps, distract him from me. "She's locked me up. Make her let me out."

Seeing did not clarify matters for the banker based on the confused expressions twitching across his face. "Why would she do that? Where's the dog?" He turned in my direction, squinting into the dark, but when his eyes found me, they went wide, displaying their full whites. "What the hell?" he trailed off, unable to find words through his drunken fog. "Waa..," he tried again.

My patience and hunger found their limit. Roaring, I grabbed his shoulders between my paws and sank my fangs into his flabby neck. Inarticulate sounds caught in his throat and became a gurgle of bloody incoherence. I tore a chunk of flesh from him and swallowed without chewing. I raised him from the floor to plant my fangs in his soft belly. Warm blood spilled over my chin, onto my chest, and dripped liberally to the dirt floor. To my horror, I found I enjoyed the familiar taste. My body tingled with energy from the sustenance. Rejuvenated, I devoured mouthfuls as I approached the doorway to confront the others. It was time to end this.

Mal backed himself and the lantern into the space adjacent to the shattered door to give me room. I tossed the dead man's corpse aside and bellowed a menacing howl at the crowd of men. They stumbled backward, trying to escape up the wooden stairs and shouting in panic.

"Get my gun!" Grogan yelled in terror. He gave the man in front of him a shove toward me and elbowed his way up the stairs two at a time.

I raked the man down the front of his face with my right claw and eviscerated him from his genitals through his thorax with the other. He split open, screaming, and collapsed on the stairs. I leaped over the body and took the steps three at a stride. Once in the hall, I spotted Flynn running from me. He made the mistake of looking over his shoulder to check my progress. "No! No! No!" He whined.

I was upon him in an instant and severed his head from his body with a mighty swipe of my razor-sharp claw. I then impaled him between his shoulder blades, holding his corpse like a shield as I propelled myself forward. I forced my way into the sitting room, where I tore into his limp body and devoured his soft middle. After a few rushed mouthfuls, I tossed his body into the crackling fireplace. I was shocked to find gentlemen and ladies of the night still positioned on the furniture, going about their business, high on opium or drunk on spirits, and oblivious to danger.

I followed the scent of Madam Crossly up the half-spiral grand staircase to the second level, bounding upstairs. The closer I got, the stronger her smell became. I crashed through a locked white door detailed with ornate gilt trim. Backed against a wardrobe across the room, Crossly whimpered in fear, clutching a lady's knuckle-duster pistol. She fired her only shot into my chest before I made it halfway to her. The small caliber bullet barely registered.

I struggled with my natural desire to kill and eat her as my clawed fingers wrapped around her throat, just tight enough to make her cough and struggle for breath. I growled in her face, baring my bloody fangs, then dragged her to the basement. She kicked at my legs and lost her shoes but landed ineffective fists on my shoulders and snout. My path had cleared, and no one but Mal and Ajiah remained below. I tossed Crossly into the room with the safe and growled with effective malice. She coughed and rose to her knees, massaging the bleeding redness my nails inflicted upon her throat.

"Please don't kill me!" She begged, raising a hand to me and staring at the blood and gore spilled over the dirt floor from the murdered banker. Mal's lantern cast a macabre glow.

"Then let me out!" Ajiah commanded in a steady tone.

"All right! All right! All right," Crossly screamed. "Let me calm down so I can remember the fucking combination." She stared at my werewolf form and shuddered at the alternative. She covered her eyes as though waking from a nightmare, exhaled, and took a deep breath.

Mal turned the lantern down so Crossly would not have to look at me in full illumination. Reassuringly, he said, "Just steady yourself and think what the combination is, miss. I can turn the dial if you're too shaky."

"Why are you helping it?" She snapped at Mal in a quavering voice.

"Because he won't leave until he gets what he wants, and what he wants is for you to release the girl. I don't want to see any more innocent people killed." Mal looked up at me, wondering if that was possible.

I stepped back and growled. It was the only intonation I was capable of. When Mal referred to me as *he*, I knew Mal understood it was me and was struggling with that realization.

I took a menacing step toward her and bared my fangs.

"Okay," she trilled. "I've got it." She scrambled to the safe door on her knees, pushing through the debris. She dusted off the dial to see the numbers and blew at it for good measure. Mal held the lantern to provide her with an unobstructed view. It took her a few tries, but I heard the internal locking mechanism click with each correct fall of the tumblers until a louder, more satisfying sound registered success. She grasped the steel lever with both hands and gave it a hard turn and pull. The bolts disengaged the door from their housings with a metallic clack and opened a fraction of an inch. Ajiah shoved the door open in her haste to escape, striking Crossly full in the face and knocking her down. Crossly touched at the tender point of impact. Her nose was bleeding, and her lip split. Ajiah looked at each of us in turn, her wondering gaze lingering on me in fascination. She sneered at Crossly and fled the cellar without a word.

"I've done what you asked. Please don't kill me!" Crossly begged, knowing she had nothing to bargain with. She looked to Mal for sympathy but pointed accusingly at me. "You know it's Kincaid, don't you?"

Mal sighed with a slump of his shoulders and gave her a slight nod.

"I won't tell anyone." She whimpered in desperation. "Please."

But I had to kill her. She knew, and I sensed the danger in that. I moved toward her, backing her against the wall. She raised a cowering hand to fend me off and screamed.

"No!" Mal pled on Crossly's behalf.

Ignoring my friend, I shanked the four claws of my right paw into her chest, stabbing through her ribs and skewering her heart. She sagged as her life drained away. Blood burbled from her mouth, thick and red, as she attempted to form a final thought she would never share.

I fed.

"Oh, Boss," Mal sobbed in despair. He shuddered in fear. "What have you become?"

33

What indeed? Mal stared at my monstrous being in open judgment. I should have felt shame, but a calm came over me instead. The rage was satisfied. Ajiah was free, and the threats, Crossly, Flynn, Saul, and a man or two I couldn't even name, had been murdered. I didn't kill anyone that didn't deserve it, I reasoned. The more I considered what I needed to do next, the more I realized I would soon naturally revert to my human form. I felt it coming. I had to flee.

I stared at Mal and gestured to Ajiah's escape route. He nodded his reluctant agreement and cautiously handed me my bloody coat and shredded trousers. By collecting the castoff garments that would identify me, Mal demonstrated his quickness of mind and loyalty despite the horror I had become. "You should go back to the fort. I'll see to the girls." Mal promised in a low voice. He was understandably upset.

There was no reason to remain to contemplate the night's events. I left the cellar dungeon while still possessing the strength and agility. I managed to slip through the maze of hallways and into the alley without being seen. Judging by the sounds and smells emanating from the great room, men with guns had arrived. There was the indistinct shouting of instructions and half questions about what occurred and who was responsible. One of the voices belonged to Captain Witwer. Was he only now entering to check on me and Mal?

Keeping to the shadows and waiting for townspeople and carriages to pass, I made my way to the fort with my bundle of clothes clutched in a claw. Fierce exhaustion overtook me like the sleepiness that overtakes a drunk slipping toward unconsciousness. I needed a secluded place to lie down and let whatever might happen next occur. I found a barn near the company livery. Therein, my presence caused the whinnying and snorting of several horses. Their excitement reminiscent of the creature's first attack. Only this time, I was the source of their trepidation.

In back, I laid down in an inviting, out-of-the-way pile of loose hay where I would not be stumbled across. Unable to fight the overwhelming exhaustion, I slipped into the seductive void of slumber. My entire body relaxed and shrank to a more familiar shape.

I awoke to the familiar chill of the mid-morning sun, well past my usual wake-up time of dawn. Around my naked body were remnants of furry gore and sloughed-off skin in advanced decomposition. It reminded me of a snake molting its too-tight skin, except it had fallen away from me in pieces instead of one long sheath. I supposed it had to go somewhere after the reverse transformation and was not reabsorbed into my body. Remaining was a thin, bloody, placenta-like substance coating my. It had dried and become flakey, like sunburned flesh that disintegrated upon vigorous rubbing. I was myself again and feeling better than I had in years. Gone were the aching bones and tired muscles from war-weary years of sleeping on the cold, hard ground in undesirable conditions. Gone was the wear and tear on the body I abused with too much exertion and too little sleep.

There was a wave of nausea I knew would not pass until I vomited up whatever was upsetting my stomach. I positioned myself on all fours as gobs of red, white, and veiny blue morsels purged from me in violent heaves. The upchuck consisted of undigested man meat and bone fragments from the mouthfuls I ingested to sate my werewolf hunger. Not for the first time, I noted a familiar flavor to it. Once the offending pieces were out, I spat the nasty dregs lingering in my mouth to one side. I needed water to rinse away the foul taste. Beyond that, I felt fine. Better than fine.

I rose to my feet with ease and found not a hint of pain in my shattered kneecap or my broken hip and ribs. I shook the leg lightly and got not so much as a twinge of discomfort. I shook it more vigorously and kicked out at natural and irregular angles as if daring the two-day-old injuries to reignite. When there was no soreness, I did several deep knee bends and leaped as high into the air as possible. I was completely healed. How was that possible?

I reached under my left armpit and felt at my side for the ugly scar of the rifle wound inflicted by the albino Andersonville guard Miller. It, too, was fully healed. Like it never existed. The five-year-old reminder of one of my worst memories melted away during the night. Next, I checked my genitals where Miller stabbed and castrated me, leaving me unable to produce children. Again, I found no scar and no twinge of the discomfort that plagued me since the brutal assault. I was fully rejuvenated. I laughed aloud at the delightful side effect.

Unfortunately, my clothing had not regenerated. My coat was serviceable but spattered with fresh blood and gore. It would need replacing but would cover my nakedness until I made it to my quarters. My trousers were in worse shape, missing all of the necessary buttons. Fortunately, my belt was intact except for a tear in the leather where my buckle strained the notch. I inserted it, intending to tie it off or slacken it to the next punch, only to find my waistline reduced by two sizes. The lost weight left my belly firm and free of the residual fat collected over the years. I pulled the belt tight to the last notch. So far, I was reaping nothing but benefits from the change.

I proceeded barefoot to the fort entrance and waved my way past the sentries. If they noticed my slovenly appearance, they kept their opinions to themselves. I needed to reach my quarters to bathe, shave, change to appropriate attire, and erase all evidence of the night's events. Many a man returned to forts in shame and embarrassment, but no one quite like me on this occasion. I made it to my quarters without running across anyone in close enough proximity that my disheveled state would draw attention. Once my door was closed, I sighed a breath of relief.

"I'm glad you made it back okay, Boss," Mal said from the chair beside my writing desk.

"You startled me, Mal," I lied. He had not startled me, and my pulse had not quickened even a beat by his unexpected appearance. However, the heightened senses experienced during my rescue of Ajiah had not remained to warn me of his presence. "I woke up in a barn covered in the remnants of last night." I undressed in front of him and showed him the dried, bloody mucous still clinging to my skin like day-old snot. "Thank you for having the presence of mind to grab my clothing. Returning nude might have raised a few eyebrows."

There was no reason to pretend it wasn't me. Although Mal didn't witness my transformation, he knew by my discarded clothing and crutch. Our review of the journal turned out to be prophetic. What caused this was the question weighing on my mind. What might be the resulting consequences?

"The girls and children are resting easy in the stockade." Mal looked like he hadn't gotten a wink of sleep. He was a bundle of conflict and guilt, though he had done nothing wrong.

"Thanks to you getting them here safely." I drank from a water pitcher on my bureau to rinse the bloody offal from my mouth and spit it into a chamber pot on the floor. Next, I filled the washbowl and scrubbed myself with a clean cloth until the bowl was so red I couldn't see the bottom. I transferred the filthy water into the pot and repeated the process until the water in the bowl was only a light shade of pink. Mal watched me with sage patience.

"You're welcome, Boss." He whispered. He had something on his mind.

"I'll want to question Ajiah as soon as I dress and have some breakfast. I'm starving." I smiled, seeing the humor in the statement, but immediately sobered at its inappropriateness. "I'd like you to join me. I'm sure you have your own."

He nodded his solemn agreement. "You weren't a dumb animal when you were like. You knew what you were doing."

"Yes," I confirmed. "I just couldn't speak."

"I knew when you brought that Crossly woman to the cellar to open the safe and pointed at the girl. An animal can't reason like that."

"No, I don't suppose they can."

"It's an abomination." Mal's stinging condemnation hung unaddressed as I slipped into my uniform blouse. I nodded acknowledgment but ignored the ramifications. "How did this happen?"

"I don't know," I admitted. Once I pulled on an old pair of boots and draped my bearskin coat over my shoulders, we headed to the mess hall.

"It attacked both of us but bit you." Mal kept his voice down as we walked. "The doctor mentioned a wolf bite."

"Major, you're up and about." Witwer approached from behind.

It hadn't occurred to me to keep up a facade of my recent injuries. So much had happened. "Yes, I'm feeling much better," I confessed. "We must have lost track of you following the commotion last night."

"I can't believe the creature made it to town and found its way to the very establishment where we had business. The local populace is in a state of terror. The Mayor visited Colonel Kirkwood this morning. The town council is demanding immediate reinforcements to protect the public. They have lost confidence in our Buffalo Soldiers and want them replaced with white soldiers." Witwer paused, realizing he, too, was being insulted by that request. "Colonel Kirkwood has requested I fetch you to discuss next steps."

"Tell him it will have to wait until after breakfast." I was unnaturally ravenous.

"Right away, sir." Witwer saluted and took his leave.

The aromas that usually drew me into the mess hall now turned my stomach. I moved immediately to the offerings of beefsteak and thick cuts of pork and loaded my plate with the rarest cuts. Mal chose modest portions of eggs and potatoes, my usual morning staples. Once seated, I noted Mal was unusually quiet, eyeing me and my plate of meat. He held a forkful of eggs in place by a skewered potato wedge and watched me shove a large, uncut chunk of pork into my mouth. The fatty juice was savory, but the spicing and texture of the meat repulsed me.

"Overcooked." I chewed, craving the rare buffalo meat stew Ajiah fed me in the wagon. My mind flashed to the satisfaction I took in feeding as the werewolf. I willed the thought away.

Mal lowered his fork without taking a bite and pushed his plate aside in exasperation.

"What's wrong?" I swallowed too much at once and coughed.

"After last night…" He looked around to ensure no one was near and lowered his voice. "Watching you devour those people." He sighed again and shook his head. "Lost my appetite."

Private Leonard arrived with a pot of coffee to refill our cups. I had only taken a few sips. "Everything to your satisfaction, Major?"

"Do you have any buffalo steaks back there?" I cocked my head toward the kitchen.

"No sir, I'm sorry. I believe Dr. Nagel ate the last one some time ago."

I furrowed my brow. Hadn't there been some on the chuckwagon? "Are you sure there isn't any left? Maybe stew meat?"

"No, sir. I'd be glad to get you something else."

"Hmm, maybe some water, thank you." Even my morning coffee tasted wrong.

"You're welcome, sir." Leonard stepped away, and I felt suddenly nauseous. I pointed at Mal's untouched plate. "If you're not going to eat that, would you mind?"

"Go right ahead, Boss." He leaned back in his chair and folded his arms across his chest as I placed his full plate upon my empty one. I thought the milder food would settle my stomach, but I felt intense nausea after a few bites of the eggs and fried potatoes. I needed the privy - fast.

"I'll meet you outside." I rushed from the building. Once purged, my stomach felt better, but the gnawing of intense hunger returned. I spit the remnants of my vomit into the pit and joined Mal outside the outhouse.

"Better?"

I nodded. "But hungrier than ever. Something didn't agree with me." Mal looked at me in disbelief. I knew what he was tempted to say, but he kept it to himself.

When we arrived at Kirkwood's office, we found Grogan in attendance. He provided a spirited description of what he witnessed. "It was the most incredible creature I've ever seen, Colonel. Truly remarkable. I've taken the liberty of cabling the Pinkerton Agency in Chicago and requested twenty-five heavily armed men to arrive forthwith."

The Pinkertons were a celebrated private detective agency established in 1850 by Allan Pinkerton, specializing in private security. I wondered what Grogan had in mind for them but figured he would make his plans known. For an instant, I was concerned his focus might be on determining the werewolf's identity. Then I reminded myself Grogan was not aware the werewolf was also a human being.

"What do you expect the Pinkertons to do for you, Mr. Grogan?" Kirkwood asked. "There's nothing to investigate. We know what's killing our men. Now, it's attacking the townspeople. Better we assemble a hunting team to track this beast down and kill it once and for all. Building searches of the town and neighboring farms have turned up nothing."

"I called for Pinkertons because I couldn't think of a faster way to get a substantial force of trained and armed men here. When might we expect reinforcements from Washington?"

"Fresh troops will likely come up from Fort Leavenworth once the orders are cut, provided they can be spared. Major Kincaid has already requested replacements, but these things take time," Kirkwood explained. "There's nothing fast about the federal government."

"Must we limit ourselves to Buffalo Soldiers?" Grogan countered, glancing at Mal and myself. "Seems this troop has proven itself ineffective against this thing. Now it's here in Lucian killing honest white folk. I think it's time we summon the real army. We've got a problem that requires a force ready for war. And you've still got a renegade Indian problem."

I flashed anger at Grogan's insult of my Buffalo Soldiers and disparaged my leadership. "It's by no fault of the men this werewolf appeared and became so destructive. Modern weapons have thus far proven useless. It shrugged off your Gatling gun like it was a child's peashooter. Spooner made it howl in pain, yes, but it kept coming and didn't stop until it killed all of your Cowboys and most of my soldiers." I looked Grogan up and down. "Or did you miss that while you were deserting your men?"

Grogan reddened, silently rebuked, then turned his attention back to Kirkwood. "You haven't personally seen it, have you, Colonel?"

"No, I haven't had the pleasure," Kirkwood said facetiously, "though I've heard quite a bit about it." He threw me a glance.

"It is the single most destructive force I have ever encountered," Grogan said with a note of admiration. "Could you imagine the value of such an animal on the battlefield doing our bidding? Our forces would be unstoppable!"

There it was: The reason behind the secrets. For as long as men have waged war, there have been efforts to introduce animals into the fray. Horses in the West, elephants in the East, and camels in the Middle East have been used to transport men and weapons from battle to battle. But to my knowledge, animals have never been effectively used in offensive attacks. Dogs are sometimes employed, but not without close-quarter combat. Dogs need handlers to direct their actions. What Grogan was suggesting and likely envisioned was training the werewolf to attack enemy troops unsupervised by verbal commands or other incentives. An ignorant animal wasn't capable of that kind of discipline. But I knew more about the beast from firsthand experience. I knew exactly how effective I could be on a battlefield in werewolf form. With only a fraction of the ability I exhibited overnight, the devastation I could have visited upon the Rebs during the war would have been incredible. At Andersonville, I could have killed all of the guards and liberated the thirty-thousand pitiful wretches singlehanded. Maybe Grogan's idea wasn't so fanciful after all.

"Besides the Pinkertons, I requested some experimental weapons manufactured by a railroad friend and the heaviest nets available. As much as I would enjoy killing this thing and adding its head to my collection of trophies, I'm convinced it would be worth a fortune to the military. Wouldn't you agree, Major?" Grogan prodded. "You've seen it up close."

"Yes," I replied, with a stroke of my beard. "I admit, I hadn't considered its military applications until you suggested it. I think it's important to note it is as undisciplined as it is unpredictable." I gave Grogan my full attention for the first time, looking the heavy man in the eye. "It would likely prove just as dangerous to its handlers as you hope it would be against an enemy." I knitted my brow. "How exactly would you train it?" It was a ludicrous proposition.

"There are men who perform miracles with animals. You've seen tigers and lions in circuses take direction. They require special trainers and motivators," Grogan lectured. He meant brutality. I was sure any cruelty visited on the creature in pursuit of compliance would be returned in kind. Tenfold.

"Even circus animals have to be carefully supervised." I pointed out. "Trainers don't trust wild animals. They can't take their eyes off them or turn their backs for an instant, or they risk serious injury and death. Other than sitting up, roaring, and performing a few simple tricks before returning to their cages, there isn't much circus animals do. Let's suppose you were in a position to train it successfully. How might it differentiate between friend and foe?" Part of me wanted to see him try.

"A bridge to cross following its capture and caging," Grogan evaded. "Once it's confined, we'll have plenty of time to contemplate training. In the meantime, we need to acquire a large, escape-proof cage. Perhaps something mounted to the bed of a railroad car for easy transport."

"I think you're getting way ahead of yourself," Kirkwood cautioned. He leaned back in his chair and folded his hands over his paunch. "We don't even know where to find it."

"It's done a pretty good job of finding us." Grogan gestured to include the three of us. "We've not seen the last of it, I'll wager. It seems drawn to that young Indian girl for some reason. What's that about?"

I looked to Mal, knowing only we knew there were two werewolves now. Grogan's facts were skewed, but he had a point. Ajiah had been nearby when the werewolf attacked. I theorized the werewolf was Angry Eagle, and he somehow infected me with his affliction. Either way, I wanted to be involved in Grogan's plan for hunting and capturing the monster, if for no other reason than self-preservation and to avoid collateral damage. "You can expect my full cooperation, Mr. Grogan."

"I appreciate that, Major."

<u>34</u>

I rushed from my meeting with Kirkwood to the stockade. Ajiah had reunited in the temporary quarters with Tanka and Plenty Wounds. The two women remained traumatized by their experience at the brothel. Ajiah sat between them with a protective arm around each to reassure them of their safety.

Aside from the violence in Lucian, I hoped for answers from Ajiah. In addition to my physical changes, I noted a mental shift. I was surprisingly undisturbed by recent events - particularly my violence. My overall health was superior to anything I'd experienced since boyhood. My debilitating injuries were miraculously healed. Would my improved and recovered state be permanent? I had no reason to believe it wouldn't. The only negative side-effect was my lack of moral indignation. I was surprised at the absence of guilt for killing those people. I chalked it up to a lifetime of carnage and justified it with the faults I found in Crossly, Flynn, and Saul. None of them would be mistaken for exemplary human beings.

Flynn sold the girls into a life of sexual slavery. Crossly purchased the girls to exploit for monetary gain. Saul maintained and supported the institution and likely made use of their services. The banker knowingly created and perpetuated the market. I absolved myself of all responsibility in their demise, convinced they deserved their violent ends. I assumed Mal saw it the same way. However, there was a time not so long ago when I would have considered my actions unjust. According to the law, the fates of those four individuals should have been determined in a court by a jury of their peers. Though, admittedly, none of them would have been found guilty of any of the crimes I convicted them of. Nor would they have been executed.

Then again, no one gave the Natives a fair trial before stripping them of their lands, removing them from their territories, killing their women and children, or sentencing them to death for failing to comply with Manifest Destiny. No one expressed remorse for the wanton slaughter and near extinction of the buffalo to starve those same Natives out of existence. I was now perceiving my years of brutality serving government interests from the point of view of our victims. Had I thought these things all along, or had my change been a mental and physical transformation? An awakening of sorts.

Bestowed with a singular power over who lived and died and possessing preternatural impunity from government justice, I saw things differently now. I saw my Buffalo Soldiers as wholey exploited. The East sent Negro soldiers west to kill the Natives and remove them from their lands. This further removed able-bodied Negro men from the South. For many of the Buffalo Soldiers, their only reward was death, which was probably the preference of the white politicians who ruled Washington.

As I walked with Ajiah for the first time since being altered, the answers to my questions about the werewolf came without asking. The werewolf was killing my men because we forcibly relocated and killed them while acting as tools of the government. The werewolf didn't care about the reasons for the actions against the Natives. It just wanted the attacks and removals to stop. It didn't care how many of us it had to kill to achieve that goal any more than we concerned ourselves with killing Natives.

Of the many questions swimming in my head, the one foremost in my mind was: "What the hell happened to me out there?" I asked, assuming she saw what occurred and understood its significance.

"You were given a gift. You should be grateful," she replied.

"I am," I said too quickly, thinking at first of my rapid healing. "But at what price? Why would Angry Eagle make me as powerful as he? When I first met him, he was filled with nothing but hate and threats of death."

Ajiah stopped walking and smiled up at me. "Angry Eagle?"

"The werewolf. I figured as much from the broken leg shackle found in the wagon. That happened when he transformed. We found the journal of drawings among the Wolf Clan's possessions."

"Drawings?" The furrow in her brow told me she was genuinely puzzled.

"Of the Indian transforming into the creature. It explains quite a bit."

Her expression remained blank and questioning, with parted lips and brown eyes searching my own. She didn't appear to know what I was talking about.

"Have you seen the sketches of the creature emerging from a Native form?"

She shook her head slowly. "I am not aware of any drawings."

"I'll show them to you. I don't understand why Angry Eagle did this to me."

"Angry Eagle is impetuous. He left with his father, Whiteman Killer. As I chose to stay and care for you." She patiently folded her hands across her waist.

"Any insight you can provide would be welcome." I wasn't hearing her. I looked down and left as I considered the possibilities. "Unless he intended me to turn the ability against my men and my people? If that was it, he failed. I know what I'm doing." I nodded the affirmation.

"It is a gift to do with as you wish but also a curse, Kincaid." She tipped her head to draw my eyes to hers. "A curse in that you will never be free of it. Its hunger will drive you forever, and you will have to satisfy that hunger whether it is convenient or not. Some of the time, you will be able to control it. More often than not, it will control you."

Just her mentioning hunger made my stomach growl. I ate a hearty breakfast with Mal about two hours ago and just as quickly threw it up. I remained famished. I needed something I could keep down. My first thought upon transforming in front of Crossly and Flynn had been the need to feed. I dismissed the notion as the power of Ajiah's suggestion. "When I came for you last night, I felt compelled. The change came without warning. It ended with overwhelming exhaustion. I fell asleep, and when I woke up, I was myself again. Miraculously healed of all my former injuries."

"That is your curse and your gift." Her sage tone was matter-of-fact.

"I don't understand." I shook my head questioningly. Did it control me as she suggested, or did I control it as I assumed? "How many of these things are there?"

"Now there are two."

I was stunned.

"You were carefully selected because of the kind of man you are." She tilted her head, moving her silky black hair with the motion. "As for learning how to navigate the ability, you must find your path."

I shook my head. "I still don't understand."

"You will." She smiled with a curl at the edges of her lips.

I changed the subject with a deep sigh. "I'll safely get you and the other girls to the reservation with your clan." I made the promise, thinking it would ease their worries.

"Better to return us all to where you found us." Her smile was gone, and her words firm.

"I can't do that." It was impossible on several levels. I was bound to my duty.

She looked me squarely in the eye, and at that moment, her wisdom seemed well beyond her eighteen years. "You can do whatever you want now, Kincaid."

I left her feeling conflicted. Reflecting on Ajiah's confusing responses regarding my new reality, I silently thanked God for Mal. I didn't know what I would do without him. We came together during the most tumultuous period of my life. And at a turning point for the country as it enthusiastically ripped itself apart. From our first encounter, Mal proved a loyal friend, asking nothing in return and putting himself at great personal risk. When I needed help, he gave it freely and without conditions. Mal saved my life. In addition to our shared history and profoundly committed loyalty, he now possessed my deepest, darkest secret. Yet Mal was experienced at keeping secrets of his own and was careful how he played his hand.

Andersonville – 1864 -Part 7
<u>35</u>

"We hear the prison's pretty bad," Mal said, unaware I had dozed off. I was unsure how long I had been out. "I don't think I ever heard of anyone escaping successful. Most get killed or took back." Mal kept his voice low, eyes on his mules and the dusty road ahead.

"Worst of the worst," I rasped through my dry throat. "Inedible food if they bothered to feed us at all. No shelter to speak of. Unsanitary to the point everyone had dysentery. Guards looking for reasons to shoot or beat us. Preyed upon by other prisoners. Locked in stocks and whipped for minor infractions." I shook my head at the cruel memories of my past few months. It all sounded so much worse as the words rolled out of my mouth.

"I hear that." Mal eyed me over his shoulder with a knowing look, tugging the neck of his tunic down to reveal a crisscross of raised scars of various ages and sizes on a patch of his right shoulder. I knew what bullwhip scars looked like, and what he showed me was just a fraction of what likely striped his back.

"My God, man, that's inhuman. What…" I blanched in shame when I realized I was about to ask what he'd done to deserve the punishment. I wondered if such harsh treatment was visited upon all slaves. "What kind of man does that to another? I wouldn't tolerate it to an animal."

Mal tugged the front of his shirt to cover the scarring and directed his attention to the road ahead. "Mr. Butler is not a patient man. I don't know that he sees a difference between the two. He refers to me and these here mules as beasts of burden."

I shook my head. "It's unconscionable." I didn't vocalize the counter-intuitive reasoning behind brutalizing the men and animals a man depended on for his livelihood. It wasn't just the moral and ethical piece. From an economic viewpoint, it was a poor way to treat people, even if they were his property. Slaves and animals were investments with value. Abuse devalued them on every level.

A few minutes of silence passed between us before he picked the conversation back up. "What's your plan now that you're on run?"

"Make it to the river. Hoped to work down to the Gulf of Mexico." It all seemed ludicrous now. My men were dead and dying. All I accomplished was trading one prison for another. An injured federal officer behind enemy lines could only draw attention.

"Ha!" he scoffed. "You'd never made it, Boss. Too many people on the river watching for a sneak attack or Northern scouts."

I hadn't thought of that. "I considered jumping a train North."

He shook his head. "Railcars are searched for runaways. You'd get caught for sure."

"How do runaway slaves make it North?"

He stiffened a bit at the inquiry. It was likely a topic he didn't discuss aloud among his peers and never with a white man.

"I've heard of an underground railroad," I said cautiously, not wishing to put him on the spot. Since my school days, I knew the Underground Railroad to be an illegal operation assisting escaped slaves on a dangerous journey north to freedom with the help of sympathetic opponents of slavery. My understanding was limited, but I knew those involved traveled at night to avoid detection. The guides who assisted the runaways were called conductors, and the locations they hid during the day were called stations. "Do you think someone with those connections would be inclined to help me?"

He considered the question for over a minute, and I wondered if I'd touched on something that might explain some of his scars. He finally cleared his throat. "That's more up along the border between North and South, away from the fighting." He paused deliberately. "I've heard. Northern troops don't go out their way to help escaped slaves." He paused again before finishing. "Be a long walk, Boss."

"Maybe we wouldn't have to walk if somebody had a wagon and mules," I offered boldly.

"Even a white man in Georgia can get arrested for taking something that ain't his," Mal countered. "But if an educated man could write a bill of sale, he might be able to pass off the wagon and mules for his own."

"Do you think the man could do the same for a slave inclined to accompany him?"

Our eyes met. The proposal was clear. Mal considered it. "Time to hide below with Private Rice, Boss. We're close to the gin. They can't see you bloody and all."

He reined the mules to a halt and helped me out of the cotton to the ground. Pain tore at my groin and gunshot wounds. Of the two injuries, the gunshot wound won as the most apparent. The blood loss, exhaustion, and malnutrition all caught up with me in a wave of nausea and lightheadedness. I collapsed in the dirt at Mal's feet. He placed a reassuring hand on my shoulder. The last few days had drained me physically and mentally. "I need a minute, Mal."

"Yes, Boss." He jumped back into the wagon and rearranged the cotton to hide my bloodstains. He dropped next to me, casting conspiratorial glances up and down the road for any passersby, then released the hidden latches to expose the compartment where Rice lay.

Flies erupted from the shadowy space in a buzzing black cloud. They accumulated over Rice in a volume I would not have expected possible in the hour or so of travel. Rice had passed. Guilt stabbed me through the heart. This was my fault. I'd gotten all of my trusting young men killed with my ill-conceived plan.

Mal assisted me to lay on the hardwood boards in the space next to Rice's corpse. Less than six inches separated my face and the wagon's floor. It was coffin-like. "Hope you're okay with tight places, Boss. Please keep quiet," He instructed. "Sorry about your man." He re-latched the door to the compartment, locking me in the semi-dark humidity with Rice. Even after our involuntary bath in the Flint River, the stench of the clothes worn since capture was apparent. That Rice released his bowels and bladder upon death didn't help.

Mal climbed atop the cotton-laden wagon, which caused a sway in the spring suspension. He yelled, "Git!" at the mules, and the wagon jerked towards its destination. I had no trouble dozing off to the gentle, rhythmic crunch of iron treads on the dirt and gravel as the comforting clomps of the mule's hooves pounded gently forward.

I was vaguely aware of the wagon stopping at some point and men working above me to remove the cloud of compressed cotton Mal was transporting. This, coupled with the sound of men joking good-naturedly, lulled me back to sleep with a rare sense of normalcy. I convinced myself there would be no reason for men at a cotton gin to search the wagon for hidden compartments and escaped Union soldiers. Even the buzzing of flies feeding on Rice's bloody remains produced soothing music. There wasn't much I could do but get welcome sleep and worry about where I was once we reached Mal's farm.

By my estimation, it was over an hour later when I woke to the simultaneous snorting and neighing of approaching horses and the bray of one of Mal's mules. The wagon came to a halt. Though there were small spaces between the boards, the false bottom was deliberately constructed so no one on the outside could see in. Nor could I see out. Only the tiniest slivers of light leaked through. Stretching, I inadvertently brushed Rice's stiff, unyielding arm. Even in the heat and humidity, he was cold to the touch. Flies stirred. Some lit on me. I spat them from my lips and waved them from my face, struggling not to gag as I considered where they had been.

I didn't think anything special occurred until I heard men talking to Malcolm. There were at least three voices belonging to white men with regional accents I was sure I couldn't mimic, even if my life depended on it. I reached for my holster and found Miller's pistol. I was surprised Mal hadn't taken the weapon from me when I fell to the ground earlier but reminded myself a Negro slave in possession of a firearm did so upon penalty of death.

"You got a pass to be hereabouts?" The white traveler asked in a voice that testified to confidence and experience. I pictured a man in his fifties.

"Yes, sir, Boss. I got my master's pass right here," Mal responded. A parched paper crinkled as he dug it from his pocket.

"God damn right you do," a second, younger-sounding man added.

One of Mal's mules brayed again.

"Shut up, you ugly mother," a third man said. He sounded further from the others.

"What's your business this afternoon, boy?" the first man asked.

"Cotton to the gin, Boss," Mal answered in a clear voice. "Headed home."

"Are you Thompson Butler's man?" The second horseman inquired.

"Yes, Boss," Mal responded in a subservient tone, telling me he was regularly subjected to this line of questioning.

"That lazy bastard's nothing but a mean old drunk that fucks his slave gals and works his bucks to the bone," the third man said. "Ain't that right?"

The paper crunched, presumably because the older man, the man I figured to be in charge, was reading it. "Malcolm. That your name?"

"Lemme see that," the younger man demanded. Paper ruffled as it passed.

"Yes, Boss," Mal confirmed, not particularly pleased with the topic of conversation.

"Which one of those things you think he's best at?" The younger man taunted Mal.

Mal remained silent.

"I'm talking, boy. You should be answering. Which one is it?"

"Boss?" Mal asked.

The man sighed audibly. "He the laziest, drunkest, meanest, or fucking-est?" He laughed.

Mal did not reply, recognizing the gibes as a no-win for him.

"Bet he fucks the shit out them gals every chance he gets, don't he, Mal-com?" The man drew the slave's name out as if talking to a half-wit.

"Leave the picker alone," the first man said, "And give his pass back."

"Just having a little fun with Mal-com," he said. The paper crackled to Mal as it was stuffed into a pocket.

"Thank you, Boss," Mal said.

"You seen any strangers round here, boy?" The first man asked.

"No, Boss," Mal answered without hesitation.

"There's a reward for escaped Yankees from the prison. Give you a cut if you see 'em and help us round 'em up," the man promised.

"Never heard of Yankees making it this far before," Mal said.

"They killed a soldier or two by the sounds of it," the older man said. He seemed to be the more professional and best informed of the three. "Substantial bounty for rounding them up."

"I'll report if I see anything, Boss," Mal volunteered.

"God damn right you will, Mal-com," the taunting man said.

"Be on your way," the leader concluded. "Get straight on home."

"Yes, Boss," Mal agreed.

The men rode off, talking among themselves. I guessed they were one of the patrols Mal mentioned. I breathed a sigh of relief they didn't have dogs with them to sniff around the wagon and hit on Rice's dead body. Nor did they seem inclined to climb down from their saddles and conduct an inspection.

"Git!" Mal directed the mules, snapping the reins. They jerked the wagon forward. Rice's dead hand jostled and brushed my exposed wrist. I caught my breath in a wide-eyed start.

Following another half hour of travel, the wagon rumbled off the main road onto something more rugged. A path to what I assumed was the Butler farm. Chickens clucked and stirred up a ruckus as they ran to avoid the approaching mules and wagon wheels. I pictured a ramshackle cabin rather than a stately farmhouse. The image the slave patrol drew of Mal's master suggested an operation existing slightly north of the poverty line. Only so because of the five slaves Mal mentioned.

"Where the fuck you been, Malcolm?" A gravelly-voiced man bellowed in a liquored slur. "I was about to come looking for you! Thought you ran off with my cotton to finance your big escape." He laughed, but there was an edge to the laugh that suggested Mr. Butler thought escape was not outside the realm of possibility for Malcolm.

"No sir, Mr. Butler. Gin and back, just like always," Mal reassured. "Patrols were out stopping wagons."

"What for?" Butler inquired.

"Escaped Yankees from the prison. They looked at my pass and checked the wagon," Mal answered. "Twice!"

I surmised Mal was lying to make up for the time he spent stopping and assisting the escaped Yankee prisoners.

"There's a reward, Mr. Butler."

"Reward?" Butler perked up at the promise of money. "How much?

"Didn't say, Mr. Butler. Just said substantial."

"You see them Yankees, Malcolm?"

"No, sir. They were from the prison. Yankees would be stupid to come south here when they want to go north for home."

"Well, no one ever accused Yankees of smart, Malcolm," Butler laughed. "Look at this war they got us in. You see them, you let me know right now! We could use the money. Otherwise, I'm gonna need to sell one of you off to get by."

Mal remained silent. He was probably wondering which of the slaves at the Butler farm would be sold off if fortunes didn't change. Mal said earlier there were five slaves, but we didn't discuss their relationships. One of the patrollers said something about two gals. They could be wives, sisters, daughters, or mothers. That left three men, who could be a father, uncle, brother, or son. I wondered if Mal considered turning me in to spare the people he lived and worked with. After all, I was the wounded enemy soldier he just met. They were likely all family to him. I placed my hand on the butt of the pistol in case things got ugly.

"I got to put up the wagon and water and feed these mules, Mr. Butler," Mal said dejectedly. He had something weighing on his mind that I wasn't sure I would like.

"Not too much feed," Butler ordered. "Hay we don't sell is money out of my pocket."

"Yes, Boss."

Mal moved the wagon slowly, and the light in the compartment dimmed. I heard Mal close a gate, and the space grew darker. He unhitched the mules and stripped them of their leather tack. Shortly after that, he unlocked and helped me out of the compartment with a look on his face that told me I might be in trouble. I felt faint again. We were in a barn that had seen better days. It was well organized but short on essentials like stacks of bailed hay, bags of seed, chicken feed, and other equipment that usually stocked a well-run farm.

What stood out was a wagon in the back with an iron cage affixed to its base platform. It would be gracious to describe it as constructed for animals, but the transportation of farm animals did not, as a rule, require a locking door and a cage top. It was designed to hold human beings who might not be inclined to remain in captivity.

"Ima hide you in a horse stall in back where he won't look. Mr. Butler don't come out here much since his wife died years back. If he does, you best keep hid."

Mal slung my good arm over his shoulder and helped me to the stall. There was a horse blanket over some old straw on the ground. I saw it was clear of dung and had not lodged a horse, mule, or cow in some time. It looked like others hid here in the not-so-distant past, making me think of the underground railroad again.

"Mia'll bring you something to eat and have a look at your wounds. She'll get you cleaned and sewed up."

"Thanks, Mal," I said, waiting to see if he had more to say.

"You're welcome, Boss."

"Mal?"

"Yes, Boss?"

"You thinking about turning me in for the reward money?"

He mulled it over for a moment. "Crossed my mind."

A wave of tension mingled with my lightheadedness.

"You suppose Private Rice is worth anything dead?" Mal asked.

I hadn't thought of that. "Sometimes rewards specify dead is just as good as alive."

He nodded acknowledgment. "Maybe I'll find a dead body on the road tomorrow and see if it's worth something."

I shrugged. "Worth a try, but if that doesn't pan out, and for what it's worth, I think I could get you and maybe the others North to freedom."

Mal's eyes aligned with mine, and he stared hard at me. "No

disrespect, Boss, but getting people to freedom isn't your strong suit."

He had a point. "You should consider the reward might not be as much as you're hoping for. What's a slave go for around here? $800?"

"Thereabouts, depending. Less, these days, with the war and all."

"If memory serves, deserters are only worth $30. Escaped prisoners $50. As strapped as the Confederacy is for funds, all you might end up with is a pat on the back and a hearty handshake."

Mal cracked a smile. "Probably no handshakes for me."

"Guess you have to ask yourself what freedom is worth."

Andersonville – 1864 -Part 8
<u>36</u>

Late that evening, as the sun set, a slave woman in her late twenties snuck quietly into the barn, holding a tray of pots covered by a rag to keep the heat in. She slung a frayed towel over her left shoulder. I caught wind of the chicken soup before she got the barn door closed behind her. My stomach rumbled at the prospect of nourishment. She stopped when she saw me across the barn watching her. Apprehension creased her features. I was a sight in my bloody clothes. I stepped out of the stall and sat on a wooden box outside so she wouldn't perceive me as a threat. I asked in a stage whisper, "Are you Mia?"

She took a deep breath and moved toward me with a deliberate stride, careful not to spill her load. "Yes, I am," she whispered back. She set the tray next to me on the box and removed the rag covering two lidless, beat-up pots. A generous helping of chicken soup was in the smaller pot, loaded with meat chunks, atop rice, carrots, and celery saturated with seasoned broth, and nestled between two dumplings. I almost cried at the sight of it. I hadn't laid eyes on real food since I reported for duty.

Steaming water filled the larger, dented pot to the brim. Mia pulled a serving spoon from her tattered apron, stuck it into the soup, and set it next to my right thigh. "You need to eat this up while I'm out here wit you," she said soothingly. "I can't leave the dishes. Need 'em for mornin'."

"Thank you," I said. "Thank you so much." I picked up the small pot by its broken wood handle and held it to my lips for a sip of broth. It was perfect in every way. Its salty goodness rejuvenated my dry throat and trickled into my empty belly. I tried to transfer the handle to my left hand and felt a stab of pain under my wounded armpit. Had it only been twenty-four hours?

"I need you to slip out that shirt so I can tend your wounds," she said softly.

I set the soup pot down and dug into the pile of food with her spoon, stuffing in a mouthful of heaven. Warm broth dribbled out the corners of my lips into my filthy beard and dripped off my chin. I chewed the succulent mix and worked to unbutton my shirt as she instructed. She helped me pull it down my arm and let out a soft gasp when she saw the swelling, seepage, and dried blood encrusted around the wound. Her eyes widened at my protruding ribs.

"You po' man," she whispered sympathetically, "Did they ever feed you?"

"Nothing you'd want to eat," I rasped.

When our eyes met, I was immediately aware of her attractiveness. She was a few years younger than me, with light chocolate skin that was nowhere near as dark as Mal's. I guessed this was one of the gals the slave patrol mentioned. She wore a dress under her apron that reached to her bare feet and had almost as many mismatched patches as original fabric. She took the rag that covered the pots, dipped it into the hot water, and began wiping at the wound. The water was warmer than the soup. It felt like it had just come off the fire at a near boil. She cleaned the injury and the skin around it, then carefully wrung the rag out in the dirt. In this way, she was careful not to contaminate the clean water more than necessary.

After a few bites and swallows, I offered, "My name is…"

"Don't," she shushed me, holding her free hand up. "I don't want to know your name. If somebody asks, I don't have to lie when I say I don't know you." She shook her head and tightened her lips. "Malcolm try to help too many people. Puts our family in danger. Now you. He been whipped raw already, but hidin' someone like you, a soldier, get us all whipped or sold off. Or worse." She was angry and unintentionally dug too deep into my bullet wound with the rag wrapped around her index finger.

I winced and sucked a breath through my gritted teeth. "Sorry to be a burden, ma'am."

"Oh goodness, I didn't mean to hurt you." She squeezed out the rag, dipped it in the fresh water, and cleaned at me with a gentler touch. "You're not the one should be apologizing. Malcolm's the one. He may be my man, but that don't mean he always knows what's best for everyone else."

So, there it was. Mia was Malcolm's woman. It added a new level of awful to what the taunting man on the road insinuated about Mr. Butler.

"He already got our son sold off at half price to replace a boy he helped along." She slumped her shoulders and clutched the bloody rag between her knees, looking down at the wet dirt in reflection. It didn't take much imagination on my part to realize Mal was more involved with the Underground Railroad than he let on. Malcolm was punished for his activities, and they lost a son over it. I knew what it was like to lose a wife and child, but to have a child sold off? How did a man let something like that go? How did a young mother?

Mia sniffled back the urge to cry and returned to work on my wound. I took a few more mouthfuls, and though I wanted more, my stomach had shrunk since my capture and was stuffed.

"Don't force it," she cautioned. "If it's been a while since you ate decent…" She gave my ribs another glance. "You're liable to sick it all up. A sudden change in diet will, too."

I smiled at her worry for my well-being. "It's delicious. Thank you for bringing it."

She smiled back, dug a knot of thread from her apron, and unsheathed a sewing needle from the fabric of her pocket. "I think I got this as clean as it gonna get. There's no medicine to give you. Best I can say is keep it clean."

I nodded acknowledgment.

"This gonna sting," she warned, threading the needle and tightly pinching the wound's edges. "This would be easier if I had some light, but I can't risk a candle, never mind a lantern."

It stung each of the seven times she forced the cold metal into my skin, pushed it through, and repeated the process. When she started on the exit wound, I was used to the pain. Within an hour, she had me fed, cleaned up, and sewn. I was too embarrassed to mention my other wound because of its location. She dabbed at my wet skin with the towel draped over her shoulder, then hiked up her skirt to her thigh and pulled a fresh shirt loose from where she had it tied above her knee. The old, gray work shirt had probably been tailored for Butler. It was a couple sizes too large, but it was clean. She helped me slide my arms gingerly into it.

"You've thought of everything," I marveled.

She smiled, wadded my bloody shirt, then folded it into the towel. As she collected everything she brought, piling it onto the tray, we heard a door open, and slam shut outside at a separate building. Based on Mia's immediate look of alarm, I guessed it to be Butler's home. Our eyes met, and Mia held her index finger to her lips. We kept still and listened. After a full minute of silence, she pointed for me to return to my stall and picked up the tray.

Before I stepped in that direction, Butler's gravelly voice bellowed out into the evening. "Mia! Where you at, girl? Come on up to the house for a piece!" He laughed, snorted the mucus from his nose, and spat.

Mia exhaled and lowered her chin to her chest. She straightened her arms, grasping the tray's handles as though it suddenly weighed a thousand pounds. She took a breath and looked up into the dark rafters of the barn. "Please, Lord, not tonight. Please, please, please." A single tear trailed from the corner of her eye.

She looked at me. "I'll have to leave this here in the barn and pick it up when he's passed out and done wit me," she lamented. "I do not need that drunken man on top of me." She walked slowly to the door and set the tray beside it. She peeked out to ensure the coast was clear and stepped out into the dark.

"Mia!" Butler yelled out.

I moved up to the door, watching after her. Directly across from my barn was a modest, two-story white house at the end of a short, graveled path. It was flanked evenly by planted rows of oak trees that reached over the driveway and met in the middle to create a canopy. Butler stepped down from his wraparound porch with a lantern, looking to my right. There, I spied five or six small slave cabins. Three of the quarters had lights flickering from flames no more significant than a candle or small cooking fire.

Mia sidled in the shadows toward the cabins to get closer to where she was supposed to be before being noticed. She almost made it when he waved his lantern toward the barn and saw her take a step. She froze in place, and I was sure he missed her until he called out, "There you are! What you doin' up at the barn?" His speech was slurred, and he was unsteady on his feet. I wondered if the man spent all day drinking.

Mia walked down the driveway from the barn directly toward Butler, determined not to delay the inevitable. "I thought I left the chicken feed open earlier and didn't want a possum or raccoon getting into it, Mr. Butler."

"Stupid girl," he scolded. "Is it put up right? That feed cost money I ain't got."

"It was right," Mia assured. "I just got to worrying before bed is all."

"Speaking of bed, why don't you come up to the house? I got a chore or two for you to take care of." He laughed to himself.

"Can it wait, Mr. Butler?" She pled. "I'm shore tired, and we gots to get up early to pick another load for Malcolm to truck to the gin tomorrow."

"Don't sass me, bitch! Get up here and do like I say," Butler thundered. "You go to bed when I say go to bed."

Her shoulders sagged, but she marched toward him just the same, muttering, "Might as well get on with it."

I pressed my forehead to the wood frame and placed my hand on the the butt of the pistol. I could fix this right now, I thought to myself. I peeked back out and saw them climbing the stairs to the house. I glanced at the slave cabins and saw the silhouette of a man standing under the overhang of a front entry. The door was ajar, and a firelight flickered behind him. It was Mal. He had seen everything. He shook his head, stepped into his cabin, and closed the door.

37

By the miracle of the modern telegraph, the Pinkertons received Grogan's message and arrived by train within a few days. With them came horses and a railcar of equipment they kept under wraps, both physically and in secrecy. There were whispers of specialized weaponry. The railcar was moved to an adjacent track, off the main line, meaning the Pinkertons owned the car and would remain when the train continued west. I was astounded at how quickly the company organized and arrived in Lucian from Chicago. The group was led by a gentleman named Detective Steve Morgan. Like all the Pinkertons, he was clad in a dark suit with a matching vest, necktie, and long dark overcoat. It was all topped off with a bowler-style hat.

Each man was supplied with a pocket watch on a buttonhole chain attached to their vests so they would not be lost. As a group, they seemed compelled to check the time frequently. Upon arrival, Morgan reported directly to Mr. Grogan.

In addition to their uniform black suits and bowlers, the Pinkerton men sported mustaches in various shapes and sizes. Some in the handlebar style, some bushy, and some short. There were no beards whatsoever. Each man was provided a black mare and polished black saddle for individual transportation. From the supply car, each was issued a rifle to sheath on his saddle. In their holsters were the newest revolvers on the market, and around their waists hung ammunition belts of polished individual rounds in black leather loops. By all appearances, every single Pinkerton detective was right-handed.

The Pinkertons were increasingly essential to government security. They protected President Lincoln during the war, though conspicuously absent the night of his assassination at Ford's Theater. Perhaps the government side of service spawned the uniformity.

I joined the Pinkertons on the train station platform beneath the large wood-carved sign announcing LUCIAN, placed for the benefit of the engineer and passengers pulling into the stop. It was a warm afternoon, casting off the last vestiges of winter and promising a sunny spring. Adjacent to the tracks were the telegraph poles set every seventy-five yards from coast to coast. Western Union was replacing the single-strand iron wire with a multi-wire system, but we were currently limited to one line. The poles were erected in areas of rugged terrain and susceptible to inclement weather, buffalo damage, and Native hostility. In the West, the latter two caused the majority of service disruptions. The Natives understood the importance of communication in military actions. Primarily the actions against them.

Upon my approach, Grogan smiled and hailed me, eager to make introductions. "Detective Morgan, this is Major Kincaid of the 9th Cavalry, Buffalo Soldiers. He may not be the ranking officer here, but he is *in charge*, as they say. The Major has encountered this thing twice. It attacked and killed several dozen of his men. Neither of us has seen anything like it." Grogan roped me into his statements to paint us as equals in the eyes of Morgan.

Morgan shook my hand firmly and gave me a steely gaze. "A werewolf," he began, getting immediately to the point. I have to admit..." Morgan stopped himself before saying any more. His first instinct was to express skepticism, but he seemed to rethink that in the presence of Grogan, his employer. Where was it last seen?" he asked instead.

"A brothel here in town called the Treasure Trove," I said. "The proprietor was killed the night of the attack, along with an employee, a BIA agent, and at least one patron."

"Were you there?" Morgan asked.

"Yes, I was," Grogan jumped in.

"How about you, Major?" Morgan never took his eyes off me.

"Yes," I answered, not looking away. "I was there with my Sergeant and Lieutenant."

"Did you see it?"

"No, I didn't see it that night," I answered truthfully.

"Why were you there?" He asked, without cracking a smile or finding salacious humor in the obvious answer as to why any man would be at a brothel.

"To collect three women illegally sold to Madam Crossly by the BIA agent, Flynn."

"I see," Morgan stated, "So, you were there to speak with at least two of the people who were ultimately murdered?"

"I was there to collect the women. I was not there to speak to the Crossly woman, though I knew it was her establishment. I was unaware Flynn would be there. That was a coincidence."

"The Indian girl seemed to know quite a bit about the monster," Grogan told Morgan.

"How so?" Morgan asked.

"She told the Major's Negro Sergeant the animal would leave if Miss Crossly released her from the safe in the basement."

Morgan reacted with a modicum of emotion for the first time in the conversation, looking from me to Grogan and back. "I'm sorry. Did you say the girl was locked in a safe?"

"Yes, apparently, Crossly was trying to bend the girl to her will and locked her in the safe as a punishment," Grogan answered.

"That's monstrous," Morgan said. "She could have suffocated." He paused before continuing. "And then what happened?"

Grogan looked to me for support, but I held my tongue. Technically, I wasn't present when this occurred. The only person who could say otherwise was Mal. Grogan licked at his lips, adding, "The beast attacked the people in the cellar, including two of the decedents. I went looking for a gun, but when I returned, the creature was gone, and Miss Crossly was dead."

"I see," Morgan said. "What happened to the girl?"

Grogan shrugged. "She fled."

Morgan looked to me for an answer.

"She returned to the fort with the other enslaved women," I said.

Morgan's eyebrows rose. "Enslaved?"

"What would you call three women sold to a brothel owner in support of her sex trade?"

Morgan nodded understanding, then asked, "Who took them to the fort?"

"My Sergeant and Lieutenant," I answered, then corrected myself, "Captain. He was recently promoted. There's been a great deal of turnover lately."

"And you?"

I considered ending the questioning by telling Morgan I needed to see to other duties. But the best thing to do with this professional detective was answer his questions and hope he went away. Being evasive and uncooperative would only increase his interest in me. "I walked back."

"You walked back to the fort as your Captain and Negro Sergeant rode with the Indian girls?" He spotted the irregularity in this immediately.

"Yes," I answered. "And some children commandeered as domestic servants."

"Why?"

"I stuck around to see what the commotion was about."

Morgan raised an eyebrow. "How exactly did the Indian girl get out of the safe?"

"It's my understanding the Crossly woman released her."

"Understanding? How did you learn of this outcome?" Morgan pressed.

"My Sergeant, Malcolm Butler, told me."

Morgan nodded, thinking something over before continuing. "Very good. I want to speak to your Sergeant, Captain, and the Indian girl. I'll have my men speak to the patrons and employees of the brothel. The Treasure Trove, you called it?"

"Yes." I knew no one at the Trove could implicate me. Mal was the only person who knew I was the werewolf. Ironically, not the werewolf Morgan and Grogan were looking for. I hadn't anticipated a crew of Pinkerton Detectives would descend on the Dakota Territory, Fort Charon, and the town of Lucian in pursuit of our werewolf. Unfortunately for me, Morgan was sharp and organized. He assigned investigators to examine the bodies for clues.

"I'll have my men question the townsfolk and see who saw what that night," Morgan informed us. Major, could you show me the way to the fort?"

"Certainly," I said. "Would you like to check into a hotel and freshen up first? Maybe get something to eat?" I was starving and still unable to keep anything down. It was becoming a problem. An illness without end. I hoped it wasn't Flynn's dysentery.

"No, thank you," he said, all business. "I would like to get this show on the road. The sooner we find this thing, the sooner we'll have a resolution." Morgan flipped his pocket watch open and checked the time yet again.

"Remember, I'll pay more if it's taken alive," Grogan said.

Morgan nodded. "You've made that quite clear, Mr. Grogan. We'll do our best."

Accompanying Morgan and me to the fort were Grogan and two young detectives dressed identically to Morgan. Their names were Samuelson and Bixby. Grogan was enjoying his investment in the werewolf hunt, as evidenced by his smile and chest puffing.

At the fort, we met with Colonel Kirkwood, who supported the

Pinkertons' efforts and was glad for the help. The Pinkerton men in Lucian would relieve the pressure on Kirkwood to act. In a way, this was the best solution to the problem. If the effort failed, the blame would fall on the Pinkertons. If the Pinkertons succeeded, the military could take credit for aiding.

Bixby and Samuelson broke away to locate and interview Witwer. I wasn't concerned about Witwer. He never entered the brothel and witnessed nothing. I stayed with Morgan. I wanted to be there when he grilled Mal, though I was confident Mal would exercise caution.

We found Mal sitting on a bench, talking with Dr. Nagel outside the officer's mess. Both men stood as we approached. I realized too late my tactical error when Nagel cocked his head and knitted his brow in curiosity. "Where is your crutch, Major?"

Probably lying in the spatter and gore of what had once been Saul, the doorman, in the Treasure Trove's parlor. "I must have lost track of it during the confusion," I answered.

"How are you able to stand? You really shouldn't be up and about on that hip. I warned you your condition is quite fragile. I wasn't joking," Nagel expressed amazement. He walked carefully around me as though I was a sideshow freak at a traveling carnival. "Your hip is broken! Your kneecap is shattered!"

Morgan was now regarding me with a great deal of curiosity.

"Perhaps I was misdiagnosed?" I exaggerated, putting all my weight on my left leg to illustrate nothing was wrong with me.

Nagel blanched and shook his head in disbelief. It wasn't in him to consider he might have made a mistake. He hadn't made a mistake, and he knew it. "No, your injuries were severe."

"Not as severe as originally thought," I said, trying to change the subject. I pivoted the conversation away from Nagel. "Mal, this is Detective Morgan of the Chicago Pinkerton Agency. He would like to ask a few about your interaction with the creature the other evening."

Mal stepped forward and offered his hand to Morgan, "Sergeant Malcolm Butler, at your service," he said, introducing himself formally.

Morgan shook Mal's hand but couldn't help but study the scar that started at Mal's forehead, valleyed under his leather eyepatch, and to his cheek. "Pleased to make your acquaintance."

"As you've noticed, I've interacted with the creature on more than one occasion," Mal smiled and laughed at his joke.

Morgan smiled. "My apologies for staring. It's an impressive scar.

You're lucky to be alive by the look of it."

"Yes, you could say that," Mal said humbly. "God's will."

"How did you happen to find yourself in the cellar of the brothel with the animal?" Morgan asked, picking up the thread of the story where we left off.

"I was entering the brothel through the servant's entrance from the alley when I heard strange sounds." Before Morgan could ask him, Mal supplied, "There was growling and snarling from a curtained parlor. When I found my way into the area, the creature attacked the doorman, Saul, with Madam Crossly aside, paralyzed with fear."

"I've no doubt she was fearful. Were you armed?" Morgan inquired.

"Yes." Mal placed his hand on the butt of his pistol to illustrate. "And I had my hand on my weapon, ready to draw, but I thought better of it because the last time I shot it, I got this." Mal pointed at his scarred face. "It's been my experience shooting makes it angrier." Mal glanced at me. "As if it could get any angrier."

"And then what happened?" Morgan continued.

"It fled the room for the cellar. At that point, everyone in residence was aware something was very wrong. The animal sounds were out of place and alarming. Men came from their rooms and rushed to see what was happening."

"I was one of them," Grogan volunteered. "I went to investigate."

"That's right," Mal continued. "Mr. Grogan called for a lantern, and I brought one past the men on the stairs and to the room where the girl was locked in the safe."

"Yes, I called for the lantern," Grogan added, eager to place himself in the thick of the action, though we both knew he was not.

"Once I was in the room, I saw a portion of the wall and safe had been dug away by the creature. It was standing in the shadows. I didn't think it smart to run and excite it."

"And then what happened?" Morgan prodded with his favorite question. I noticed he was skilled at not putting words into the mouths of his interviewees.

"The girl asked to be released and said Madam Crossly had the combination to the safe."

"Did she say anything else?"

Mal looked to me for reassurance. I gave him a slight nod to proceed. Mal continued. "She said if Crossly released her, the thing would leave."

Morgan started at the statement. "Pardon me. How could the girl know that?"

"I don't think she did," Mal said. "I think she just said that to get out."

Before Morgan could ask his go-to question again, Grogan said, "And then it waded through us, killing a few men, including the BIA man, Flynn, and located Miss Crossly. I went to find a gun and didn't see anything after that."

Morgan eyed the pistol on Grogan's hip suspiciously but did not ask if it had been there the night of the attack. He looked to Mal, waiting for him to continue.

"It came back with the Crossly woman in tow. I told her if she wanted to live, she needed to release the girl from the safe," Mal said.

"Why did you tell her that?"

"Because I believed it to be true," Mal told Morgan, looking at me accusingly. "After she opened the safe and released the girl, the monster killed her anyway."

Because she knew my secret. I hadn't realized how hard this was on Mal.

"And then it fled," Mal finished, swallowing hard at the memory.

"Are you telling me the girl was somehow able to communicate with the monster?"

Mal took a deep breath and rolled his eye around as he considered the question. "I never saw actual communication between them as much as I observed intelligence on the part of the creature. When the girl indicated she needed Crossly to get out of the safe, the creature went and got Crossly. Its goal was to get the girl out of the safe. It never threatened me in any way."

"Interesting," Morgan said, stroking his bushy mustache. "Extraordinary. I've never heard of an animal displaying that kind of intelligence, patience, or presence of mind. Extraordinary and deeply concerning." Morgan rechecked his pocket watch. I wondered if there was more to it than a fidgety affectation. Morgan didn't strike me as the fidgety type.

"Neither have I," Mal agreed.

"Nor I," Grogan piped in. "And I've killed a lot of wild animals."

"Quite." Morgan acknowledged, dismissing him.

Morgan studied me as he made his final request. "I would like to speak to the Indian girl. From what you've told me, I expect she does not require a translator?"

"No, her English is excellent."

Morgan cocked his head in thought. "How is that, exactly?"

"Settlers adopted her after a skirmish with Natives on a wagon train west."

"Sounds like a story in itself," Morgan remarked.

38

As we entered the enclosure, Morgan took careful inventory of the defeated people, seeing to various personal tasks. Their apathy and aversion to interacting with us reminded me of my internment. As a prisoner, you didn't want to draw attention to yourself or inadvertently offend your captors and suffer the consequences. Given our shared experience, I went out of my way to treat them with respect and humanity. But, in the end, a prisoner would feel adversarial no matter how accommodating their jailers.

Morgan stopped walking and surveyed the stockade's tightly set timbers. The girth of each log had been milled to a uniform eighteen inches. It was twenty feet tall to discourage climbing. For the first time, it occurred to me how devastating it must be to a people accustomed to vast open space to have the outside world blocked from view.

Morgan shaded his eyes to look at the guard shacks at each corner and couldn't help but notice that only two were occupied by our skeleton crew. "Ever have anyone make it over the wall, Major?"

"No," I answered, intuiting his next question.

"In your opinion, could this creature escape if cornered here?"

I could easily scale the walls by sinking my talons into the wood and climbing over. I was just as sure I could leap to the top and vault the rest of the way over, but I answered, "I've never seen it leap or scale a barrier. As a rule, wolves are not known for their climbing ability."

Morgan acknowledged without expressing whether he agreed or disagreed with my assessment. "I assume these Indians are destined for the nearest reservation?"

"That was Flynn, the BIA agent's responsibility. He was killed at the brothel. I'm not sure where things stand with the transport of these folks."

We found our way to the liveryman's office, where I first interviewed

Ajiah. She was seated in the same chair as before, but now Morgan was asking the questions, with me as the observer. I tried to give her a reassuring look. She kept her gaze on Morgan with a singular focus. Her face remained impassive as she sized him up. Only her brown eyes moved as she took her measure of the man. It wasn't fear she was exhibiting; it was confidence and defiance.

"I'm Detective Morgan with the Pinkerton Agency of Chicago." His tone was pleasant and even. He offered his hand, but hers remained in her lap.

"I know what the Pinkertons are," Ajiah said in a cold, deliberate tone, her eyes continuing to meet his. "Hired guns."

Morgan's eyebrows climbed halfway up his forehead. As they slowly lowered, he remarked, "Your English is better than I expected."

"I was with a white family for several years. They insisted I speak and understand their language, study their ways, and do their bidding." Ajiah's last four words had an ominous tone. I could only imagine what she meant, and what came to mind was unpleasant.

"What became of that family?" Morgan asked innocuously to make conversation.

"They died on their wagon journey to California," Ajiah said. Then added, "Violently."

Grogan was unsettled by the statement and raised his arms across his barrel chest as though suddenly chilled.

Morgan handled it better than Grogan, but a raised eyebrow and a slight tipping of his head revealed the statement also struck a chord. "Was your wolf friend responsible?"

"Partly," she confirmed, "But anyone venturing west is somewhat to blame for their fate, wouldn't you agree?" She paused to let that sink in. "I was later taken in by the people here."

It was clear Morgan had not anticipated the interview progressing this way. He struck me as the type of man who mapped out his questions in advance, anticipated answers, and had follow-up questions at the ready. She was throwing him off his game.

"Some of the men on the wagon train were intent on abusing me sexually," she said in an even tone. "They told me they could do whatever they wanted with pretty Indian girls. They had done so before, and I could do nothing about it. If they had not acted in that way, they might not have been killed." Ajiah had not previously relayed those details. It was hard to hear, but I took her word without question.

"So, in your opinion, they're responsible for their deaths because of what they did to you?" Morgan clarified.

By the blank look on his face, Grogan did not seem to understand the cause and effect of what she was explaining.

Although Morgan struck me as a professional who took his duties seriously, I also appreciated he was a just man with a sense of integrity. It undoubtedly came from his pursuit of truth in ordinary criminal investigations. He seemed troubled by the image Ajiah painted. "I'm sorry that happened to you," he offered.

She shrugged. "They got what was coming to them."

Comeuppance was the word she used before.

Morgan regarded her, but his lips parted as his confidence faltered. "Maybe we can skip ahead to the other night when you were in the safe at the brothel. Tell me about that."

Ajiah nodded. "Madam Crossly, the woman who ran the house, planned to auction off my purity to the highest bidder." Ajiah stabbed a finger at Grogan. "He was one of them."

Grogan ruffled at the accusation. "I never...," he stammered. "That's a lie." His blanching confirmed otherwise.

"I refused, and she locked me in that tiny safe to force me. She told me I would remain there until I changed my mind." Ajiah shivered at the memory. "I hate confinement. It was clear from the filth inside I was not the first. I prayed for the Wolf to rescue me."

Morgan let the silence hang until Ajiah picked up where she left off. "And it did come," she concluded. I noticed a slight smile curl at the corner of her lips and got a sinking feeling about my state of being. Was that all it took to summon the monster in me? A prayer?

"Did you tell someone the animal would leave if the Crossly woman let you out?"

"Yes," she said with a slight nod. "Whoever was outside of the safe."

"Was it Sergeant Butler?"

She shrugged. "If that's who was there. It didn't matter who received the message."

"How did you know the creature would comply with that promise?" Morgan asked.

"I didn't, but it never stays long."

"Do you call on it often?" Morgan continued.

"It comes when it's needed."

"Where does it hide when it's not needed?" Morgan asked pointedly.

"You're not going to catch it sleeping if that's what you're thinking," Ajiah warned. "It knows you want to kill it, but you will fail."

Grogan recovered from the accusation regarding his lascivious intentions and seemed somewhat amused. "What makes you so sure?"

Ajiah looked at Grogan evenly before answering. "Because you always do. This is not a safari animal that rolls in sunny grass, oblivious to danger. It does not sit idly by waiting for you to bait it into a trap while you hide behind ugly weapons. It knows you want to extinguish its life and mount its head on your trophy wall." She gestured to each of us in turn. "It has killed dozens of Major Kincaid's soldiers. It has killed your men, and it will kill these new men." She indicated Morgan. "And there is nothing you can do to stop it." She paused for emphasis, "Unless…"

"Unless what?" Morgan swallowed, forcing a stoic front.

"Unless you release my people where you found them and never return."

Grogan laughed outright, while Morgan merely chuckled and shook his head. They considered her a silly young girl with an unrealistic worldview. Once something is shattered, it cannot be reassembled. She was repeating Angry Eagle's threats. He promised the creature would follow us to our fort and keep killing until we released the Natives and returned their lands.

"It will kill all of you if you don't heed my warning," she cautioned. "You can't beat it. You can't kill it, and you won't catch it."

"We will," Grogan said, sharing a glance with Morgan. "I have a lot of experience with this sort of thing. Now that we know what it is, it's only a matter of proper preparation."

Morgan's sudden presence had not been a haphazard cry for help from Grogan. There was a far-reaching plan in place that I was not privy to.

A loud, piercing whistle came from the Lucian train station, interrupting the tense calm in the interview room. Morgan pulled out his pocket watch and smiled in satisfaction. "Almost to the exact minute." He held the watch up to show me the displayed time of 3:01 PM.

"Would you like to see how we'll do it?" Grogan taunted.

"I would," Ajiah said, accepting the challenge.

Curious, I knitted my brow but didn't ask what was in store. I expected it would all be revealed to me shortly. The four of us made our way to the gates, where Bixby, Samuelson, and Witwer joined us. Bixby had the journal of drawings and handed it to Morgan. I felt immediately uncomfortable. I didn't want Morgan aware of what the book suggested.

"You might find this of interest, sir," Bixby said, handing the journal to Morgan.

Morgan strolled at an average pace as he paged through the journal. When he reached the sketches, his gait slowed until he came to a complete halt. He carefully studied each graphic drawing with patient interest, taking the information seriously.

"You flip it at the edge there," Witwer said helpfully.

"What?" Morgan asked, somewhat irritated by the interruption.

"May I, sir?" Bixby took the journal from Morgan and showed him how to flip the pictures into animation. Morgan's mouth opened in amazement.

"It's consistent with the European legends," Bixby said softly.

"Unbelievable," Morgan responded. He took the journal back and did what we all had done: He flipped it a few times forward and then in reverse.

"Is your wolf friend a man who becomes a monster, or a monster who becomes a man?" Morgan addressed Ajiah.

All eyes were upon the beautiful young woman who looked upon us without deference or fear. "It seems to me your people revealed themselves to be the true monsters long ago."

Admittedly, she had a point. Slavery, genocide, war amongst ourselves, wholesale slaughter of various species for their furs. Her words were not lost on Morgan either. The message bypassed Grogan completely. He responded, "What's that supposed to mean?"

Says the man who kills for profit and for the sake of killing.

We continued to our horses, tied up outside Kirkwood's office. I waved to Mal to join us. Grogan couldn't wait to show us. I pulled Ajiah onto Styx with me rather than take the time to find and prepare a mount.

"Whatever they have in mind, they're going to regret it," Ajiah assured me.

I wasn't sure what she meant by that.

"Were those the drawings you mentioned?" She asked me.

"Yes."

"I've never seen them," she offered.

I found that hard to reconcile. "But they are accurate in both detail and representation."

"If you say so."

As we rode out of the fort's common area, I saw Nagel eyeing me suspiciously from the bench he occupied with Mal earlier. He shook his head with disbelief and continued talking excitedly with the Pinkerton, Samuelson. I couldn't hear what he was saying, but every so often, he pointed at me with finality. It could only mean he was troubled by my miraculous recovery. I

214

offended his professional integrity by not feigning continued injury. I tried to shrug it off.

Ajiah nudged me and passed something wrapped in a swath of coarsely woven cloth that may have been from an old feedbag. "Eat this if your stomach is still unsettled."

I unwrapped the package and found several lengths of medium red jerky. It was more of the buffalo meat. I eagerly bit into a piece. My mouth watered as I chewed and swallowed the lightly salted meat. Once it hit my stomach, I experienced immediate relief from the ever-present hunger pangs. "It's the only thing I can keep down. You'll have to show me how it's prepared."

"This portion will get you by until your body adjusts to the trauma." I tried to eat the stick slowly, but it made me feel so good I gobbled it all. Determined not to waste any if it was to come back up, I wrapped the rest and shoved it deep into my pocket for later. We arrived at our destination before I could ask her what she meant by her statement.

39

Upon our arrival at the train station, I looked on in amazement at the smaller engine and ten railcars filled with another fifty men, horses, supplies, and weapons. The entire ensemble was privately funded and not attached to either major railroad company. This was essentially a private army of severe-looking mercenaries. All the Cowboys were similarly clad as Spooner, Tarling, and Grogan's deceased, former Confederate soldiers who met their deaths under the arrows and claws of the Wolf Clan and their werewolf. They, too, wore the sand-colored dusters and CSA accouterments. From snatches of their conversations, I noted they all spoke with Southern or Texas drawls. Grogan was going all out. I was calculating the expense when I spotted the brass plate attached to each railcar: Wilcox & Associates. A name that popped up with some regularity. Grogan had secured the backing of serious East Coast money.

Among the Cowboy contingent was a familiar man whose impossible appearance startled me. He was more weathered than the last time we met. His skin burned a leathery brown from too much sun. He looked like Spooner, the man who first rained fire upon the werewolf with the Gatling gun and had his head ripped off as his reward. Same stance, same manner, and facial expressions. It testified to the circumstances and atmosphere that my first thought was of resurrection rather than the logical conclusion I was staring at a relative.

"You look like you seen a ghost, Boss," Mal observed.

"More like a vendetta," I whispered.

Mal studied Spooner's double, and his face went sour. "I see what you're getting at."

Most of the Pinkertons were assembled at the station. Whatever this was, it represented the reason for their constant consultation of their pocket watches. This particular train and the additional men, weapons, and supplies were impatiently expected. Grogan and his silent partners were intent on capturing the werewolf and sparing no expense.

Spooner's lookalike greeted Grogan, and I got my first confirmation when Grogan said, "Captain Spooner, I'm glad you could make it on short notice. How was your trip?"

"Bumpy," Captain Spooner complained in a gravelly voice. This man appeared older than his dead twin, but it was from hard miles rather than years. Everything about him cried, war veteran. He was the kind of man that likely dug in and fought to the last man. He was here with an army committed to hunting a werewolf he probably didn't believe existed.

Ajiah and I dismounted to follow Morgan, but Grogan wanted to make the introduction.

"Major, this is Captain Spooner. He commands my Cowboys," Grogan said with pride. "His brother was one of the men…"

"Twin," Captain Spooner interrupted. "Tim was my twin, and the way I see it, you and your incompetent… soldiers got him killed."

A flash of anger reached deeper than usual as I immediately disliked the man. He embodied everything I stood against, and it set the tone of our relationship. At West Point, we received training to ignore emotions because they interfered with sound judgment. My anger was something I still struggled to tamp down.

"That's what happens when you send their kind to do a white man's job," Spooner finished. "And how is it you escaped without so much as a scratch?" He looked me up and down suspiciously, accusing me of cowardice to boot.

I took a menacing step toward Spooner and narrowed my eyes. He didn't back away as most bullies did, which cemented my impression of him as a stand-your-ground maniac. I could smell the death on him. I wondered how many of his soldiers died in the war, forced to hold meaningless inches because Spooner lacked the good sense to back off. I reminded myself his brother unnecessarily started the chaos that got so many of our combined forces killed.

"You'll want to watch your words around my soldiers," I warned. "Your brother got himself killed by starting a firefight just as I was initiating a peaceful surrender."

"Bullshit! Renegades don't negotiate. They're next to animals for intelligence, and your fort is full of them. Fish in a barrel, as far as I'm concerned." He glanced dismissively at Ajiah, who squinted with disapproval.

She was getting the same read I was.

"You an Indian lover, Major? This your squaw? Don't you know Indians kill whites on sight? This is a white man's nation. Once we cage this animal, whatever it is, I'm gonna get some payback for their part in killing my brother." He closed the gap between us.

Grogan raised his arm across Spooner's chest. "Hold on there, Captain. First things first. We don't need to antagonize the army."

"An army of darkies ain't no army," Spooner spat. It's a stampede that needs corralling."

"Any attempt to harm my prisoners will be met with force," I warned.

Mal remained tightlipped in his stewing resentment. He struggled to keep the metaphorical steam from seeping out of his ears. He was necessarily practiced at holding his tongue. The only outward expression of his anger was the slight shake of his head.

We had drawn the attention of everyone around us. This happened when former Rebs and former Federals squared off, each side spoiling for a fight to reignite the war. The difference was I represented the victorious side and had everything to lose by engaging in a fistfight with a hot-headed mercenary.

Morgan, the experienced law enforcement officer, intervened by changing the subject. "Shall we get on with this?" He eyed me, Grogan, and Spooner.

"By all means, Detective," Grogan agreed.

I nodded but didn't bother offering Spooner a hand in friendship.

Morgan led the way, with Bixby and Samuelson following behind him to the Pinkerton railcar. Mal whistled at the sheer scope of the operation. The car's interior was packed with items tightly wrapped and loosely covered in canvas tarps. Grogan pulled back a flap of crisp vanilla fabric and gestured for Ajiah. "If you look here, you'll see how we'll achieve our goal."

I looked around in wonder. Were there more Gatling guns? I detected the scent of gun oil, gunpowder, and other heavy artillery odors. Ajiah ducked under the flap entrance. Grogan pushed the canvas flap aside and slammed a heavy metal door I recognized as a cage. He turned the oversized key in the lock, engaged the mechanism, removed it, and slid it into his pocket. Spooner's Cowboys pulled the larger canvas covering off what I assumed was a box or large crate to reveal a small cage inside the larger cage where we were standing. The small cage was a cell for one constructed of flat vertical steel bars about four inches apart and welded firmly into place. It's what small-town jails and prisoner transport wagons used. In Georgia, they confined unruly slaves. The larger cage looked like it came from a zoo to contain elephants and lions.

"What the fuck's going on?" I demanded.

"No," Mal echoed. "No, boss, this isn't right. This is barbaric."

"Sometimes you got to sacrifice a small animal to catch something bigger," Spooner said snidely. "It's called bait."

Ajiah looked upon me with accusing eyes and pursed lips, wounded and betrayed but without fear. I stepped to the cage door and grabbed the cold bars. They were close enough together she could not slip between them. She looked at me without judgment.

"I didn't know this was going to happen."

"I believe you," she said. "I expected something like this."

"You would think by now I would know better," Mal said under his breath.

"I'm sorry it has to be this way," Morgan told Ajiah. But what I've gleaned from Mr. Grogan, the witnesses, and the army's reports is the one common denominator in this mess is you." He pointed at Ajiah. "The werewolf always comes when there is danger to you."

"I'm not sorry," Grogan said in a bullying tone. "You should start praying for your Wolf god to show up so we can catch it." Grogan's Cowboys and a good portion of the Pinkertons laughed as only those with the upper hand could, like a gang of toughs who tease their prey.

Morgan ignored Grogan's chiding. "We'll keep you as comfortable as possible until this ordeal ends. We may resort to shackles to give you a measure of freedom outside the cage. If there is anything you desire, ask, and you shall receive it. Food, water, bedding…"

"You're making a mistake, Mr. Morgan," she interrupted. "This will end badly for all of you. You can still release me and let us return to our land."

This drew more laughter from the crowd of men.

"Fat chance!" Spooner sniped.

"Then you should all find comfort in the few hours you have left to live," she announced to the Cowboys and Pinkertons encircling the cage. She didn't have to yell to be heard. The power of her words silenced every man within earshot. "Pray to your God while you still can. He is ever absent, in my experience."

"Big talk from a trapped rat," Grogan goaded, trying to laugh off the looming unease in the air. He would have had an easier time dismissing the threat if he hadn't seen the supernatural danger with his own eyes. He wasn't as sure of himself as he attempted to project.

"You won't escape its wrath, Mr. Grogan. It has ignored your cowardice twice. Next time, you will die in excruciating pain as it eats you alive." She pointed at Spooner. "Like his brother."

Grogan was stung and swallowed hard.

Spooner gritted his teeth, refraining from a verbal response. He quick-drew his pistol and struck the iron bar nearest her face with the ivory butt. Ajiah did not flinch and maintained her defiant demeanor. She pressed her cheeks to either side of the bars. "Once it is here, there is no stopping it. You have until that moment to release me."

"I think we're done talking to the bait," Spooner announced, spitting tobacco juice onto the planked floor inside her cage.

I could only wonder how Ajiah expected to foil this trap. Did she realize she had confirmed their plan would work as they had laid it out? That she seemed as confident the Wolf would come as they did?

I was the werewolf who rescued her. Angry Eagle was the menacing Wolf they prized, but that Wolf had not ventured far from the wooded area where the Natives were captured. I wasn't about to allow myself to be taken prisoner. There was no doubt the large animal cage would hold me, but I valued my freedom and would fight to maintain it.

Yet, I felt compelled to rescue Ajiah from the brothel, turning unwillingly into a monster. Could she summon me again? Had she known she was walking into a trap when we accompanied Morgan and Grogan to the railyard? She was so calm about it. Courageous.

40

I took a mental inventory of the large items unwrapped within the Pinkerton railcar. The obligatory Gatling guns and a massive stockpile of the necessary ammunition were present. There were cannons unlike anything I had ever seen. These newer models had wider mouths and shorter barrels. Nothing like the famous smoothbore Napoleon cannons we used prolifically during the war to launch twelve-pound cannonballs to level Rebel strongholds and buildings. Smaller charges hurled exploding projectiles to inflict devastating injuries on foot and mounted soldiers, mimicking the short-range effects of a short shotgun.

These new cannons were built for close-quarter combat using minimal powder for propulsion and designed not to shred the target. In this case, a large animal. It wasn't until several crates were opened to reveal bundles of tightly wadded, heavy-gauge, wire-reinforced nets that I understood. They planned to launch the special nets at the creature. Best case scenario, they hoped to lure it into the large animal cage where Ajiah was locked up and slam shut the door behind it. Did they expect it wouldn't harm her at that point? I didn't see how they planned to free her once the creature was locked in the cage. Spooner made it clear that was not his priority. I had to remind myself the Wolf they were hunting was not the werewolf that came to her rescue at the brothel. The creature from the woods was a raging monster motivated by revenge.

"I've never seen cannons like these, Boss," Mal's thoughts echoed my own.

Grogan's Cowboys worked at offloading the Big Mouth cannons, as they were calling them. The railcar, with the two cages and Ajiah, was moved along auxiliary tracks to a warehouse where unused cars were stored and repaired. This provided an enclosed area to protect the occupants from the elements and set up a contained space to prepare for the arrival of their quarry. Big Mouth cannons were positioned to cover the two exterior doors from either side of the opposing warehouse interior walls. The east wall Big Mouth covered the south entrance, and the west wall Big Mouth covered the north. Each crate was packed with four specialized charges beside each station and operated by a two-man team. The Big Mouths were tested to ensure they would swivel ninety degrees for aiming purposes under Spooner's supervision.

Outside the warehouse, a Big Mouth was positioned at each of the four corners and set to swivel under one hundred eighty degrees to prevent each team from hitting another. If these outdoor teams could not net the creature outside the warehouse, they would have easy access to the interior cannons. Gatling guns were set up on tripods to support each station. I noted no provision was made for locking the weapons to avoid accidentally strafing the other teams.

The setups were positioned strategically at each corner in a two-block radius around the warehouse, including alleys. Gatling guns were set up on rooftops overlooking the streets, giving the gunners a wide area of influence. Other men with rifles, either Cowboys or Pinkertons, would support those high-ground positions.

"They think they covered every inch, Boss, but I see lots of opportunity for crossfire if it gets chaotic like that first night," Mal pointed out.

"They don't understand how fast it can move or how erratically it behaves."

The Lucian townsfolk busied themselves, boarding up business fronts and nearby homes in preparation for trouble. They stockpiled their own ammunition and dry goods. Something ignored in the military-style planning. Some were caught in the siege between the states, and that conflict likely resonated in their minds.

In the middle of the broad Main Street, a short distance from the last point of attack, the Treasure Trove brothel, Morgan, Grogan, five Pinkertons, and an equal group of Cowboys led by Captain Spooner set up a Big Mouth for demonstration. The cannon was primed to launch one of the specialized nets. The gunner then prepared the triggering mechanism so a simple cord jerk would ignite the powder and fire the bundle.

Cowboys and Pinkertons gathered around to see how the Big Mouth worked. An older, former Reb gunner saw to all of the preparation but looked to Captain Spooner for instruction.

"Ready when you are, Captain," the gunner said in a voice too loud, verifying what I assumed was deafness from firing cannons without ear protection during the war.

Under ideal conditions, operating a cannon took up to ten men. If each man performed his duty to the best of his ability, the team could fire up to four shots in one minute. More often than not, ten men became five, with the fewer men doing double duty. We didn't need two observers, two ammunition runners, a sighting man, and two primers to clean and load the barrel. This was not war. A skeleton crew of two or three could do the job effectively. Chances were, they wouldn't get a second shot if they missed their moving target.

Captain Spooner led a broken-down mare into the middle of the street approximately one hundred feet away, dropped her lead to the ground, and stepped out of the way. The animal looked around in confusion, rolling her lower jaw and snorting at the fresh air.

"Fire when ready, Sergeant Griggs," Spooner ordered the old gunner.

The wiry old man took a firm grip of the triggering cord and warned, "Cover your ears. Gonna be loud!"

Just as his words registered and everyone in attendance raised their hands to cover their ears, the gunner yelled, "Fire!" And yanked the cord.

A deafening explosion echoed through the block and off the buildings lining either side of Main Street. The old mare startled at the unexpected boom and took a few pre-emptive steps in flight. The billowing smoke emitted an expanding blur as a circular net lined about its perimeter with small lead weights materialized. The net grew in circumference as it unfolded into a fifteen-foot-wide oval. It spiraled to envelop the terrified horse. As the animal tried to flee, it was wrapped up in tangling squares of reinforced netting from muzzle to hooves, tripping her up and sending her staggering into the dirt. The horse whinnied with fright at her uncooperative legs and the hindrance entangling them.

The crowd of gunmen cheered and clapped at the success of the Big Mouth net and the experimental capture of a sitting duck that in no way approximated the nightmare of claws and fangs they were pursuing. The Wolf would not stand idly waiting to be shot with a cannon because the Wolf would know what it was facing and be in motion. However, I saw how the invention might work. Two nets hitting me at once could bring me down fast, allowing a couple of fearless horses and determined riders to attach ropes and drag me to the large cage.

The horse was crying out in real pain and terror, fighting frantically to free itself from the netting. Spooner, who led the flailing test subject into the street, approached from behind to avoid getting kicked. He had his Bowie knife out to cut the mare free but found the net was better reinforced by the wiring than anticipated. He looked to the crowd of spectators and yelled out to be heard over the struggling animal. "Anybody got a pair of wire cutters?" His tone was one of irritation at the inconvenience.

Receiving no immediate response, Spooner grew increasingly annoyed with the incessant shrieks of the desperate mare. He turned his attention to the horse and yelled, "God damnit, shut the fuck up!" With the order, he drew his pistol and shot the animal twice in the head.

An appalled silence fell over the crowd as all fight left the horse, and a small cloud of gun smoke wafted above the street. I turned to nearby Morgan. He looked as though slapped hard in the face by the utter cruelty. "Interesting bunch you've thrown in with, Detective. Not so hard to understand why the Natives fear us."

Morgan side-eyed me but did not disagree.

Too late, a man called from the crowd, "I found my wire cutters. Where you need 'em?"

Mal shook his head in disgust.

Grogan took the lull as an opportunity to jump up on a nearby wagon with a big smile on his bearded face. "That last part was unfortunate, but now you all see how this will work." He addressed the crowd of Cowboys, Pinkertons, and town folk. "For those who don't know me, I'm John Grogan, your employer. You can call me Little John. Everyone does!"

There was light, scattered laughter, as always when the heavy man referred to himself by the nickname no one used.

"The point is to capture this thing alive." He looked around for emphasis. "Alive! You hear me? I'll double the wages of the team that accomplishes that goal."

At the utterance of more money, an enthusiastic cheer went up.

Captain Spooner moved in closer to Grogan, appearing unmoved. "Fuck that," he mumbled, making it clear he wanted to kill the monster that took his brother's life.

"The Gatling guns are for your protection and the protection of the good people of Lucian, but they are also a last resort. Alive, I want this thing. Understand?" Little John raised his eyebrows to indicate how seriously he intended this mission to be taken. He gave Spooner a prolonged stare.

"What exactly are we hunting here?" A Cowboy in the back asked cautiously.

Grogan smiled in a way that should have served as a warning to everyone listening. "Something as rare as a unicorn, my friends. But a lot less friendly. It looks like a wolf but stands like a man!"

A hush fell over the assembled men, followed by uncertain grumbling and nervous laughter that grew steadily in intensity.

"Bullshit!" An unseen speaker called out.

"Right," drawled another skeptically.

"No joke!" Grogan raised his voice in all seriousness. "No joke at all." The crowd quieted down.

"I cannot adequately describe how dangerous this animal is. Whether you believe my words or not, I have one piece of advice." He paused for effect. " If you freeze to stare and convince yourself your eyes are lying, you will die before you can blink."

There grew an atmosphere of mumbled uneasiness and uncertainty among the crowd.

"I shit you not," Grogan concluded. "Now, everyone, to the saloon for a last drink and to receive your assignments. Thank you!" Grogan jumped to the road and lumbered toward the Broken Spoke as the crowd cheered for the free booze.

Spooner climbed up to replace Grogan. "Belay that order, gentlemen! No drinking! You're gonna need to keep your wits. This ain't a bunch of under-trained Yankees wishing they was home sucking their momma's teat. This is a wild animal that relishes the kill. We aim to take it alive, but if that becomes untenable, I'll be the one to kill the motherfucker for murdering my brother." He strove to make eye contact with every man around him and drive his point home. "Go get your assignments and see me if you have questions."

A less enthusiastic crowd dispersed.

Over Mal's shoulder, I saw the Pinkerton Samuelson pull Morgan aside and whisper in his ear. They entered the Treasure Trove. Though closed for business, the building was now the temporary headquarters due to its centralized location.

"Mal, I got a bad feeling. If this doesn't turn out the way they hope, we got a lot of outsiders disinclined to recognize the authority of Negro soldiers. Our being understaffed makes the situation worse."

Mal nodded. "This Captain Spooner is the worst of the old Confederacy, Boss. These Cowboys look to be a lot of ex-Rebs, and I don't like the looks we been getting."

"I'm worried about our guests," I added. "Spooner wants to avenge his dead brother, and I think he'll take it out on them if the Wolf doesn't arrive to satisfy his timeline."

"I don't like how they tricked the girl into that cage." Mal shook his head. "Brings up a lot of bad memories. Using her as bait. It's inhuman."

"They don't look at Natives as human, Mal." I agreed with Mal's compassion. But from a strategic standpoint, this was a stroke of genius. Morgan drew some insightful conclusions. The Wolf always appeared when Ajiah was in dire straits. Grogan and Spooner might have a nasty surprise or two up their sleeves.

"We're not going to let anything unfortunate happen," I assured him. "I want you to find Buff if things break bad."

"Buff?" Mal asked, not following.

"Yes. If this goes awry, I want you to send Buff to where this all began. Tell him to find Whiteman Killer..."

Mal jerked away from me in shock. "The renegade Indian? They'll kill old Buff! He's a traitor to them. You heard that kid, Angry Eagle."

"Not if it means saving his people from a slaughter," I explained. "He'll need you to get them safely out of the stockade and help retrieve their horses."

Mal looked at me like he didn't know who I was anymore, assessing me for a lunatic. "You gonna let them go, Boss?"

"I'd rather release them than keep them locked up where they're defenseless. You heard Spooner call them fish in a barrel. That sound like a massacre in the making to you?"

We considered each other. His lone eye searched both of mine.

"Worst case scenario, we capture them all over again. Maybe without all the killing."

"What about these Cowboys, Boss? You gonna turn into that thing again?" He asked with clear apprehension. "You gonna kill us if we get in your way?"

I hung my head, not knowing how to answer. We never discussed what happened or if it would happen again. "I could never kill you, Mal. That will never happen." And I meant it.

"How can you promise? When you're you, you're you, but when you're that thing, you're a monster."

I couldn't explain how I maintained my full consciousness when I changed. I knew what I was doing. But I also knew I couldn't kill Mal under any circumstances.

"And those men," Mal continued, "Some of them Cowboys may have it coming, no doubt about it, but I'm sure just as many don't. Those Pinkertons are just doing a job, like us. They don't seem like bad sorts," Mal implored. "Innocent until proven guilty. Not all Southerners are guilty of atrocities. Even I know that, and I got scars to prove it. Not all of them picked up the whip. Not all of them owned slaves."

"You should've been an attorney, Mal," I said, trying to make light of it.

Just then, Morgan exited the Treasure Trove with a handful of his Pinkerton underlings behind him. They marched toward Mal and me.

"What now?" I said under my breath.

Mal followed my line of sight. "Looks like somebody got a bee in his bonnet."

Morgan caught my eye and didn't look away. "Can we talk, Major?"

"Certainly."

"Inside, please?" Morgan jerked a thumb toward the Treasure Trove.

Mal and I traded reluctant glances and entered behind Morgan. We noted the other men boxing us in. Did they think we might flee, or were they simply eager to impress their boss? I felt overall calm, but Mal was getting tense. Sweat beaded at his temples.

We entered Beth Crossly's gaudy little office. It looked like the kind of sanctuary a businesswoman in her profession might piece together. Red velvet curtains blocked prying eyes and the slightest rays of sunshine. A flattering oil portrait of Crossly hung behind a carved business desk depicting dragons, knights, ladies with fans, and oriental symbols. The desk was cluttered, but Morgan had created an efficient workspace by shoving piles of newspaper and correspondence to the outer edges.

"What's this about, Morgan?" I was becoming impatient.

Morgan cleared his throat, then tapped his index finger to his lips. "Several pieces of information have come together from our investigation into the werewolf matter that I must address with you," he began.

I kept my mouth shut, allowing him to fill the silence.

"First off, Dr. Nagel is adamant you suffered grievous injuries as a result of your confrontation with the creature." He glanced at some notes on the desk in front of him. "Broken hip, shattered kneecap, broken ribs, concussion, and a bite to the neck. He confined you to bedrest, administered a splint, and prescribed you laudanum for pain."

"I'm fine," I said, shrugging it off. "My injuries were not all that serious."

"Would you mind showing me the bite mark, Major?"

I didn't anticipate the request and stood in stunned silence.

"Major?" He asked again.

I reluctantly unbuttoned my collar and pulled it to reveal my unblemished neck. There was no sign of the bite Dr. Nagel treated.

"Mr. Grogan saw the animal standing over you, which supports Dr. Nagel's statement you were bitten."

"Little John wasn't exactly close when the creature knocked me down," I pointed out. "He was fleeing for his life. I'd be surprised if he were in a position to see much of anything."

Morgan nodded acknowledgment but turned to another statement among his notes. "Secondly, while searching these premises, my men located bits of torn, bloody clothing."

A Pinkerton I could not name stepped out of the office, rummaged through a nearby cabinet, and returned, holding bits of my blood-spattered shirt in his gloved hands. It was privately tailored and not military issue. Many officers preferred a more comfortable and expensive weave. There wasn't enough left to indicate origin or ownership. Mal must have picked up my crutch, splint, and boots and discarded them.

"Thirdly, on the morning following the murders at the brothel, you entered the fort in a disheveled state. According to Lieutenant Carpenter, who was on duty at the gates. He mentioned your coat was spattered with what appeared to be blood, and you were barefoot." Morgan laid out the case as though presiding over a murder trial. Something he had no doubt been a party to in life under normal circumstances.

"Do you have anything to say for yourself, Major?" Morgan demanded.

I took a deep breath and assumed a deferential and embarrassed demeanor. "Come now, Detective. Surely you don't believe me to be the first army officer to return to barracks in an unkempt state, having lost his footwear? Boots get hot." I was being flip, but I read doubt in his expression and thought it worth exploiting. "After all, I was in a brothel." I tried to sound conciliatory and self-conscious.

He deliberated without responding.

"You're not suggesting I'm a werewolf, are you?" I asked indignantly, confronting the unmentioned accusation head-on. Morgan stared at me, bobbing his focus from one eye to the other as he considered my words.

"If my injuries were as grave as reported, how could I possibly have healed in a matter of hours? It's impossible," I said with what I considered the right amount of incredulity.

"Unless it's some sort of side effect," Morgan suggested.

It was an astute observation. I had to give him credit for that one.

"The Major's not a werewolf," Mal proclaimed in my defense. "We've been together since the war. If he were other than an honorable man, I would know."

Morgan took a more measured tone. "Normally, I would agree with your assessment, Sergeant, but I'm being paid to conduct a thorough investigation. There is something dark and sinister at work here. Several soldiers and civilians have been murdered. Dr. Nagel conducted autopsies. My men have examined the recent bodies, and the violent injuries inflicted upon them. A large, unidentified predator attacked all of the victims. That is not in dispute."

Morgan swallowed hard and continued. "We've done our research. As limited as the information is, and as fantastical as it seems, the legends are clear the bite of a werewolf results in the victim becoming a werewolf."

"You're suggesting I could be a werewolf because I was attacked?" I asked.

"What of the other men who survived?" Mal asked, "Me for one. Are we monsters, too?"

"Wouldn't several werewolves be running about if that were the case?" They weren't, and I wasn't sure why.

Morgan struggled. "The whole transformation piece is difficult to accept, but the drawings and the torn, bloody shirt are too persuasive to ignore. I can't take the chance there's nothing to it." He sighed, "Especially those drawings."

For an instant, I thought Morgan might order his men to clap me in irons and toss me into the cage with Ajiah.

"The drawings?" Mal asked.

"Yes, they're precise. My wife is an artist, and my young daughter has taken up sketching in charcoal. If there is one thing I've learned about art from them, it's that art evolves."

"Evolves?" I asked.

"Yes. Artists experiment. There are variations, even if they repeatedly draw or paint the same thing. Sometimes subtle, sometimes not so subtle, especially when the subject matter is a product of imagination and not a still life." Morgan pulled out the journal of sketches and showed us various pages. "There is no variation here. The artists were in agreement. The subject is unchanged throughout, except in style. Identical in appearance. The ears are the same length and shape in every iteration. As are the teeth, the claws, the proportions. It has a tail. The artists drew the same creature every single time without improvements or variants. But there is only one. Never two together.

229

One.

"What I'm suggesting, as strange as it sounds, is this creature may have the ability to masquerade as a man, and that same man may be walking among us. It was at the brothel the night of the murders. It entered and exited undetected. All of our men will have to be vigilant," he explained. "I can't fathom how to advise them what they're looking for unless it arrives in its werewolf form. It's most dangerous form."

I almost exhaled an audible sigh of relief. Morgan was very close to surmising my secret. If he continued to examine the accrued facts, he might draw a very different conclusion about me. His mistake was giving me the benefit of the doubt. His apparent disbelief came from not seeing it himself. But that might eventually change.

I glanced at Mal sideways. The beads of sweat ran below the strap of his eyepatch.

"What's your plan moving forward?" I asked.

"It's a waiting game. We've assigned men to stations. They'll work in shifts to achieve full coverage. It will likely attack at night. That is its pattern. We'll have to stay on our toes."

"I'll authorize as many men as I can spare."

"Appreciated, but please steer clear of Captain Spooner and his men," Morgan advised. "This is a powder keg that could go off any time."

"Agreed."

41

Walking into the street with Mal reminded me of my prison escape. Relief, with danger ever present. Morgan would continue his deductive thoughts, eventually leading him to the correct conclusion. "He was close to figuring it out." The words were more for me than for Mal. I feared ending up in a cage for the rest of my life. A cage like Ajiah's. She was there because of me, making her safety my responsibility.

"I'm going to the warehouse to guard Ajiah personally," I informed Mal. "You find Witwer and have him assign a detail to assist in Morgan's action but maintain enough men to watch over the Natives at the fort. Pass my message on to Buff."

"I hope you know what you're doing," Mal sighed.

"It's a work in progress."

We parted ways, with Mal heading to the fort and me riding to the warehouse. Styx reacted no differently to me after the transformation, which I took to mean he sensed no danger. Animals are more sensitive to threats than men. How deep inside me did the danger lurk?

As day blurred into evening, I felt the undeniable draw to Ajiah, though not with the urgency I experienced the night of my metamorphosis. I wanted to be near to keep watch, but I was neglecting my professional responsibilities in favor of her well-being. I steered Styx to the warehouse where she was contained. Two and three-man teams of Spooner's Cowboys crewed the Big Mouth cannon and Gatling gun stations. Former soldiers doing soldier work as Western mercenaries. The ex-Rebs eyed my Union uniform with barely concealed hatred. Those wounds never heal. They were spoiling for the fight Spooner wanted, and I worried where that energy would lead if the monster never appeared. One thing was for sure: nothing was going to enter the warehouse unnoticed. Cowboys and Pinkertons milled everywhere.

I found a safe livery nearby to water Styx and get him hay and grain. I might be away for a bit, and there was no need to keep him uncomfortably bridled and saddled. I kept to the shadows as I crept to the trap.

The interior of the warehouse stood in stark contrast to the exterior. For all the talk of teams keeping watch over every square inch in expectation of the werewolf's arrival, the dusty warehouse itself was deserted. The poor girl was staked out in the cage like a lamb for sacrifice. She sat cross-legged, her back straight, hands on knees, deep in thought. Though I strode lightly, her eyes were immediately upon me. I quickened my pace toward her. "I'm not going to let anything happen to you."

She smiled pleasantly. "I know why you're here, Major."

Seeing her caged brought me shame. A warm flash of rebuke washed over me. "Detective Mogan can't bring himself to believe a man can transform into a werewolf."

"They always realize too late what has been staring them in the face," she said.

"There's more going on here than I understand," I said in frustration.

"You're different from the others, Major. You understand very well what is happening. The question you should be asking yourself is what you will do about it."

She was right. I was fed up with the killing and wrongness of war well before I was taken prisoner. That's why I signed up to lead black soldiers to take the fight back to the Rebs, not just as payback for my incarceration but to give former slaves a measure of power and retribution over their tormentors. Slaves were prisoners robbed of their dignity and freedom by men with the wealth and means to enforce a brutal system of subservience. It's why I conscripted Mal and others like him to be Buffalo Soldiers when the war ended. The westward expansion was my way of breaking loose from the old ways. The West may have appeared serene and awe-inspiring in its beauty, but I deluded myself into thinking it would be a peaceful escape.

Soon, we were escorting interlopers from the East to the promised land of the West at the expense of people who already occupied it. The Natives were looked upon as a nuisance and inconvenience by white invaders. With the escorts came confrontation, skirmishes, and more death. Later, our mission became the extermination and relocation of the rightful owners. Their children were taken and educated to become servants. The ex-slaves were enslaving others.

"We just want to live in peace on our land, Kincaid," she said, interpreting my thoughts. "We're not asking for anything that wasn't already ours."

I nodded my agreement. I understood her words. They sounded simple, but she didn't understand how the white world worked. It was all take. There was no giving back.

I sighed in exhaustion and looked for a place to sit and rest. Not far from the cages was a manager's office. In it, I spied a cot and chair to keep an eye on her. My standing outside her cage would draw suspicion.

"Can I get you anything to eat or drink?" I peered into her uncomfortable quarters and reached into my pocket to offer the jerky she provided me earlier.

"I'm fine," she assured. "It won't be long. I gave that to you to keep you sated."

I weighed the wrapped meat in my hand and stuffed it back into my pocket. "I'll be in there," I said, pointing to the office. "Just shout if you need me."

She nodded. "I won't need to shout."

I only intended to sit briefly but laid down on the narrow cot within minutes. My anxiety evaporated with her proximity. Without intention, I quickly drifted off and into a dream. In it, I was free of my uniform and responsibilities, running across the open prairie in my powerful wolf form, looking for deserving men to kill and devour. "Don't kill anything you aren't going to eat," my grandfather's words echoed in my mind.

When I awoke, it was dark. The office door latched sometime during my nap, muffling any peripheral sounds. There was a muted conversation coming from nearby. I strained to determine if it originated outside the warehouse office or from the exterior wall separating me from the outdoors. It was a bit of both. Men outside the building kept each other company and occasionally laughed at traded jokes.

From inside the warehouse, the conversation was coaxing. Someone tried to convince another to do something they might not ordinarily consider. A pair of vaguely familiar voices worked in tandem at persuasion. At first, I wasn't sure I was fully awake and hearing correctly because the conversation was so out of place.

"Come on, honey, you want to take a break from that cell?"

The other voice said, "We'll get you something to eat, and maybe you can show your appreciation." The two men chuckled in unison.

"Yeah, I been wanting to see what's under them Indian clothes since the first day I laid eyes on you," the first voice soothed.

The voices belonged to Axil and Private Jackson. Their propositions were directed at Ajiah. Their overt sexual advances made me angry, but instead of bursting into the warehouse and ordering them back to their assigned duties, I opened the latched door quietly to see what was happening. She would likely tell them to fuck off, and that would be the end of it.

Illuminating lanterns were now dispersed around the warehouse, primarily at the open gates and around Ajiah's outer cage. They provided more than adequate lighting should anything appear but were spaced at safe distances from the Big Mouth cannons and their flammable powder sacks. Jackson and Axil were assigned to light and position the lanterns. More likely, they volunteered for the assignment, knowing it would put them close to the girl.

The Big Mouth and Gatling gun stations within the warehouse were still unmanned. I assumed if the fight reached this inner sanctum, men would move in from the stations on the exterior of the building. I wondered if those self-same gunners thought they could move fast enough to get in front of an advancing enemy.

Jackson and Axil stood on either side of Ajiah's cage, looking in. They wanted her to choose which she preferred. She didn't seem interested in either. Nor did she register fear.

"For any of that, you would need the key," she said playfully.

"Damn, girl, I'm not stupid," Axil said, stepping forward and removing a unique iron key from his pocket. He smiled and slipped it into the lock. Before turning it, Axil took his hand off and looked Ajiah over earnestly. "Before I let you out, I need assurances I go first."

"What the fuck?" Jackson complained.

"I ain't been with a woman as fine as you in forever," Axil explained. "This was my plan. I told the Cowboy you needed out for some food, facilities, and fucking." Axil grinned widely at his clever alliteration. "Well, maybe I didn't mention the last one."

"You seen the Major round?" Jackson asked.

"No," she lied.

"I seen Stick at the livery. Major, don't just leave him any ole place. He love that horse," Axil explained.

"The horse's name is Styx," Ajiah corrected. "It's the river that separates the world of the living from the world of the dead."

"Who gives a fuck?" Axil said in annoyance.

"Maybe he's walking the perimeter of this cluster fuck," Jackson suggested.

Ajiah stared at the unturned key and shrugged. "Seems you better get on with whatever you have in mind before someone checks." She gave him an alluring smile of perfect teeth.

Axil swallowed in anticipation and rubbed his crotch. "What I got in mind just grew seven inches," he chuckled salaciously.

I looked on in fascination, trying to understand her behavior. She wasn't leery at all. She was toying with them.

"Before I let you out, I did promise that Cowboy one thing."

"What's that?" Ajiah asked coyly.

"Gotta cuff you," Jackson said, displaying a pair of police-style handcuffs he'd been holding at his side.

"We're supposed to use leg irons," Axil scoffed, "But that would make things difficult."

Jackson smacked a hand on the food port. "Hands, stick 'em through

She nodded understanding and got on her knees in compliance. Before sticking her hands through, she wiggled out of her clothing. Her pert, full breasts swayed seductively back and forth with her quick, deliberate movements. Axil and Jackson were on fire with desire. She folded her clothes neatly atop her hide footwear and pushed the articles aside.

"Oh Lordy, I died and gone to heaven for sure," Jackson whispered eagerly.

Ajiah stuck her hands out the port, and Jackson ratcheted the cuffs snuggly around her small wrists. "Hurry, hurry," Jackson said, backing away so Axil could open the door.

Axil stared at her nude body in open-mouthed lust. "I can't wait to go balls deep in that," he said, giving the key a clumsy turn. The locking mechanism simultaneously unlatched the iron door in three places. Axil pulled the door open a few inches and asked, "Why you being so accommodating?"

"Because I'm starving and you offered to let me out," she explained.

"I thought you hated us," Jackson added.

"I do," Ajiah agreed in a deep, guttural voice. "I hate all of you." She shoved the cage door hard into them, sending the men staggering backward in stunned shock.

Inky darkness enveloped her as thick black hair flowed from every pore of her perfect skin, wrapping her in pitch uniformity. Muscles rolled and thickened under the sprouting hairs. Bones cracked, and tendons popped as her body reshaped into a larger, more powerful being. Her perfect teeth sharpened and elongated. A wet snout pushed from her face, and velvety ears speared from the sides of her head into horn-like appendages. She held the cuffs, securing her wrists above her forming muzzle, and watched as the pressure from her thickening forearms pressed against them. One hinge sprang and then the other. The cuffs dropped to the ground with a metallic clink - the loudest sound in the warehouse.

Axil and Jackson reacted much the same as Crossly and Flynn. Their jaws slackened, and their eyes widened. They were paralyzed with stupefied wonder instead of running for the cage door. Axil was the first to scramble in flight and was thus the first to have his throat seized. Claws dug into his throat, choking off his cries.

Frozen in fear, Jackson made a steady, high-pitched whining sound. The jet-black Wolf snarled and clutched him by the neck in the same bullwhip quick manner as Axil. She lifted their flailing, strangling bodies off their feet with ease as she grew in size, looking from one set of bulging eyes to the other. Both grabbed instinctively at her powerful wrists, ignorantly expecting this would somehow force her to release them. They kicked ineffectual blows to her legs and torso, drawing only snarls of irritation.

She bit into Jackson's face and crunched through his skull and into the soft cavity of his brain. Dark red blood spewed in the hue of molten lava down the front of his uniform in the lantern light. His legs kicked involuntarily for a few seconds before going limp. Satisfied he was dead, she tossed him out the door of the large cage and onto the dirt floor of the warehouse.

Seeing what was in store for him, Axil kicked at her body and pounded on her forearm with renewed vigor. He tried to scream for help but could utter no more than choking gurgles under her vice-like grip. She bared her blood-covered teeth and growled as Jackson's blood dripped from her mouth and down her chin. She grabbed his thigh with her empty paw and raised his torso to her widening jaws. Axil could only moan.

She snapped her teeth together and bit out a crackling hunk of his ribs and belly. Spontaneously, I cried out, "NO!" at the awfulness of it. Is that how I looked when I did those brutal things? If she heard me, she paid no notice.

Axil's face went ashy with the trauma of being eaten alive. She swallowed and took another deep bite as the life drained from his face. His hands dropped from their death grip around her wrist. She swallowed and took a third mouthful from his lifeless form, dragging most of his entrails out to dangle as she chewed his warm flesh. She transferred her hold on Axil's throat and thigh to his ankle. His head thumped on the wooden platform. She dragged Axil to where Jackson lay and grabbed his ankle, glancing at the warehouse entrances. Detecting no danger, she stood fully erect. She directed her attention to me, witnessing her transformation and bloodthirsty actions.

Of course! I thought to myself. All this time. Why hadn't I seen it? She all but told me it wasn't Angry Eagle. Ajiah was the black Wolf. This is what killed those settlers who kidnapped and abused an Indian girl on the wagon journey west. She posed as a helpless orphan upon whom they bestowed pity and lust. They were enticed to take her in, thereby falling for her ruse.

I opened the door to expose myself in full. The longer she stared at me with her narrow red eyes, the more apparent her human intelligence and cunning became. It was the same for me in the wolf form. Was she trying to communicate? Call me to join her? She knew who and what I was. She took a deep breath that billowed her chest and the thick black mane covering her breasts, shoulders, and upper back. She was going to roar and summon the men lying in wait. I had to warn her of the danger.

"Wait!" I stepped from the small office. She exhaled and tossed me the freshly murdered body of Corporal Jackson as an offering and growled softly. She wanted me to change and eat him. Deep down, I felt an obscene hunger pang.

Though Grogan, Spooner, the Cowboys, and Pinkertons had gone to great pains and expense to capture the Wolf, they had mistakenly assumed the monster would arrive from without. All their specialized weapons and preparations were pointed in the wrong direction. I chuckled to myself. Leave it to Rebs to leave their asses exposed in a fight. We weren't all General Sherman on a southern march straight through Georgia, destroying everything in our path. They stupidly baited their elaborate trap with the very thing they sought to catch.

"Ajiah, those cannon fire steel-reinforced nets. They mean to capture you and lock you in the larger cage." I pointed to the Big Mouth cannon aimed at the north door and gestured toward the cage. "You have to avoid those nets. Grogan wants you alive to use as a weapon, but Spooner wants to kill you outright for murdering his brother."

She growled acknowledgment and waved her free claw at Jackson. She wanted me to change and feed. Why didn't she reveal herself to me before? I sighed in frustration. I had so many questions. "I know you want me to join you, but I can't." I implored. I thought of Mal's pained expression when he asked if I would kill him and our men to help her.

She took another deep breath, filling her lungs to capacity. She meant to do it this time, and there was no way to stop her. She balled her free, splayed claw into a fist and thrust her jaws open to emit a loud, angry roar. It developed into a foreboding howl meant to terrify every man within earshot. Her dark, hulking form moved to the north door and bellowed into the night.

Instantly, horses whinnied, dogs barked, and men yelled unintelligible words. But nothing more meaningful than, "What the fuck was that!?" and "Where did that come?"

Cowboys appeared at the doors bearing lanterns and rifles, wearing soiled dusters and sweat-stained ten-gallon hats to keep themselves warm against the falling temperature. Upon first visual contact with the Wolf, they did what all men do: They froze and stared in disbelief. That she stood there clutching the ankle of a half-eaten human being didn't make it any easier for them to move their leaden feet.

"What the hell!?"

"Fucking shoot it, dummy! Shoot it!" Cried another. "What are you waiting for?"

A man without a duster, wearing stained suspenders to hold his pants up, bolted for the nearest Big Mouth and Gatling gun. "One of you assholes want to help me out?"

Another man ran to assist. Ajiah swung Axil's mutilated body at them like some morbid boomerang. The corpse swirled awkwardly through the air at a velocity neither man could avoid. It knocked them through the wooden planks of the warehouse wall. Ajiah grabbed the nearest lantern handle with a curved talon and flung it after them. The lantern shattered and exploded into flame against the Big Mouth as the men struggled from under Axil's body. Flaring kerosene splashed into the crate of netting and gunpowder charges.

As the powder ignited, I dropped to the ground and was deafened by each furious charge, exploding in succession. The two men were set ablaze and screamed in agony. The final explosion silenced them, but the fire spread quickly across the dry wooden planks.

"It's here! It's here!" A man yelled. "It's in the warehouse!"

Every bell in the area began ringing in a cascading panic as if judgment day had arrived and the rapture had begun. The bells summoned the volunteer fire brigades into action. Yet, the incessant clanging intoned desperation, warning no matter how many men came to assist, there would never be enough to handle the dire emergency.

42

Detective Morgan was the first familiar face to arrive at the north door. He came to a halt, wearing his clean bowler and dark suit, and held a pistol pointed safely skyward. "My god, it's the Devil himself!" He exclaimed, with a look of shocked wonder. He was flanked by two Cowboys who shouldered their rifles, took quick aim, and fired repeatedly at the looming black Wolf. Though the bullets struck their target squarely in the chest and torso, the gunfire had no visible effect other than to produce greater rage. Seeing the futility of small arms fire, Morgan did not bother to level his pistol for a shot of his own. "Man your cannons!"

The spreading fire consumed the dry planks that made up the structure. An undulating wave of bright yellow and orange flame crawled along the interior surfaces upward and outward, mimicking water lapping at a seashore. Only this tide did not retreat. It advanced and spread its fiery scope by the second. The rising temperature in the warehouse prohibited safe entry to operate the cannons, though attempts were still made.

The black Wolf grabbed another lantern and lobbed it at the west wall, where a Cowboy hesitantly tried to get to the opposite Big Mouth or Gatling undetected. This wall, too, burst into flames following the spattering path of expelled kerosene. The Cowboy cloaked himself in his duster and exited the building just as the charges beside the second Big Mouth detonated. A large hole of flaming planks collapsed to the ground.

Instead of exiting toward the men crowding at either of the two doors, the monster darted toward the flaming maw of the first hole. She leaped through, pulling her knees into her chest and tucking her head like an expert gymnast.

"Where did it go?" One of the Pinkertons called out.

"It busted through the west wall," a Cowboy responded.

Men ran to pursue the creature, while others shielded their eyes to get a look into the inferno from which the beast emerged. The fire reached the rafters in less than a minute and lapped at the ceiling. As the men were preoccupied with the beast and the spreading fire, I moved to the edge of the railcar. I retrieved Ajiah's carefully folded clothing from her cell. Once I had them, I raced toward the door furthest from Morgan, holding my coat up to protect my face from the intense heat, choking smoke, and licking flames.

I knew Ajiah could take care of herself, so I turned my attention to the safety of my horse. The men crewing the Big Mouth stations outside the warehouse were in the same predicament as those who tried to get inside. The fire was making their stations impossible to reach and maintain. A dark figure ran cloaked in shadows on the opposite side of the trainyard and knocked kerosene-fueled streetlamps to the ground. Unless the town had a first-class fire brigade with pressurized water pumps, all of the buildings on the block would soon be engulfed.

I ran to the livery, where men were already opening gates to usher the horses into the corral and away from the stored hay bales. I found my saddle and tack and stuffed Ajiah's buckskins and moccasins into a leather pouch. I threw the protective blanket over Styx's back, tossed my saddle over it, and cinched it securely above his belly. Next, I got the bit into his mouth and the bridle snuggly over his head. With reins held tight, I jumped in the saddle and dug my heels into his ribs. The stable boy swung the gate open for me and ten mares that followed.

From the next block over, there came the distinct sound of at least two Gatling guns firing in tandem. That could only mean Ajiah was spotted. I raced Styx in that direction, careful to avoid any trigger-happy Cowboys and Pinkertons along the way. The panicked men were descending into chaos, firing their weapons indiscriminately at anything moving to take action in the face of unknown danger.

As I drew closer, I heard men yelling instructions to each other.

"Watch the fire! It's spreading!"

"Where'd it go?" was a question asked repeatedly.

Here and there, I saw unfamiliar men eviscerated or mortally wounded. Except for a handful, the Cowboys and Pinkertons were strangers to me. Identifiable only by their uniforms. The scene was taking on the impersonal devastation of war. Men were injured, dead, or dying, but because I didn't know them, they were meaningless to me. Through the carnage, I saw where Ajiah had been, and by tracking the staccato Gatling reports, I tracked her location.

I slowed Styx down and proceeded cautiously. A man atop a building behind a Gatling swung it from side to side in terror. "Where's it at?" He was so determined to open fire he didn't respond sensibly or take note of his surroundings.

On a corner below and across from the man on the rooftop was a Gatling gunner swinging his weapon around wildly. From somewhere down the same block, a mighty roar erupted. Both men turned their guns in that direction and immediately started firing. I wasn't convinced they knew what they were firing at. Men screamed in response, but was it from a werewolf attack or indiscriminate gunfire? Both gunners fired until their magazines were spent. Instead of immediately reloading like they were trained, they squinted through the haze of gun smoke, anxious to see if they'd hit anything.

From an unidentified location closer than the last roar, a bone-chilling howl escaped Ajiah's powerful lungs. The man on the roof slapped at his weapon, not understanding why it wouldn't fire. "Fuck!" He yelled before inserting another magazine into the receiver. The empty ammo stick clattered to the ground below as he discarded it in favor of its replacement.

A shadow leaped into view near the man on the street, struggling with his reload. The creature was upon him before he completed the necessary task. Men around him backed away and started firing at the monster with their rifles and pistols. Undaunted, the creature roared angrily and attacked the man at the Gatling with crisscrossing claws and gnashing jaws.

Unfortunately, the man on the rooftop above also spotted the creature and only had eyes for killing it. He cranked the handle and sent high-velocity missiles from the spiraling barrels toward his compatriots below. The strafing trajectory of the bullets was marked by dirt kicking up in a search for the elusive werewolf, but they only found men in the path of the ill-aimed gunfire. At least three men, in addition to the gunner, were shot to pieces, dancing the machinegun waltz as their bodies were riddled with hellfire from above. It wasn't until the magazine was empty that the gunner realized his error, and the Wolf took note of his location.

"Stop! You're shooting our guys!" A Cowboy shouted from a position of cover beside a building a quarter of a block away. He pointed his rifle at the Wolf but thought better of firing and drawing attention to himself.

The Wolf dropped the gunner's body and barreled toward the building where the rooftop Cowboy was perched. The Cowboy swore and hastily swapped out magazines as the creature vaulted from the street to the side of the building. She dug her claws into the brick face and clung with the ease and skill of a macabre spider. Ajiah sank her claws into the mortar

241

between bricks and methodically inched her way up the side of the building just as the Cowboy slapped the new magazine into place and grabbed hold of the crank to fire.

As Ajiah reached the Gatling post, the Cowboy learned the hard way the Gatling on his tripod was not engineered to point straight downward. Though able to fire the gun, he could not shoot at an angle that allowed him to strike the stalking creature.

Two men got into position across the street, primed a Big Mouth cannon, packed a charge, and inserted the priming tube. The gunner had the triggering mechanism ready.

"Fire!" He warned, yanking the cord with more force than necessary. The net sailed behind the explosion toward Ajiah. As the lead weights expanded the wire-reinforced web into a spiraling circle, one of the edges caught the flagpole protruding from the face of the building between the cannon and its target. The net wrapped harmlessly around the obstruction.

"Fuck!" The gunner swore. "Almost had the mother!" The team repeated the loading and priming process as quickly as possible, giving Ajiah plenty of time to dig her nails into the thigh of the man fighting to angle his Gatling down at her. The Cowboy screamed in shock and pain as the creature sliced his leg open and snarled in his face. He managed to crank the handle of the weapon and spit gunfire uselessly into the street.

"Ready!" The Big Mouth team loader announced.

"Fire! The gunner yelled, pulling the ripcord and launching the package.

Ajiah turned as the second net flew toward her in an ever-widening web. Perceiving the threat, she flung the screaming Gatling gunner into the advancing mesh. The net wrapped around the man and dragged him to the ground below, where his head struck a brick step, cracking it open to silence his agonized cries.

Before the team could take another shot, Ajiah dropped to the ground beside the netted dead man and lunged directly at her attackers. Instead of running away as they should have, they chose the riskier path and attempted to fire another net. Ajiah slashed their throats and nearly beheaded them before they could get another projectile into the mouth of their cannon.

Escalation came in the form of a Gatling gun mounted to the bed of a double horse-drawn wagon. The setup resembled the tripod positioning the first Spooner twin attempted before being spectacularly decapitated at the buffalo field. Only this time, the attacker was in motion. The wagon passed the black Wolf with a teamster reign-whipping the horses into a frenzy to gain speed. A machine gunner was strapped into a harness to prevent flying over the clapboard side and into the graveled street. Unlike the other Gatlings, this one had an ammunition man to feed fresh magazine sticks into the receiver. The ammo man's greatest challenge was not keeping the machine gun fed but keeping himself low enough to avoid being knocked from the wagon by the gunner swinging the rotating barrels side to side.

The wagon gun did better in finding its mark than any stationary arrangement. I couldn't follow on Styx without risking us taking stray fire. But the creature only took a few rounds before adjusting her course in stops and starts, darting behind whatever cover was offered by posts, barrels, and streetlamps. When a bullet found its mark, the animal barked in pain but was not wounded in any visible way. Unfortunately, the waggoneers underestimated the creature's speed. Ajiah was fleeter of foot and steadily gaining.

I galloped Styx at a distance to safely watch while avoiding gunfire. As she closed in on them, I heard the ammunition man yell to the gunner and the teamster, who occasionally stole glances back at their pursuer. "Let's try this one!" The ammo feeder shouted. He slapped a fresh clip in place.

A more menacing tone accompanied the discharged rounds as the gunner cranked the weapon handle. Fiery missiles erupted from rotating barrels. Red tracers glowed behind every fifth round to show the gunner where his bullets were streaking. The only thing that created this effect was phosphorus, which I knew would burn at a few thousand degrees. Upon embedding in her hide, the rounds flared to life. She screamed like a dog run over by a racing wagon. She batted her paws at the burning ammunition, which did nothing to diminish the angry flames. Were they firing magnesium ammunition? It was the one element that detonated when placed in liquid. Did that mean the rounds successfully pierced her hide, and the magnesium ignited upon contact with her blood? That could only result in searing, flesh-ripping pain.

Ajiah changed course and tore the wooden rail from a nearby hitching post. She ran the boardwalk past storefronts, clutching the five-foot length of timber like a club in both claws. She timed the swapping of magazines, increased speed, and thrust the thick lumber into the nearest wagon spokes. The post carried upward and wedged against the undercarriage, causing the wheels at both ends of the rear axle to lock and drag. Wooden spokes shattered into kindling, and the rear quarter of the wagon dug into the ground. The ammunition man, a Cowboy with a thick and bushy mustache, rolled in the dirt with an angry werewolf bearing down on him. Before he could get to his feet and run, the creature seized him and tore him apart in one angry bite.

Unable to get the wagon moving, the teamster pulled the lynchpin linking the wagon to the team. Freed, he jumped into the tack and was carried away at an accelerated speed. The action was made without regard for the gunner, who remained harnessed in place with an empty gun and stationary wagon. The Cowboy worked frantically to free himself from the harness while watching the progress of the approaching creature. Even if he had been able to give the buckles all of his attention, there was no time to release himself and avoid a violent death.

Ajiah finished the man off with three swipes of her menacing claws and took a few seconds to consume portions of his flesh. She crouched low over him and watched for further threats from the mercenaries. In chasing the wagon, she rapidly cleared the kill zone set up to contain her. She successfully defeated their offensive with an unexpected attack from within.

Tiny tendrils of gray smoke curled from the extinguished wounds in her torso. The magnesium and phosphorous burned through her fur. The men and women hiding in the shadows of the homes and businesses around her kept quiet. Of course, she knew they were there and growled to keep them in fear. In the distance, the fire from the warehouse crested and spread to nearby buildings as yellow and orange fingers reached skyward. Billows of dark smoke filled the air, signaling destruction. Screams and yelps called for help that would never arrive. The fire whooshed in an angry wind of embers intent on sweeping the helpless town away. With it came an oppressive rise in temperature.

Bells continued their frantic alarm and call to arms. The fire threat was now the greater danger to the town and its residents. Fire was an ever-present enemy in every prairie town slapped together with parched lumber and poorly designed buildings positioned too close together.

Ajiah rose and twitched her moist nose at the air, me, and the buildings around her. I wasn't sure if she was sensing danger or seeking new targets to vent her wrath. There was the expected yelling and unintelligible calls for assistance in the distance. But beyond the destruction, there was no immediate peril. Where were the Cowboys and Pinkertons? What were they up to now that their best-laid plans had imploded in failure?

43

The Black Wolf moved into the shadows with practiced stealth, constantly checking the rooftops up and down the street for attackers. I spun Styx around to ensure the roads and alleys were clear in all directions. Ajiah's muzzle jerked in the direction of something in the distance, toward the fort and opposite the fire threatening the town. A crackling sound echoed that had no place within the confines of Fort Charon. The bursts were overlapped at the end by a grouping of screams and terrified protests. The cracks began again and became the recognizable, rapid-fire staccato of a Gatling gun in deadly operation.

Ajiah's long ears perked up as she recognized it for the horror it was. She broke into a dead run toward the fort, taking long, powerful strides, claws curled into fists and arms pumping in determination. The speed and stamina of the monster were astounding to behold. If it had been necessary for Styx to retreat, I knew it was a race my Appaloosa would not win. He was lucky to keep her in sight as he struggled to follow. Ajiah worried the machine gun fire was directed at the helpless people of the Wolf Clan. It was the first fear to take root in my mind as well. With a battle against the werewolf raging in Lucian's streets, there had been no sign of Grogan, the great white hunter, nor his vindictive henchman, Captain Spooner.

They were willing to use Ajiah as live bait to attract the werewolf. Though some of us had, in one way or another, entertained the possibility the werewolf transformed in and out of human form, none of us had guessed the young Native woman was the demon's vessel. But if anyone should have drawn that conclusion, it should have been me. Looking back, I realized I had missed obvious clues by unconsciously assuming a woman incapable of abominable acts of violence generally attributed to men. Now, I was confronted with the reality Ajiah was the most vicious and powerful being in existence. Was there another creature alive that intentionally sought out human beings to attack and devour?

I experienced a sudden sinking sensation of profound realization at my query. There was one other such creature, and we were now constant companions. Again, I experienced the gnawing ache of ravenous hunger that I was consciously suppressing. I pressed my left hand into my gut as though it might satisfy the growing void. I wanted to reach for the jerky in my pocket and eat, but there was no time.

It was easy to guess what was happening at the fort. With the bulk of the forces committed to the warehouse trap and surrounding trainyard, it was simple for them to lay an alternative trap using the draw of the creature's protective instinct against it. The entirety of the Wolf Clan itself. After all, hadn't Ajiah explained the Wolf protected the Natives? As we raced to the fort, I grew anxious about the slaughter we might find.

Within sight of the fort, the gunfire became localized as coming from within the pine-walled stockade at the far end of the parade grounds. The gates stood open and abnormally void of guards. We operated with a skeleton crew since most of the men were assigned to the downtown area. Spooner and Grogan had taken advantage of the lack of soldiers to set up an alternate. Ajiah did not slow her gait as she raced inside. She abandoned all caution, intent on protecting her adopted people.

Styx slowed to a cautious trot as I maneuvered him through the fort gates and hastily secured him to a secluded hitching post near my quarters. The only illumination came from the stockade. There were no Buffalo Soldiers at any of their usual posts. Those left behind had likely deployed to assist the townsfolk with their firefighting efforts when the bells rang. Then I saw Cowboys and Pinkertons lurking in the shadows where my Buffalo Soldiers should have been.

Spirited shouting came from the outermost corner guardhouse overlooking the stockyard where the prisoners were detained. I crept closer, not immediately understanding why the atmosphere of my fort appeared so foreign. The kerosine lamps that generally lit the area were dark. Replacing them as a light source were torches wrapped with cloth and dipped in pitch. They flickered and spat, giving the scene an eerie noir quality of sinister threat. The firelight enriched the shadows and brought them to inky life.

I wrapped myself around the righthand gate, sticking to the shadows and away from the confrontation within. To my horror, I saw Spooner and Grogan had set up Gatling guns in the three guard towers. There were a handful of bloody victims sprawled on the dusty ground below. The others were bunched up in frightened groups with their backs against the reinforced pine walls. Spooner had no doubt surmised he would draw the creature in if he started wantonly killing the prisoners. What puzzled me was how he planned to capture and imprison it. The cage shipped for that purpose was at the center of a firestorm in town.

I was surprised when Ajiah entered with blind determination. I would have expected her to attack from the outside and pick off the interlopers individually. Instead, she was drawn to put herself between the lethal danger of the Gatlings and the people she chose to defend. All the white men looked upon the magnificent beast with awe and disbelief. It was indeed a wonder to behold, a majestic animal never before seen by civilized eyes. The Natives breathed a collective sigh of relief as their prayers were answered. Those who were uninjured dropped to their knees and clasped their hands in gratitude, bowing as if to their Creator. They mumbled and cried words that intoned thanks.

"Take it alive, Mr. Spooner!" Grogan bellowed. "We didn't go to all this expense to come up emptyhanded."

"And do what with it?" Spooner contorted his face in anger, asking the obvious question. "Our cage is engulfed in flames."

"At the end of the day, it's just a dumb animal," Grogan turned with a scowl, dismissing by his tone the creature could have any intelligence or sentience. "We'll chain it up and pin it down until we either recover the cage from the fire, ship a new one out, or make do with a reinforced railroad car. But we are not going to kill it."

Spooner shook his head in vehement disagreement and growled, "It killed my brother. It has to pay." He grasped the Gatling with determination and cranked the handle to shoot an isolated elder woman into oblivion. Her slow shuffle toward the stables for shelter had drawn his attention.

Ajiah roared and barreled straight toward Spooner's perch in the guard tower. She vaulted upward, fully intent upon eviscerating him with fangs and talons. Spooner did not react as expected. Once he saw her taking the bait, he didn't flee or fire the remainder of his magazine into her. In an admirable act of courage or insanity, Spooner stood his ground behind the Gatling. His face broke open to reveal a mouthful of tobacco-stained teeth, smiling with maniacal glee as he yelled, "Fire!"

Four Big Mouth cannons exploded in unison with deafening booms from hidden positions at the corners of the stockade. No wonder everything was so ominously dark and cloaked in shadow. They didn't want her to see what they had in store.

The nets flew at Ajiah's airborne wolf body like giant hands reaching out to capture her in heavy gloves. The way one net after another surrounded and entangled her was an engineering work of art, although in this case, it was no more than dumb luck. Three of the four nets hurled at her through the sooty gray gun smoke hit their mark. Each improved upon the effectiveness of the last in orderly succession, mimicking a group of Venus flytraps closing one set of jaws after another around the same hapless victim. Ajiah could not redirect her attack in the drag of the heavy nets. Her forward motion propelled her into the ungiving, tightly crowded pine timbers that made up the interior walls. She dropped to the hardpacked ground, confined in steel-reinforced meshwork, struggling to get herself into a defensive posture or work out an escape. Attacking her tormentors was now secondary to escaping the cocoon ensnaring her.

As she rolled around in the dirt to gain purchase on all fours, five brave Cowboys moved in with a thicker and visibly heavier rawhide net. I wasn't the one being netted, but what they brought down upon her was so overwhelming I easily imagined the weight of it upon her, accompanied by a crushing sense of defeat. The Cowboys clipped and tied leather keepers on the mesh to hold the nets in place. They threaded saddle-grade rawhide ropes of various shades of tan through the squares to further secure Ajiah. She wiggled her talons between the squares and managed to slice a few of her bindings at multiple points. She would eventually work her way free if she were merely tied and left to her own devices. But the mercenaries weren't going to give the werewolf time.

The Cowboys wrapped her with thicker rawhide ropes of up to eight braided strands. Each was about thirty feet long and of an uncommon quality on the parched prairies of Indian Territory. The thicker lines would not be snapped with brute force or a flick of sharp nails. Four horsemen secured ropes to their saddle horns and coaxed their mounts backward to tighten the bindings. They spread out to the four points of the compass as though in preparation for a draw and quartering. The ropes and nets constricted as expected, further confining the great black Wolf. Instead of quieting and exhausting her into surrender and submission, the effort further enraged her. Her growls and roars grew in intensity and began to take on a tone of desperation. With each jerk and tug of her powerful body, she dragged each horse inward a step or two.

"Jesus, this motherfucker's strong," one of the werewolf wranglers drawled.

"Meaner than a bag of rattlesnakes!" Another added.

Spooner spat from his gunner station on the wall. "If you want me to crank a few rounds into it for good measure, let me know, but I can't promise I won't kill one of you or your horses in the process." He laughed behind the cruel warning.

The monster eyed the men around her with hatred and menace. She was determined to find a weakness or opening and make them sorry. Her wild-eyed frenzy found me with a glowering gaze that reached my soul. I immediately shared her anger and rage. They were taking her freedom and bending her to their will in a way akin to rape, yet without the further indignity of a forced sex act.

"Those of you standing around need to get your asses in there and lend a hand," Spooner shouted. "Four men ain't gonna do it!"

In a way, Spooner, Grogan, and the Cowboys had fallen into Ajiah's trap, sprung by their flippant cruelty. She needed to feed to replenish her strength, and the more I thought about her unrelenting hunger, the more I could not suppress my own. It was the thought of feeding that triggered the transformation inside me. It was orgasmic in its rush and wantonness to be fulfilled. There was no holding back. My second metamorphosis exploded outward. There were no thoughts of preserving my clothing or hiding what was happening. I did not take the time to inspect the stages of my conversion this time, as I was too focused on our enemies. Anyone who cared to look in my direction on the periphery of the werewolf engagement had an unobstructed view of what was happening to me. The only thing not apparent to a random onlooker was the unadulterated euphoria I felt as my skeleton cracked, and my muscles swelled with girth and strength. My skin exuded hairs in what felt like individual razors prickling outward from beneath the surface. The elder, Little Bear, was the first to notice me and alert the others to my presence as an elated grin of missing teeth grew on his face. When Spooner and Grogan went down to inspect their struggling prize, the Natives were intoning a soulful chant to welcome the second werewolf rising to their defense and reinforcing the first.

"What are the fucking Indians going on about?" Spooner growled in response as their haunting harmony rose around the stockade.

I reached through the dust clouding the air between the struggling Cowboys, who were incapable of pacifying Ajiah. With a firm grip, I seized upon one of the taut ropes, binding a saddle horn to the bundle of nets confining her, and yanked it with a force fueled by wrath. The horse lost its footing and fell hard into the dirt. Its otherwise focused Cowboy flew toward me in bug-eyed shock. I roared at him as I grasped his throat with my claw and raked him into my waiting jaws. I bit into his shoulder and chest and tore out mouthfuls of his flesh and bone. He screamed and flailed, but I was oblivious to his pain as I consumed his flesh to sate my lust for live meat. As I swallowed, I felt my hulking body respond with flashes of rejuvenating energy. The more I ate, the more I wanted. I dropped the dribbling ruination of the man and turned to the other men struggling to hold Ajiah at bay as they became painfully aware of me.

The fight with Ajiah became a two-front assault. The three remaining Cowboys shifted their efforts, trying to keep the ropes tight on her while avoiding me. To keep her under control, she had to remain at the end of their ropes. It was a losing proposition. One of them would have to occupy the leg of the tripod closest to me, and that man would be the next to die.

"Two!?" Spooner yelled in shock over the commotion. Real fear lined his face around his open mouth and creasing forehead. There had been no contingency for two. He pulled a pistol from his holster and fired a shot into Ajiah's face and another into mine. The resulting twinge of sensation did not register as pain, but the affront of the futile act further outraged me. I snarled and yanked a second Cowboy out of his saddle by his left arm, nearly tearing it from its socket. As I drew him toward me, I bit deeply into him, ripping half his ribcage from his convulsing body. With it came an unconscious familiarity in its flavor.

Spooner froze in his saddle. His eyes widened, his jaw dropped, and his horse trotted backward to escape me. I took another deep bite of the second Cowboy, which tore the screaming man in half. I threw the leg half into Spooner. Spooner was knocked from his stirrups and into the dirt, fighting to maintain a grip on his pistol and reigns. He lost hold of both. His horse whinnied in wide-eyed panic and bucked wildly away toward the open gate.

As I circled them, the remaining horses became frantic about freeing themselves from the monster to which they were bound. The riderless mare thrashed enough to loosen her saddle cinch and kick the leather off. Free of Ajiah, she, too, bolted for the exit as quickly as she could.

Grogan looked from me to Ajiah. This was an eventuality he had not anticipated nor remotely prepared for in his greedy calculations. He'd seen what kind of destruction one werewolf could perpetrate, but a second, working in concert with the first, was no-win. Had I not been needed to free Ajiah from her bindings, I would have torn the fat fuck to shreds.

"Shoot them!" Spooner screamed. "Shoot the motherfuckers!"

On cue, every man with a weapon started shooting indiscriminately at the two of us. The Indians, as a group, managed to back clear of the terrified horses, fighting monsters, and random gunfire but confined their self-preservation to a distance that allowed them to see what was happening. In the thick of it, I ripped the third Cowboy from his saddle and bit out a maw full of flesh from his throat and chest. Blood poured over my chin and down his front as he screamed and shook in a death throe. I swallowed the chunk of muscle, bone, and tissue between ravenous bites and tossed his corpse against the stockade pines with all the force I could muster.

I speared the netting confining Ajiah with my claws, then sliced through two layers with a swipe of my wrist. With three Cowboys down, the netting became noticeably slack. Ajiah worked from the inside, and between us, we sliced through a good portion of the cocoon in short order. The fourth Cowboy looked like he wanted to flee but seemed bound by some obligation to duty. Without his efforts, Ajiah would have regained her feet and likely shrugged off the remnants of the tattered nets. As it worked out, the Cowboys and Pinkertons opened fire on us. They only managed to kill the one man who maintained control over Ajiah. She tore free in a fury of growls and snarls.

"We need troops! I'm going to the telegraph office!" Grogan called over the din, looking for a dignified exit that didn't paint him as the utter coward he was.

In the fray, Spooner returned to his vantage point above and cranked the Gatling back to life. Red tracer rounds rained down upon us. At near point-blank range, there were few misses. The bullets stung, but they did not pierce our werewolf hides or retard our momentum. "Eat that, you hairy motherfuckers!" Spooner screamed. "Fuck you! Fuck both you ugly fucks!"

As a team, we waded into the slack-jawed mercenaries and drew the gunfire away from the defenseless Wolf Clan. Both of us were focused on killing as many of the men as we could get our claws and teeth into. Spooner unintentionally chewed up several of his Cowboys with his indiscriminate machinegun fire and swapped magazines between epithets.

We slashed and clawed into the men. Some ran and tried to hide, but neither of us was inclined to show mercy and allow them to escape. They had become a nuisance that needed to be eliminated. Somewhere in the chaos, I lost track of Grogan. But as the gunmen thinned out, our collective attention turned to Spooner, firing upon us from above. When we both turned our focus upon him, he visibly registered his mistake in remaining to fight. This was a battle he would not survive. I growled and crept toward the wall, gauging the ease of scaling it.

Spooner defiantly pulled a pistol from each of his holsters and fired at us, one after the other with each hand, one trigger pull after another, right, left, right, left. I leaped upward with minimal effort and grappled the tip of the pointed pine nearest him as his hammers fell on empty chambers. I grasped him by the throat and yanked him over the edge toward Ajiah below. As he tumbled from his gun turret, he pistol-whipped my muzzle, gritting his teeth to emit a sound not unlike a child throwing a temper tantrum.

Ajiah caught him roughly in her claws and sank them through his ribs before his boots could reach the ground. He brought the butts of the pistols down hard on her shoulders but not with any force that would inflict injury. She responded by sinking her fangs into his throat and upper chest, ripping flesh and bone away to reveal his esophagus, chest cavity, and lungs. His screams softened into wheezing as she robbed him of his larynx. Spooner flailed his arms and legs as she bit deeper and deeper into his chest, one bone-crushing bite after another. His eyes rolled back as his head lolled into an unnatural tilt with his chin in the air. Unsatisfied with his mere death, she tore him in two with her claws, making him a symbol of the fury she felt at the indignities he had inflicted upon her in his cruel attempt to take her freedom. She mutilated him to the point he was a man no more and erased him from existence.

We scanned the yard for any remaining Cowboys but found that those who survived had fled the enclosure. It troubled me that I had not seen any Buffalo Soldiers since entering the fort after Ajiah. She sniffed the air, flaring her nostrils and twitching her ears as though trying to find something via bat-like echolocation. She froze, intent, eyes darting from side to side in deliberate consideration. Then, she raised her chin upward and released a deep, resonating howl.

She listened for a response, velvety ears perking up and pivoting to find sound. Getting none, she repeated the process twice more, patiently checking for an answer. From a distance came a much weaker, less forceful howl, clearly produced by a human being imitating a wolf. This communication was followed by the howls of several men at different locations outside the walls of Fort Charon. Ajiah howled again in a drawn-out octave from one end of the scale to the other to let the men know she heard them. Her bushy tail swept the air behind her in delight.

The remaining Wolf Clan members instinctively picked up their meager belongings and followed Ajiah to the stockade gate. She eased it wide, enabling their freedom. The wounded were assisted as best they could be managed, but the dead had to be left behind with brief prayers of remembrance. Some cried, and others uttered last words I could not understand. However, the tones of condolence, sorrow, and reverence were unmistakable.

44

We met no resistance as we left the fort. Beyond the walls, we found Buff and Mal with Whiteman Killer and the hunting party that eluded us from the beginning. They had not been so far away after all. Beside the lead Indian sat Angry Eagle with a sour look on his face. The muscular warriors wore wolf skins as capes, with the upper portion of the animal's skull hollowed out to provide an ominous cowl. The ears were enhanced into an exaggerated, horn-like position to mimic those of the black Wolf. The apparel was an homage to the Wolf entity that protected them. I noted a few of their horses bore a prominent WW brand on their flanks. They must have belonged to the William Wilcox prospectors, but that detail was unimportant now. After all, what more could Wilcox possibly have to do with this matter? His men and equipment lay in ruin all around.

Backing Mal was what remained of my Buffalo Soldiers. I was struck by the picture of my soldiers on horseback working alongside the Natives. Mal and Buff had done as I requested and gained the cooperation of Whiteman Killer. They managed to locate the warriors and escort them to the fort. They would provide security for the captives on their journey back to their point of capture and protect them in case of retaliation. My contingency plan had come to full fruition.

All in attendance were astonished and uneasy in the presence of two hulking werewolves. The Wolf Clan's buzz of conversation and attention told me they had never seen two creatures together before, which created questions in my mind. Only our shades differentiated us in the spitting torchlight. Ajiah black, and I brown. The Natives knew instinctively I was the outsider.

Having never seen a werewolf before, Buff was the uneasiest of the group. He kept checking the reactions of the Wolf Clan braves and took his cues from them. They registered no fear, so Buff followed suit, though he tried to hide his apprehension. Only Mal showed reluctance to accept the black Wolf that wounded him and took his eye, even if she appeared to be in league with me. His look for me was one of reassessment.

"Your horses are in the livery over there," Mal pointed out the building to Whiteman Killer, with Buff providing the translation. "They have been well fed and watered. Only the weak and injured were slaughtered for meat. We will assist you in reclaiming all that is yours."

"Take any wagons you need for your injured and old," Mal continued at a cadence Buff followed with ease. "There are no words adequate to express our apologies."

Whiteman Killer heard the words, but his demeanor was not one of acceptance or forgiveness. His response to Buff was curt and to the point.

"He says if it were not for the Wolf, you would not be so sorry."

"Got that right," Buff agreed under his breath.

Whiteman Killer spoke, and Buff translated. "They desire only to be left in peace and their lands respected per the treaties signed by our government."

"Guess we'll see how that works out," Buff directed at Mal, expressing his skepticism.

I was still working out a manageable plan but vowed to make Whiteman Killer's wishes so. In the meantime, there was an urgent matter to address in Lucian. Ajiah would remain with the Wolf Clan and accompany them home. There was no way for me to impart my short-term plans to her in my werewolf form, but I was sure she understood my intentions. As I moved away from the men, they pulled their reins to back their horses away from me. Wild-eyed and heads elevated, the animals were anxious in my presence.

Mal inched toward me. "Boss?" He looked at me questioningly as though trying to discern the identity of a man in costume. Some identifying characteristics to prove I was still the man he knew. I gave him the barest of nods and a soft growl, the only communication I could manage. I then looked toward Lucian, scowled, and broke into a run for town, figuring my plans would become apparent if he followed. If he didn't, I would explain later. He chose the latter and only followed briefly to see me off. A distance, his mount, Luthor, was only too relieved to see increase.

Half the town was on fire or burned to the ground, but it looked like the townspeople had the disaster under control. By the looks of things, the majority of the buildings survived. Fire in prairie towns was a fact of life. That a portion of Lucian survived at all was a miracle. A thick haze and stench of wood smoke hung in the air.

The closer I got, the better I could detect Grogan's scent. He was sweating profusely, pushing his horse to escape the werewolves. What had he planned for Ajiah that was so important? I knew he thought there was some military application for which the monster was suited. But I wasn't sure how he planned to achieve compliance or move forward with that plan. He likely assumed what he told Spooner, that a werewolf was nothing but a dumb animal. Did he think he could train her to work in concert with soldiers like a dog? Would he continue to entertain the notion if he knew who she was in human form?

What of me? I could actually do the things Grogan envisioned. Trained in military tactics and understanding objectives, I could be of great value in combat. However, no one would ever trust me once they knew what I was and what I could do. At the first opportunity, the commanding generals would lock me up, confine me, and abuse me for compliance. I shuddered at the prospect. It would be Andersonville all over again. Worse, I would be all alone and forced to kill. A hellish existence I could never bear. I increased my speed, knowing what Grogan planned.

Grogan made a beeline for the telegraph office. There, he would wake a balding man named Zwart, who gained his communications experience during the war. Zwart could tap out Morse Code messages without pausing as another man dictated. I couldn't have Grogan convince someone to send more troops. It would only result in more dead soldiers.

I eyed the pole erected behind the telegraph office and the iron line connecting it to the outside world. I was amazed that such a small, innocuous thing could hold so much power over future events. I considered severing it first, but in the time that would take, they might manage enough of a message outbound to ensure disaster.

"Hurry, Goddamnit!" Grogan's fists pounded the door's wood frame. The centered glass rattled. Zwart, the small man inside, fumbled to insert his key and get the tiny, one-man office open as quickly as possible. Sweat dripped from the tip of Grogan's bulbous nose as he glanced over his shoulder. He was lucky the office still stood. The fire could have just as easily devoured it. "We need to get a message off before it's too late!"

"I don't understand the urgency, Little John. Why can't this wait until morning? I'm exhausted from working the bucket brigade." The glass between them distorted Zwart's voice. He jingled his keyring and got the door to unlock. "No one will respond in the middle of the night." Zwart pulled the door open as Grogan pushed inside.

"You better hope they do," Grogan huffed. "You have no idea what we're up against."

I bellowed a threatening roar as I closed in. I wanted Grogan to know I was coming.

Grogan turned with a start and glared out into the darkness surrounding him. His features creased with dread as he considered his fate.

"What in God's name was that?" Zwart asked, suddenly wide awake to the danger.

"You must be the one person in town with his head so far up his ass he doesn't know what's been going on," Grogan said testily. "Time to get busy!"

Zwart sat in a high-backed oaken chair at a sturdy matching desk. The desktop was strewn with newspapers, memo pads, and stubby pencils. He lit a lamp on the desk with a sulfur matchstick, which I could smell from my advancing position a quarter of a mile away. The telegraph apparatus was affixed to a glossy rectangle of wood and a piece of equipment with which I only had passing familiarity. Zwart casually slid the equipment up to his chest as if preparing to enjoy a leisurely bowl of soup. I knew there was a battery attached to the key somehow and that the wire screwed down behind the key ultimately transmitted the Morse code signal to the iron line stretching miles east. However, I was unaware of how it worked or what each component accomplished.

"You know it's a dollar a word, right?" Zwart informed Grogan. There was no urgency in his tone or actions.

Grogan stared at Zwart incredulously. Zwart did not grasp the dire nature of the situation.

"I don't give a shit how much it costs. Just start sending the fucking message!"

"Certainly," Zwart smiled. "You don't have to cuss at me. And I'd like the money in advance, please."

I had seconds to stop them and roared again. The street in front was dark and deserted. I imagined anyone attached to the shops and rooms near the telegraph office was likely assisting with what remained of the fire.

I glimpsed my reflection in the large plate glass window adjacent to the door. In gilt lettering, Zwart's name glowed above the words *Telegraph Office*. A seven-foot furry devil with a pronounced brow over deep-set eyes, high pointed ears, a barrel chest, and ivory fangs glimmered in the low light. I was more fearsome than I ever regarded Ajiah. No wonder the initial reaction was for people to stare in disbelief.

Both men looked out at me. Zwart and Grogan froze with terror, registering my imposing form as I approached. Grogan slammed the door shut and locked it as if that would stop me. I crashed through the window, sending shards flying like daggers. I shook the tinier bits off my coat like tinkling rain onto the bare wood floor. Panicked, Grogan shoved Zwart, chair and all, into me and dashed to the back of the business, hoping to find escape.

Zwart screamed, "No!" and put his hands up defensively, closing his eyes in anticipation of my attack. I batted him out of the way with the back of my paw so as not to mortally wound him. He and the wooden chair tumbled across the room, where he spilled out onto the floor. I tore at the telegraph key with my claws and ripped it loose from the wires connecting it to the outside world. Unsure if that would render it permanently inoperable, I clawed at every wire in the office until satisfied it would take hours, if not days, to repair. Zwart lay in a fetal position on the floor with his hands waving in the air to ward me off, screeching, "Please don't hurt me!"

I ran to the back of the office and found a wooden door standing open to the alley where a poorly constructed outhouse stood. Grogan was running down the alley, looking over his shoulder to mark my progress, squealing in fear.

I eyed the long, slender pine pole that supported the telegraph wire. The line from inside the office poked out of a drilled hole in the backside of the building and snaked up the pole to its connection at the top. I placed both paws against the timber and pushed at it with all my strength. The pole cracked, then snapped off at ground level, tearing it loose from the wire above.

Grogan made his way to Main Street to find help, but it, too, was deserted. Several black, saddled mares belonging to Pinkertons were hitched to posts outside the Broken Spoke and the Treasure Trove. They whinnied and snorted, detecting my approach. Burning lamps illuminated both buildings' interiors and a few windows on the merchant's street side.

I checked all directions for Cowboys, Big Mouth cannons, or other surprise traps and found none. Grogan made it to the boardwalk that conjoined the two businesses and lurched toward the Spoke and then the Trove, trying to decide which to enter. I growled to goad him along. He chose the brothel, remembering the armed Pinkertons were headquartered there.

Upon entry, Grogan slammed the great door shut and threw the inside bolt into place. I crashed through with my shoulder and pushed it off its hinges and into the foyer formerly guarded by Saul, the doorman. The heavy perfumes that once scented the operation had faded and been replaced by the odors of mouse droppings, mold, and poor hygiene. As I entered the great room overshadowed by the fresh buffalo head over the fireplace mantel, the gift bestowed upon Crossly's establishment by Grogan, I found the man crouching behind a couch once occupied by escorts and their suitors negotiating terms. Grogan was frozen in place, knowing he could not escape me. I growled and raised my lengthy arms outward to impart to him my area of influence was greater than his, and there was no point running. He huffed, unable to catch his breath. He may have been close to a heart attack based on the pounding of his heart. My teeth throbbed as I began to salivate.

A group of Pinkerton men at the bar, sooty in face and clothing and stinking from the fires they had been fighting, backed away from the confrontation. They held glasses of whisky, bourbon, and other spirits. Some set their glasses down and reached for their weapons, while others flattened their backs against the wall in shock and indecision.

"Don't just stand there! Help me!" Grogan pled. "I'll make it worth your while!"

A group of men rushed out of Crossly's office with their revolvers drawn. Among them were Detective Morgan and Colonel Kirkwood. Not surprisingly, it was Morgan who took charge of the situation. "Don't shoot!" He ordered. "You'll only make it angrier!"

I growled to warn them back and emphasize Morgan's directive.

"My God, man! Are you insane?" Kirkwood stepped forward and took aim.

"NO!" Morgan shouted. He reached for Kirkwood, but the Colonel fired into me anyway.

With reflex rather than malice, I stepped into Kirkwood and batted him to the ground with the back of my paw as I had Zwart, only with greater force. I hit him in his right shoulder and unintentionally broke his collarbone with a tender crunch. His weapon went tumbling across the ornate carpet and under a table. Kirkwood clutched his injured shoulder with his left hand and squinted up at me, biting back the pain. He scooted away as best he could, fearing another blow or worse.

Some of the Pinkertons instinctively raised their weapons as per their training.

"Don't do it!" Morgan yelled. They lowered their weapons but kept their eyes on me, struggling to process what they were dealing with.

Grogan took advantage of my diverted attention, drew and fired his pistol. The bullet struck me in the face below my left eye. The bullet dropped to the floor without drawing so much as a drop of blood. I snarled and advanced upon him. The other men in the room gave us a wide birth, none wanting to become the object of my ire. None moved to rescue Grogan.

I flung the couch between us out of the way and swished my tail without a thought as to why or how I'd done it. Advancing upon Grogan, I thought of all the animals he mercilessly slaughtered, now feeling a kinship with them. How many millions of buffalo died because of Grogan and profiteers like him so their skins could be taken and their meat left to rot on the prairie? All the while, people died of starvation from their hunting grounds being stolen from them. How many exotic animals were obliterated so those same profiteers could puff up their chests as though killing God's creatures somehow made them worthy of envy? Grogan embodied everything I hated as both man and beast.

He clasped his hands in front of his chest and screamed, "Please, no!"

I swiped at him with my long black nails and hit him with the full force of my right and left paws. I seized his shoulders as his hands flew to his gaping throat. He gurgled incomprehensibly as his life's blood sprayed out of him, spilling down and staining the front of his suit. I lunged and bit into him, severing his spine from his skull. His fingers stopped wiggling to stem the bleeding as his body drooped to the floor and soiled the carpet. I held his dripping head between my paws, stared into his face, and watched the color drain. With it, the flickering light of life faded from his eyes. I wondered fleetingly if his brain registered me there, watching him slip away.

"Jesus Holy Christ!" Morgan uttered in a stage whisper.

A ravenous hunger seized me, and I recalled a threat made by both Ajiah and Angry Eagle that I intended to make good on. I set the head aside and tore Grogan's clothes away to feast on his fatty tissue until my belly was full. I heard at least two of the Pinkertons retch somewhere behind me. Savoring his meat, I came to a hard realization. It had the same texture and flavor as the rare cuts of stew meat and jerky Ajiah fed me. It was the only thing that sated my hunger. Human flesh was my only digestible food. It was my curse. Who better to go first than Grogan?

Once I'd eaten my fill, I took Grogan's head firmly between my paws and moved to the cold fireplace. I raised it high above my horn-like ears and forced it into place. It made a meaty squishing sound as I impaled his open neck onto one of the great horns of the bison head Grogan supplied to the brothel. I took a step back to consider what I had done, and it occurred to me how stupid it looked—a man's head mounted like that. How do you like it,

Little John? How do you like being violated?

I turned and swept my tail to warn the men in the room of my intention to leave. I looked them each in the eye so they would know it was deliberate and that there was an intelligence behind their being spared. They would remember this night, that werewolves exist, and that ill actions are taken into account. As I strode out into the night, I heard and smelled Morgan approaching cautiously from behind. I whirled on him with my claws shoulder high and my teeth bared. He stopped in his tracks, raising his empty hands to the same level. After a brief silence between us, he asked quietly, "Kincaid?"

I tilted my head and marveled at his deductive abilities.

"It is you, isn't it?" He paused as though expecting a response. Realizing I was incapable of speech, he continued, "The girl is the black one, isn't she?"

I considered giving him a nod but decided against it.

"We should…" He stopped talking, searching for the words.

I gave him an unyielding stare. We should what? Keep in touch. Talk later? Work together? Come to an arrangement? Of course, he wanted to suggest all of those things. I would have laughed in his face if I had been capable. Instead, I ran into the pitch of the moonless night.

Andersonville – 1864 -Part 9
<u>45</u>

I spent most of the night worrying how to get out of Georgia. Before I knew it, I was blinking awake to Mal kneeling beside me with a cloth of warm buttered biscuits. "You awake, Boss?"

I sat up, nodding. My wound felt stiff and tight from Mia's stitches.

"You need to stay inside and not let anyone see you," he whispered

"You keep feeding me like this, and I'll never leave," I smiled, reaching for one of the biscuits. In addition to butter, they were loaded with honey.

"Mia's a good cook, that's for sure," Mal stood and rubbed his hands, looking determined. "Ima find Private Rice on the road today as far from here as possible. Soon as I get to the gin or run across a patrol, Ima report a dead Yankee escapee. That'll stir things up away from here."

"Won't that cause you a problem with Butler and his reward money?"

"Can't be helped. They'll have all kinds of men swarming the area for anyone they expect he be traveling with. That can't be here."

I understood what he was getting at. A search for me would immediately start where the dead man was found and work its way out. If he brought the body to Butler, the search would begin at the Butler farm no matter where Mal said he found it. It was good thinking, but I wondered what kind of suspicion it would bring on Mal.

Mal hooked the mules up to the wagon and rode out into the morning. By the look of things, Mia and the others hit the field before daybreak and stuffed their ten-foot-long canvas harvesting bags full of cotton. Each of the slaves bore a strap over one shoulder across their chests and under the opposite arm with the mouth of the sack about midriff. This made it easy to stuff handfuls of the white blossoms one after another in endless repetition, leaving the unopened bolls on the plant for next time. They dragged their bags behind them, moving steadily, snatching the tufts off the six-foot-high stalks up one row and down the other, careful not to break branches because broken branches don't yield further crop. The work had a precise rhythm as they each systematically picked the plants clean, staying out of each other's way, missing nothing. Occasionally, each of them winced, shook the pain out of a pricked finger, and continued without breaking stride. It was unimaginably brutal, monotonous work, mercifully not made worse by an overseer chiding them to pick faster. Only because Butler could not afford one.

Mal pulled the wagon to the edge of the field, where he jumped down and collected a stuffed sack he must have picked before waking me. He swung the sack into the back, climbed in after it, and unloaded the cotton into the bed, walking back and forth to tamp it into place. Once he got the load matted satisfactorily, he returned to the field to resume picking himself. He intermittently assisted Mia and the other slave woman in the hoisting and unloading their sacks. Mal accomplished twice the work of the others, though none were slacking.

It was close to noon before Butler showed up on horseback to check on his labor. He wore a wide-brimmed straw hat and light-colored clothing to protect himself from the oppressive sun. He occasionally dragged his long sleeves across his forehead to mop the sweat on his brow. The instant he showed up, the five slaves increased their pace and productivity. This was likely calculated as proof they did not require supervision.

After an hour of observation, Butler moved his horse to the wagon and peered into the bed to check the mounting progress. Butler wriggled his nose and glanced around at the field as though detecting a foul odor. He was within mere feet of Rice's putrefying corpse in its hidden compartment. He trotted around the area searching for the smell's source, likely thinking he would find a dead deer or some other animal. He gave up or decided it was not worth the effort and rode back to the house for lunch or whatever small-time cotton growers do during the day. His slaves breathed a sigh of relief and slowed their activities down a notch.

By midday, the wagon was filled to capacity. Mal climbed into the driver's seat to begin his long drive to the gin and back. I silently wished him luck and hoped for no unforeseen problems in offloading Rice's body.

I finished off the biscuits Mal brought me that morning and noticed Mia made her way to the farmhouse, presumably to cook Butler his evening meal. The other slaves looked after the livestock, tended the vegetable garden, drew water from the well, and conducted other necessary chores. There was never a moment free of toil.

It was well past the time of day Mal delivered me to the Butler farm when I got an inkling he was overdue. It came when Butler erupted from his home. "Where the fuck is he!?"

Butler burst through the door and stormed onto his wraparound porch, checking for any sign of Mal approaching from the main road. He shaded his eyes with his hand to cut the glare. "Christ Almighty!" He swore in frustration, returned to the house, and shouted something else.

Within the hour came the cadenced trot of mule hooves hitting the dirt and crushed gravel of the driveway. I stepped to the barn door to watch Mal drive the team in. Butler barreled out of the house carrying something I couldn't quite make out. Mia appeared at the door behind him, her body language softening with relief at Mal's return. Butler strode to confront Mal before he could guide the mules to the barn.

"Christ, Malcolm, where the fuck you been? It's after 8 o'clock!" Butler's drunkenness fueled his fury. He uncoiled the object he brought from the house, revealing a black leather bullwhip. It whistled through the air as he drew it over his head and threw everything he had into forward motion. Mal raised one hand to ward off the blow while maintaining his grip on the reins with the other. The whip cracked as it connected with Mal's face. Mal cupped his left cheek and covered his eye in self-defense. The mules brayed in fear at the whip crack and drowned out whatever Mal said in response to the unearned punishment.

I drew a breath between my gritting teeth, a sympathetic response to the defenseless man taking a savage blow to his face. I took a step forward to intervene but stopped myself. That wouldn't be prudent. I restrained myself and hung back.

"Malcolm!" Mia called in alarm and shuffled toward her man.

Butler pulled the whip back. It's swish through the air heralded another stinging blow.

"Boss, no!" Mal cried out. "I found a dead Yankee on the road just like you told me to watch for!" Mal continued to hold his hand to his face.

"What?" Butler let the whip fall to his side. A leather loop on the handle encircled his right wrist.

"I found a dead Yankee. There's a reward."

"How much?" Butler's tone became conciliatory and curious. The curl of an unexpected smile appeared at the edges of his mouth. "Hand it over!"

"Forty dollars, Mr. Butler! But you have to go to town to pick it up."

"Forty dollars?" Butler scowled. "Forty dollars? That ain't shit! Give it here!" Butler reached out, oblivious to what Mal had just informed him.

"You have to see the Sheriff. They don't give money to Negroes," he explained. Mal dabbed his fingers at a bleeding welt on his face.

"Fucking Christ!" Butler swore. "Why didn't you just bring the body here so we could turn it over to our Sheriff?"

Beyond Mal's actual reason, that he didn't want to lead the authorities to me, there were several explanations. By moving the body and reporting it later, Mal would be looked at for possibly helping the wounded man escape in the first place. He had done the right thing for an honest man who happened upon a body.

"Been dead a day or more by looks of him, Mister Butler. He was ripe enough to fall apart and worthless if they couldn't identify him." Rice was a day or more away from that kind of decomposition. But Mal knew it was money that motivated Butler. He climbed from the wagon, knowing his master would be displeased if he remained seated high in the wagon, and forced Butler to look up at him. Mal tried to appear as subservient as possible.

The commotion between Mal and Butler drew the other three slaves from their cabins. Butler noticed them approaching, too, and something about it set him off. Maybe he felt threatened or surrounded, but whichever it was, coupled with his drunkenness, it clouded his judgment. "Y'all go back inside. There's nothing to see here but an uppity pickaninny taking his medicine."

Butler sliced the air with the whip, then threw the handle forward with a practiced wrist flip. The end cracked and slapped Mal's back. Mal covered his face with his hands as best he could and backed away.

"Don't you run from me, Malcolm!" Butler ordered. "Don't you do it!"

"No!" Mia screamed.

"You shoulda brought that Yankee here. Christ all!" Butler drew his whip back.

"Boss, we can get the money," Mal pled. "They just won't give it to me!"

Butler swung the whip. Mal snatched at the strap as if he might catch it. Instead, the end caught his face with another cutting smack. Mal doubled over, clutching his bleeding face.

"Mister Butler, please stop!" Mia wailed, becoming hysterical, daring to move forward.

This is my fault, I thought as I stepped out of the barn pulling the pistol from its holster and cocking the hammer.

Butler drew the whip again. Mal staggered, preparing to break into a run and take whatever punishment followed rather than endure the beating.

"She said, STOP!" I yelled angrily. All six sets of eyes were upon me, the unexpected white man emerging from the barn. I leveled the gun at Butler. If he saw I was armed, he didn't acknowledge it.

"I don't know who the fuck you think you are, mister, but that's my shirt, and you can just back the fuck off while I discipline my nigger!" Butler grimaced, stepping in to deliver another bite of the whip.

I pulled the trigger, and the back of Butler's head exploded. A red hole in his forehead dribbled blood. His head lolled backward, following the whip and his suddenly limp arm into the driveway gravel. I continued forward, cocked the hammer to rotate the single-action cylinder, and kept it pointed at Butler in case he wasn't as bad off as he looked.

Both the women screamed. Mia inched forward, conditioned to aid her tormentor, loyal even upon his death. "No!" she cried out, kneeling next to the bloody mess. She reached for him but didn't know how to fix him.

"Oh, Boss," Mal said, looking at me with his hand pressed against the left side of his bleeding face. "What have you done?"

Realizing Butler was a hopeless loss and no longer someone she owed allegiance, Mia moved to the man she loved. "Malcolm, let me see." She pulled his hand away, revealing nasty welts and an open wound from his forehead to his left cheek that mercifully left his eye uninjured. It would result in an ugly, lifelong scar.

The older of the two remaining men took comforting hold of the hysterical woman and stared at me. The younger man glared at my pistol, still leveled at Butler, and raised a cautious hand to wave off any violence. "You gonna kill all us, mister?"

"No," I said softly, easing pressure on the trigger and slowly lowering the hammer with my thumb as I re-holstered a safe weapon. I eyed each of them with what I hoped they saw as reassurance. "No, I just couldn't stand here and do nothing."

I shook my head in disbelief at what I had just done. I had effectively destroyed the world of these five strangers and now found myself responsible for them. Should I have just watched Butler beat Mal with a bullwhip? Too late to rethink it now. "You should all pack up. We need to get out of here by first light. Once we make it North, you're free."

<u>46</u>

I awoke the next morning naked in my barracks bed, finding remnants of the night before sloughed off in tufts of fur and dried blood. Again, my skin was coated with a thin layer of the dried, bloody, placenta-like substance that crumbled into a gritty material as I brushed it away. Remembering what I had done to Grogan, I anticipated the wave of nausea that previously hit me after feeding on a human being. When the nausea didn't come, I surmised the flesh had been fully digested. Human flesh. There were no nagging hunger pangs for the first time in a long while and no uncertainty about why. Although I tried to push it out of my mind, I predicted a recurring acceptance of that fact.

I poured a bowl of water and cleaned myself. Once the grit was removed, I found my skin supple, smooth, and free of dryness and blemishes. It was the healthiest it had ever been. I detected the same baby-fresh scent about myself that I noticed with Ajiah. After cleaning up and shaving my neck below my beard, I put on my last remaining uniform. It fit loosely, even though it was years old and tailored for the man I was four years ago. I was leaner than ever before.

I found Lieutenant Carpenter and Captain Witwer in Colonel Kirkwood's office. Before asking why, I recalled injuring Kirkwood the night before at the brothel. They both stood at attention and saluted me as I entered. I returned the courtesy. "Good morning, Major," they said in unison, startled by my sudden presence. They appeared weary and dirty, with ashes lightly smeared on their faces and uniforms. Lingering remnants of their firefighting efforts in town.

"Gentlemen," I greeted.

"Major," Witwer said, "Sergeant Butler took the balance of the men to escort the Indians back where we captured them. He said they were your orders?" He seemed unsure. "We thought you went with him." Witwer looked to Carpenter, who nodded in agreement.

"Yes, that's exactly what I ordered," I confirmed. "It's the only way to solve this werewolf problem for good." Once more, they exchanged confused glances.

I changed the subject. "Any idea what our guests are up to this morning?"

"The Pinkertons and Cowboys left about dawn," Witwer explained. "Following Mr. Grogan's death and the slaughter of so many of their men, they couldn't leave town fast enough."

I raised an eyebrow. "Strange." They didn't strike me as the sort to leave a job unfinished. I half expected Detective Morgan might linger and follow up on his theory concerning Ajiah and me. Apparently not.

"I assume the Colonel is in the infirmary?" I asked.

"He's in his quarters. Broken collarbone and a dislocated shoulder," Carpenter advised. "Dr. Nagel is treating him. Looks like you're in command, sir."

"Looks like," I acknowledged. That outcome had not occurred to me.

I made my way to Kirkwood's quarters. Dr. Nagel was indeed treating him. Kirkwood appeared unconscious. The doctor eyed me up and down with an expression of disapproval and mumbled, "You'll have to explain to me how you did that sometime."

"Did what?"

He stopped adjusting Kirkwood's bandages and locked eyes with me from across the room. He huffed. "Made a full recovery overnight."

I shrugged, trying not to provoke him. "Not so badly injured, fortunately." I suspect he had a pretty good idea but couldn't wrap his clinical mind around a supernatural explanation. After all, how would a medical doctor in the nineteenth century come to a scientific conclusion that a man who becomes a werewolf also gains the residual benefit of spontaneous healing?

"I'll need to speak to the Colonel alone, Doctor."

Kirkwood opened and rolled his soupy eyes, then licked at the dried spittle coating his chapped lips. I spied half a bottle of laudanum on his nightstand next to two empties. Kirkwood had been indulging liberally in the pain medication. Nagel took a deep breath and exited the Colonel's quarters, slamming the door behind him to express his displeasure.

"Congratulations on your battlefield promotion," Kirkwood slurred with a hint of relief. "I met your werewolf last night. I'm lucky it didn't kill me." He nodded at his bandaged shoulder.

Luck had nothing to do with it. If I wanted him dead, he'd be dead. I was sorry I'd injured him. That wasn't my intention. His condition would make it harder for me to desert him.

"That's what I wanted to talk to you about," I said.

"Taking command of the werewolf?"

"The Natives want their land restored to them. I ordered Sergeant Butler, Buff, and what's left of the men to escort them back to where they were captured."

"You did what?" He tried to sit up in bed but winced at a stab of pain.

"You saw it last night," I pointed out. "You saw what it did to Grogan and his mercenary Cowboys. The Natives promised if we return them to their lands in peace, they'll take the werewolf with them."

"And you believe a bunch of lying redskins?" Kirkwood thundered, slurring again.

"Yes," I said without hesitation. "I don't know if Detective Morgan told you, but there were two werewolves last night. We honestly have no idea how many more there are. Grogan's special weapons were useless. If anything, they made the creatures more destructive. I'm ready to try it the Wolf Clan way. I don't see we have a choice."

"We don't have the authority to negotiate an agreement like that," Kirkwood pointed out.

I scoffed. "Our government breaks and renegotiates treaties with the Natives all the time. An arrangement that favors them and saves us a conflict we can't win will be worth it."

"What do they want? Define *their* lands," Kirkwood demanded.

"The Dakota Territory and south to the railroad tracks." They didn't ask for that. I came up with it off the top of my head because it seemed fair.

"Jesus Fuck!" Kirkwood thundered, wincing again. He grabbed his laudanum bottle, took a hard pull, and wiped his lips with his sleeve. "Washington will never go for that!"

"Better go easy on that stuff, sir," I cautioned from experience. "The Indians don't want our railroad. They want to be left alone, hunt buffalo, and live in freedom. Maybe we can relocate all the tribes to the Dakota Territory. It would save both sides a lot of grief and suffering."

"Washington will never agree," Kirkwood repeated, emphasizing *never.*

I thought for a moment. "It would be to our advantage. I don't know that the Dakota Territory is considered particularly hospitable. The land is worthless by our standards. There's nothing of value up there." I shrugged for effect. "What Congress might want to consider is what if that thing you saw last night shows up in Washington and starts killing Congressmen and Senators opposed to an agreement."

Genuine fear clouded Kirkwood's face as he contemplated that scenario. He swallowed hard. "Would they do that?"

"Do you think the local police, Secret Service, or even the Pinkertons could stop it? Hell, Grogan hired a small army of ex-Confederate mercenaries, and it literally tore them apart," I pointed out. "Half the town burned down. Three-quarters of our men have been killed. It's a menace. A deadly, invulnerable menace."

Kirkwood hesitated. It wasn't his decision. All he had to do was pass the message up the chain of command to the newly minted President Grant. I hoped the former general might be open to sparing the Natives. Rumor had it his drinking problem stemmed from guilt over the thousands of men he led to their deaths during the war. Ultimately, it was for the DC politicians to hammer out. I figured persuading Kirkwood was a good start. As the man on the ground, he might hold sway over those above him. And if he didn't, I could guarantee more bloodshed directed toward various government officials until they agreed.

"Look, sir, it's not like we'd be returning the entirety of the Louisiana Purchase, just the worthless flatland in the northwest that nobody wants anyway. At one time, Jefferson proposed leaving everything west of the Mississippi River to the Natives." However, President after President, since Jefferson chipped away at what was allocated for them. The discovery of gold in California certainly didn't help when it came to impeding westward expansion.

Kirkwood nodded acknowledgment. "I can run it up the flagpole, but what makes you think the Indians will keep their part of the bargain?"

When had the Natives ever not held up their part of the bargain? We'd never given them much choice to do otherwise. When they didn't comply with our broken agreements, we stuck guns in their faces and told them *tough shit.*

"We never heard of these things until we captured the Wolf Clan. Since then, we've had nothing but murder. Trouble Washington can't afford to ignore as a Territory problem. We can solve this for them in short order."

Kirkwood took a lengthy pause before nodding in inebriated agreement. "True enough."

"In the meantime, I propose sending Buffalo Soldiers to the edge of the territory to maintain a buffer, keeping the Natives in the Dakotas and the settlers, prospectors, and especially the military out. White soldiers might view it as a shit detail, but the Buffalo Soldiers? They would embrace the challenge of a unique mission. Maybe bring their families out and establish a community all their own." There were hundreds of Negroes who would see open land, free of the white establishment, as an opportunity worth considering. A renewal of the reneged Forty Acres and a Mule promise. Southern states would be more than happy to see freed Negroes migrate west and never return.

"You make a persuasive proposal, Major." Or maybe it was the laudanum.

"I'll leave it to Captain Witwer to meet with you and write up the necessary paperwork."

"Witwer? Why not you?" Kirkwood rumbled.

"I think it best if I escort the Natives myself. Get things up and running, so to speak."

"Live in exile?" He asked. "With that thing out there?"

I ignored his concern. "I'll return to check in with you and make progress reports, Colonel. Rotate with Sergeant Butler when I check on the new Buffalo Soldier recruits scheduled to arrive. This is the right thing to do. We stand a chance of lasting success. I'm certain of it."

I'm sure Kirkwood thought me a fool with a short lifespan, but I had him as close to convinced as I could get.

<u>47</u>

As I rode Styx out of Lucian, I experienced an exhilarating sense of optimism. I resolved to break from the old ways that forced me to commit atrocities to advance the goals of those who viewed the world as something to conquer and exploit. If I could negotiate this agreement and establish a haven for the Natives to live in peace, I would achieve something enviable for once in my miserable life.

A short time after concluding the thought, Styx and I became simultaneously aware of the canter of a pony approaching from behind. I reached for my pistol and pulled the reins to see who it was. I relaxed and re-holstered my weapon when I saw it was just Zwart. He looked out of place on his tan, white-maned palomino he called Scribe. When I saw him removing nothing more threatening than a telegram page from his vest, I approached at a slow trot. His wire-rimmed glasses flashed in the sun with every movement of his head and gray bowler.

"You headed out, Major?" The telegram fluttered in the breeze as he held it out to me. "Captain Witwer said this goes to you while Colonel Kirkwood is laid up," Zwart said.

"What is it?" I was a tad annoyed. I wanted to hit the trail but took the telegram and read Zwart's carefully transcribed words. Disbelief and dread took hold of me. Zwart's raised palm was open, awaiting a tip. I dug into my pocket and gave him a quarter. His face soured in disappointment. Scribe snorted at Styx.

Zwart pointed at the paper as I read. "He's talking about the monster that ripped up my place and went after Little John, isn't he?" Zwart shivered involuntarily.

I didn't answer but marveled at how quickly Zwart had gotten his essential business up and running in record time.

"Glad it didn't kill him in my office," Zwart shook his head. "So much blood over at the Treasure Trove. I would've had to tear up all my cedar planks."

The message was more than I bargained for. I knew Grogan had a tenuous connection to Wilcox and thereby surmised Wilcox was funding Grogan's operation in pursuit of the werewolf. But this telegram reached much deeper.

I glanced at Zwart with mounting anxiety. "How much to respond and tell him the mission has been accomplished? We don't need more mayhem."

"Oh, I already responded," Zwart grinned. "I told him Little John was killed, and the beast and the Indians are on the loose." Zwart thought for a moment, furrowing his brow. "I heard there might have been two of them. That true, Major?"

"You've already responded?" I was incredulous. Styx read my mood and became restless, raising each hoof a step in turn.

"Mr. Wilcox paid ahead for an immediate. He's a rich man. Owns a chunk of the railroad." Zwart spoke of the man as if they were acquainted.

A fresh army was on its way. Fuck. I had to immediately get to Ajiah, Mal, the men, and the Wolf Clan.

48

I pressed Styx West as hard as I dared all day. The pressure from the telegram was inescapable. While I tried convincing myself there was still ample time to prepare, the implications lingered. A more significant threat had emerged.

When I arrived at the wooded area near the clearing where we attacked and captured the Wolf Clan, Ajiah was alone on a light-shaded Appaloosa mare. The twilight of sundown silhouetted her. The usual judgment and cynicism were gone from her features. She seemed genuinely pleased to see me. Styx halted beside her, bringing us face to face. No pleasantries were exchanged. Her confidence amazed me. She was the embodiment of fearlessness.

Before I could speak, Luthor clomped from the woods with Mal in the saddle. There was no welcoming smile on his face when he saw me. His gleaming sidearms, ammunition belt, and sheathed rifle contributed to his grim demeanor. I detected the scent of gun oil in the air. He'd recently cleaned his firearms. "Boss," he nodded and glanced at me but eyed Ajiah questioningly. I realized there had never been a conversation between the three of us.

"There's a problem," my dust-coated throat rasped.

"What kind of problem?" Mal sighed, his shoulders slumping slightly as if suddenly laden with another heavy load. I reached into my left inside pocket, retrieved Zwart's folded telegram, and passed it to him. His solitary eye scanned the words etched in my mind.

TO: Little John Grogan, Lucian, Nebraska,

I haven't heard from you in some time, my friend. It is my sincerest wish this telegram finds you well. Please respond soonest. Considering the magnitude of my investment in our operation to capture the creature that murdered my son and punish the Indians in league with it, I am disappointed by your lack of tangible results. For your sake, I hope your news is good.

As Mal read, Ajiah gazed over the vast prairie from which I came. "There have been challenges for as long as I have lived, " she volunteered. "When the white men first arrived in their so-called New World, they initially stayed for short periods, scouting, exploring, and returning to their lands across the sea. When they returned, they always brought more men, stayed longer, and left men behind, making their intentions clear."

"When they brought their women and families, it became evident the outsiders meant to make permanent homes here, but it was a struggle for them. Many died trying to survive in conditions for which they were not prepared. At first, the men fought us and killed us, seeing us as the enemy even though they were the uninvited. Theirs was a hard life, and they later looked to us for assistance. We aided them, hoping friendships could be forged. Over time, they expected our help. Later, they demanded it."

Mal's gaze shifted between Ajiah speaking and the words on the paper.

Vague accounts from the region recount a costly battle that left half the town burned to the ground and many dead. Shades of Sherman in Atlanta! A strange animal running amok was mentioned. I hope this message finds you regrouping.

Ajiah locked eyes with me. "It was then I knew they would never leave and meant to take everything of ours. Have you ever felt that Kincaid? That a change had come, your world would never be the same, and there was nothing you could do about it?" A smile crept to her lips.

Yes, when you first attacked us, I didn't say aloud. An unstoppable force. She wasn't expecting a verbal response and went on. "Even more arrived after they built their towns and cities. And still, they kept coming. Then, they began moving west in their wagons."

Should the receiving telegraph office fail to locate Mr. Grogan, or he is incapacitated, please deliver this telegram to the highest-ranking military officer in the area and have him reply forthwith. Failure to receive a timely response will compel me to finance a sizable expedition of military personnel, horses, and specialized weapons to renew our endeavor.

"I used my pleasing appearance to lure them. They eagerly welcomed a comely Native maiden. And that was their undoing. At night, I attacked. I believed if I killed enough of them, they would stop coming. But no matter how many I killed or how horrifying I made their deaths, it did not affect the flood of invaders." She held my gaze. "There was a time when I believed I could kill all of you but realized I could not do it alone, even if I had started centuries ago. I was but one lone force. One Bringer of Death. I needed help but could produce no children."

She paused to let her words sink in. As my mind and emotions caught up, I grasped what she was revealing. Her view of the European invasion of America from the Native perspective was a concept I had never contemplated. She spoke of the steady onslaught of colonization as though she had seen it with her own eyes.

Mal lowered the message to his saddle, his brow furrowing with gloom. He'd read it more than once. "It's signed: William Webster Wilcox, New York City," he finished.

"That was one of the men I killed," Ajiah informed us. "The prospectors you asked about when we first spoke. I howled to warn them off, but they kept coming, hoping to photograph me with their boxy camera. When I came to their camp in this form and told them they did not belong, they thought they could do what they wished with me." She nodded, her eyes distant in the memory. "They were wrong."

"When I bit into you, ready to end your life, I sensed a deep morality I had never encountered in another, Kinkaid. Yours was not a gift I knew I could give until that moment. I will need your guidance as you will need mine. From you, I've learned that selectively killing will be better. There is a strategy to it. You live by a code of ethics I do not entirely understand. I hope for more like you and fewer abusers. We are kindred in our desire to protect animals from senseless slaughter and defend helpless people from slavery and abuse."

She glanced at Mal for the first time. "Together, we will destroy those who threaten us. Our world will be safer and just for all."

We exchanged glances. Mal shot me a glare. He wanted to talk privately, but I was full of questions for Ajiah. "Are there others?" I asked. "Like you?

Her face remained emotionless. "I don't know. I've never met another, but I find it unlikely there is just one like me." She paused in deep thought before continuing. "When I came, a land bridge existed at the furthest point north. That lonely journey is one of my oldest memories." She shrugged. "There could be others. Others who made an agreement with Kayute, the One with Horns. But the ocean rose and took the land bridge long ago."

My brow furrowed at the implications of that statement, prompting me to ask, "How long have you... been?"

She smiled widely and laughed with a hint of mischief in her tone. "Since the beginning."

Mal reined Luthor to me and whispered, "A word, Boss. Please?" It wasn't until then I realized how distressed Mal was. His voice quivered with emotion. He used Luthor to edge me away from Ajiah. "Are we going to kill everyone who comes after us, Boss? Is that who we are now?"

My gaze shifted from his remaining eye to his leather patch. "Do we have a choice? Isn't that what we've done to others this past decade? Isn't that what's been done to the three of us?" I gestured to include Ajiah. "We've all been hunted at one time."

Mal's brow rose above his eye and patch. "Boss, she just told you she sold her soul to the Devil. She killed over half our men. She's corrupted you to join her in more killing."

"That's not how I took it." I shook my head. "This benefits all of us. We will stop the *indiscriminate* killing," I emphasized, "But if they come after us, if they don't respect the boundaries, we protect ourselves." And feed, I didn't say aloud. That was a curse I would learn to navigate and keep Mal out of as much as possible.

"We trust each other," I said to the two of them. "You're the only two people I trust." I tried to smile to reassure them both. "Ever since you picked me up and saved me at Andersonville," I told Mal.

I locked eyes with Ajiah. "Ever since you changed me in a way that I can make a difference."

Mal eyed Ajiah from Luthor. His stony expression told me he wasn't convinced, but I was determined to convince him. "I see a path. Let's see where it takes us."

LITTLE BIG HORN, MONTANA – 1876

<u>49</u>

It was a warm summer day in late June when they entered the Indian Territory, violating the treaty of 1871. Touted by many as the Final Indian Treaty, it did not stop the sporadic encroachments of those who wanted to test the boundaries painstakingly established by the United States Congress and the Nation of United Tribes. The Indian Territory was defined by their proposed statehood names, the Dakotas, Wyoming, and Montana. Nebraska was the last state admitted to the Union in 1867, and Colorado was on track to be next. Non-Indians were not allowed into Indian Territory without express permission from the United Tribes Tribal Council. No permits had been granted except to the Buffalo Soldiers and their families. Prospecting, hunting, and settling by outsiders were crimes punishable as the Council saw fit. Entry by uniformed military personnel was considered an act of war.

In November 1875, a group of trespassing prospectors discovered a small deposit of gold in a place called Deadwood Gulch in the southwest corner of the Dakotas in an area known as the Black Hills. It was a locale named for the dark earth and thick trees. We began monitoring the group upon their illegal entry from the northwest corner of Nebraska. Their use of dynamite alerted us to the threat they presented. There were rumors of gold in the Black Hills long before the Fort Laramie Treaty of 1868 was made with the Great Sioux Reservation, which forbade white settlement even then. Those terms and language were assimilated into the Final Indian Treaty of 1871, so there was no reason for the men to be there.

The discovery of gold and its accompanying greed would always threaten the established boundaries. When the prospectors mysteriously disappeared, it was thought the discovery was contained until the 7th Cavalry arrived with over 200 soldiers led by a showboat and dandy known to me from my war years. His name was George Armstrong Custer. Following the war, his rank was reduced from General to Lieutenant Colonel, and he was put in charge of securing the Union's Northern border.

I rode out with Mal and twenty Buffalo Soldiers to head off the problem trespassers. Custer graduated at the bottom of his class at West Point in1861 but managed to win some significant battles during the war, besting the likes of J.E.B. Stuart and Jubal Early. He was present for Lee's surrender to Grant at Appomattox in 1864. After the war, he was assigned to Fort Riley, Kansas, to address the Indian problem. He had a reputation for brutality against the Natives in that he did not differentiate warriors from defenseless women and children.

Upon our arrival, Custer was eating a light lunch of roasted rabbit with his general officers in the shade of a canvass tent his men hastily erected before our arrival. Outside were the stars and stripes and Custer's 7th Cavalry banner. It amused me that Mal and I were dressed in our aging army uniforms representing the United Tribes, unlike Custer. The former general was clad in an immaculate suit of light buckskin, representing the Union, as he was known to eschew a proper uniform while assigned to the West. He did not look up from his meal to greet us. We did not salute, nor did Custer or his subordinates.

"We've met, haven't we?" Custer was curt in his nasal tone. "Major Kincaid, isn't it?" He said *Major* in a way that signaled he did not consider me worthy of the rank.

"Yes, sir. During the war," I replied. "Maybe once at Fort Riley."

He smiled and stuck another forkful of meat into his mouth under his bushy blond mustache. He thought he had one up on me, but he was informed long ago I was out here. He looked up as he chewed, shaking his long, cinnamon-scented locks back, and furrowed his brow in thought. Always conscious of his appearance, Custer asked, "My God, Kincaid, you haven't aged a day. What's your secret?"

"A simple life. Mind the buffalo. Discourage trespassers."

Custer's expression toed the line between confusion and concern. I was sure my youthful appearance was off-putting, but my health had improved to perfection, and I had not aged since my first transformation.

"I thought the buffalo wiped out," he said with a smile, spearing another chunk of meat. "Not for lack of trying," he laughed, and the men in the tent laughed with him.

"They've made a strong comeback since the treaty. Same with the tribes. The Natives are experts at managing their game. Adept at agriculture, too. Everything is much better since the treaty." I glanced at Mal. "Thriving, wouldn't you say, Sergeant?"

Mal nodded in agreement. "Most definitely, Major. Since the treaty."

"Speaking of the treaty, Colonel," I said, giving Custer my full attention, "You're in violation. You and your regiment are trespassing in the Territory of the United Tribes. Under the Articles of the Final Treaty…"

"Act of war," Custer finished. "We're just here to take a look around, Major," he said reassuringly, gesturing with a bone from his meal. "One of those *things* wandered into Nebraska. Killed some innocents."

"Well, you're in Montana, about 400 miles from the Nebraska border. You've done enough looking around. If something like what you're describing occurred, I would know about it. Believe me," I emphasized. "So, I suggest you decamp and return to Union territory as soon as possible."

Accusations of Natives wandering into Nebraska were common ploys to justify breaking the treaty's terms. Any mention of a werewolf was a rare act of desperation. Custer sought a reason to see how far he could push us.

"Or else?" Custer laughed, dropping his fork onto his empty plate. "Or else what? You and your twenty Buffalo Soldiers going to kick us out of here?" His men again joined in their commander's laughter.

"No," I smiled, stiffening at the implied slight. "The three thousand Indian warriors backing us up will do that." I jerked my right thumb over my shoulder.

"Three thousand," Custer scoffed.

"Colonel?" A worried-looking Lieutenant stepped into the mess tent, addressing Custer. He saluted, and Custer saluted back.

"What is it, Lieutenant? I'm in an important meeting with these Buffalo Soldiers."

"I'm sorry, Colonel, but there's something out here you should see," the young Lieutenant said anxiously.

"What's that?" Custer rose and hastily wiped his mouth with a linen napkin. "What's so goddamn important you had to interrupt my lunch?"

Custer stepped out of the tent to find every one of his men with their backs to him, shading their eyes with their hands to cut the glare and get a better look at something in the distance. He shuffled around them for an unobstructed view. Lining the nearest hill, less than a mile from our position, stood well over three thousand mounted warriors. Their silhouettes showed them armed with various weapons, including spears and rifles. What wasn't apparent from the distance was the mix of tribes living under the Nation of

United Tribes banner. It was an impressive display of force led by Angry Eagle in an elaborate war bonnet.

"Jesus Christ!" Custer swore. "Where did all those fucking Indians come from?"

"More where they came from," Mal added ominously. "You're in violation."

"Jesus can't save you," I cautioned. "God helps those who help themselves."

Custer turned to me in anger, but there was a note of fear in his voice, and the color had drained from his face. "You can't do this to me, Kincaid. It will be all-out war. There will be repercussions!"

I raised an eyebrow in mock consideration. "I don't think so. You've violated the treaty. The Natives are well within their rights. I'll give you an hour to be on your way and twenty-four to make it into Nebraska. After that…" I shook my head as a subtle threat. "It may be your bones being picked clean tomorrow."

Custer simmered as he considered a cutting retort but nodded to his subordinates, who nervously awaited orders. They looked relieved when he said, "Pack up, we're breaking camp."

"Smart move," I said. "After such a storied career, why make the Little Big Horn your last stand?"

"Word of advice, Colonel," Mal added. "Don't stop to camp overnight. If you hear a howl in the night, you'd best abandon your equipment and ride out as fast as possible." Mal kept both eyes trained on Custer and gave him a tight smile. The regeneration of his lost eye and the erasure of his long-time bullwhip scars made him look vigorous and more intimidating.

"You won't get away with this, Kincaid," Custer blustered.

"Leave peacefully, George. It's not just your life you're saving. Your men will be eternally grateful." As an afterthought, I shrugged and added, "Who knows? Under different circumstances, this could have gone another way."

THE END

ABOUT THE AUTHOR

Jeff Howard is a Nebraska-based writer specializing in dark fiction. Now retired, he spent many years working on Indian Reservations, collaborating closely with members of various Native American tribes. His extensive experience working for government entities often serves as rich inspiration for his writing, adding depth and authenticity to his work. Jeff is the author of five novels, with his upcoming release, *Gargoyle City*, set to be published in 2025. He has also written several scripts for movies and television in the horror genre. Currently, he is developing ideas for future projects, continuing to explore themes that blend horror, suspense, and insight drawn from his unique career and experiences.

Printed in Great Britain
by Amazon

62881049R00167